Winter's Crown

The Winter Murders, Book 2

E.L. Johnson

ARE YOU SIGNED UP FOR DRAGONBLADE'S BLOG?

You'll get the latest news and information on exclusive giveaways, exclusive excerpts, coming releases, sales, free books, cover reveals and more.

Check out our complete list of authors, too!

No spam, no junk. That's a promise!

Sign Up Here

www.dragonbladepublishing.com

Dearest Reader;

Thank you for your support of a small press. At Dragonblade Publishing, we strive to bring you the highest quality Historical Romance from some of the best authors in the business. Without your support, there is no 'us', so we sincerely hope you adore these stories and find some new favorite authors along the way.

Happy Reading!

CEO, Dragonblade Publishing

Additional Dragonblade books by Author E.L. Johnson

The Perfect Poison Murders
Winter's Poison (Book 1)
Winter's Crown (Book 2)

The Perfect Poison Murders
The Strangled Servant (Book 1)
The Poisoned Clergyman (Book 2)
The Mistress Murders (Book 3)
The Deadly Debutante (Book 4)
The Betrayed Bride (Book 5)

The Lyon's Den Series
The Lyon and the Bluestocking
A Lyon to Die For
In Service to a Lyon

Chapter One

Outside Lincoln, in the Year of Our Lord Eleven Hundred and Forty-One, February

BEING A COOK in Empress Maud's camp wasn't so bad, Bronwyn decided. It was even exciting. Except when a knife was aimed at her throat.

Bronwyn Blakenhale was one of hundreds of refugees living in the empress's camp. She helped cook, clean, wash clothes, and hem garments—a bit of everything. With each day that dawned and she awoke, not from the straw pallet she'd known in her family's bakery in the city of Lincoln, but from a rolled-up bundle of cloth on the ground, it was a constant reminder that her life had changed, and not for the better.

She knew the land well, down to the trees by the brooks where she used to gather water for her family's bakery, to where the ground was loose underfoot from where she'd run and played as a girl. But unhappiness grew like a weed in her heart.

Rumors flew that soon they would travel to Gloucester, to the empress's court, and leave Lincoln—the only home she'd ever known—entirely.

Earlier that month, King Stephen had been captured at Lincoln, along with a handful of his knights. Those who'd stood by his side and hadn't fled for their lives in the face of the Welsh fighters the empress had hired to win her the day.

Bronwyn had grown up to the ripe age of eighteen and had thought she would have led a quiet, ordinary life. She might have, had she not faced her father being accused of murder. And then, after having cleared his name and dealt with the battle ravaging her hometown, then trying to assume a quieter life as best she could, she came to the empress's attention a few weeks back. One afternoon she had been washing her hands in a stream, when she had come across a woman urinating. Bronwyn would have left the woman to her privacy but for the armed man she'd spotted coming out from behind a tree, a dagger in his hand. Without thinking, she'd lunged at him.

He hadn't been expecting a young woman to come at him. They'd tussled, only for him to die by accident. The fight had ended with him dead, and Bronwyn surrounded by guards, their spears pointed at her throat. It had been a bit awkward as the man had collapsed on top of her, and he'd been heavy. Bronwyn had grunted and shoved him off, then swallowed at the many pairs of eyes narrowed at her.

As it had turned out, the woman she'd saved had been no ordinary person. In her hurry to save the woman, Bronwyn had overlooked her fine dress, plaited hair, delicate veil, as well as the circlet atop her head that had shone in the afternoon sun, in the face of the more immediate danger.

"Back off, you'll kill her," the woman snapped. She stood and arranged her skirts, standing to her full height. She surveyed Bronwyn with hard eyes. "Who are you? What do you want?"

"Nothing. I'm Bronwyn Blakenhale. I'm nobody."

The woman wore a dark-crimson dress, and she had a veil and circlet over her hair and a thin belt to accentuate her waist. She was very finely dressed and stunningly beautiful. Her skin was clear and fair, her eyes sharp with intelligence. For a moment.

The woman's eyes narrowed, her mouth pursed. She took in Bronwyn's long, blonde hair, tied back in a kerchief. The ordinary clothes that marked her as a peasant. The work apron tied around her waist, the plain, brown woolen dress she wore that was laced up to cover her bosom. And her skin, once pale and free of blemish, now slightly tanned and spotted from weeks on the road and by the hazy, English winter sun.

Bronwyn's gaze darted to her hands, which had once been frequently covered in flour but now were dirty from the tussle with the man, covered in mud, dirt, and his blood. Sharp rocks and pebbles bit into her skin, and she wiped her hands nervously on her apron, not that it helped.

The well-dressed woman raised her chin. She looked down her nose at Bronwyn, her round jaw set in an arrogant tilt.

Her skin was clear and fair, her eyes sharp with intelligence. For a moment. Before she snorted and said in French-accented English, "I'll be the judge of that. Your name. Welsh?"

"No, I'm English. But the name is."

"Good name. The Welsh are good fighters." She felt at her pockets but had no coin purse.

Her face darkened. "What were you doing there? Were you spying on me?"

Bronwyn shook her head. "No. I saw the man start to sneak up on you. It looked like he was going to attack, so I jumped him."

The guards exchanged uneasy looks. The woman shot them all an annoyed look. "That is what happens when you're not alert." She tossed a long, thick, light-brown braid over her shoulder. "God, I hate the outdoors. Give me a castle any day. You, Bronwyn Blakenhale. Come along. You're with me." She snapped her fingers and walked off.

Bronwyn watched her go and got to her feet. She asked one of the guards, "Uh, what?"

One guard glanced at the woman departing and said quietly, "You're not nobody anymore, not now. That was the empress. You just saved her life."

And that had been her first meeting with Empress Maud.

Since Lincoln had fallen in February, Bronwyn had lived a nomadic life. The city had been razed to the ground, and she had joined the camp of refugees for weeks now. She had been lucky to fall in with the company of the cooks and staff who accompanied the empress's entourage. No one had known where the camp was going until word came, like a whisper through the ranks.

They were due to head south, to Gloucester, but tarried as the empress rallied her forces in Lincoln.

The camp filled as armed men, fighters, and a few noblemen arrived or traveled in great carriages and on wagons. *Ladies never lower themselves by walking on foot*, Bronwyn thought as a wagon passed by, ladies chatting as they looked out the windows. Bronwyn had to watch her footing as she stepped around dung; the horses had come through here too.

Her shoes were not made for this and she soon developed hard blisters on her feet. At night, she stayed with the other cooks and servants: the potboys, the scullery maids, the men who cooked with pride and specialized in sauces and soups. So different from her brief time working in the royal kitchens of King Stephen and Queen Matilda, she realized now how privileged a life they'd lived behind those stone walls.

She missed her father. Back in January, they had sold some expensive bread rolls to a nobleman and brought them to court, only for Bronwyn to see a stranger messing with them, adding some suspicious topping. She had raised a fuss but was ignored. The rolls had ended up poisoning the nobleman and an unlucky cook, and had been considered an attack on the king and queen. It had landed her father in prison, despite his innocence. Bronwyn had worked in the castle kitchens to make up for the loss, and had been tasked by the queen privately with finding out who really had been behind the poisonings. She had succeeded, just as the siege of Lincoln had taken place.

A little over a month ago, she had made the acquaintance of Lady Alice, a noblewoman of similar age to Bronwyn who'd been a spy in King Stephen's court, unbeknownst to most. Lady Alice had taken her into her service as Bronwyn had looked to prove her father's innocence and find the poisoner behind the nobleman's and cook's deaths. Theirs had not been a friendship, per se, but they had respected one another. But since their separation at the Battle of Lincoln, as people were calling it, Bronwyn had not seen her again, or Rupert Bothwell, the squire about whom she'd thought often, thinking of his golden hair that shone in the sun.

With her father and friends—Lady Alice, loyal to the empress with pale skin, shining, jet-black hair, and a haughty demeanor, and Rupert Bothwell, whose caring ways and golden hair had captured her heart—they had been lucky to escape with their lives, but Bronwyn and her father had been separated, and she'd seen nothing of her stepmother, Margaret, and their apprentice, Wyot, a lad of ten years old, either.

Since then, Bronwyn had slept beneath a starlit sky, baked and cooked what she could find in the woods that morning, and had never been so happy to rest after a long day's work. She slept like the dead. The daylight and working hours did not change, but she felt an exhaustion creeping over her limbs like a bad dream. Her arms, legs, and feet ached from all the walking, cooking, and scavenging, and she felt bone-tired at night.

She did not dance or join in the revelry that took place in the evenings, or admire the bonfires that offered a much-needed warmth in the cold February nights. She kept to herself, mostly.

This resulted in her not making many friends on the journey, and she did not share laughs or jokes with the other men and women at camp. She didn't know what it was that kept her from joining in the others' revelry. It was not for lack of feeling or coldness. She simply felt empty and dull inside. How could she give flirtatious glances and smiles at other men when Rupert had captured her heart but was unavailable, and her family might well be dead?

Bronwyn had searched amongst the camp for her father and stepmother, but there among Empress Maud's retinue, and the sheer number of people who had fled the city and had nowhere else to go, were more than she could count. There were hundreds of them, possibly more.

Did her parents miss her? Were they even alive? She didn't know.

When she had escaped with her father from the castle prison, her father had been so weak and frail; almost a month in the jail seemed to have aged him ten years. They had escaped through the chaos through a midden chute and had landed in a cesspit, literally. Anyone would have smelled them a mile away. But they'd been alive, and together, even if they'd smelled like refuse. Being alive was all that had mattered.

But she didn't even have that now. They had all been separated and she was alone. And whilst she'd been used to the occasional attempts at flirting from men before, being surrounded by hundreds of men at the camp made her wish for her former life selling bread at the market in Lincoln. At least there, she'd always had her father or Wyot as protector. She had no one now. But she found that she rather wished for Rupert, even just his smile, to brighten her day.

At the day's end, once the servants had shared an evening meal and fed all those who were hungry, she slipped away and made up a small pallet for herself with some of the other women for safety. They usually slept close together, or near enough as the fires would allow. The men had women they slept with, but she was not one of them. Nor were the empress's ladies-in-waiting.

A few days later, she was working in the cooking tents when a page tapped her on the shoulder and said a lady wished to speak with her. He motioned for Bronwyn to come outside the tents, and she did, wiping her hands on her stained work apron.

"Yes?" Bronwyn said, then the breath *whooshed* out of her as Lady Alice embraced her.

"Oh." Bronwyn hugged Lady Alice back. She felt awkward. Lady Alice smelled clean, whereas she stank of flour, cooking smoke, sweat, and probably worse. Their worlds could not have been more dissimilar.

Bronwyn at times felt they were not friends, but then a part of her doubted whether that was true. They had been through an ordeal together. Escaped with their lives through a cesspit together. If that did not bond people in some way, then she did not understand human relationships and was clearly no judge of character.

Lady Alice released her. "Heavens, I thought I'd never see you again. I had to come and see for myself. Are you all right?"

"Yes. You?" Bronwyn glanced back at the tent. "And what of Rupert? Have you seen him?"

"We got separated. But I know he cares for me. He said he would find me once the battle was over, so I know it's only a matter of time before we are together again." She gave Bronwyn a beatific smile. "I'm so grateful to you for introducing us."

Bronwyn tried not to wince. Her smile was bittersweet. She just hoped Lady Alice wouldn't notice. "You seem to be doing well."

Lady Alice looked over her shoulder. "I always land on my feet. Like a cat. My mother always said so. I could get you a place serving us ladies if you wanted. A better position. It must be an improvement on working in the cooking tents."

Bronwyn looked at her fondly. "I've no doubt it would be, but I think I'm better off where I am. If they're anything like the ladies of Queen Matilda's court, I doubt they would like me, and I'd probably be the fool of their japes. I'll stick to where I'm wanted."

Lady Alice bit her lip. "About that... I mentioned you to the empress."

Bronwyn raised an eyebrow.

Lady Alice adjusted a wrinkle in her skirt. "She mentioned that a mere servant had done her a favor, and I asked who, and when she gave your name, I said that I knew you very well, for you used to be a maidservant of mine.

"They were interested, especially since they learned that you had saved the empress's life, although she did not say how, and I said how you used to be in the court of the queen. The empress got mad at that, then amused." Lady Alice gave Bronwyn a serious look, meeting her eyes squarely. "I think she means to use you in some of her schemes. How, I do not know, but you should be on your guard."

Bronwyn laughed.

"I do not joke, Bronwyn." Her expression was calm and un-moving.

"No, I'm just laughing at the absurdity of it all. She is an em-press. What use would she have of me, aside from bringing her bread rolls?" Bronwyn shook her head. "No. You are mistaken. I am no one. A nobody. I'm surprised she even remembers my name. Not when she has a kingdom to run."

"You speak kindly of the empress," Lady Alice pointed out. "That is wise of you. Have your loyalties changed?"

Bronwyn pondered this. "I hardly know my own thoughts half the time. I couldn't say." She curtsied to Lady Alice and went on her way.

Bronwyn smiled. Lady Alice was wrong about the empress's interest in a mere servant girl, but it was good of the lady to warn her. *She's like a curious but haughty superior, well-meaning, who doesn't realize her actions are like that of a friend*, Bronwyn thought. And they came from different worlds. What use would Lady Alice have for an ordinary baker? For that matter, what use would an empress have for her?

Lady Alice called after her, "Wait. There is one who wants to meet you."

Bronwyn turned. "Who? And why?"

"It's Lady Eleanor. You'll like her; she's the nicest of Empress Maud's ladies," Lady Alice said.

Before Bronwyn could ask more, an older woman joined them. She stood taller than average, slim, in a fine grey dress and veil, with a peek of wispy, faded, blonde hair peeking out from her hat. She looked at Bronwyn with interest, and her brown eyes sparkled as she smiled and showed a pair of dimples.

"Lady Eleanor, allow me to introduce Bronwyn Blakenhale," Lady Alice said. "Bronwyn, Lady Eleanor Cheswick."

Bronwyn curtsied, and Lady Eleanor gave her a polite curtsey in return.

"Well met, Mistress Blakenhale," said the lady. "I wonder if we might walk together and get some air?"

Considering they stood in an outdoor camp, there was nothing but air, but Bronwyn surmised the lady had some reason for seeking her out. "Of course."

"Good." Lady Eleanor took her arm. They began walking, and Lady Eleanor guided her through the camp, walking along the grounds as if there weren't guards and people everywhere.

Bronwyn felt wary as they walked through a nicer area of the camp, where well-dressed knights, fighters, and women strolled, but none stopped the pair.

Two tents stood apart from the others. One was grand and had multiple guards posted inside and out, and there were voices of murmured conversations. The second tent was also well guarded but stood apart from the others.

"What is in those?" Bronwyn asked.

Lady Eleanor followed her gaze. "The first is where the empress stays. It is where she sleeps, keeps court, and makes her decisions. The other, smaller tent is where the empress's belongings are kept. You know, her traveling trunks, her dresses and jewels, her crown."

"She brought a crown with her?"

"Oh, yes. Do you know, when we came here from France, she brought two crowns and the mummified hand of St. James?"

Bronwyn shuddered.

Lady Eleanor laughed. "It's not like she carries the hand around. It's a holy relic. One of her crowns is so heavy, it requires her to wear two metal rods on her shoulders, just to hold it up. In any case, one of them is in there." She pointed toward the tent that was manned by a pair of guards. "I wouldn't go poking around in there. Not unless you've got a good reason and don't value your head."

Bronwyn nodded. "I'm surprised she brought a crown with her to Lincoln."

"An empress never travels without her crown. It's the single most important symbol of her right to rule. Without it, she might have a harder time convincing people that she is a ruler." Her cheeks were rosy.

"But surely, the people would know."

"Would they? Would you recognize a king or queen, or an empress, if you saw one?"

Bronwyn scratched her head. The first time she'd come across the empress, she had mistaken her for just an ordinary woman looking for a quiet place to urinate. "I guess not."

"Exactly. And from what the empress tells me, you did not recognize her upon your first meeting. Although I am glad you were there to help." Lady Eleanor gave her a little grin and whispered, "She told me everything. How you saved her life. She's most grateful."

Bronwyn couldn't help it; the noblewoman's impish smile was infectious. Lady Eleanor took her arm and chatted like they were old friends, much to the curious looks of the other ladies-in-waiting. One in particular, a young woman with thick, brown hair, a round face and chin, and narrowed eyes, looked at Bronwyn, her mouth twisting in distaste.

"That lady doesn't seem to like me much," Bronwyn said.

"Never mind Morwenna. She doesn't care for anyone. To her, people are either to be used or envied. I don't know which is better—or worse."

They passed by two knights who walked by. One, Lady Eleanor whispered, was Sir Edward, a good and kindly gentleman knight. Sir Edward, a comely, stocky fellow with a head of thinning, blond hair and an alert gaze that seemed to miss nothing, gave Lady Eleanor a flirty wink.

Lady Eleanor blushed, but her smile quickly faded as Sir Bors gave her a leering grin. Sir Bors, Bronwyn recognized, had survived the battle of Lincoln, she noted unhappily. She knew it was harsh to not wish to see another person again, but so many innocent people had died in that battle, and possibly her own family. For this boorish, rude, crass knight of King Stephen's to have switched sides to the empress did not surprise her, but she disliked him greatly. With a deep, booming voice that he loved to raise and a manner of standing in people's way and making demands, he was one person she wished to avoid.

His beady eyes raked the length of her, and he laughed as Lady Eleanor turned away, steering Bronwyn in a different direction.

"You do not like him," Bronwyn said.

"I do not care for the way he looks at me. Or at the other ladies-in-waiting. He leers at us as if we were nothing more than objects of desire, not real women with minds and hearts, worthy of respect."

"And you, Lady Eleanor?" Bronwyn asked. "Why are you being so kind to me?"

The good lady smiled. She was of about forty years, closer to the empress's own age, and whilst she carried herself with confidence and grace, there were one or two lines on her face that came from seeing many summers.

"Because when I heard that a humble servant had saved my empress's life, I was keen to meet her. You did a wondrous thing, and I wanted to see you with my own eyes."

"I didn't do anything so great as you make it out to be, milady. I just…"

"Attacked an armed man twice your size—and ended up killing him."

Bronwyn tensed. "I never meant to… It was an accident. I only meant to stop him." Shame and sorrow filled her. She hadn't meant to kill anyone. He'd fallen on her dagger and his own weight had crushed the life out of him. She would have done the same for anyone in danger, empress or not.

"I could guess as much. But the fact remains that you saved the empress's life, and that has not gone unnoticed. Another person might have been struck dumb or frozen at the sight. Not you, Mistress Blakenhale. Not you. You're special, and the empress sees it, even if you do not."

"Lady Eleanor, the empress needs you," Lady Morwenna called, eyeing them with another lady-in-waiting.

"I'll be anon. Tell her I'll join her presently," Lady Eleanor said.

The young women inclined their heads and left, whispering among them.

"I swear, that young woman is like a crow with that dark hair of hers, always muttering and whispering about something." Lady Eleanor snorted. "I'd best get back. It was a pleasure to meet you, Mistress Blakenhale."

"And you, Lady Eleanor."

Lady Eleanor's dimples deepened in her cheeks when she smiled, and her warm, brown eyes were kind. "Do not doubt yourself, Bronwyn. I came from a simple family too. A potter's daughter, and now I count the empress to be one of my closest friends. You too can rise, if you wish it."

Bronwyn laughed. "You jest, milady. I know my path. I will be a baker, and maybe a wife and mother someday."

"Perhaps. But you might do something before that, or during, or after. You are special, Bronwyn Blakenhale, I can just see it. Good day." Lady Eleanor squeezed her hand and walked away.

That evening, Bronwyn sat at one of the campfires with the other cooks. The men laughed and teased one another as they dined on hot, thin potage, a sort of hot mash mixed with nuts, berries, and whatever they could find. The lords and ladies never went hungry, and as the saying goes, an army marched on its stomach. She well understood its meaning now.

She found herself alone at the small cooking fire. The smells coming from the pot were delicious, but it had long since been scraped clean. With the pot removed from the heat, it was now a small fire.

Perched at the end of a log, Bronwyn felt the rough timber beneath her bottom and shifted uncomfortably. Most of the cooks had gone to drink, gamble, or sleep, but she stared into the flames and the darkness, watching the orange sparks crackle and fly. She wished she could see Rupert again. To see his smiling face and golden hair, even just for a moment. It would give her something to be happy about.

A woman sat down nearby, saying nothing. She was of an average height but appeared black when silhouetted against the firelight, appearing like a being made of shadow, until she moved aside her thick fur mantle of her cloak and the light revealed her face.

Bronwyn opened her mouth to speak when the woman raised a hand.

"Do not speak until I have asked you to." The empress's firm voice was clear. "Why do you not drink with the others?"

Bronwyn shrugged. "I have things on my mind."

"Such as? A handsome young man, perhaps?" Her voice was teasing. "Life on the road can lead to romance, you know."

Bronwyn shook her head. "Not for me."

She cocked her head, inquiring.

A chill wind blew, and Bronwyn hunched her shoulders against it. Even when curled up near a fire, she still found it cold at night. She said, "I got separated from my father during the battle. I don't know where he is, or my stepmother, or our apprentice, Wyot. He's only ten. I don't even know if they're still alive."

She stared moodily into the flames, forgetting briefly to whom she was talking.

The woman's teasing smile had faded. "How old are you, girl? And what is your name?"

"Bronwyn Blakenhale."

"A Welsh name."

She had never liked her name. Not a Jane or Mary, hers sounded far too much like Wynn for her liking. The old irritability of having a boyish-sounding name felt like a flickering candle in the dark, a whisper of a life that had ended long ago. Her childhood, perhaps.

"I am eighteen years old." She would celebrate nineteen summers in June.

"Well, Bronwyn of Blakenhale, when I was your age, I had already been married—for quite some time. Today, my son is in France, and my foolish husband is fighting to keep a hold of our territory. Each day that passes, I do not know if or when I will see them again. So you see, war separates us as well. You are not the only one affected by this anarchy."

Bronwyn met her gaze. Her dark eyes were fixed on her face, but her mind was elsewhere. But then the fire cracked, and Empress Maud's sharp attention returned to her. "I have heard your name mentioned by my ladies. I did not know it was you of whom they spoke."

"My lady?" she asked, wincing at seeing the empress's bristling expression.

"You address me as 'Your Grace,' or in private, 'Empress.'"

"Yes, Empress."

"Better." She nodded. "A lady-in-waiting of mine, Lady Alice Duncombe, mentioned you. She says you were a servant of hers for a time, when she was looking for a new maid." Her hard gaze seemed to assess Bronwyn to see if that was true.

"Yes, Empress."

She narrowed her eyes, perhaps trying to tell if Bronwyn was mocking her. When Bronwyn stayed silent, Empress Maud said, "I have also heard it said that you are quite capable, and smart for a baker. You work in the cooking tents but also proved your father innocent of murder. Did that truly happen?"

Bronwyn had just opened her mouth to answer when an arrow flew into the fire, sending up a flurry of sparks. She and the empress shot to their feet together, looking around. A pair of fighters tumbled and fell into the fire, making Bronwyn and the empress fall back with a cry.

A man warned, "It's an attack!" and the empress looked at Bronwyn, her eyes wide.

They were engulfed in chaos. Suddenly, they stood on the outskirts of a battle.

A voice called out, "Protect the empress!"

Empress Maud said, "Dear God, they're after me."

Chapter Two

BATTLE WAS A horrid business. Darkness made it worse. The fire lit up men's forms, dashing in the night, like black demons out of hell, Bronwyn imagined.

The empress fled. The loud neighs of horses provided a chaotic, noisy backdrop against the cacophony of blades crashing, the whistle and hard blows of arrows that arched through the air and the muffled cries as they landed and hit their targets. Blades tinged and echoed with loud rings as swords beat and clattered against shiclds. Men groaned and cried out in agony as blades sank into their flesh.

Men and women ran, screaming. Some were trampled, others shot dead by the arrows that fell, fiery harbingers of death. Some fell where they stood, cut down by invading marauders.

She could not tell what was fired or who was an enemy in this mess, and the air filled with smoke as fires were disturbed beneath charging hooves and men's boots. Others began running, fighting, calling for help.

Bronwyn stood by, timid and terrified as a dormouse. She shook, almost frozen in place. If only Rupert were there to protect her. He'd know what to do. At that moment, she felt helpless, and indecision stayed her feet. She didn't know where to go, what to do. It struck her then, that of course, Rupert would run to protect Lady Alice, not her. If she wanted to survive, she'd have to look after herself. She swallowed, straightened her shoulders, picked up one foot, and began to run. Dashing into the darkness as fast as her feet would carry her, she stumbled over two men fighting. Her feet slipped on the wet ground, slick with mud and blood. She slid on her hands and knees, her hands splayed out into the muck as she tried to stop and gain some purchase on the ground.

The earth was soft. She got to her feet. Groans filled the air. Her foot nudged something hard—a weapon—and she picked it up, the pommel slippery against her wet hands. It was a short mace and heavy. Grasping it firmly, she grimaced and wielded it with both hands as a warrior crashed into her with a loud cry.

They fell to the ground with a hard jolt, and the breath rushed out of her. The man crushed her, pinning her against the mace. Its deadly weight began to press firmly into her middle. Would she be crushed to death?

She grunted from the weight and struggled to breathe. They slipped on the wet grass, the mud, and who knew what else that flew against her face and mixed in her hair.

He stiffened suddenly and didn't move as she shoved, yelled, and finally kicked him. Warm liquid spilled on her dress, and she fretted that he might have loosened his bladder. But as two hands pulled him off of her, she blinked in the moonlight and saw she was mistaken.

Her weapon had taken him in the lower gut, and he was now bleeding steadily on her dress. A helpful hand was extended to her in the darkness. "Here, mistress. You're safe now."

She couldn't see but took the hand. Anything was better than lying in this muck.

The hand lifted her up easily, her fingers gliding over the stranger's warm and callused grip. She dropped the mace and caught her breath, releasing the hand. As the moonlight hit, she saw a familiar face. "Rupert?"

"Bronwyn? Good God, is that you?" He stared in disbelief.

She grinned at him and gasped with relief.

His face lit up as they clasped arms, and he pulled her into a hug. His facial hair tickled her cheek and nose as he held her tightly for a second, then released her. He smelled like sweat, horse, hay, and blood. "Are you all right? I saw that man come for you." He looked dispassionately at the dead body at her feet. "Come on. We've got to get somewhere safe." He pulled her by the arm and led her over to a series of tents. "We'll have shelter here."

She instantly felt comforted as he kept an eye out, sword at the ready.

"You're sure you're all right?" he asked.

"I'm fine." Her heart pounded as they watched men run past. A few more cries and yells, then nothing.

As some fighters passed by, it was clear that the attack had ended.

"The battle's over," he said. "You're safe now."

She let out a sigh of relief. She wiped her hands on the wet grass, then dried them with her apron. "What happened to you when we got separated at Lincoln?" she asked.

His face grew long. "You know that my master was taken prisoner, along with the king. I'm still in his service, even if he is prisoner here in the enemy's camp. I would visit him, but he and the other prisoners are under watch at all times. I think the French wench would have killed them if she did not have so many people around. I heard she plans to make a show of it and receive the king as a prisoner at her court in Gloucester.

"When we came to the camp I... hid my allegiance. Lady Alice promised to keep my loyalties secret. I work wherever I can, waiting at tables, working with the groomsmen, scouting— anything to keep busy. Lady Alice has done a fair sight better. She dines and laughs with the other ladies, from what I can tell." He looked away.

Was he blushing? A pang of sadness filled her at the thought. He really did care for Lady Alice.

He looked back at her. "What are you doing here? I thought you would have returned to the city to find your parents, or hidden till the soldiers were gone."

She shook her head, her thick blonde braid brushing against her shoulder. "Once we got separated at the battle, I joined the camp. I thought my family might have too. But I haven't found anyone. Yours and Lady Alice's are the first friendly faces I've seen for weeks. She only found me a few hours ago."

His expression softened. "I've heard the city is not a safe place anymore. And tonight? Why didn't you run and hide?"

"I tried but couldn't see in the dark and didn't know where to run."

He nodded, and they fell into a companionable silence as they walked back into the camp. Torches burned from men's shaking hands, and small campfires burned, tiny beacons in the darkness.

Rupert touched her arm. "You're cold. Are you all right?" The warm firelight nearby flickered, revealing that his eyes were wide with concern.

Bronwyn let out a shuddering breath. "Yes. Glad to be alive. Who was behind the attack?"

"I don't know. I'm going to check on my master, make sure he's all right. I'll leave you now, but I'll find you again, I promise. Where can I find you?" He lowered his hand.

She felt oddly bereft as his touch disappeared.

"In the cooking tents. You can find me there most days," she said with a smile.

They clasped arms and she watched him disappear into the darkness.

She meant to join up with some of the cooks but instead got waylaid. Drawn by the sounds of the injured and dying, she knelt to help one man who was bleeding steadily from a nasty wound in his thigh. A blade had stuck him through his woolen clothes and he sweated, even though it was a cold night. The air was rich with the coppery scent of blood, and the heady smells of fire and wood smoke.

She tended to him as best she could, moving bloody strands of hair out of his face, when he grasped her wrist, his eyes wide and white with fear.

Blood leaked from his body as he stared at her, a hollow, sunken gaze. "Did we get it? The crown?"

"I'm sorry? What do you—"

He cut her off. "The crown, blast it. Did they take it?"

"I—I don't know."

"Find out, girl, or this will all have been for nothing. You have to find out. Does Henry live?" He gripped her wrist harder. It hurt.

"I don't—" She tugged at her wrist. "You're hurting me."

He looked past her and cried, "You must not let her reclaim it. You mustn't. Death to the empress. Death to the false queen! Let the king take his rightful throne—" The cry died in his throat as a blade thrust into his heart.

Bronwyn shrieked and backed up, tugging hard to free herself. The man's grip loosened on her wrist and fell away.

"He's dead now," a low voice said over her shoulder.

She turned, tense at the blade so close to her. "He was already dying."

The young man pulled out the blade and wiped it on the dead man's jerkin.

Bronwyn watched in distaste; it felt like adding insult to injury. The man was already dead; why soil his clothes more?

It was a young man who looked at her in the moonlight. He raised his head with a self-satisfied air. "You're safe. He's no trouble to anyone now." He walked off, whistling to himself.

Rubbing her wrist, Bronwyn stood and left the dead man staring up at the sky. She could no longer see his warm breath in the light; it had gone cold with death.

But the crown. He had been talking about the empress's crown. Bronwyn ran, hearing screams. She dashed toward the sound—a lady's cries rent the night air. But amidst the chaos, Bronwyn quickly lost sight of where and what direction they'd come from.

There was a commotion by the tents, and she found herself

near the tents belonging to the ladies-in-waiting, and where the empress had her belongings. But an arresting sight stopped her in her tracks. There, at the tent that bore the empress's traveling trunks, jewels, and crown, the torch light was very bright, for all to see. No guards stood in front.

Her feet moved with a mind of their own, and despite the people running around, she found herself picking up speed, hurrying toward the tent.

Bronwyn stumbled and walked sideways trying to avoid people who ran. It was dark, it was chaotic, but something about the empress's storage tent made her pause. Just as she hurried forward with trepidatious steps, she saw three figures lying on the ground.

Bronwyn ran forward. A guard, Sir Bors, and the third was a woman.

She bent to her knees. The light from the torches within the tent lit it up clearly. The faint scent of roses lingered in the air. A perfume of rosewater, if she wasn't mistaken.

"Lady Eleanor," Bronwyn said, shaking her. "Are you all right? Lady Eleanor?"

Lady Eleanor's head rolled to the side and she stared at nothing, revealing a deep-red line against her pale neck.

"Oh, no." The empress's voice came from behind her. "Eleanor?"

"She's dead." Bronwyn said.

"And you killed her," a male voice challenged, grabbing Bronwyn's arm.

Chapter Three

B RONWYN PULLED AND jerked at the beefy hand on her arm. "Let go of me. I didn't do this."

"Sure, you didn't. We just happen to find you standing over the body."

"Don't be a fool, Ranulf. I know this girl," the empress said.

The gruff man hauled Bronwyn to her feet.

She eyed the man, meeting his glare. If this was who she thought it was, she was among infamous company. Sir Ranulf de Gernon was one of the two men who, just a few months back, had tricked the chatelains of Lincoln Castle and had taken it over in the empress's name. Then whilst King Stephen had brought his troops and retaken it, Sir Ranulf had left his comrade Sir William de Roumare to rot in jail whilst he rode to fetch help. He bared his teeth at Bronwyn, evidently disliking what he saw.

Two men entered the tent. Sir Bors and a young man at arms.

The man who gripped her arm, Sir Ranulf, towered over her, and stood, with a plain, wooden cross around his neck over his tunic, which was belted at the waist with a sword and scabbard and a small purse hanging at his hips. He moved with assurance and had short, brown hair turning to grey, curled at the ends. He had a thinly trimmed mustache and beard, and narrow, slightly sunken eyes that seemed to miss nothing. They reminded Bronwyn of a raptor that flew in the sky.

She recognized the young man instantly. He was the one

who had stuck his blade in the body of the dying man mere moments earlier, and who'd scared her half out of her wits. She recognized his dark, curled hair and the arrogant tilt of his chin. She felt it was particularly unfair that for one so sure of himself, he was also exceedingly handsome.

She saw he recognized her too, as he glanced at her chest, followed by her face, and then ignored her.

She glared back at Sir Ranulf, who gripped her arm. "Let go of me."

"Not until you tell us what you're doing here," he demanded.

"I was helping one of the wounded when he mentioned the crown."

"What man?" the empress asked.

"A soldier, I think. I don't know who he was. He was dying and wouldn't let me go. He asked if it had been taken. Then *he* killed him." She met the curious gaze of the young man with black curls.

His head jerked back for an instant, then he stared at her. "I do not know you." He looked at her curiously. "Wait. You're the girl whose life I saved. Now you're accusing me of killing? That's rich."

Bronwyn continued, ignoring his sarcasm. "I heard a lady scream. I came here and saw that there were no guards. I thought that was odd and then I found Lady Eleanor."

"A likely story," Sir Ranulf said. "You just thought you'd check on the crown, eh? A maidservant like you? Why do you care?"

Bronwyn glared at him.

He grinned. "I like a girl with spirit."

She uttered a noise in disgust, earning a laugh from him. He squeezed her arm harder.

"Ranulf, release her. You're about to squeeze the life out of her," the empress said, standing in the tent entrance. She entered the tent and looked around. "Sir Bors."

Heads turned toward the sight of a burly man lying on the

ground. He groaned as the guard went to him. Bors sat up. "Back off, knave." He clapped a hand to the side of his head. "Oh."

"You, guard the entrance. No one gets in," the empress ordered, and the guard left.

Sir Ranulf released Bronwyn. "What happened to you? Your face."

Sir Bors touched his face, then his head. He grunted and got to his feet. "How is—oh. She died."

"Sir Bors, tell us what happened," Empress Maud said.

He gingerly touched a hand to his chin, which bore bloody scratches. "I don't know. It all happened so fast. I saw a scuffle in the tent and came to investigate. I saw the good Lady Eleanor..." He paused.

"What is it?" Empress Maud asked.

"You will not like this," Sir Bors said. "She was... struggling. Fighting. She was fighting with a guard. I didn't recognize him."

"What? Why?" the black curly-haired young man asked.

"She had the crown in her hands. She was trying to steal it."

"No. No, no. That cannot be. I don't believe you." Empress Maud swayed slightly on her feet. "Lady Eleanor, steal from me? She would never. She loves me."

"*Loved*, Your Grace," Sir Ranulf said heartlessly.

The empress blinked back tears. "Oh. We shall have to tell Sir Edward. He will be saddened by her loss."

She turned her head, her hair and veil whipping around her left shoulder and crossed her arms beneath her chest. "Tell me what happened. Leave out no detail."

Sir Bors said, "When I came in, she had the crown in her hands and was attempting to steal it."

"How do you know?" the empress asked.

"Because the guard was trying to stop her. She kicked him in the groin and he went down, and she would have gotten away with it, but I cornered her. Got my face scratched thanks to her. I would have stopped her, but someone hit me from behind. The next thing I know, one guard is dead, the other is gone, she's dead, and you're all here. Did you see who did it?"

"No. This servant girl found her."

Sir Bors glanced at Bronwyn. "You look familiar."

"We've met before." She remembered him from King Stephen and Queen Matilda's court. One of their trusted men, or so he'd claimed to be. But even then, he'd struck her as untrustworthy, and he'd had a way of bellowing orders first, asking questions later, that had gotten under her skin.

"Of course. I expect you've heard of me."

Her eyebrows rose and she opened her mouth, when the empress said, "That isn't important. I want to know what Lady Eleanor was doing in here with my crown, and where is it now?"

Silence was her answer.

"I demand someone answer me. Where is my crown, and where are the guards?" the empress asked.

"There are normally two guards stationed in front of this tent. Where is the other?"

Bors shook his head. "I didn't see him. He must have been hiding or fled. When I was struggling with Lady Eleanor, one of the guards was already dead. It was probably the other one who hit me in the head."

Empress Maud breathed in noisily. "This cannot happen." She looked down at her dead friend and sniffed. "Right. Tell no one what happened. Get the bodies out—quietly. Say they were unfortunate tragedies in the battle."

"As they were, Your Grace," Sir Bors said.

Bronwyn spoke up. "They weren't."

Everyone looked at her. She swallowed and pointed down. "Look at the dark-red line on Lady Eleanor's throat. See how it shines around her neck?"

"What of it?"

"I think her death was no accident. She was... What's the word? Garot?"

"Garroted." Empress Maud hissed. "What makes you say this, Bronwyn?"

Sir Ranulf interrupted. "The girl speaks nonsense, Your Grace. She is trying to deflect attention from herself, to save her own neck."

Bronwyn shook her head and shot him a dirty look. "I think she was killed on purpose. It was no chance result of the chaos. Look at her eyes—they're red and bloodshot. Her fingernails are bloody. I think she struggled with whoever did this to her."

Sir Bors growled, "You don't believe me? I told you, the woman scratched me." He touched his cheek.

Bronwyn nodded. "But you don't garrote someone by accident or even in self-defense. She could have just fled after Sir Bors was knocked out."

Empress Maud sniffed. "Theobold. In the absence of your master, have a look at the body. See if Mistress Blakenhale is telling the truth."

"You would task a mere squire for a serious matter like this?" Sir Bors asked.

The empress's eyes flashed. "He is not just *some squire*, Sir Bors. And he has some experience with these things. Do not question my decisions, or do I need to wonder why you only so lately came to my court?"

Sir Bors muttered under his breath, then stayed silent.

The curly-haired young man stepped forward. He bent down and examined Lady Eleanor, turning her head this way and that. He picked up one of her hands and gently laid it down. "The girl speaks the truth. Lady Eleanor's body does bear the signs of a struggle, like she says."

"You don't take me at my word, boy?" Sir Bors bellowed.

The young man gazed at Sir Bors with a steely gaze.

"Let me see." Sir Ranulf stepped forward and peered at her body. "I don't see anything."

"I am not lying. Neither is the girl," Theobold said.

Sir Ranulf picked up her wrist, then let it drop like a doll's.

"Have a care, de Gernon," Empress Maud said, her voice tight.

Sir Ranulf sneered at Theobold. "You *would* have knowledge of dead bodies, wouldn't you, boy?"

Theobold's face flushed. "What are you saying?"

"Only that with your family, you've probably had your fill of bodies, eh? Bet you got to know women's bodies very well. Bet you like a bit of cold, dead flesh like that…" Sir Ranulf grinned.

Theobold stood face to face with him, almost seething. Then his eyes rested on Bronwyn, and he took a breath before stepping back. "By your leave, Empress. I will go."

"Oh, aye, go. Don't dally here when there's work to be done. Only bodies to clean up," Sir Ranulf said, grinning.

Sir Bors snickered.

A well-dressed, middle-aged man entered the tent. He stood tall and thin, with a lanky but wiry strength about him, and gripped the handle of the short sword that hung at his belt. His short-cropped brown hair reminded Bronwyn of a monk's tonsure. "My empress, I'm sorry. What happened? I am glad to see you are unhurt."

Empress Maud said, "We have suffered a loss, Sir Miles. One of my ladies is dead, Sir Bors is hurt, and my own crown stolen."

His eyes widened. "How?"

"Repeat what you told us, Sir Bors."

Sir Bors relayed the story.

Sir Miles's gaze hardened as he stroked his thin mustache. "Could Lady Eleanor have been involved in a plot to steal the crown?"

"No. I cannot believe it," Empress Maud said.

"I agree," Bronwyn said. "Lady Eleanor was kind and spoke of a friendship with Your Grace. She didn't strike me as a traitor."

"Do you know many traitors, girl?" Sir Ranulf asked.

Sir Miles snapped, "Have a care for the way you speak, de Gernon. You are in the presence of an empress."

Theobold's mouth curled into a slight smile. He winked at Bronwyn.

Bronwyn bowed her head. She felt unfriendly eyes on her,

judging, assessing.

The empress began talking to the knights in French. The conversation went over her ears. She did not know their language, which she supposed was their intention.

Theobold approached Bronwyn and spoke quietly. "You wish to know what they are saying?"

She shrugged. "I've said what I know." She curtsied and turned to go.

"Wait." The empress's voice rang out.

Bronwyn stopped.

"I have not dismissed you. Stay."

Bronwyn looked at the empress and held her tongue.

Sir Miles frowned. "I would not advise this."

The empress looked back at her. "What do you know of our route?"

Bronwyn glanced at the men.

"These are four of my most trusted men. Mistress Bronwyn Blakenhale, meet Sir Bors, Sir Miles, Sir Ranulf, and Theobold Durville, squire to Sir Robert."

She nodded to the men and gave a slight curtsey.

The older knights looked bored, whilst the younger gazed at her with some interest.

"Tell us, girl, what do you think you know?" Sir Miles asked.

"I did not know her well, but I spoke to the lady before she died. Lady Eleanor was kind, and she struck me as loyal to Her Grace. I think she stumbled across the theft and was killed for her trouble."

"Sir Bors? What say you?" the empress asked.

"The girl is mistaken, Empress. I clearly saw Lady Eleanor with her hands on the crown, trying to steal it. No doubt the maid's love and affection for the sweet lady is clouding her judgment. She shows a womanly compassion, which is why women do not belong in decision-making. Except for yourself, Your Grace." He cleared his throat.

The empress remained quiet.

Theobold said, "So if I understand correctly, Sir Bors found Lady Eleanor stealing the crown and fought with her, until he was attacked, then woke to find one guard dead, Lady Eleanor dead, and another guard gone. Is that right?"

"Yes," Sir Bors said.

"Then, Sir Bors, what were you doing there?"

Sir Bors paused. Then he blustered and said, "Same as the maid. I heard the noise and thought it odd, then went in and found Lady Eleanor stealing the crown. The other guard ran away. He must've taken the crown and run." Seeing Theobold's expression, he added, "You don't think I had anything to do with this. I was hurt." He rubbed his head.

"No one is doubting your loyalty, Sir Bors," Sir Miles said.

Bronwyn pursed her lips. There was something she disliked about Sir Bors's story.

Sir Miles looked Bronwyn up and down and wrinkled his nose. "Empress, I do not like this. Why are we discussing such serious matters before a servant? She is covered with flour. Does she work with the cooks? She is not one of your ladies."

"No, she is not. But I have a mind to make something of her." The empress looked at Bronwyn, her gaze raking her from head to toe. "She is smart and could be useful. My lady Alice tells me she was something of a pet of Stephen's wife."

The men eyed Bronwyn.

The fact that Empress Maud did not call the woman in question "Queen Matilda" did not go unnoticed by Bronwyn. Even so, she did not consider herself to be anyone's pet. But she also felt unsafe—and she wanted to leave.

"Pardon me, Your Grace—"

"*Pardonnez-moi.*"

"Come again?"

"If you are going to be of use to me in my court, you will learn a bit of French. The saying is '*pardonnez-moi.*' Say it," Empress Maud commanded.

"*Pardonnez-moi*, Your Grace."

"Your accent is terrible. But carry on. What is it?" Empress Maud asked.

"*Pardonnez-moi*, Your Grace, but I should be getting back to the cooking tent."

Sir Ranulf growled. "You'll go when she says you may go."

Bronwyn tensed slightly.

"This man you attended on the battlefield. The one who spoke. What did he look like?" Sir Ranulf asked.

"It was dark. I couldn't really see."

"Try."

She thought back to the man's strong grip on her wrist, his wide eyes. He'd been older—but still fit. He might have even recovered from his wounds, had Theobold not stuck him through with his blade.

"He had short, dark hair and a wide, round face, but he was dying." She nodded toward Theobold. "He cut him and ended it before he could say more."

The knight and the empress looked at Theobold.

"The man had his hands on her. I was saving her life."

"He was already dying," Bronwyn said.

He shrugged. "I know what I saw."

"What was he wearing?" Sir Miles asked.

"Cloth and chainmail," Bronwyn clarified.

"He was not one of ours, Empress," Theobold said. "I didn't recognize him."

"Mistress Bronwyn. What you heard, forget. You heard the ramblings of a dying man," the empress said.

"Yes, Your Grace."

"Tell no one what you saw. Now go. Back to the cooking tent with you."

Bronwyn curtsied and left. As she exited the tent, the older knight said, "Your Grace, how can we be sure she will keep her mouth shut?"

The empress gave a haughty laugh. "She won't talk. She's smart enough to know what will happen if she tells people what she heard. It will be the worse for her later."

Bronwyn left quickly, not wanting to hear more.

But she had not taken many steps before she realized she was being followed. The crunch of a man's boots on the hard ground made her pause. She turned on her heel.

It was Theobold, who held up a hand. "Don't mind me. I'm walking this way too."

She felt a prickling between her shoulder blades but turned back and kept walking.

"Wait." He hurried to keep up with her, and due to his long legs, caught up to her in no time.

"What is it?" she asked. "What do you want?"

He flashed her a winning smile. "So direct. I like a woman who knows what she wants."

She kept walking.

"I wanted to talk to you."

"So talk."

He stood in her way. "You don't like me."

"Whether I do or don't doesn't matter." Now why had she said that?

His eyes were dark and glittering. "Why not?"

She put her hands on her hips. "You're in my way."

"Tell me and I'll move. Why do you not care for me?"

She pursed her lips in annoyance, and his gaze darted to her mouth.

"You killed that man when he was already dying," she said. "He wasn't a threat. Why'd you do that?"

He blinked and looked into her eyes. It seemed like he hadn't expected that response.

"He had put a hand on you and wouldn't let go. I wanted to free you. Is that a crime?" he asked.

"You caused him more pain," she said.

"I put him out of his misery. He had a quick death, an honorable one. If he had lived, the empress's men would have tortured him."

There was an unspoken message: I *would have had to torture him.*

"And are you one of the empress's men?" she asked.

"Of course. Everyone here is. Just as you are the empress's woman." His gaze darted to her lips again and dropped to her bosom. "I—"

"Good evening."

He stood there, smiling. She growled and walked away.

"Good morrow. I'll be seeing you soon, Mistress Bronwyn," Theobold called after her.

She felt like an angry cat, swishing her tail in warning, except on her it was her braid. She felt like a fool. She could not get the image of Theobold's eyes darting to her lips out of her mind.

But she had to wonder. Had the kind Lady Eleanor been involved in a wider plot against the empress? Had she caught the guard stealing the crown and tried to stop him? Had she and Sir Bors been in a plot together, and their so-called dislike of each other all a farce? So many possibilities. She needed to think, and not about the curly-haired young man who'd winked at her.

Chapter Four

THEOBOLD TENSED AS he stood by his horse, using a brush to gently rub down its back and sides. Grooming his horse was a chore he didn't mind, and as squire to Sir Robert of Gloucester, he needed to look after his master's horse, anyway.

But even as Theobold glided the brush over the tawny hide, gently grazing the velvety skin of the mare, its blonde mane reminded him of the blonde-haired girl, whom the empress had called "Mistress Bronwyn." She was an interesting one.

Of an average height for a woman, but maybe an inch or so shorter than most, he'd been ready to overlook and dismiss her as just another pretty face. But when she'd challenged him on the field of battle, taking him to task for saving her life and running through that traitor, it had made him pause.

And then of all things, she'd spoken to the empress, as if it were no great thing to address an *empress*, the very ruler of a country. She was brash and had spoken quickly, but her words had sounded true when she'd repeated what the dying man had said. He regretted killing him now.

Well, almost. He had not wanted to put a man to torture, and that was what would have been in store for him. The empress had no qualms about questioning a man to get answers, and she simply paid others to do the dirty work for her. By any means necessary, she would find out what she needed, no matter if literal heads rolled or not. Once he'd learned that, early on in his master's service to her, he'd made a point of taking no prisoners. He didn't have the stomach for it.

When the young woman had left the tent, the empress had called Sir Bors; him; his master, Sir Robert of Gloucester; Sir Ranulf; and Sir Miles, for a quick counsel. There in the quiet, with naught but the ordinary sounds of people talking and milling about outside, he stood with the three knights facing the empress, waiting for his master to arrive. The fight had been unexpected and bloody. His master would be working with scouts and men-at-arms to tally up the casualties and the dead.

The empress sat on a squat, wooden chair lined with furs and asked, "Whilst we wait for Sir Robert, what think you all of this matter?"

Theobold was first to speak up. "I fear the girl is right, Empress. The crown was taken."

Maud's pretty face went from fair to ferocious in an instant, and she hissed, "And how did that happen? Who let it happen, and why are they not before me?"

Sir Ranulf stood at attention. "I'll get them, Empress. I'll bring them in and—"

"A worthy sentiment, de Gernon, if only we knew who *they* were," Sir Miles said, cutting him off. He clasped his hands like a worthy advisor. "Empress, we know this was a concerted attack on the camp. But the number of casualties and fatalities is of such a number that... I do not know that this was done with any other purpose than to cause confusion and steal your crown."

"But why? Why come after my crown and not try to free my cousin?" she asked.

Sir Miles shrugged. "That I couldn't say. Sir Robert is looking into that as we speak."

Theobold pondered this and rested his hands along his belt, where his sword hung, sheathed. What did it mean, for people to have died, all for the sake of a theft? He didn't understand it, either.

"Theobold? What do you make of this?" Empress Maud

asked.

"He's but a squire, Empress," said Sir Ranulf. "Surely, he can stay outside with the others and—"

"I will choose who gives me counsel, de Gernon, and I do not recall asking your opinion," Empress Maud snapped. Her French accent grew heavier, a sure sign of her distress. Her gaze fixed on Theobold. "Tell me."

It was not a request, but a command.

Theobold ran a hand through his black curls. "I do not know, Empress. I think that Sir Miles is right, and stealing the crown must have been the object. But I do think this wasn't just one person. The attack and the theft came at the same time. The crown wasn't discovered missing till after we had killed the attackers."

"Could whoever did this have simply been waiting for the right chance, and the battle a mere opportune moment to make an attempt?" Sir Miles asked.

Theobold shrugged. "I am not sure. It's possible but unlikely, as they would have had to subdue the two guards outside the tent, and the one within. That a mere woman could single-handedly fight two armed guards is... not impossible, but unlikely, especially as Lady Eleanor was no warrior. Fighting the guards alone would require a warrior with considerable skill. Barring the present company, only a few of the knights in the company could have accomplished such a feat. But out of those, I would not hazard a guess as to who would dare turn against you, Empress. I believe your knights are good, loyal fighters."

"Of course we are, *boy*," Sir Bors said, thumping the empress's armchair with his fist.

The empress nodded, but Sir Ranulf smirked as Sir Robert of Gloucester entered the tent. He was tall, swarthy, with light-blond hair and a bushy, long mustache that needed trimming. His eyes were bright and alert, and his jaw square, like his torso. He strode in wearing a mix of armor over chainmail and carried a sword like he knew to use it. He wore no helmet but presented a fearsome enough exterior that Theobold pitied the enemy who dared aim a spear at his head. He nodded to the other knights, bowed to the empress, and said in a low voice, "Empress. We got off lightly. Fewer than a hundred dead. Some sick and wounded, but our fatalities were few, thank God."

"And the prisoners? Stephen?" Empress Maud asked.

"Secure. Their guards are still in place. Any attempt at escape you can be sure would have met with swift action. But strangely enough, there was no attack on their guards, or by the prisoners to leave."

"Odd. Why else then would we be attacked like this, if not to confuse our men whilst Stephen's bandits attempted a rescue?" The empress rose from her chair and began pacing around the tent.

"I do not know, Empress. It is indeed strange."

Sir Ranulf smirked, eyeing Theobold.

"Something amuses you, de Gernon?" Sir Miles asked.

"Only that before Sir Robert came in, you took Theobold's word as if he were some great warrior, when he's just Gloucester's squire. He's barely a man." There was a note of challenge there.

Theobold stepped forward. "I will take you on the field right here and now."

Sir Ranulf grinned. "You'd like that, wouldn't you? Show everyone how good you are with a sword."

"Peace, men. Not in my tents. You want to fight like children, do it outside," Empress Maud said.

Sir Robert's expression darkened. He shot Sir Ranulf an annoyed glance, and the man calmly rested his hands on his sword belt, below his belly.

Theobold stepped back, his face hot. He'd taken Sir Ranulf's bait and proven he was one to rise to the merest insult.

Sir Robert said, "Let us have no more of this fighting. What I want to know is this: how did the man or men, whoever it was, steal the crown at all? And what happened to the guards who were supposed to be looking after it?"

Sir Miles said, "We were just discussing that. Lady Eleanor and a guard were killed and one disappeared. I assume he fled rather than face the empress for his crime."

"Lady Eleanor? What was she doing here?" Sir Robert's forehead wrinkled as he looked to Theobold for clarification, then down at the body. He crossed himself. "That dear lady."

Sir Bors relayed his account of the theft.

Sir Robert stroked his chin. "I find it hard to believe the lady would try to steal the crown."

Empress Maud clasped her hands. "I agree. But aside from that, these men who attacked us—what if they were working with Stephen's men? His knights?"

"But they are imprisoned, Empress," Sir Miles said. "We know that during the attack, the prisoners were not tampered with, and no one escaped."

"Did any try?" Empress Maud asked.

"Yes. But not for long," Sir Robert said.

"Question them," she said. "I want to know if they saw anything, or if they were working with the thieves. Someone must have seen something."

Sir Ranulf harrumphed and hitched his belt up higher. "I will find the thieves for you, Empress."

"Good. You can work with Theobold to find out who is behind this."

Theobold grimaced, Sir Ranulf scowled, and Sir Bors grinned. Sir Ranulf said, "Empress, I need no help." He looked down at Theobold as if to say, *not from him.*

"Two heads are better than one, and I want answers. Ranulf, question the prisoners. Theobold, find my crown. I want it back. You have until we leave for Gloucester, which shall give you about five days. I don't need to tell you to keep this news quiet. No one must know it's gone." Her dark eyes demanded action, obeisance, and absolute loyalty.

"Yes, Empress," Sir Ranulf and Theobold chorused.

"What of the girl, Empress? The maid?" Sir Bors asked.

"What about her?" Empress Maud asked.

"She knows something. Or she thinks she does. I've seen that look on a woman's face before. She's either a busybody, or she has a secret she doesn't wish us to know."

"Hmm." The empress tapped a delicate finger against her round chin. "Our expressions do not betray us all, Sir Bors."

"We could kill her. Make sure she doesn't go talking," Sir Ranulf said.

Theobold stiffened. To kill a young woman so heedlessly for sharing what she knew? "No."

The others looked at him.

Theobold shook his head. "She's just a servant."

"Exactly. No one will miss her," Sir Ranulf said. "We could put a knife through her guts and drown her in the river, make it seem like she fell in. No one would be the wiser."

"No," Theobold said. "She could be useful."

The empress looked at him thoughtfully, a small smile on her face. "All right. I have decided. The servant lives. Stay close to her, Theobold. Report back if she does something untrustworthy or suspect. Get close to her if you can."

Sir Ranulf grinned. "Oh, he'll have no trouble with that. I hear he's slept with half the servant women in camp already."

The men laughed, the empress loudest of all. "Take care you do not break the hearts of all my ladies-in-waiting, Theobold. I would hate to have to exile that handsome face of yours."

Theobold took the laughter in stride, feeling his cheeks warm. "I will not disappoint you, Empress." He bowed and at a nod from her, he quit the tent.

As he walked out, he overheard Sir Ranulf sulk. "Don't see why you involve him in your plans. He's just a boy."

"That may be," said Empress Maud, "but he's quite a useful one, and he's a very competent squire. Sir Robert, wouldn't you agree?"

"Aye, Empress. He's a good lad."

"Why do you want him to get close to the servant, anyway?"

Empress Maud said, "With his looks and honeyed words, he'll have the woman wrapped around his finger in no time. She'll tell him all her secrets just to keep him interested, I expect. Besides, I want to keep her close. Alice tells me she was something of a pet of Stephen's wife, and so now that she is in my camp, I will have her. I will enjoy playing with what was hers, that is now mine."

He could hear the smile on her face. And yet, it sent a chill through him.

This should be an easier task than he could have asked for. Charm a young woman, keep her close, report back if she did anything odd or suspicious. And she had a pretty face and was nice to look at. He'd have her eating out of his hand in no time.

But that hadn't happened yet. Not exactly.

He'd flirted with her, talked to her, given her his best smiles.

She was proving a harder challenge than he'd thought. But never mind. Her affection would be the balm to soothe his nerves once he was finished with the prisoners.

He'd gone to them, the men tied up and under heavy guard. The empress did not want Stephen to have access to his knights, so she had separated them and kept Stephen hidden away in a small, private tent of his own. The guards she used were trusted men. Only those she knew would happily give their lives for the cause were trusted with watching over him. Not that he did anything worthy of note.

Theobold swallowed. He did not relish what he had to do, but he needed to know if there was anything to be learned from the prisoners. He first went to the knights, who were kept tied up in a pen, like pigs, and made to suffer the indignity of living out in the open air, beneath the elements, in each other's company with no nearby latrine to speak of. As he approached the prisoners' pen, he could smell them before he could hear them.

The air was scented with the harsh stink of unwashed male body odor, sweat, urine and feces, and as he approached, he saw six men sitting in the pen, watching. It was humiliating treatment, and not something he had much stomach for.

The huddled figures of the imprisoned men shivered in the cold. That was the problem with caging in the men like this. They were all knights and with noble blood and titles, yet here they were penned in like dogs or wild animals. In no time at all, their good natures and breeding would desert them, and they would act like feral beasts.

"What do you want?" one knight asked as Theobold stopped before the cage.

"To speak with you. Why didn't you try to escape during the battle?" he asked.

The man's mouth curled into a sneer. "That weren't no battle, boy. That weren't even a skirmish. And it's not like we can do much here."

The men started calling out abuse to him, so he turned to leave, when the knight asked, "Why'd you ask? Is it because the French wench is missing something?"

Theobold paused. "Where'd you hear that?"

The man tapped his nose. "Free us and I'll tell you."

"Don't think so. I'm just surprised none of you tried to escape the other night."

The man shrugged. "Give us some ale." Seeing Theobold's dubious expression, he said, "Give us a drink and I'll tell you."

Theobold fetched a cup of ale and gave it to the man. "Talk."

The man drank, the ale running down his mouth. He passed the cup to another man and wiped his mouth on his sleeve. "We didn't try to escape. Too tired and cold. When it happened, most of us were asleep. And in no time at all, the fight had ended."

"So you know nothing."

"That's not what I said. I told you we didn't try to escape. That don't mean we didn't hear anything."

"Like what?"

"Like men talking about stealing the crown."

Theobold breathed in through his nose. "Who?"

"Two men."

"What'd they look like?"

"Couldn't see, as it was too dark. But they were talking about it. Said they had to move fast, before it's over." The prisoner's voice was dull.

"What does that mean?"

"The battle. They were timing whatever they were doing with the fight." The prisoner scratched his leg, searching for a wary flea.

"A likely story. Why would two men just happen to talk about that in front of you?" Theobold asked.

"Search me," the man said. "But a lot of people act as though we're not here and overlook us. They forget we're there. Like servants."

"What is your name?" Theobold asked.

The man raised his head. He was middle-aged but looked older. His hair was scraggly and grey, with a growing beard. "I am Sir Grossetete. And I am a knight of His Grace. The true ruler of England, King Stephen." With each word, he spoke with defiance and his eyes flared with a dangerous light.

Theobold knew better than to test him. This was a man he would not care to cross in a fight, unless he had to. He nodded and left.

If what Sir Grossetete said was true, then these two men, whoever they were, had plotted to steal the empress's crown during the fight. The timing of it all was too perfect to be a coincidence. So they'd been behind the staged battle and the theft. But how had they done it? There were dozens of people dead and wounded. This had to have been more than the work of two men.

Now, more than ever, he decided he needed to stay close to the baker Bronwyn and learn everything she knew. But how to do that without alarming her? He blinked. It was like how the empress had said all along. She expected him to charm her and lower her guard with his flirtatious ways.

He sighed a little. He knew he was considered attractive, but he wished to prove himself as more. He was squire to the empress's half-brother, Sir Robert Fitzroy of Gloucester, a man who demanded excellence. It wasn't just anyone who could train to become his squire. But as he wandered through the camp, dimly conscious of the women's admiring glances as he walked by, he did so wish to be more than a handsome face.

He had more skills than as a lover of women, and he would prove it. He headed for the training ground. There, he'd be sure to find someone with whom to fight. As he strode toward the training space and nodded to the other men practicing, he pulled off his shirt and looked around. Maybe Bronwyn might see him.

❦

Chapter Five

Ｉf Bronwyn caught a few hours' sleep before dawn, she was surprised. She was enlisted into helping care for the wounded and dying. She worked with mainly women, tending to their needs. But it was her first battlefield, and even though the fight had not lasted longer than a few minutes, maybe less than half an hour, men and women had died, mostly those who'd been defenseless and unarmed.

She held an old man's hand as he took his last breath, and called for his daughter. She wiped blood from a child's forehead and the hours flew by as one after another, people died. Not all, however. Some only needed their wounds re-stitched and rebound tightly, but there was almost no linen to be had.

She'd already used her kerchief and torn her work apron to rags to bind wounds for lack of fresh linen, and she was on the verge of tearing the hem of her brown, woolen dress, when a hush came over the infirmary tent. She turned to look at the cause of such silence.

The empress strode in, her face set and commanding. She wore a thick, fur-trimmed mantle around her shoulders, above a rich, burgundy-colored cloak. Her dark-blonde hair was plaited in a long, thick braid intertwined with a plain circlet that marked her as a ruler. Her shoulders were back and her pale face was set in a stern expression.

Two guards preceded her, spears at the ready.

Empress Maud marched around the tent of the sick and wounded and happened to look Bronwyn's way. Their eyes met, and the empress approached.

The middle-aged man to whom Bronwyn was attending gasped. "Do you see? That's the empress." He hissed, touching her hand. "She's coming this way." His hands trembled in excitement.

Standing before them, the empress looked down at Bronwyn's patient. He had suffered a blow to the chest, and a sword cut to his abdomen. He had been bandaged, but the blood had soaked through the wrappings, and Bronwyn had been about to change it when the empress's arrival had paused everything.

Seeing the empress, the patient attempted to sit up, when Empress Maud held up a gloved hand. "Stay, my good man. What happened to you?"

As he told her, the empress's gaze grew darker and more serious. She turned and her voice, loud and clear, called out, "This is what comes of loyalty to Stephen. Senseless attacks in the night, and only dead men, women, and children to answer for it."

She paused to let that sink in.

"He cares nothing for you good people. Not your families, your siblings, your children. He hasn't a care for your loved ones. He only wishes to hurt and does not care who gets in his way. He will push and fight and attack you all, until everyone who does not swear allegiance to him is dead." Her voice carried amidst the warm breaths that plumed like steam in the cold, wintry air.

Empress Maud leaned forward and touched the wounded man's shoulder. "Rest, my good man, and with God's blessing, I hope you will rise and fight again. We need good men like you." The look she gave the man was almost maternal. Then she gave him a saucy wink.

He beamed and squeezed Bronwyn's hand.

The empress stood by as the guards cried and others took up the call. "Three cheers for the empress. Hurrah! Hurrah! Hurrah!"

The empress smiled faintly and glanced at Bronwyn. "When you are able, do return to the cooking tents. I hear from one of my ladies-in-waiting that you make the most delightful white bread rolls."

Bronwyn bowed her head as the empress left.

The wounded man whistled once she had gone and turned to Bronwyn. "Did you see that? She touched me. The empress touched me."

Bronwyn smiled at him. "Now you'll have to get better."

He nodded and looked off in the distance, in the direction the empress had taken. "I'll never wash that shoulder again."

Bronwyn laughed. She sincerely hoped he was joking.

LATER THAT DAY, Bronwyn stood at the outskirts of the camp, collecting rosemary from some bushes and running her hands over the plants, pulling the delicious blades of green herb from the stalks. She wanted a moment to her own thoughts. Lady Eleanor, dead. Her loss seemed hard for the empress to bear, but perhaps more so the idea that someone close to her would betray her trust. And Sir Bors, saying she had been trying to steal the crown. It seemed wrong. What would Sir Edward say? She wanted to speak with him. And what about the scent of roses that had hung in the air when she'd arrived at the tent? Had that signified anything?

She looked down at the rosemary blades in her hand and dropped them into her basket. The plant had released a wonderful spicy scent into the air. Bronwyn heard heavy footfalls behind her.

"If you're hungry, go to the cooks," she said without looking.

"It's you I was looking for," a male voice said.

She turned around to find Theobold smiling at her. "Oh. What do you want?"

He grinned. "So rude. Never a good morrow for me?"

She didn't trust him. She couldn't say why. "Good afternoon," she said pointedly before turning back to collecting rosemary.

"What are you doing?" he asked, coming closer.

"Collecting herbs." She put more spicy blades into her small basket. Then she stopped. Maybe Theobold had heard more of the dead man's words than she'd thought. "Last night, after that man died, after the battle. He asked about the crown, implied that it had been taken. Why would he ask that?"

"Why would a pretty young woman like you trouble herself with a dead man's ramblings?" He gave her a winning smile.

Bronwyn rolled her eyes, huffed, and stood, brushing down her skirts. "Good day." She hoisted her basket and walked.

"Oi, wait. Mistress Bronwyn, wait. I meant no offense." Theobold trotted after her. "I was trying to give you a compliment."

"By calling me 'pretty' and 'stupid.'" She glared at him.

"No. Not at all. I only meant…" He ran a hand through his curled, black hair. "I didn't mean to suggest you were dumb. I only meant that you're pretty and have other things to worry about than…" He cursed. "Oh, never mind. Fine. You're really hard to talk to, you know that?"

"I'll just say it's one of my prettier qualities. Unless you disagree?" She cocked her head, batted her eyelashes, and gave him a sickly-sweet smile before she kept walking.

"Dash it, wait. Wait, blast you," he said, catching up with her easily. "Most young women I know aren't like you."

She kept walking. "So now I am odd. What an attractive quality."

"Bronwyn."

She faced him. He squared up to her. They stared into each other's eyes. His were brown. His gaze seemed to explore her face and drifted down to her curves. It made her blush.

"I am to look into this business," he said, "the matter of the stolen item. Will you help me?"

She blinked. "Gladly. Tell me about the battle."

He let out a small laugh and stepped back. "How much do you know about the attack?"

"Not a lot. I was with the empress when it started. I'm guessing it was an attempt by King Stephen's men to free him from capture."

"That's the most obvious presumption. But we found something different." He had her full attention now. "You know that once the men and sick have a chance to rest, we go to Gloucester, yes?"

"Everyone knows," she said.

He raised an eyebrow, evidently unhappy with her tone. "What you may not know is the empress plans to be crowned in London, at Westminster."

"So Gloucester, then London."

"But she needs her crown if she is to be crowned the rightful empress and Queen of England."

"So the attack…" she started.

"Was a diversion as someone attempted to steal the crown. It was not an attempt to free Stephen."

She let out a noisy breath. So it was true. Stealing the crown had been the object of the attack. Her heart began to pound at the knowledge of this. No longer a thought or a rumor, it was confirmed. It was fact.

He added, "The empress wears a circlet to show whoever might be watching that the loss of her crown does not bother her, but no one is to know the truth. I risk a lot just telling you this." He rubbed the side of his face. "If word got out that some rebels managed to steal her crown, it would look bad. It'd make the followers and the people in her entourage think she was less of a leader, to let her crown go missing."

So that was why the empress had bid her to silence, Bronwyn realized. Of course she was afraid of the secret getting out.

"And the man you killed?" Bronwyn asked.

"He hinted at what we later confirmed. When the battle happened, we immediately thought it was an attempt to rescue the false king, or to kill the empress. No one thought to check on her belongings, much less her crown. We found you, and the rest you know."

"So you killed the man because he would be of no use to you," she said, a bitter note in her voice.

"I killed him out of mercy. I did not wish to be tasked with making him talk. Better to die in battle than spend hours on the rack." Theobald's voice grew dull, and his eyes took on a faraway look. He shivered.

Perhaps torture is as grueling for the torturer as it is for the victims, she thought.

"Why would the empress ask *you* to investigate?" she asked.

He swallowed. "My family's history. It's in the blood."

She looked at him.

He turned his head and glanced at the ground, then over his shoulder, as if to check that they were alone. "My father was a hangman. An executioner, and a good one. Like his father before him. It runs in the family. I'm different. I cast my lot to be a squire in the empress's army. But my family's profession and reputation followed me. Some might think I have a taste for murder and killing, but I detest it. I have no stomach for it." He pushed a dark curl out of his eyes. "So you see, I am not so black-hearted as you think."

"I never said you were," she said.

"It's written all over your face. That and your pretty smile," he said, again trying to charm her.

She raised an eyebrow and shook her head. She had no time for flirting. Or rather, she didn't want to. Not with him.

"Why did you decide to tell me all this? Surely, the empress wouldn't want me to know."

"Probably not. But you asked. And she trusts you. She thinks you're a lot smarter than a lot of the people 'round here. And I trust her. We are both loyal to her cause, you and I, so it seemed only right to share what I knew." He offered her a slow smile that to her surprise, seemed genuine. "Besides, maybe it might make you not hate me so much."

"I don't hate you," Bronwyn said. She wasn't loyal to the

empress, either, but felt glad he thought so, for her own personal safety.

"Maybe not. But you don't like me, either."

"Why do you care if I like you or not?"

His look was warm, his gaze darting to her lips again, and he ran a hand through his wavy, dark hair. "Most young women like me. It's odd that you don't."

She snorted at that. "So that's it. I must be odd because I'm not fawning all over you."

"Yes. It's confusing."

She rolled her eyes and readjusted the basket in her arms. "You're right. I don't like you. You're arrogant and full of yourself. Especially if you think that all young women should like you just because." With a toss of her head, she flicked her blonde braid over her shoulder and stalked off like an angry cat.

He laughed and called after her, but she was too annoyed to listen. The arrogance of it all.

So why did she find herself thinking of him later?

His brown eyes had danced when he'd talked to her, and she remembered the way his mouth looked when he laughed. The self-assured tilt of his chin, the confident way he walked.

It was foolish. She didn't like him. But she did appreciate his honesty.

And yet, she pondered what he'd told her about the empress's stolen crown. So it was indeed missing. She knew the reason behind it—without the crown, the empress might not be able to assume the throne—but wanted to know more.

OVER THE NEXT few hours, bodies were laid out and buried. The healthy men had dug a great pit of rows like they would have a latrine and laid the dead in there without ceremony. The ground, however, was hard and in many places, frozen. It made for hard, sweaty work. There were too many bodies to burn and nowhere to safely store them until spring. Leaving them would attract wild animals. What to do?

In the end, the army's plans to march were put on hold. There was an urgency, but the fighters had been caught unawares and with so many wounded and needing attention and rest, they had to stay.

So the men buried some, lit funeral pyres for others, and made plans to move soon. At the burning of the pyre, the healthy people stood by and watched in silent tribute as the local priest gave a few words prayer.

Bronwyn stood among the crowds, shivering in the late-afternoon sun. The sight of the great funeral pyre with so many bodies chilled her. She watched as the shrouded body of Lady Eleanor, carried with great reverence and tenderness, was laid upon the pyre by Sir Edward.

The pyre's flames bloomed, enveloping the bodies whole.

Theobold appeared beside her. "Will you look at that?"

The sun shone and the flames gave off a great heat, but there was no denying the tears that rolled down Sir Edward's cheeks.

"He loved her, I think," Bronwyn said.

"Of that, I have no doubt," Theobold said. "We'll need to speak with him. We should do it now, whilst he's distracted."

"Why? Can't we leave him to mourn her in peace?"

"Because she is in his thoughts. He won't appreciate our questions, but the shock of it all might make him answer honestly. Come." He led the way toward the knight.

They approached, but Bronwyn didn't feel comfortable about it. She stood quietly as Theobold cleared his throat. "Sir Edward, I wonder if we might ask you about the good Lady Eleanor."

"Leave me. I'll have none of your questions now, lad. Begone." Sir Edward's voice was gruff.

"I am tasked by the empress—"

"I don't care about your blasted investigation. Clear off and leave me to my thoughts."

Theobold shot Bronwyn a glance, bowed to Sir Edward, and left.

Bronwyn gave it a moment before she said, "I'm sorry."

"He is impertinent." The older man rubbed at his eyes. "What is it you want?"

"She was very dear to you, wasn't she?"

He paused, for so long that Bronwyn wondered if he would ignore her, but then he sighed and said, "She was a lady. We were affianced. I would have married her years ago and raised a family together in Lincolnshire, but she would stay with the empress. She felt a life at court offered no stable home for a child and did not want to leave Maud's side. And now…" His voice was gruff. "Lady Eleanor was beloved by all. She had no business in that tent, none at all."

"What do you think she was doing there?" Bronwyn asked.

"I don't bloody know. Don't you think I've been asking myself that? Why a good, Godly Christian woman would be in the empress's tent. It doesn't make any sense. And I don't believe a word that Sir Bors says, either."

Bronwyn glanced at him.

"He's lying. She wouldn't have tried to steal the crown. What would she do with it? She's innocent. She would never steal, especially not from the empress. She loved her like a sister."

"Why do you think she was there?"

"She must have seen something amiss and gone in. And if she fought with Sir Bors…" He gritted his teeth. "The man is a liar and a lecher. He has no respect, no gentlemanly love for women. And he is a turncoat. He used to be one of the empress's knights and instead turned to Stephen's camp. Then, after she wins the battle at Lincoln, he is back, as if nothing ever happened. And she welcomes him back with open arms. It's not right. I thought we might be rid of him, but I was wrong."

"I'm sorry." Bronwyn turned to leave, then paused. "Would it help if I brought you her rosewater perfume, to remember her by?"

"Pardon?" He looked at her. "She never wore rosewater. Only lavender scent. It was her favorite."

"My mistake."

"Leave me. Just know she was innocent. She was an innocent." He wiped his eyes again.

Bronwyn left him to his thoughts.

WHEN SHE GOT a free moment, she went in search of answers. She wanted to relay to Theobold what she'd learned, but the camp held hundreds of people, and there was little sense or order to it, at least beyond the most important people of the camp.

The tent of the empress was shadowed by her ladies, who slept in a tent together, as befitting their station. Their servants were not far away. More servants, peasants, and common folk were near. The horses were looked after by groomsmen, and the knights, men at arms, and squires rode and trained together.

After half an hour of walking through the camp and looking, she spotted Theobold, training and mock-fighting with another squire. His tall figure was unmistakable, as was his curly, black hair that shone in the cold, winter sun.

A circle of men stood around, cheering, watching as Theobold fought with wooden swords against an opponent. Theobold moved, dashing, almost dancing, as the clash and hard knock of wooden swords broke the still air.

Some men laid bets; others called out encouragement or insults.

As a mere servant, Bronwyn was ignored, so she stood by and came closer for a better view.

Theobold stood, his dark hair sweaty and plastered against his face as he towered over his opponent, a shorter, stocky, young man whose reddish-blond hair flashed like burnished gold in the sun. Rupert, she realized. Her heart began to pound. He was shirtless, and the sight of his bare, muscular torso sent a thrill through her. But then so was Theobold half-naked, and there was no mistaking the hard strength he brought to the fight.

The young men faced one another and had stripped down to their shirts and trousers, the boots cuffing the hard earth as they circled each other within the ring of cheering men.

Bronwyn observed she was not the only young woman in attendance. A few of the peasants, and even some ladies-in-waiting, were calling out or clapping their hands. Bronwyn idly wondered where Lady Alice was, for she was missing a chance to witness Rupert fight.

One stood nearby, and as they nodded to each other, the young woman said, "He's so handsome, isn't he?"

"Who?"

"Theobold. He's squire to Sir Robert."

"Sir Robert?" Bronwyn repeated.

The young woman shot her a look, surprised. "Sir Robert Fitzroy, the Earl of Gloucester? I'm surprised you don't know. He's the empress's half-brother. He and Sir Miles FitzWalter led her forces at Lincoln. Not that those people could stand a chance against Her Grace. They were in sore need of her help, the poor things." She *tsked*.

Bronwyn said, "I'm from Lincoln."

The young woman looked her up and down, noting her thin, brown woolen work dress, apron, and thin shoes. She didn't need to speak for Bronwyn to take her meaning.

Bronwyn ignored her and looked on at the fighting. She'd never asked Theobold about his master, or his position in the empress's court.

The young men attacked and parried with their wooden weapons, the steady hard beat and loud clap of the blades making hard knocks as they struck at one another again and again.

Finally, now sweating profusely and breathing hard, the men crashed into each other, but Rupert put a foot wrong. He slipped and stumbled, dust and dirt flying.

Her heart beat in her throat, and her right hand drifted to her chest. Would Rupert lose? Would it be out of the question to comfort him? But she wanted to speak with Theobold. And he wasn't wearing a shirt. She held a hand up to her warming cheeks. Could she look him in the eye without blushing?

In seconds, Theobold had knocked his wooden sword away,

sending it out of reach. He had his blade at Rupert's throat. The dust cleared, and the young fighters were at a standstill. The point of Theobold's blade rested against Rupert's throat. It was held there lightly, but if he wanted to, Theobold could cause Rupert harm and not be criticized for it.

His voice was loud and clear in the swirling dust. "Do you yield?"

"Yes." Rupert's voice came, resigned. He was still.

Theobold lowered his wooden sword with a half-smile and offered a hand to help Rupert up. Rupert took it and got to his feet in an instant, shaking hands.

Bronwyn licked her lips. Both men were sweaty, dusty, and dirty. The sun beat down on them, and there was no mistaking the muscles both had. Theobold was taller, slimmer, but Rupert had a stockier build. Bronwyn knew she should have looked away but didn't want to.

The knights watching declared Theobold the winner, and men and women clapped, laughing and talking. The young fighters both turned, Theobold to the loud cheers of the men and women present, Rupert to the silence of defeat.

As Theobold grinned and accepted their congratulations with thanks, he seemed to spot Bronwyn amongst the crowd. He'd handed his wooden sword away and had a linen shirt in hand. He'd been about to pull it over his head when he glanced at her.

She nodded to him, when there came a voice at her shoulder.

"Bronwyn. Looking for me? Did you see the fight?" Rupert said.

She turned. He looked handsome but very sweaty in the midday sun. "Yes. I'm sorry you lost."

"It happens. I'll beat him next time," Rupert said with an easy smile. "I'm glad you came. Most women come here to watch Theobold, so it's nice to have a real supporter. You're not swayed by his pretty face. You're smarter than that."

Bronwyn bit her lip. "I—" she started, just as Theobold stood before her and interrupted.

"There you are. I thought I saw you standing there." To Rupert, he said, "Oh, sorry, mate. She's here to see me."

Rupert's eyes widened. "Is this true? You came looking for him?"

"I wanted to talk to him," Bronwyn said.

"Oh." Rupert's shoulders slumped a fraction.

Bronwyn's heart fell. She could practically feel his disappointment. How could she make it up to him without revealing her true feelings? Even though he was romancing Alice, she still cared.

Theobold shot Rupert a triumphant smile. He grinned as Rupert walked away, shaking his head.

"Ask away, beautiful," Theobold said loudly.

Bronwyn rolled her eyes. "Stop that. This is important."

He grinned. "It always is." He flexed his arm muscles and used the plain, linen shirt in his hands to wipe the sweat from his face and neck.

The fact that he was shirtless had not gone unnoticed by Bronwyn, but she had no wish to give him the satisfaction of looking at his body. Besides, it felt rude. She kept her gaze fixed on his face. Unfortunately, this only made him smile more.

"What did you want to talk about? How much you like seeing me sweat?" he teased.

She shook her head. "The crown."

His smile disappeared, and he put a hand to her back, guiding her away from the crowd. She tensed and felt her cheeks grow warm.

His voice grew quiet. "Leave it, Bronwyn. It's done. Some little fool stole it. And when we find out who, they'll wish they'd never left their mother's womb."

"So we know whoever took it likely thinks that without her crown, the empress won't be able to be crowned ruler of England," Bronwyn surmised. "They hope to prevent her taking the throne by literally denying her a crown to wear. What does the empress think of this?"

"You know as much as I do. She hopes to hide it from the camp entourage and the men. It's no surprise to anyone that there are rebels here hiding among the people. But what they will do next is anyone's guess." He glanced at her. "Why do you care?"

She didn't know. From what she had seen, the empress could be hard, blunt, and arrogant. And yet there was another side of her. The empress had a way with people, if the man in the sick tent was any sign. He and others seemed to view Empress Maud as not a woman, but a leader, and a powerful one at that. And she couldn't ignore the way the empress had come to talk to her at the campfire, woman to woman, almost as if they were equals. She'd warned her, then raised her up as if she were important. It was dizzying.

"I spoke with Sir Edward. He says she was innocent. They were affianced. He says she'd never have stolen the crown, for she loved the empress."

"He believes Sir Bors was lying?" He turned his head to the side.

She nodded. "But what I find most interesting is the smell."

"What smell?" His eyebrows furrowed.

"When I entered the tent and found her dead, there was the scent of roses in the air, but there were no flowers in the tent, it is not the season for it. And Sir Edward tells me that Lady Eleanor never wore rosewater, only lavender scent."

He frowned. Did his eyes flash with recognition?

"The smell doesn't matter. The camp is full of odd smells. Likely, Sir Bors was dallying with a maidservant before the battle. You shouldn't stick your nose where it doesn't belong."

Her eyes narrowed. "You asked for my help!"

He met her gaze. "Then stick to the facts. Fewer smells and more bodies. Sir Bors has been tasked with finding the crown, but I'll wager there's no telling where it's gone. It may be fifty miles from here by now. Likely, that guard who fled took it."

Bronwyn started to turn.

"Hey. Aren't you going to stay?" Theobold asked. He pulled his shirt over his head.

She looked at him properly, noting how his broad shoulders filled out the shirt, and the way it pulled against the outline of his muscular arms. It was an enticing sight, and she looked away. "I've seen the show."

He laughed, and she walked away, leaving him to his group of admirers.

Rupert soon found her. As the loser of the mock fight, fewer people wished to speak with him. Bronwyn sensed him as he fell into pace beside her.

"What was all that about?" he asked.

"I had a question for him."

"What was it?" Rupert looked at her.

She opened her mouth to speak, then remembered the empress's warning. "I can't say."

"Can't or won't? Just admit it, you like him," Rupert said. He gave her an intense stare.

"It's not that." She paused and bit her lip. He thought Alice was beautiful, so why was he accusing her of liking another man?

"No? I saw the way you looked at him with his shirt off. You fancy him, don't you?" Rupert let out a forceful breath.

"No." Her lips pursed tightly. She didn't dare speak the truth.

"Come on, you can tell me. I'm like a brother to you. Lady Alice said so." He nudged her with his shoulder, and she missed a step, then nudged him back.

"What about you and Lady Alice? Are you two…?" She left it hanging, but her shoulders drooped. If only he didn't view her as a sister.

He blushed and rubbed the side of his face. "That's none of your business."

Her heart fell a little, but she hid it behind a smile and thumped him on the shoulder. They laughed and teased each other, joking around. But as they parted ways, with him returning to the makeshift training ground and her to the cooking tents, she cast a look back at him, at his reddish-golden hair that shone in the sun.

She couldn't bring herself to tell Rupert how she really felt about him. *But it doesn't matter*, she thought bitterly. It wasn't like she was able to compete with Lady Alice, anyway.

As she walked back to the servants and cooking area, she decided to instead focus on the mystery before her. So there was a rival court amongst the people at camp. That was no surprise. But why take such a risk, all to steal a crown, when people had died in the fight? It did not seem right. To risk the lives of refugees like herself, of innocent women, children, old men, all to prevent a ruler from being crowned... It seemed wrong.

BRONWYN WENT TO the makeshift cooking tents in the camp. They were little more than hastily constructed tables and pots and cauldrons hoisted over cooking fires. There was little to go around, but somehow, the people in the camp made it work.

One of the cooks had been injured in the battle and two of the scullery boys had died from the arrows, while others had been trampled underneath those fleeing the chaos.

Their numbers were fewer, but there were still so many of the servants. From one day to the next, the faces of the cooking staff changed, but the work remained the same.

Each day, they scavenged for herbs, set traps for animals, and collected and killed deer, rabbits, squirrels, wild hares, pheasants, ducks, and geese. The pheasants were especially dumb, but their plumage was beautiful, and they used the long tail feathers to decorate the platters on which they served the food.

When the sun warmed the river enough to melt the ice, the men would fish, but it was still winter and the nights were cold, the animals often thin and scrawny. Milk, butter, cream, and cheese were hard to come by, for cows were rare, unless the empress bought one. Similarly with flour—they only used what they could buy from villagers and markets they passed by.

Empress Maud was quick to capitalize on this misfortune,

often blaming King Stephen's influence. As if he, a prisoner, were to blame for the scarce food, the poor harvest, and the lack of flour.

THE NEXT DAY, Bronwyn stood by the riverbank, watching the waters ebb and flow. She sat on the cold ground, feeling the brittle soil break beneath her, and hugged her knees to her chest. There, a short distance across the river, sat the city of Lincoln, and her family's bakery. Or what was left of it.

Since escaping the city during the Battle of Lincoln, she had neither seen nor heard anything of her family. Nothing from her father or her stepmother or their apprentice, Wyot, a boy with a mop of blond hair and a love of honey cakes. What of them? Were they alive? Were they well? Did they miss her? Had they looked for her? She watched and wondered. She wondered if she could go back.

"Penny for your thoughts," a male voice said behind her.

She glanced back. It was Rupert, which instantly made her cheeks warm and her shoulders tense. He made her nervous, especially when he plopped himself down on the stunted grass next to her.

"Thinking of having a swim? It's a bit cold for bathing," he said with a grin.

She shook her head. She didn't know when the last time she'd had a bath was. She usually woke up early in the morning before dawn and swam in the river. She'd come out shivering but clean, and despite smelling like pond, it was better than trying to swim in the daylight, when someone would always be watching. And after long days of walking, cooking, cleaning, and sweaty work, she often felt dirty when the day was done.

"I was thinking about my family," she said, her voice dull.

"Oh." He sat quietly, not saying a word. Then, as many young men were wont to do, he took a bit of grass and played with it, fiddling as he bent and made it into a jumbled-up pile in his hands.

That was good about Rupert. He didn't pry.

"I wonder if I could go back."

"What do you mean? They're just across the river. Of course you can."

"But it's hard to enter the city now. And I'm with the empress's camp. I'm needed in the cooking tents. I can't just leave."

"Sure, you can," Rupert said. "People leave all the time. Each night we spend camped out here, people leave."

She stared at him, admiring his handsome face, his strong chin, before looking away. "Where do they go?"

"Anywhere but here. They go home, or to another town or village to start over. Some join Stephen's forces. Bronwyn, there's no one forcing you to stay. If you want to go, go."

She looked down at the grass, the muddy riverbank. Could he truly say goodbye to her so easily? Once they parted, they might never see each other again, and she couldn't bear that. "It doesn't feel so easy as that."

"It's not," another male voice said behind her.

She and Rupert looked up.

"Theobold," Rupert said, with a touch of dislike.

"Rupert." Theobold inclined his head. "Shouldn't you be attending your master?"

"He is well enough."

Bronwyn studied Rupert. His master, Sir Baldwin of Clare, had been captured at the battle and imprisoned with his lord, the king. The men loyal to him were kept nearby, but not close enough to arrange any plots of escape or attack. She wondered how often Rupert was allowed to see his master and how well attended the prisoners were.

"And the Lady Alice?"

Rupert blushed.

Bronwyn looked at Rupert, feeling her heart pound in her chest. She remembered Lady Alice thanking her for introducing them back in Lincoln, before the battle. Rupert and Lady Alice had instantly enjoyed each other's company, much to Bronwyn's regret. Had this truly grown into something more? Was it so obvious that others had noticed?

Rupert tossed the blade of folded grass away and stood, brushing down his tunic and leggings. "I don't see how that's any of your business."

Theobold stood by, hooking his fingers in his belt, along which hung a purse and a sheathed blade. "I only ask, as I assume she's wondering where you are. I did not know you and Mistress Bronwyn were friends."

Rupert shot him a dirty look. "We are."

Bronwyn's heart lifted. She moved to stand.

"We—I—" Rupert walked away, shaking his head, then turned. "Bronwyn, if you want to go visit your family, I'll go with you. That's what I wanted to say."

Bronwyn and Theobold watched him disappear into the crowd of people. "Why did you have to interrupt like that?" she asked, hands on her hips.

His mouth curled into a smile. "Why does it matter to you? Do you like him?"

She turned her back and sat down, refusing to say more.

Theobold gave a light laugh and sat down beside her. "Never mind. I can guess the answer well enough. So why are you planning to go into the city?"

She picked up a blade of grass and began to shred it into tiny pieces before throwing it away. "My family is there. I mean, they were. I don't know if they still are. But I want to go see."

He was quiet. She realized he was thinking.

"But I'm part of the empress's camp and don't think I can just go into the city, especially now, after the battle. I don't know how easy it will be, and whether there's anything still there. I don't even know if my family's still alive." Her voice shook, and she blinked hard, surprised at the sudden tears in her eyes.

Theobold rubbed her arm. "Hey. It's all right. Were they supporters of the king?"

She wiped her eyes on her sleeve. "I don't know. We were

caught up in a downright nasty business and…" Suddenly, she found herself telling him everything almost, how an innocent order for expensive bread rolls had landed her father in jail and led to her working in the castle kitchens, tasked with finding a murderer.

"Then the battle happened and Lady Alice rescued us from prison and we got out of the castle, but it was such a mess, people everywhere, and we got separated and… and…" She let out a quiet sob. "That was the last time I saw my pa." She swallowed and sobbed again.

He pulled her close and held her, rubbing her back as she wept. It was the first time she'd cried for a long time, and he held her, not so tightly to hurt or be uncomfortable, but just to comfort her. He held her like a man held a woman, and it was something she'd never experienced before. It felt… nice. But grief, worry, and the emotion and fear of not knowing about her family's whereabouts plagued her mind, and her body trembled as she cried.

He stroked her back with his right hand and murmured words of comfort in her ear, nonsensical noises, like one might calm a mewling animal or wild beast.

She cried and got his tunic damp with her tears, and then her sobs began to quiet, and she pulled away.

She blinked hard and wiped her eyes on her other sleeve. "I'm sorry. I didn't mean to get your tunic wet."

He looked down at the damp patch on his shirt. "Oh, that's all right. It'll dry. And I can just tell the men that I had women crying over me, which is true now." He grinned.

Bronwyn laughed a little. It felt good to laugh. She needed it, and after her cry, she felt empty almost, like a limp rag that had been wrung out. She was tired and wanted to sleep. What to say?

His eyes looked full of concern. "Are you all right?"

She nodded. "I will be." She got to her feet and wiped her cheeks. "Thanks."

"No problem." He stood. "So when are we going? You'll need

an escort."

"I will? But it's my home city."

He gave a knowing look. "That's just been under siege and retaken by the empress. A young woman like yourself shouldn't be walking around the streets alone."

She frowned at him. "But it's my city."

"Not anymore. It's Empress Maud's city now."

She turned her head and watched the sun set, its golden rays fading to a sky blue before it sank below the horizon. The trees stood out stark and black against the sky, like grizzled reminders of winter—and of war.

Their eyes met, and Bronwyn felt something pass between them. She felt more aware of herself. "You'll help me?"

"Yes. Just don't do anything foolish. When do you want to go?"

"Tomorrow?"

"We'll leave at first light."

∎❧∎

Chapter Six

THE NEXT MORNING, Bronwyn met Theobold on the outskirts of the camp. He came leading a horse in tow. "I thought we'd need this. I can always say I'm on the empress's business."

She looked up at the horse. It was so big, and with simple trappings. She'd only ridden a horse once before and had found it a very unpleasant experience that had left her sore. She did not relish repeating it.

"Um, can't we walk?"

"And take ages? You want to go or not?" He tilted his head to the side. "You're not scared?"

"No." The animal in question was tall, a light-grey mare with a snowy-white velvety coat and silvery mane.

"You do know how to ride, don't you?"

She hitched a shoulder in a half-shrug. "I rode once, but that's it. We don't often ride horses when we're baking." She gave him a slight smile.

He grinned back at her. "Of course not. And here I was, thinking all bakers are talented riders as well." He rubbed his cheek. "Learn something new every day. All right, come here. I'll give you a foot up."

He stood by and tied the horse's reins to a tree as he helped her get a foot in the stirrup and then helped boost her up into the saddle. She was ungainly, awkward and ungraceful, but after some harried fumbling and rearranging of her skirts, she was there. She sat up, seeing him snort, and pulled her skirts down over her legs as best she could.

"Stop looking at my legs," she said.

His gaze darted to her legs. "I wasn't, but I am now."

She furiously tried pulling her skirts down more to cover her legs and wobbled in the saddle, almost slipping.

He laughed and put a hand on her thigh to steady her. "Whoa there. I promise not to look at your legs if you agree to stay in the saddle, all right?"

She frowned at him. "It's not like I was trying to lose my balance," she said grumpily.

He smiled again.

"What's so funny?" she asked.

"You." He left her side and went to untie the reins from the tree. He easily climbed up into the saddle behind her, which made her tense, and settled his weight behind her, wrapping his arms around her waist as he held the reins. "Hold on."

She stiffened at the feel of his arms around her. They were warm, and a part of her wanted to relax, but she couldn't. She felt nervous all over again.

"Relax, I won't let you fall," he told her.

That's not what I'm afraid of, she thought.

He nudged the horse gently with his heels and the mare started to walk. They took a path out of camp, away from the large encampment, and slowly picked a way across and around a bridge to the city's entrance.

"Why were you laughing at me?" she asked.

"Because. Usually, it's women who are *trying* to show me a glimpse of their legs, but not you. You're the opposite."

"Oh."

They kept riding. In no time at all, they were at the castle gates. The guards didn't recognize them, but Theobold tossed one a coin and announced they were there on the empress's business. The guards let them in, and as they passed through the stone gates and under the arch, Bronwyn took a deep breath.

Part of it was seeing the city from a new height, but also, some of the city had changed. The battle had only been about a fortnight ago and yet things were already different. Some buildings had collapsed and fallen from the destruction, the streets had new people wandering them, different folk. Bronwyn recognized no faces at all. It was like entering a new town, and yet one where she knew the layout.

But the streets were dirty, and the scents of human waste, butchery, blood, and smoke were in the air. It wasn't pleasant, and it wasn't the normal city smells, either.

"Let's halt for a moment." Theobald pulled back on the reins.

"What is it?" Bronwyn wanted to turn in the saddle and look at him, but to move too much made her lose her balance. She contented herself with looking straight ahead, eyeing the buildings and rubble of places she'd once known.

"I don't think we thought this through."

"What do you mean? We're here." She turned in the saddle to face him and he locked his arms around her so she wouldn't fall. She glanced up at his eyes. "If you don't want to go any farther, then fine, but I mean to see my family's bakery. I want to know if they're still alive."

"But—"

"Enough. Thank you, Theobold. You've been very kind." She faced forward and began to lift her leg, when he stopped her.

"For God's sake, Bronwyn, just wait a minute."

"What for?"

"Think for a moment. How do you know they're still alive? You don't. They could be…"

"Dead?"

"Yes. I don't want you to go in there and see their bodies if that's the case."

She stiffened.

"I'm sorry. I didn't know how else to say it." He let out a small sigh. "I'll take you wherever you want to go. Just stay on the horse, and let me go in first, all right? Just to make sure it's safe."

"It's my family home. Of course it's safe."

She felt him let out a noisy breath. "You haven't seen a city after a battle until now, Bronwyn. I have. It changes things. The people, the places. They're different after a battle. You think things may be the same as before, but I assure you, they're not. No one thinks the war will ever reach them, but it can and it does, from Southampton to Lincoln and back. Their Graces brought their war here, and Lincoln did not escape unscathed." He nudged the horse on. "Tell me which way your family's home is."

She gave him directions, and they took the streets at a slow walk, the mare's hooves striking the ground in the early morning.

"What if they're still alive?" he asked.

"That's my hope," she said quietly.

"But if they are, what will you do?"

"Return home. Live with my family. What else?" she asked, thinking of Rupert. He would never have a future with her, anyway, she realized with a pang of sadness. They were besotted with each other, if Rupert's shy blushes and Lady Alice's smiles were any indication.

"But you're a part of the empress's camp now. Will you give that up to return to your life here?"

"Of course I will. I—" She paused.

She had wanted her independence, to see other parts of the world. The empress's camp promised to do just that for her. In another day or so, they would begin traveling to Gloucester. It was another part of the country, and a part she had never seen before. She'd never been out of Lincoln before. It was an enticing prospect. But then she felt guilty for thinking that.

"I just want to know if they're okay. Anything else can wait."

"Are you sure? What if they're—"

"I want to know. Wouldn't you want to know if your family is alive and well?"

"I know. My family is..." His voice was dull. "I don't want to talk about them."

"Oh. All right." She let the conversation stop for a beat. They were likely dead. "I'm sorry."

"'S all right." He nudged the horse on. "Promise me you won't make any rash decisions right away."

"I promise," she said as they turned around a corner. "Oh."

The bakery was a ruin. Bronwyn slipped off the horse, ignoring Theobald's protests. She walked toward the building, quiet as a spirit. Her footsteps were light against the dirt road, and yet she felt as if she were returning home, and for a split second, she wanted to turn and tell Theobold it was fine, her family was here, safe and sound. She'd invite him to dinner and they'd all laugh about what a worrier she'd been.

But that wasn't the case.

The door hung off its hinges, and leaves fluttered inside the building. An ill wind blew, sending Bronwyn's hair across her face. She brushed the strands away and opened the door, pushing it aside.

Inside, the shop was empty. It was cold. No fires had been lit; the stone oven she had known to burn since she'd been a child sat abandoned. The worktables were empty, bare of bread rolls and loaves. The wind blew the door open, making it squeak and groan against the doorframe.

Bronwyn's eyes adjusted to the shadows and the darkness, and she saw a few huddled figures there, curled up for warmth. The air smelled of urine and feces, with none of the traces of bread, flour, or baking she'd known. It was as if her family had never existed, and all that was left of the home she'd known was an empty shell.

The figures were sleeping. She wanted to know… was her family among them? Was Wyot there?

She stepped forward—and paused. None of the figures there she recognized. They were refugees, having fled from the battle. All traces of her family were gone.

She climbed up the ladder to her family's room and peeked

her head above the floor space. It was bare, and empty. A few poor souls slept in what had been her parents' bed, and her old pallet. No one she knew was up there.

She climbed back down and saw a few of the people awake, watching her with cold, sunken eyes. Their faces were long and drawn with hunger. She stepped back.

"Please…" A man stood and came toward her. "Do you have any food?"

She shook her head. "No. No, I don't."

He reached for her and she shied away, stumbling backward. Bronwyn landed on the floor and hit her rump hard, banging her elbows. She bit back a cry and scuttled back on her hands like a crab before Theobold burst through the door, his sword out and gleaming in a small ray of sunlight. Dust floated in the air as the sword flashed with warning. "Get away from her. Get back."

The man, an older man of some middle-age years, whom hunger and the cold had clearly worn down, lowered his hand and drew away. Some of the shadowy figures clung to each other and retreated farther into the dark corners of the room.

"Are you all right?" Theobold asked.

"Yes."

He held out a hand and she took it, allowing him to help her up. With his sword still extended, they backed out of the bakery, until she said, "Wait."

"What?"

She re-entered and made eye contact with the man. "There's a storeroom downstairs. below ground. If you open it, there might still be some flour, some old loaves."

The man looked. She pointed to where, and he fumbled, looking for the trap door opening.

"Bronwyn, let's go," Theobold said at her shoulder.

"But we could bring something back—"

"Now." His voice held a note of finality, and she listened to it. He meant business. "We've stayed long enough."

"All right." She turned and followed him out into the light.

Once outside the bakery, she breathed in the air, letting the early-morning rays fall on her face. She closed her eyes for a moment and breathed but did not feel comforted. When she opened her eyes, Theobold was watching her.

"I'm ready," she said.

He had tied the horse's reins to a post outside the bakery and helped her climb into the stirrup and atop the saddle again. Once they were both safely on, he asked, "Did you find what you were looking for?"

She shrugged. "I think so."

"Did you see your family?"

"No. They're gone. There's nothing there for me now."

He nodded, made a noise to the mare, and touched her sides gently with his heels. The mare started to move, and they rode, with Theobold leaving Bronwyn to her thoughts.

"Why did you want to go? We could have looked for some spare flour. There might've been some in the storeroom," she said, feeling slight comfort in his arms around her and his solid presence at her back.

He shook his head, a motion she felt against the back of her head, almost as if his chin touched her hair. "I didn't like that place. No offense, but that's no longer a bakery or a home. It's where people are sheltering for the winter, and you took a risk going in there. If someone had attacked you, I could have rescued you, but I wouldn't want to fight against so many people. There were too many."

"They weren't fighters. Just men and women who were hungry."

"Hunger makes people do dangerous things, Bronwyn. I hope you never have to see that."

They exited the city and once outside the gates, Bronwyn took a deep breath. She felt hollow, tired, and rejuvenated slightly.

"You all right?" he asked at her shoulder.

"Yes. I feel better now. At least now I know they're gone. I don't know what I was expecting."

"What will you do now?"

She shrugged. "I guess I'll stay on with the empress's camp. I wanted a bit of adventure since my pa and I first got involved with the castle, but it's been danger ever since. Not quite what I thought my life would be like."

"Would you return to them?" he asked. "I mean, if you could turn back time, and none of this would have happened. Would you stay there with them in the bakery if it meant a life with no adventure?"

"No. I wouldn't know what I know now, and I'd still be wanting to get away and see a bit of the world. I used to think that going out of Lincoln would be a big change, but now I think I might have been wrong about that."

"The world can seem very big and very small at the same time."

"You're a poet. Like a minstrel." She leaned closer to him.

He laughed. "As long as you don't call me a 'fool,' we'll get on fine."

They returned to the camp. As he pulled the horse over to one of the lines of the creatures tied together for safety, he tossed the reins to a stableboy and climbed down. Theobold waited a second, then as Bronwyn began to dismount, he took her by the waist and lifted her from the horse, setting her on the ground.

"Thank you." She shivered.

"You're cold. Here, take my cloak." He untied his cloak and put it around her shoulders.

She felt comforted at the gesture but shook her head. "I can't—it's far too big for me. I'll trip over it." She laughed and handed it back.

"Then I'll just have to find you one that fits."

Their eyes met, and he smiled. His black curls shone in the early morning sun.

"I'm glad you've decided to stay with us."

"You are?"

"Of course. Who else would I have to tease?" He lowered his hands from her waist and nodded. "Till we meet again, Mistress Bronwyn." He gave her a courtly bow and waved, walking away. "Call on me whenever you fancy a ride on horseback."

She clapped a hand to her cheeks, which felt overly warm. Was she blushing? No. It wasn't possible. It was her body's reaction to the cold chill of the morning, surely.

She walked and immediately felt sore muscles ache in her legs. She rubbed her thighs, trying to ease the muscles to relax.

"What do you think you're doing?" Rupert's voice came from behind her. "I saw you two ride off together. Did he try anything with you?"

"Rupert." She shaded her eyes from the morning light. "What are you talking about?"

"You. Him. What are you doing spending time with Theobold? Don't you know he's close to the empress? He's not someone you want to dally with. What were you doing together, anyway? Did he promise you a romantic ride on horseback?" His eyes were sharp, his mouth firm with disapproval.

Bronwyn's eyes narrowed and she squared up to him. "No, he didn't. He was helping me."

"With what?"

"Not that it's any of your business, but he took me into the city to visit my family's bakery. I wanted to see if they were still there, or still alive."

They stood close now. Too close for courtly propriety. You could slide a piece of parchment between them, she surmised. Not that it mattered.

His eyes bored into hers. "I don't like you seeing him. You should be more careful."

"Why? What do you care with whom I spend time? You ought not to care at all," she challenged. He wanted to be with Alice, didn't he?

"You're right, I don't care. I just don't like seeing a smart woman like you make foolish decisions."

They stood inches apart. She had to crane her neck up to glare into his eyes, and she felt her chest lightly brush against him. He stiffened at the touch. Rupert glared back at her, and then to her surprise, his gaze darted to her lips.

What did that mean? He repeated the action. This time, she could not ignore it.

"Bronwyn, I..." he started.

"Yes?"

She breathed in, when a voice called out, "Mistress Baker! My lady wants some bread rolls now for her breakfast. For some reason, she asks you deliver them yourself, so make yourself presentable."

A young, broad-shouldered woman with long, thick, brown hair; a round, doughy face and chin; and darting eyes that narrowed at the sight of her appeared in front of her. The Lady Morwenna, if Bronwyn remembered correctly from Lady Eleanor.

This young woman spelled trouble, Bronwyn knew within a second. How, she didn't know. She just knew it in her gut.

Lady Morwenna's face was unmistakable, as was the way her eyes danced with delight. "I do hope I'm not interrupting."

Rupert stepped back. "No, you're not."

Bronwyn turned to Lady Morwenna. "I'll go. Excuse me." She did not bow, simply marching away toward the cooking tents.

Lady Morwenna caught up to her. "My, my, what was that all about? If I didn't know better, I'd say he was about to kiss you."

"You're wrong. We were arguing."

"If that's what you call arguing, I'd love to see more. Where can I find a knight like that who'll argue with me?"

Bronwyn shook her head, her blond braid flying over her shoulder. "He's not a knight. He's a squire."

"Is he? What a pity. Very well. I'm sure he'll become a knight soon. I know the type, you see."

"What do you mean?"

Lady Morwenna fluffed her thick, brown hair, so dark, it was almost black. "Well, my family happens to be a major supporter of the empress. We own hundreds of acres in Kent, not far from Leeds Castle. We also are patrons of young men who show promise to the crown and prove their worth in battle. Everyone who is anyone wants my family's patronage," she said with a self-satisfied smile.

Bronwyn raised an eyebrow. Why did this young woman care about Bronwyn and Rupert?

"That's nice."

"Yes, it is. But then I don't expect you to understand. You've probably never had a patron in your life. We only take the best, so I don't imagine our paths would ever cross. But all the same, you would be wise to be good to me. You don't want me as your enemy." Lady Morwenna faced her, standing in her path. "And please address me properly. *Lady Morwenna.*"

Bronwyn ducked her head. "Lady Morwenna." Something about this young woman sent an eerie prickling between her shoulder blades. She smelled like trouble.

"Good. It seems you know your place. Don't cross me and we'll get along just fine." She tossed her hair and with her nose in the air, swept away, her skirts in her hands as she walked with her shoulders back.

Bronwyn watched her go.

"Don't mind her. Lady Alice was talking you up to the empress, and Lady Morwenna felt threatened. She's the empress's favorite."

Bronwyn turned. There stood another of the empress's ladies-in-waiting. This one was plump with dark-auburn hair and a rosy hue to her cheeks, with a smattering of freckles across her nose. She smiled at Bronwyn. "You probably don't remember me. I'm Lady Susanna. I don't like to put on airs like the other ladies do."

"I'm Bronwyn." She paused. "Just Bronwyn."

"I can see that. Your dress is clearly homespun and you're wearing an apron. You're a servant, yes?"

Bronwyn nodded. "I'm Bronwyn Blakenhale. I'm a baker by trade, from Lincoln. My family…"

"Oh, yes. Were you in the battle? Did you see the king fall?"

"I was there, but not at the fighting." Bronwyn's shoulders slumped as she thought of visiting her family's bakery with Theobold. "They're gone."

"Your family? Where are they now?" Lady Susanna tilted her head.

"I don't know. Theobold took me to see, but—"

"Oh, don't mention him. You shouldn't even talk to him." Her lips pressed together in a slight frown.

"What do you mean? Why?" Bronwyn's brow wrinkled. "I thought he was popular amongst the women at camp."

"He is. But he and Lady Morwenna don't get along. There's a long story there, but she fancies him and he doesn't care for her, no matter how much she tries. So now they're at odds. If she sees you two together, well… She might try to make your life miserable," Lady Susanna said.

"Why? I haven't done anything to her."

"Lady Morwenna has fancied Theobold for the past three years. She even got her family to patronize him as he trained as a page and then a squire, to Sir Robert of Gloucester. Sir Robert is a trusted knight of the empress, and ever so bold. Lady Morwenna's family paid a lot for Sir Robert to take him on."

"Why doesn't his own family pay for his position?" Bronwyn asked.

"Don't you know? They aren't well liked, considering the family profession. He was sent to be a squire and bring prestige to their name." She giggled. "I shouldn't be telling you all this. Lady Morwenna wouldn't want you to know. But… she has hoped that they would wed. Although it doesn't seem like that now."

"No?"

Lady Susanna shook her head, her auburn hair shining in the sunlight. "Since arriving at camp, Theobold has been stepping out with all the young women. He charms them and takes them on horseback rides, maybe steals a kiss or two, then he loses interest and breaks their hearts. Don't let it happen to you, is all I'd say."

Bronwyn nodded, taking this information in. Had Theobold been trying to slowly seduce her, or had he just been being kind, by taking her to see her family's bakery? She didn't know.

Bronwyn made rolls. There was no precious white flour to be had, but they did have some salt, so she prepared an ordinary brown flour roll with rosemary and a touch of salt. it wasn't a sweet bread roll, but she hoped it would be tasty.

Normally, she would've asked why, but she had an idea. The empress wished to speak with her, and she had information to share. But she did not know at that moment where her loyalties lay.

She didn't know if she was allied with King Stephen and Queen Matilda or Empress Maud. The king had imprisoned her father for a crime he had not committed, and if Bronwyn had not found the killer, and the battle had not thrown their world into chaos, he would have been hanged on a feast day and died an innocent man. Could she really pledge allegiance to such a cold-hearted ruler?

So why did she feel a sense of loyalty to the queen, his wife? She wasn't sure.

Bronwyn saw the weary and wary glances of the other cooks and kitchen hands and one of the older cooks bid her go. Bronwyn swallowed and followed the page, brushing her hands down on her plain work apron.

He led her through the camp, past groups of men training, some wrestling and play fighting. Other groups of men and women, non-combatants, sat around cooking fires and talking. The people looked exhausted. Their clothes were dirty and worn, their faces pale and drawn. Some were walking injured, and there was little help to be had until they reached Gloucester.

She was led to a grand tent, where they were let in by a pair of guards with spears. The light clink of cups and women's muted laughter filtered outward from inside, and Bronwyn tugged at the top of her dress, trying to loosen it from her collarbone.

A page ushered her inside, and her eyes drifted to the floor. She glanced up at the people in the tent as the voices quieted. The women appraised her, taking in the sight of her floury work apron, her hair tied back in a kerchief, and the light dotting of sweat across her brow.

Flanked by two guards, and with two more standing behind her, she felt almost like a prisoner. At the opposite end of the room sat the empress on a round, wooden chair laid with furs. Tables and chests were behind her.

Near the empress in a half-circle sat Lady Morwenna, Lady Susanna, and Lady Alice, who looked at Bronwyn with recognition, but no hint of warmth. Instead, she cast a bored gaze and examined her nails.

She sat beside Lady Susanna and a lady-in-waiting with soft-brown hair and a pert nose who idly ate an apple whilst whispering to Lady Morwenna.

The young woman smiled and whispered again, making the empress laugh. "Susanna, Morwenna, you young ladies are too much." The empress giggled. Fastening her gaze on Bronwyn, she said, "Well, Mistress Blakenhale. So good of you to join us. Tell me, what are these?" She gestured to the pile of rolls set aside on a plate.

"They are rolls of rosemary and salt, Your Grace," she said.

"And why did you not prepare sweet white rolls with honey? Alice tells me they are something of a specialty of yours." She tapped her foot.

Bronwyn bowed her head, then met the empress's eyes. "There is no white flour or honey to be had, Your Grace."

"I see. Such is life on the road, I suppose. I will tolerate that for now, but once we reach Gloucester, I will expect you to prepare some of these rolls I keep hearing about. I gather Stephen's little wife is fond of them." She smirked and motioned to Lady Susanna. "Hand those here. They will do, for now." Her voice held a note of idle warning.

Bronwyn swallowed. The empress may have seemed sulky at the idea of there being no fresh, white flour for fine bread rolls, but she was also the leader of the invading army. Bronwyn realized she would be wise not to get on Empress Maud's bad side. The rolls were plain but good enough, she hoped.

The empress took one and bit into it. "Good, but not as good as what we would have at court. Be sure to have the cooks teach you how to make the sweet white rolls with honey, and other delicacies."

Bronwyn nodded.

"I have heard a rumor that you entered the city. Don't you know it is dangerous?"

"Yes, Your Grace." Her pulse began to race. The fact that the empress knew about her and Theobold's trip to the city made her nervous. Who had watched and informed the empress about their movements?

"Why did you go?"

"To see my family. I wanted to know if they were still alive." Her heart began to pound in her chest, loudly, like a drum.

"And? Are they?"

Bronwyn bowed her head. "I do not know, Your Grace."

"What do you mean?"

"They were not there. The bakery was empty." She did not mention the refugees and hungry people there. Somehow, she felt that would not be welcome information to receive.

"A pity. Then you could have gone home. I'm sure your family would be looking for you," Lady Morwenna said with false sweetness.

"A very kind thought, Lady Morwenna," Empress Maud said, bestowing a smile on her.

Lady Morwenna practically preened from the attention, shooting Bronwyn a self-satisfied smile.

"How did you get to the city?" the empress asked.

"Oh, a squire gave me a ride on his horse."

The ladies grew interested.

"Who?" Lady Alice asked.

Bronwyn swallowed. If she were to lie and name Rupert, Lady Alice would get jealous. If she named Theobold, she would incur Lady Morwenna's ire. What to say?

Lady Susanna tapped her chin with a dainty finger and shot her a warning look.

"Um, I cannot remember," Bronwyn lied. "It was a young man who was kind and took me there, then back again. He must have been on an errand for Your Grace."

The ladies nodded. Lady Susanna said, "Very kind."

"Your Grace, I should get back. *Pardonnez-moi.*"

"Go." Empress Maud waved a hand in dismissal. "Oh, Bronwyn. Be sure to gather your things. We leave for Gloucester in the next few days."

Bronwyn left the plate of bread rolls, curtsied, and left, thinking, *What things?* She had nothing but the clothes on her back, and even those she suspected would be stolen if she were not careful.

Word quickly passed through the camp about the upcoming travels. Gloucester. So it was finally happening. They would soon be on the move.

After luncheon, which for the staff, was a thin potage made of whatever they could find, scavenge, and buy from the city of Lincoln, having raided its stores, she spent the day cooking, cleaning, washing linens and dishes, using her fingers and bits of smelly soap to clean the trenchers and serving plates.

"Psst." Lady Susanna stood at her elbow.

"Hullo. What are you doing here? Did you need something?" Bronwyn asked.

"No. Only to say that was very smart of you to stay vague about who took you into the city. I was worried for you for a minute there."

"Thanks. I don't like to lie."

Lady Susanna agreed. "So what are you doing?"

Bronwyn was currently up to her elbows in dirty dishwater

and was scrubbing clean a used serving dish. "Cleaning."

"Oh. That's less exciting than I thought. I figured you would be fishing or hunting. Something more interesting than needlepoint."

Bronwyn smiled. "Not really. Is that what the ladies do?"

"Often. Or we play music, sing, or read."

Bronwyn let out a quiet sigh. "I wish I could read."

"I know a little. My mama always said I didn't need to, but my father says I'd need to learn how to run a household someday, so he taught me a little about figures. I'd like to learn more, though."

"Lady Susanna. What are you doing here? Associating with the servants?" Lady Morwenna strolled by and saw them. "Don't you look like a little pair of thieves."

Lady Susanna flushed. "I…"

"Not to worry," said Bronwyn, improvising. "I'll bring some more rolls as quick as I can. Thanks for letting me know."

"Uh, of course. Don't forget." Lady Susanna turned and walked away with Lady Morwenna, chatting.

Bronwyn watched them go. She felt she had a slight friend in Lady Susanna, but at the same time, she was a servant and Lady Susanna was a lady. Bronwyn felt slighted, but not surprised that Lady Susanna would want to keep their budding friendship a secret. If that was even what it was.

Bronwyn worked until nightfall, helping the cooks and servants pack up the serving pots and dishes, but only some, as they'd still need to feed the camp before leaving the area soon.

That night, she was delivering a plate of rolls to the ladies-in-waiting, as the empress had expressed a wish for some, and was holding the platter, when Lady Alice accosted her.

"Lady Alice? What is it?" Bronwyn asked.

"Um, I need your help. Can those wait?"

"Well, they're for the empress. I should deliver them right away."

Lady Alice pulled her arm. "Come here." She turned to a

page and said, "You. Come here."

The youth approached. Lady Alice took the platter of bread rolls and pressed it into his hands. "These are for the empress. Deliver them now. I'll know if you steal one."

The page's eyes widened and he turned and hurried in the direction of the empress's tent. Once he had disappeared, Lady Alice said, "Come with me."

Bronwyn let Lady Alice pull her away, to another tent, smaller, which she apparently shared with another few women. She pulled her inside and closed the flap, looking behind them.

"What are we doing here?" Bronwyn asked. "This is your tent?"

"Yes." Lady Alice's movements were flighty, nervous. Like a bird darting or a crow hopping. She pushed a black tendril of hair behind her ear. "I was in here, when I saw something odd."

"What?"

"I was looking for a shawl when I found this." She pointed toward a blanket and pillow, stuffed with hay. "Look."

"What am I looking for?"

"You'll see. Just look."

Bronwyn took a hesitant step toward the grey, woolen blanket that was swaddled up messily. She pulled it back. Nothing. She peeked beneath the pillow. There, sat beneath it, lay a golden crown.

Chapter Seven

B RONWYN HISSED AND stepped back. "Alice. What in the world were you thinking?"

"I didn't take it, you dolt. I found it here."

"You mean…"

"Someone took the empress's blooming crown and put it amongst my things. They planted it here, no doubt to try to make it appear as though I had stolen it. But I didn't."

Bronwyn thought quickly. "We have to get rid of it."

"Well, obviously." Lady Alice's voice was short, clipped, and laden with sarcasm.

Bronwyn gave Lady Alice a level look and put her hand on her hips.

"Sorry. I'm very anxious about this. I need your help. What are we going to do?" Lady Alice bit at her nails.

"'We'?"

"It's no longer *my* problem, it's *ours*. You're essentially my maid. If I am found out, or if anyone finds us with it, we'll hang together."

Bronwyn inhaled through her nose and let out a breath. She hadn't been Lady Alice's maid since they'd been together at Lincoln. "Right." She covered up the crown quickly. "Tell me what you were doing and how you found it."

Lady Alice d tapped her nose with a dainty index finger. "I was at dinner with the empress and the other ladies, and then we stepped away for some dancing. Rupert was there," she said, recalling with a fond smile. "He complimented my hair, and ... Never mind. I went to use the privy, and when I came back here to fetch a shawl, I found it."

"How did you know to look under your pillow?"

"I don't know. I just thought something was wrong. I knew as soon as I came in that someone had been here."

"How?"

Lady Alice tilted her head, her nose slightly in the air. "When I am without a maid to look after my person, I… often clean and make up my own bedding. I fold the blanket and plump up the pillow so it's nice and tidy. It doesn't do to be messy and unruly. It's the height of uncleanliness."

"So you came in and found your bedding disturbed."

"Yes, that's it exactly. I saw my pillow had been moved, so when I went to straighten it, I found *that*." Lady Alice seemed not to even want to say the word.

"Hmm."

"What are we to do? Rupert will be wondering where I am," Lady Alice said.

"Did you see anyone else leave the dining area?"

"No. But I wasn't paying attention. I mean, aside from the usual."

"What do you mean?" Bronwyn asked.

"Well, only that when Lady Morwenna goes to the privy, then Lady Susanna will go too, as Lady Susanna doesn't like to go alone. But then Lady Morwenna told her *no*, she'd had enough of her constant company and said she wanted to be alone. She used some very rude words and Lady Susanna was a bit shocked and hurt, I dare say, so she let Lady Morwenna go. You should talk to Lady Susanna and see if she saw anything."

"Can she be trusted?"

"Hmm, I'd say so. She's kind enough, even if she does like to natter on. I have to go. We must hide this. I cannot go to sleep knowing that thing is amongst my bedsheets. It's a death sentence." She looked at Bronwyn. "Can you… take it with you? Hide it somewhere?"

"*Me?*" Bronwyn's eyes widened.

"Yes. No one would suspect a servant girl. Especially one covered in flour. You smell like bread."

There was a rustle of noise outside.

Lady Alice tensed, wadded up the crown in one of her dresses, and said loudly, "This dress of mine has a stain on it. Clean it for me. I must look my best before the empress." She pressed the crown and dress into Bronwyn's hands. "Go. Now," she whispered.

The tent flap opened. It was Lady Susanna. "Oh, hello. Are you taking clothes for washing? I have a dress too. Would you mind, terribly?"

Bronwyn shook her head.

"She is *my* maidservant, Lady Susanna, not yours," Lady Alice pointed out.

"Oh." Lady Susanna blushed.

"I don't mind, Lady Susanna," Bronwyn said.

"Oh, good. That's ever so kind of you." The tent was large enough to hold four makeshift beds and two chests. Three of the beds hadn't been made up, with ladies' clothing strewn around. Lady Susanna took a shift and dress from one of the unmade beds and handed them to Bronwyn. "You sure you don't mind?"

"Yes, my lady."

"So kind. Thank you." Lady Susanna gave Bronwyn a warm smile.

"I'll be off, then." Bronwyn ducked her head, lifted the tent flap, and stepped out into the night.

Her thoughts scattered like leaves. She now had in her possession Empress Maud's very crown. A gold crown. People had died over it. Men might have been tortured for it. She needed to think. She needed a plan—and fast.

She untied her apron from her waist and, wrapping the crown in one of her old dresses, she went out into the woods, near where she had gathered rosemary before and dug a hole with her hands, getting the dirt beneath her fingernails and on her skin. She had no spade or gloves, and the ground was hard. She'd made hardly a dent in it, for the ground was still brittle from the winter freeze. No, this wouldn't do. She couldn't bury it.

She'd have to keep it on her person, which was a dangerous prospect in and of itself. But that alone would be near impossible, for it wasn't a small, little band. This was a heavy, gold circlet. She went to wash her hands by the river and thought over her options. She'd have to hide it. With any luck, it would not be noticed. And even then, what to do with it? Could she return it? Just having it was a death sentence. She had to get rid of it—somehow.

But that still left the matter of the fact that the crown had been returned and found in Lady Alice's things. She believed Lady Alice. The lady had no reason to want to steal the crown, for she was loyal to the empress. So if she was innocent, why would someone have put the crown amongst her bedding?

Someone who wanted to hurt her, have the empress impris-on or possibly kill her, or perhaps someone who'd also found it amongst their things and wanted to avoid suspicion by hiding the crown amongst someone else's. What if Lady Alice had not been the intended victim of this crime? For a crime was what it was.

Bronwyn thought back to the night when the crown had first gone missing. There had been only two guards manning the tent, and one had been killed, while the other had disappeared. Where had the other gone, and why had he fled? She needed to talk to Theobold about this again. But how much could she trust him? Could she tell him of their discovery of the crown? Would he believe that she hadn't stolen it herself?

She frowned. He'd like her questions entirely too much, for he was pig-headed and rather full of himself. No doubt he'd find her questions an attempt to talk to him, and he already got far too much attention. She found him attractive, but she did not like how arrogant he was. Still, she needed help, and answers. But could she trust him?

She wasn't sure. One thing she could do was talk to Rupert. Her palms sweated at the thought. But she needed help and knew he would give it. Even if she had to ignore her feelings for him.

Bronwyn washed the ladies' dresses in the river, wringing them out with her cold, wet hands. The crown was in the washing too, and she took care to make sure the circlet was well hidden. She took the whole lot to her spot by the fire, where the other women servants were preparing to sleep, and sat on a log, stuffing the crown beneath her dress, still bundled in her now-damp apron. Feeling the solid, wooden log beneath her rump and wishing she could have a cushion, she shook out the ladies' wet dresses, letting the woolen cloth steam and dry by the open flame. Once the other women had fallen asleep, she quickly wadded up the crown in one of the ladies' dresses and shook out her damp apron to dry.

Looking around for any prying eyes, Bronwyn put the entire bundle as a makeshift pillow, and slept on it for safekeeping. Lying down, she looked around warily. Was anyone watching her? Had any of the ladies seen her switch out the crown and were only pretending to sleep? Bronwyn laid on the ground, stiff. Her limbs couldn't get comfortable. But then sleep took her, and despite waking multiple times in the night, she eventually got a few hours' rest until dawn.

The next morning, she sat up, sore and aching in different muscles, having slept on the hard ground again and with a crown bundled up in her makeshift pillow. She'd barely slept, for fear that someone would notice, or she'd somehow reveal it in her sleep, and wake up surrounded by spears. But so far, her morning was unremarkable. People walked through the camp as normal, and no one paid her any attention. She let out a small sigh of relief.

The problem was that when she went to work in the make-shift kitchen area, there was no safety or security for her personal belongings, and more often than not, her things would have been disturbed or stolen during the day. It meant she couldn't just leave the crown there—it'd be found in no time.

She looked around. The women with whom she'd slept at the campfire were all still asleep. It was dawn, after all. They would be waking soon. She made a quick decision. Rising, she quietly took the ladies' dresses, along with her apron and the crown, and took the lot with her.

She found a familiar tree with great holes and knots in the gnarled wood and twisted tree roots, which looked as thick as ankles, as if some great tree grandfather had come to life and sunk his fingers into the soft ground, then hardened in place.

She carefully wrapped the crown tightly in her apron, making it small and practically unnoticeable, and tucked it within the small holes of the tree. Its beige color made the bundle blend in, so it was invisible. If she hadn't known it was there, she would have missed it entirely.

Satisfied, she took the dresses and went to the ladies-in-waiting's tent. She didn't dare leave the fine dresses unattended, for they would disappear in no time. She peeked her head inside. The ladies slept, with Lady Alice sleeping soundly and Lady Susanna snoring, her mouth hung open. Lady Morwenna's bed was empty.

Bronwyn snuck in, set the dresses down to the side, where the young women would find them, and left, heading to the cooking tents.

ONLY A SHORT time later, one of the kitchen boys came in, shaking his head. "'Pon my word, those ladies are fighting like cats. I thought high-born ladies were supposed to be kind. Not these."

"What do you mean?" Bronwyn asked. "What ladies?"

The boy, a tawny-haired youth of about age ten with dirt on his nose, looked at her and jerked his thumb. "Over near the empress's tent. Something about…" He scratched his head. "Nah, I couldn't have heard that right. It almost sounded like they were talking about a crown."

Bronwyn hurried away. If the ladies were arguing openly about a crown, so loudly that the kitchen boys could hear, that was a problem. She ran as fast as she could without causing comment and slipped through the milling crowds of people to the direction of the ladies-in-waiting tent.

But as she arrived, she stopped short. Guards stood outside the tent, holding spears. Bronwyn froze.

The pair of guards looked at her. She'd come too close to the tent to turn around now without causing suspicion. She said, "I thought I heard my mistress calling for me." She called, "Lady Alice? Do you need me?"

Lady Alice strode out of the tent, past the guards. Her eyes widened at the sight of Bronwyn. She came up to her and said, "Oh, thank the Lord you're here. Help me."

"What is it?"

"They think I stole something."

Theobold, Lady Susanna, a guard, and Lady Morwenna stepped outside. Lady Morwenna put a hand on her hip, a sly smile on her face. Theobold met Bronwyn's eyes briefly but only nodded to her. "Do you know something about this, Bronwyn?" Theobold asked.

Bronwyn swallowed. "If Lady Alice says she did not steal, then I believe her."

"Hear, hear," Lady Susanna said. "I agree. In fact—"

Morwenna cut in. "No one asked, you, Lady Susanna. Nor would I base any judgement on the word of a servant. What are you doing here, anyway, Bronwyn? Shouldn't you be back with the cooks, where you belong?"

Bronwyn's cheeks grew warm. She'd never had so many insults as when she mixed with highborn people. Some really were rude.

She said, "I thought I heard Lady Alice calling for me. When was Lady Alice supposed to have taken this… stolen item?"

The guard, a thin young man in his twenties with a limpid

expression and weak chin, gazed at Lady Morwenna with interest.

"Lady Morwenna?" Theobold asked.

Lady Morwenna shrugged. "I don't know. All I know is she was acting very mysterious the other night and seemed nervous, like she was hiding something. I thought maybe she might have done or taken something she shouldn't have, and I think we all know what that would be. The crown. I heard from someone that it had gone missing. And as Lady Susanna and I have been with the empress for months, it only stands to reason that someone new to her retinue might want to take it for themselves."

Bronwyn's eyes grew wide, and she glanced at Lady Alice, who shook her head emphatically, her black waves swinging. "You forget, Lady Morwenna. I too have been working for the empress these past few months. I've been on a mission for her, in Stephen's court."

"Aha, so you've been spying. And you admit it. How are we to believe you didn't switch sides while you were there? Perhaps you were caught and made a deal, your life for the empress's crown."

"I most certainly did not," Lady Alice said hotly.

"I think you did. I think you took the crown and hid it so you can use it later to barter with. Maybe to gain more riches or wealth," Lady Morwenna said snidely.

"And so that is why you are going through her things?" Bronwyn asked.

Lady Morwenna glared at her. The guard paused. Theobold crossed his arms. He looked none too happy to see Bronwyn, his jaw set. "That is why we must take this seriously. Any accusation of theft of Her Grace's possessions is a matter of grave importance."

Bronwyn lifted her chin. "But what if it's not true? What reason would Lady Alice have to want to steal the crown? She just rejoined the empress's court. By my understanding, she is grateful to Her Grace for the opportunity to prove her loyalty.

She wouldn't steal."

Lady Alice muttered behind her shoulder, "Don't make me sound like a blooming beggar, Bronwyn. Let's not give them any ideas."

"I believe Lady Alice," Bronwyn said, ignoring Lady Alice's quip. "If she said she didn't steal, then I trust her word."

"Me too," Lady Susanna agreed. "In fact—"

"No one asked you, Lady Susanna, or you." Lady Morwenna addressed Bronwyn. "Get out of here. This is no business of yours. Go mend a shirt or cook something."

"I'll stay if Lady Alice needs me," Bronwyn said.

"Stay." Lady Alice stood beside Bronwyn and put her hands on her hips. "I have nothing to hide."

"Very well. Go on," Lady Morwenna said to the guard. "I'm sure you'll find something." She smirked at Lady Alice.

The guard rummaged through Lady Alice's bedding and spare linens and dresses, finding nothing out of the ordinary. He looked at Lady Morwenna, who turned pink. "Keep looking."

Why would Lady Morwenna be so adamant that the stolen crown was hidden amongst Lady Alice's things? She wouldn't openly accuse Lady Alice, unless she'd known it had been there. Most likely, because Lady Morwenna had put it there herself. But that would mean that she had stolen the crown. So why had no one seen her?

The guard approached Lady Susanna's things, checking her dresses and shifts. He turned to Lady Morwenna's bedding when she held up a hand. "Stop."

"My lady?" he asked.

"You're wasting your time. I don't understand it. It must be here. I know she took it," Lady Morwenna said, her voice rising.

"Lady Morwenna," Theobold started. "Enough. It's not here."

"No, it is! I'm sure of it. She's guilty. She was acting suspicious. I know she's up to something." Lady Morwenna went forward and threw Lady Alice's bedding and spare dress in the air, the very one she'd had Bronwyn clean the night before.

"Oi! That's my dress," Lady Alice said, hurrying forward to claim it. But before Lady Alice could whisk it away from the ground, Lady Morwenna trod on it, stepping down hard on the fabric. When Lady Alice tried pulling it, there was a slight tear, and Lady Alice let go.

"How clumsy of me," Lady Morwenna said, stepping back.

"*Lady Morwenna,*" Theobold admonished.

The guard stood, dusting his hands on his tunic. "There's nothing here. I have to report back."

"Tell the empress it was a false alarm. An innocent mistake." Theobold's voice was even, but his dark eyes were like daggers at Lady Morwenna.

The guard left. Lady Morwenna grimaced, shooting little darting looks at Lady Alice. "I know you're behind this."

"That's enough." To the others, Theobold said, "Would you excuse us? I'd like to speak with Lady Morwenna in private."

Bronwyn ducked her head and followed Lady Alice and Lady Susanna from the tent. Lady Alice held the dress, now crumpled, torn, and dirty again thanks to Lady Morwenna's malicious treading, and handed the bundled-up material to Bronwyn. "See if you can restore it. Wash it too."

Lady Alice walked away with Lady Susanna.

Bronwyn, the torn dress in her hands, walked around the tent and hung toward the back. She slowed and stood still, listening. In seconds, she could hear their voices clearly.

"That was a foolish thing to do," Theobold told Lady Morwenna.

"Nonsense. That Lady Alice has a stick up her rear end, and she's a traitor. It's about time someone proved just how rude she is."

"Your accusation could have cost her her life," Theobold said. "And you were wrong. She didn't steal the crown. She could have died because of your words. Do you realize that? You're playing a dangerous game, cousin."

Bronwyn started. Cousin? They were related.

Lady Morwenna huffed. "Doesn't matter. I can accuse whomever I want, whenever I want. I'm protected. Her Grace trusts me. She likes me. Now that Lady Eleanor is gone, I'm her favorite."

"Don't expect that to save your hide if you go around accusing everyone of robbing Her Grace. She'll only tolerate your attitude for so long," Theobold warned.

"Worried about me?" she asked sweetly.

"No. More worried what your family will say when I tell them you've made a fool of yourself in front of the empress. They won't be pleased with you."

Lady Morwenna made a sulking noise. "I'm protected. Besides, you promised my father you'd look after me."

He snorted. "That didn't mean I'm to clean up all your messes. Stop causing trouble. I've got enough to worry about without you stirring things up."

Bronwyn knew Theobold was smart. Did he also suspect Lady Morwenna of planting the crown in their tent? Or was he distracted by their history together and didn't think she would have done it? An uncomfortable feeling squirmed in Bronwyn's belly, accompanied by a thought she didn't want to admit. She also didn't like that Theobold and Lady Morwenna had a history. If he had made her father a promise to look after Lady Morwenna, what was he getting in return?

"You just want that pretty servant to keep making eyes at you. I saw the way you looked at her. You fancy her, don't you?" Lady Morwenna asked.

Bronwyn's heart began to pound. She listened intently.

"Don't be ridiculous. Why would I fancy a servant?" Theobold said rudely.

Bronwyn's heart dropped into her stomach. His voice was so cold, like the frost air. He didn't care about her at all.

She thought about this and looked at the wadded-up bundle of dress in her arms. Why did she care about this? Why did she care what he thought of her? And why did it hurt to know he didn't care for her at all?

⚜

Chapter Eight

Bronwyn worked in the cooking tents on the grounds. It was good, hard work that demanded attention but also let her mind wander and therefore think. But that didn't last.

"Who are you? I don't know you." A tall, middle-aged, skinny woman with a mean glint in her eyes looked Bronwyn up and down. Her voice was cutting and brooked no argument but had a snide tone. "I'm the head cook here. You one of them people fleeing from the fight?"

"Yes. My name is Bronwyn."

"I don't care about your life story, only what you're doing here." The woman had an abrasive manner, and no sense of personal space, or boundaries. She stood less than a foot away and looked down her nose at Bronwyn and her work. "What makes you think you can cook in my tents? You're barely a slip of a girl."

"I'm eighteen. And… I've cooked for the queen and the empress before. They like my bread rolls."

The woman's nose twitched, and her smile didn't meet her eyes. "Did you now? Isn't that a feat. Hear that, everyone? We here got ourselves a proper cook. 'Parently, the queen and the empress like her bread rolls."

A few of the other cooks looked over, a few smiled.

Bronwyn's face grew hot. "I only meant—"

"Listen here, Bronwyn." The woman took her by the arm

and pulled her away from the worktable. "I'm the head cook here. You do what I say, when I say it and you don't give me any problems, understand? I don't care if you've worked for the bloody Queen of Sheba. This is my kitchen, and we don't have anyone here who isn't gonna pull their weight. Understand?"

Bronwyn nodded.

"If I find you're making trouble or you ignore my orders, you're out."

"But—"

"No *buts*. Now get back to work. I'll be watching you."

Bronwyn bit the inside of her cheek to keep from speaking out and marched back to the worktable, where she'd been washing dirt from carrots. She felt the woman's eyes on her as she worked.

Silence reigned in the cooking tents as the cooks worked steadily, barely speaking. The woman huffed and walked on. Five minutes later, one of the other cooks, a thin woman in her twenties, joined Bronwyn at the worktable. She took some of the pile of clean carrots and began to chop them. "These'll make a nice stew."

"Mm-hmm." Bronwyn murmured.

"That there's Mary Anglesey. She's head cook back at Gloucester Castle. She's been with the empress for years. She's good, but she's got a mean way about her. Stick to your work and do what she says, you'll be fine."

Bronwyn glanced at the woman.

"And don't go on any more about cooking for kings and queens. We all have. Anyone who puts on airs like that or tries to make themselves seem better than anyone else, well... They won't last long here. Not in Mary's kitchen, anyway."

Bronwyn kept her eyes down, washing. The purple carrots were very clean. "I didn't know."

"Now you do. Where are you from, anyway? You're not from Gloucester."

"Lincoln."

They worked together quietly. Bronwyn learned that Mary Anglesey, who ruled the cooking tents with a mean twist of her mouth and eyes that danced where there was trouble, was a dab hand in the kitchen and could make all sorts of good dinners that pleased the high-born people at camp.

That first impression however, had ruined things. Mary did not care for Bronwyn, which made life difficult. But Bronwyn found that if she focused on her work, she could ignore the idle chatter and gossip that prevailed amongst the kitchen staff. At the present moment, the crown sat hidden in her apron, safely tucked away in the nook of a tree. With any luck, it would stay hidden. She whispered a quick prayer for luck and got to work, as they were short-staffed, as usual.

She scrubbed pots, baked bread, wiped down hard trenchers and platters for serving, and once she got a spare moment, she was enlisted amongst the pages and serving boys and girls to bring platters and trenchers out to people.

That afternoon, Bronwyn cut herself gutting a fish, the small blade slicing into her palm. She cursed and the cooks sent her to find the nearest surgeon. They had bandaged her wound with a rag, but it was filthy and the cut hurt. She joined a small queue of people wanting to see the healer, an older person with a younger male assistant.

When it was her turn, the older healer, a short man well past middle-age with a balding pate and gentle hands, carefully unwrapped the bandage and *tsked*. "A nasty cut. Edmund, take care of this."

He left her and moved on to the next person. Bronwyn was approached by a young man. He had clear, blue eyes and a deft touch. The young healer cleaned her hand thoroughly, hardly speaking. In minutes, he'd wrapped her hand in a fresh clean bandage and tied it tightly. "You are a cook?"

"I help in the cooking tents. And I bake sometimes."

"No more gutting fish until this is healed. Come back in three days' time. If it hurts more or smells, see me sooner. Do you understand?" He met her eyes then, his voice dispassionate. He almost sounded bored.

"Yes, thank you." She looked at him. He was young. Older than her—in his twenties, perhaps. He had a light mop of sandy-blond hair that flopped, a thin face, and a spot on his chin. He was tall, thin, and lanky.

"Was there anything else?" he asked.

"Um. Why is this…?" She looked around. There were stores and small jars and pots laid out, but it was as if a wind or mighty force had swept an arm out and knocked most things to the ground.

"Someone broke into the stores," the healer said. "We didn't bring much—just enough to help with any wounds, aches, or pains—but people will take anything they can."

"When did this happen?"

"The other night, during the battle."

"Was anything taken?" Bronwyn asked.

"You ask a lot of questions," the young healer said, looking at her sharply.

"I was just wondering."

"Well, a few things might've been, but that's no business of yours. That's for the empress's ears alone. Now if there's nothing else…" His gaze wandered to the next patient.

She rose, thanked him, and left. His dismissal of her was clear.

As the afternoon sun lowered on the horizon and the blue sky was starting to fade to a subtle blue-grey hue, Bronwyn finished serving queues of people and scraped a bit of potage onto a small stale bread trencher, eating it with a hunk of day-old crusty bread. Her hair was still tied back with a strong kerchief, and her apron was dusted with flour and food stains, but it was her first chance in hours to sit, and so sit she would.

She took a spot at an empty cooking fire and perched on the edge of a log. People milled about in camp, always talking, walking, some in laughter, some in good spirits, some low. The

Battle of Lincoln stayed in their minds, if not their hearts, and for some, they had lost their homes and family members.

Bronwyn ate, her gaze fixed at a spot in the distance, when a familiar voice asked behind her, "Is this seat taken?"

She looked and almost dropped her trencher. "Uh, no."

Rupert sat down on the log beside her, with a trencher of his own. He gave her a pleasant smile, drinking from a small wineskin. He asked in a low voice, "Is it true that the empress's crown was stolen?"

Bronwyn froze. Bits of potage dripped from the small bit of hard bread she held in her right hand. She blinked. "Where did you hear that?"

"The other night, after the battle. The next day, the king was summoned for a private interrogation by the empress, and then after him, my lord, and one or two other knights loyal to His Grace."

Bronwyn's eyebrows rose. "Oh?"

Rupert nodded. "Aye. The men were all talking about it. Seems like someone tried to steal the crown during the battle."

"Did they succeed?"

"That's what I want to know. Have you heard anything?"

She swallowed and ate more. "I would've thought the battle was an attempt to free the king from his guards."

"I thought so too, but no. He and his men were left un-harmed. The guards weren't troubled at all. It's strange, is it not?"

Bronwyn nodded. "I…"

"What I cannot think is why anyone would want to start a fight just for fighting's sake. Unless they had another plan in mind. The empress wasn't attacked; the king was left alone. So why would men attack the camp if not for one of those purpos-es?" He scratched his chin.

"Do you know who attacked the camp?"

"Marauders. Mercenaries. Men paid to. It was only a small band of fighters, but it was enough to scare people and create chaos in the camp. People died when they didn't have to." He drank more from his wineskin and set down his empty bread trencher.

"Rupert," she began.

"Yes?"

She swallowed and gripped her trencher, balancing it on her knees. "There's something you should know."

He looked at her.

"It was stolen. The crown. You were right. It has gone missing."

"What?" His eyes widened. "When? How?"

"The night of the battle. It was stolen. But there's a problem because it—"

"There you two are. My, my, what a sweet picture you both make, sat together. Like a pair of lovebirds, I dare say. I wonder what Lady Alice will think." Lady Morwenna stood behind them, a wide smile on her face.

Bronwyn set her trencher down on the ground. "Lady Morwenna…"

"Do not address me unless I talk to you first, girl," the woman snapped. "I am your better and you will remember it."

Rupert stood.

Lady Morwenna fixed him with a smile. "Hello there. You must be the knight I've heard so much about. Rupert of Bothwell?"

"That is my name, but I am no knight. And you have insulted my friend."

Lady Morwenna smirked. "You're friends with a servant? Curious taste in friends, Rupert."

Rupert's blank expression disappeared and his jaw began to set. He picked up Bronwyn's empty trencher and his own. "I'll be going. Bronwyn." He nodded to her and left, walking past Lady Morwenna, who sniffed loudly.

"Well, I never," said Lady Morwenna. "He is handsome enough, but what manners. He's very rude. I wonder what Lady Alice sees in him. But then perhaps she likes a bit of roughness in her men.

Bronwyn stood. She had no desire to spend time in Lady Morwenna's company. She also couldn't forget that Lady Morwenna was very likely guilty of hiding the crown and trying to frame Lady Alice for the theft, so she was involved somehow. She was a person to be wary of, Bronwyn decided.

"Wait."

Bronwyn arched an eyebrow.

"I'm watching you. I know you took the crown from Lady Alice's things. I knew she was hiding it somewhere and now I know you two are in this plot together. Why else would she ask a mere servant to stay for that confrontation?"

Bronwyn opened her mouth to speak, but Lady Morwenna cut her off.

"No. You two are thick as thieves, I know. But I know something else."

"And what's that?" Bronwyn asked.

"She's a lady, like me. And like me, she won't take kindly to other women being overly friendly with her man."

"Rupert is his own person, and besides, we are friends. There is nothing between us." Bronwyn held her hands loosely behind her back.

"Nonsense. Don't lie. Your cheeks tell a different story, no matter what falsehood you tell yourself. Answer me this: does Lady Alice know of your fondness for Rupert?"

"We are simply friends." But Bronwyn's cheeks warmed at the words.

The right side of Lady Morwenna's mouth curled into a smile. "Say that if you like, but I saw the way you were looking at him. Like a prize tart you wanted to eat. You would be wise not to cross me again, little baker. I have powerful friends."

It took all of Bronwyn's reserve not to roll her eyes.

"Laugh all you want, but I know the truth. You stole the crown and you're hiding it somewhere. And when I find out, I'm going to turn you both in. See what the empress thinks of your precious rolls then." She gave a little laugh and tossed her brown, frizzy hair over her shoulder, walking away with a haughtiness to her step.

Bronwyn exhaled and sat back down on the log. Now what was she to do?

IT WAS LATER that night when Bronwyn was helping close up the cooking tents, tidying wooden trenchers, scrubbing more pots and pans, and wiping down the worktables for the next day. She worked under the watchful eye of Mary and the other cooks. She learned later that many refugees had joined the camp, and the cooks had all come together from the empress's household in Oxford and knew each other already. To them, Bronwyn was an outsider, and to receive orders from the empress and her ladies made it seem as though she were trying to elevate herself beyond her rank. It would take time to earn the cooks' trust. It might take years before they allowed her to do more than wash vegetables and scrub pots, but she hoped that her situation might be different by then.

She paused in wiping down the worktable. That was a thought that hadn't occurred to her before: what her life would be like outside of Empress Maud's camp. They wouldn't travel forever, and much as she liked being with Rupert and Lady Alice again, she'd need to figure out a future for herself, especially once the fighting between the king and empress ended. Would there be peace in England? She didn't know.

She imagined she would save up her money to buy a small bit of land and build on it, have a small house to herself. Or she could rebuild her family's home and start over in her family's bakery in Lincoln. She'd need help moving the people squatting there on, and cleaning it and arranging deals with merchants and the local mills so she could get started, but there was something about that life that held a certain appeal.

Not yet, however. She felt a little thrill being in the empress's camp, and whilst she didn't feel safe at all times, she wasn't alone.

She would like to see a bit more of the world first before she settled down somewhere and set up shop. Besides, her family's bakery had a proper oven, but the building was in disrepair now, thanks to all the fighting. She would need money to survive, save, and rebuild. And that was assuming the building hadn't been destroyed or taken over by someone else, and that it would even be available, considering the refugees sheltering there. Although would she even return to Lincoln? It was the only home she'd ever known, but now... She didn't even know if her family was still alive. Her foray into the city had shed no light on the matter, and it was an unanswered question that nagged at the back of her mind. Would she ever see her family again?

Bronwyn worked and later went to sleep, but she slept fitfully, thinking of how to save for a new life.

Someone shook her awake. "Bronwyn?"

"Eh?" She woke in an instant, eyes wide. She started and stared, scrambling back. The campfire she'd curled around was still warm, its embers still red hot in the chill wind. "W-What do you want?" Her breath was cold in the night air.

"You serve Lady Alice Duncombe, right?" A young woman's pale face looked down at her. Her thin dress hung on her bony body and she was no stranger to hunger, for her cheekbones were sharp, and her cheeks looked hollow, instead of healthy. She stood of average height in her twenties, with a pinched expression and blonde, wispy hair. Her breath steamed in the cold.

"Why? Is she all right?" Bronwyn asked, sitting up straight.

"She's crying her eyes out but won't say what or why. Making a right mess of herself, she is. A right spectacle." The young woman said the last word carefully, as if he'd heard an older person say it and was trying it on for size, like a new shoe.

"Where is she?" Bronwyn rose to her feet.

The young woman pointed. "Over there with the horses. She's spooking them, but she won't leave, and whenever one of the grooms asks her to go, she snaps at them, fierce as anything. Clear takes their heads off if they don't leave her alone."

"I'll see what's wrong," Bronwyn said.

"See that you do," the servant said imperiously. "I'm Mabel. I serve the Lady Morwenna, and you wouldn't see her acting in such a state. She's a proper lady. Not one for theatrics, unlike some I could name." She waggled her eyebrows.

Bronwyn rolled her eyes. "Fetch Rupert Bothwell, quick as you can."

"I'm not your servant. Fetch him yourself," Mabel said.

"He sleeps with the most handsome men at camp. They'll want to know why you're on such an important errand."

Mabel thought on this and patted her stringy, mouse-brown hair. "All right. But you owe me a favor."

Bronwyn swept past the maidservant in the direction of the stables, ignoring the maid's snicker.

There she found the groomsmen standing around uselessly, not speaking, all eyes elsewhere, yet very aware of the young woman crying into the soft, velvety hide of a horse.

Lady Alice's cries and muted sobs cut through the quiet of the night and could be heard from not far away, echoing amongst the trees. As Bronwyn approached, Lady Alice heard her footsteps and said, "Go away. Leave me if you know what's good for you."

Bronwyn came closer and waited silently.

Lady Alice turned and said, "Didn't you hear me? I said—" She stopped. "Oh, it's you." And she crumpled into tears.

Bronwyn held her in a tight hug and patted her back, letting the lady cry. "What's happened?"

"Oh, it was horrible." Lady Alice sobbed into her shoulder. She babbled and cried, her tears dampening Bronwyn's thin tunic.

"Sssssh." Bronwyn held her and let her cry until her sobs faded into slight tearful hiccups and fits and starts. "You're going to frighten the horses half to death. Tell me. Are you well?"

"No, I'm not bloody well. Not at all." Lady Alice stepped back and put a hand on the horse, rubbing its side. "I... I was going to use the privy and had just come back when some man, I didn't see who, but he stank of onions and sour wine, like an expensive one, not the stuff the regular men drink... He shoved me in the dirt and pinned me down. I didn't see his face, but he pulled my hair and held a knife to my throat."

Bronwyn reached for her, but Lady Alice shook her head. "He said I'd stolen the crown and he wanted it back. He demanded to know where I'd hidden it."

Bronwyn swallowed.

"I didn't tell him. I didn't give him your name." Lady Alice let out a shuddering breath that sounded too close to a sob. She cried a little and sniffed, wiping her eyes. "I told him I didn't know what he was talking about, but he was so serious and I was frightened. He said he knew I'd taken it, and he wanted it back. 'This doesn't concern you, Lady Alice,' he said, as if he knew me." Her voice shook.

Lady Alice patted the horse's side again, and the animal nickered. She sighed. "That's what scares me the most. He acted as if we were acquainted somehow. As if I'd know the kind of man who attacks a harmless young woman in the middle of the night."

"Are you all right?" Bronwyn was surprised, considering she'd first met Alice when she'd been a spy in King Stephen's court. She should have been used to a life of danger, surely.

"No, I am not all right. But I will be." Lady Alice huffed and rubbed the horse again, patting its side. "The person demanded to know where it was. I told him I didn't know, but he didn't believe me. He said it was me who had it, and he'd cut my throat if I didn't tell him where it was."

"But you don't know," Bronwyn said.

"I *know*," Lady Alice said sarcastically, shooting her an annoyed look. "That's why I didn't tell him anything. It was smart of me to involve you because then I can't tell him what I don't know."

"So what did you say? How did you get away?"

Lady Alice traced her hand gently against the horse's side.

"Lady Alice?"

She swallowed. "I gave him Mabel's name."

"Mabel, Lady Morwenna's servant?" Bronwyn stepped back.

"Yes. I didn't want to give him your name. Then he'd come for us both. So I told him she'd taken it, and I didn't know where it was or what she'd done with it."

Bronwyn stared. "But, Lady Alice, he might come after her next."

"I know." Lady Alice looked down at her feet. "But I didn't know what to do, or what to say. It just came out of my mouth. I was so scared." She shuddered. "It was terrifying. He said he'd come back for me if I was lying, and he left." She hugged her arms. "I'm so cold. It was so frightening, I..."

"Bronwyn? Lady Alice? A maidservant said you were looking for me. Is everything all—" Rupert made a loud *ooof* noise as Lady Alice flung herself into his arms.

"Oh, Rupert, it was so frightening. I was so scared." Her voice shook and she teared up all over again.

"Shh, what happened? Why are you spooking the horses?" he asked, holding her.

Bronwyn's nostrils flared.

Lady Alice crumpled in his arms, weeping. It was as if the human touch brought her to tears again.

"There, there, tell me what's happened. Did you have a bad dream?" he asked.

Lady Alice looked up at him, posture stiff. "No. I didn't *have a bad dream*. I was bloody attacked, that's what."

His eyes widened. "Tell me everything."

Bronwyn stood by as Lady Alice relayed her tale again but omitted any mention of the crown or giving Mabel's name. It didn't sit right with her, Lady Alice giving Mabel's name to her assailant. And the fact that the assailant had seemed to know her suggested they were acquainted.

"How did you escape?" Rupert asked.

"I... He heard some people and ran off. But it was terrifying. I was so scared." Lady Alice clutched at his arms.

As Rupert held her close, Bronwyn asked, "Lady Alice, what

did the man look like?"

"I couldn't see his face. It was too dark. But..." She paused. "He smelled like onions and sour wine. Not the cheap drink the fighters and men like to drink. Good wine. The sort we ladies drink with the empress."

"Was he slight? Tall? Stocky? Thin or fat?" Rupert asked.

Lady Alice shook her head. "I think he was stocky, but I couldn't tell. It all happened so quickly, and he took me by surprise. He shoved me in the dirt and now I've got mud all over my dress." She frowned and looked at Rupert. "Give me your cloak. I can't wear this. I'm covered in mud. I'll be a laughing stock and someone will take me for a servant."

Rupert complied and gave her his cloak. Lady Alice put it on, turned away, and slipped out of her dress, tying the cloak closely around her before handing her muddy dress to Bronwyn. "Can you wash this for me? Now I'll have to change dresses. Honestly, whoever is behind this is ruining all my clothes." She wore a simple, white shift and turned, clasping the cloak around her chest.

Rupert eyed her, then averted his gaze.

"What?" Lady Alice said. "Oh." Her mouth curved into a grin. "Why, Rupert, are you blushing?"

"No."

She laughed.

He blushed more. "I'll escort you back to your tent," he said, looking at the ground.

Alice beamed and curled her hands around his left arm. They walked away together without another word.

Bronwyn let out a breath and walked in the opposite direction, her cheeks warming. Part of her felt bothered by the fact that Rupert and Lady Alice were together, and that Lady Alice had found time to give her orders while making eyes at Rupert, but she had too much to think on now, and she had agreed to wash her dress. She didn't want to fall into the role of Lady Alice's maidservant again like she had before, but a part of her realized she already had, and there was a blurring of their relationship that needed figuring out. Were they lady and maidservant, or were they friends?

She needed to figure this out. And to warn Mabel to be on her guard. But first, to wash two of Alice's dresses. The one just now and the one that Lady Morwenna had torn earlier.

Bronwyn slipped away in the darkness and snuck out to the tree, digging amongst the roots until she found the crown. The dirt covered her hands and the roots bruised her skin, but she didn't care. She heaved a sigh of relief as her fingers curled around the hard, metal circlet. Pulling her kerchief from her head, she tied it around the crown, and stuffed it in the dirt and gnarled tree roots with Lady Alice's soiled dresses. No one would think to look there. But it was too dark to see easily, so she joined the other women by the campfire and found herself a spot nearby. She'd wash the clothes at first light, when it was safe to see.

She slept poorly again, worried about the crown. But even if it was found, no one would know that the kerchief and apron it sat bundled in the gnarled tree roots were hers. But if they found Lady Alice's dresses, they would both be accused. She sat up, body aching. Rising in the dawn's early light, Bronwyn crept to the tree, retrieved the dresses, and went to the riverside. She carefully walked down the bank to wash Lady Alice's dresses, coming to stand at the water's edge. In the early hours, the water looked dark, like glass. She rinsed and washed the dresses carefully, working the mud out of the stiff, woolen cloth with her fingers. But it was cold and her fingers soon felt numb. She needed to warm up. She blew on her hands and rubbed them together, stamping her feet and jumping up and down. The air was still chilly and her breath was visible as she warmed her body.

After a few more minutes of washing and freezing her fingers, Bronwyn aired out the clothes and shook them in the air to dry. They would be slightly damp but were cleaner than before, and at least Lady Alice would have something to wear besides her bare shift. The young woman must have been freezing, even if she also wore Rupert's cloak.

It had been clever of Lady Alice to ask for it. She wore it like it was a prize possession, or a mark of the fact that she and Rupert were together. As the sun rose and Bronwyn shielded her eyes from the golden brightness, she turned and, with the dresses in hand, made her way carefully back up the riverbank.

She dried the dresses and went to return them, then remembered she was meant to repair a tear in one of them, thanks to Lady Morwenna's spiteful footing back in the ladies' tent. She took the slightly damp dresses with her as the sun properly rose and the camp came to life. When the other women she'd slept near woke up, she was sat by a log, mending the tear. A short while later, she met Lady Alice coming out of her tent.

"Oh, Bronwyn. Good morning. I see you have my dresses."

"Yes. Here you go." Bronwyn returned both dresses. "I sewed up the tear as well."

"Brilliant." Lady Alice took the dresses with rosy cheeks. "Oh, Susanna wanted me to give this to you. She didn't need it anymore." She handed Bronwyn an old, purple dress.

It was dull, worn and needed washing and mending, but it was pretty in the light. "Thank you."

"Don't thank me. You can thank her yourself." Lady Alice gave a happy sigh.

"What is it?" Bronwyn asked.

"Oh, nothing. Just..." Alice giggled. "When Rupert walked me back to my tent last night, after I was so horribly attacked, well... He wanted to make sure I got back here all right and then we ended up saying goodnight..." She hugged the dresses to her chest. "We kissed."

A pang of hurt struck Bronwyn's chest like an arrow. "Oh."

"Yes, it was wonderful. I mean, I don't go around kissing every young man who pays attention to me, but Rupert is different somehow. He's noble. I have no doubt he'll be made a knight soon."

"And then?"

"Then we'll find a way to marry, of course. One has to think ahead about these things. I can't very well waste my time on a young man with no prospects." She nodded. "Thanks for these."

Talk was rife that within a day or two, the camp would pack up and move on to Gloucester. The empress had men installed back at Lincoln, so now she had no reason to stay, not when she had her own castle to which to return.

Bronwyn returned to the cooking tents, the dress in a small bundle in her hands. Her shoulders slumped. Lady Alice and Rupert, married. She'd never imagined Lady Alice would be thinking along those lines so soon. Stepping into the cooking tents, she set aside the dress beneath the worktables and began helping where she could, hardly saying a word unless asked a question. She wanted the work, any work, to busy herself. Anything was better than thinking about the possibility of Lady Alice and Rupert together forever.

She set to work quickly, taking a bit of fish and arranging it on a platter to serve.

"What is this?" a loud voice demanded from a few feet away.

Heads turned to see. It was the head cook Mary, who looked down her pointed nose at Bronwyn. Her eyes danced, her mouth in a nasty smile, and Bronwyn knew she was in trouble.

Mary came to stand by her and poked at the fish she was arranging. "What, pray tell, is this?"

Bronwyn looked at the offending platter. "It's what I was working on, mistress."

"I must say I'm surprised. I thought you knew how to cook. Didn't you say your family ran a bakery in Lincoln?" Mary's eyes danced again, filling Bronwyn with dread.

"Yes, they did." Her cheeks warmed.

Mary smirked. "If this is the sort of muck they were producing, it's no wonder they got taken over. What a bunch of fools. This is a mess. Chuck it and start over." She flicked a bit of rosemary sprigs from the platter. "We are serving the empress and knights, in case you forgot. I wouldn't serve the scullery maids with this rubbish. It looks hardly cooked." Mary gave a loud laugh. "And you even tried to hide it with rosemary. I half-expect the fish to jump and try to swim away."

A few half-hearted laughs responded to this.

"Now wait—" Bronwyn said.

"No, you shut your mouth and listen." Mary stood in her face, her light-blue eyes full of malice. She smelled like sweat and bad breath. "You see here? This is wrong, all wrong. You cannot serve Her Grace a piece of barely cooked fish and expect her to like it. I don't know where you learned to cook, but this is poor work, and I won't have them thinking I allowed this out of my kitchen when we can do better. When I tell you to get rid of it, I mean it."

Bronwyn's blood began to rise.

Mary's mouth gave a nasty curl as she flicked the dish off the worktable and onto the ground. It, of course, landed face down, so the meal now lay in the dirt.

Mary snickered. "You can't serve that now. Throw it out and start again, like I said. Unless you've got something to say?"

Bronwyn's mouth withered. Any retort she had died on her lips. She wanted to speak up but didn't dare. She fumed, her eyes wet and her cheeks flaming. She shook her head.

"And before you think of having a word with the ladies-in-waiting, I'll have you know that I have the ear of Lady Morwenna Banbury, the empress's favorite. I've known her for years. And they always enjoy, nay *love*, my little rosewater treats. You know what that means?"

Bronwyn met her eyes. "What?"

"One complaint from me and you're out of here. See who takes you on then. You can't contribute, so you'll be kicked out of the camp. You'll either freeze to death, starve, or be forced to make your way on your back and clean the latrines, if it wasn't thanks to my generosity in letting you work here. Now get out. I don't want to see your face here again unless it's to clean up this God-forsaken mess." Mary pointed, and Bronwyn bit her lip and knelt to pick up the overturned fish, her cheeks flaming.

She cleaned up the mess, conscious that Mary's feet hadn't moved. The woman stood there, barely two feet away, watching as she cleaned. Never mind that they had to cook for hundreds of people, and there were some poor wretches out there who didn't care how pretty the fish looked. Mary had wasted good food, and with much of the river having frozen over, fresh fish was hard to come by. She hated Mary's treatment of her. Even the sight of Mary's muddy shoes filled her with annoyance. And she didn't dare look up, as she knew that Mary was standing there, watching. Making sure Bronwyn did as she was told.

It was humiliating, but Mary's words sent a chill through her. If she were kicked out, she'd beg Lady Alice to take her on as a servant, or Lady Susanna—she seemed nice. She'd walk to the nearest village or town and offer to work, doing washing, cleaning, baking, anything she could. She'd run away and take her chances back in Lincoln rather than stay here.

Mary smirked again. "See what happens when sloth and laziness take hold? It's like a sickness." She turned to the tent at large. "Don't let me catch any of you being lazy or not following orders around here; otherwise, you'll end up like her. And believe me, none of you wants to be like Bronwyn." She laughed again and walked away. "Now what are you doing, Eloise? Burning something, from the smell of it."

Her face hot, Bronwyn slowly picked up the platter, taking the bits of cooked fish and rosemary from the ground. It had been meant to be a pleasant morning dish for the ladies-in-waiting, but never mind. She disposed of the food, tossing it outside to where cats and dogs would fight over it, and set the platter aside.

She went to fill a bucket from the river and took her time filling it. Mary was nothing but a bully who seemed to take pleasure in belittling her fellow cooks. But her snide laughter and jibes had set a standard of behavior in the cooking tent, and the bullies were in power. Bronwyn hated it and wondered about just walking away. But where would she go, and what could she do?

Could she really set out on her own? She could ask Lady Alice for help, but seeing her fawn over Rupert all day and night made her sick to her stomach. Maybe not Lady Alice. But then if she asked Lady Susanna for work, that might hurt Lady Alice's feelings. And she certainly couldn't ask Lady Morwenna.

As she stood outside the cooking tents, she overheard Mary say, "God, that Bronwyn winds me up. Everything she does 'for the empress this' and 'for my Lady Alice' that. She is such a horrible nuisance and yet we have to tolerate her sticking her nose in the air and acting like she's God's gift to the kitchen, all because the empress likes her bread rolls. I bet I could cook them just as well and Her Grace would never know the difference. She might even like mine better."

Bronwyn's spirits plummeted. Her sweetened bread rolls were a recipe her father had taught her, and they had been enjoyed by Queen Matilda and Empress Maud alike. She'd never imagined she'd be so disliked.

"You should do it, Mary, and prove it to Her Grace that Bronwyn is no better than the rest of us. She'll be sure to kick her out then," one cook said.

"Aye, I should. And then where will she be? If she's not sniveling in a corner and begging me on her knees to keep her, she'll be sulking and scrubbing pots, like she's better than the work. It's good, honest work we do and you don't see us complaining."

"Don't matter. Women like that can always get by on their beauty," said a woman. "And with her pretty face, Bronwyn'll be some man's bedfellow in no time."

Bronwyn clapped a hand to her mouth.

"Did you hear something?" someone inside the tent asked.

"No. You really think she'll stoop to being some man's slut?" Mary asked.

"Sure as the sun rises, I'm sure. There're a lot of men who would pay for a young woman like that to keep their bed warm."

Bronwyn's blood ran cold as the cooks laughed at her expense. Her heart sank and her shoulders slumped. Maybe her fish dish truly had been terrible. Maybe Mary was right, and she really was just an average cook at best.

But the horror and fear of being kicked out of the cooking tents chilled her, and she decided to stay out of Mary's way as much as possible. She was learning when to pick her fights and while defending herself might lead to her feeling respect for herself in the situation, it might also land her exiled with nowhere to go. Except for Lady Alice, where she'd face her and Rupert's romance constantly. She sighed. Would that she had a home to return to, but that was gone. So she had nothing, and no one. Only herself that she could trust.

Bronwyn swallowed as she returned to the cooking tents.

Seeing her, Mary ordered her to scrub pots for the rest of the day and turn the spit of the roasting animals. It was hot, sweaty work, but Bronwyn went to it without a word.

After the noonday luncheon, Bronwyn slipped away in search of Mabel. She had to warn her, and now that the other cooks were busy, this was the perfect time. She hastened toward the ladies-in-waiting tent and found Mabel inside, rummaging through Lady Morwenna's things.

"What do you want?" Mabel asked, barely sparing Bronwyn a glance. "Got your lady quieted down, I see. Was it that cloak of hers she's got now? She's acting like it's some holy relic, practically. Not that it suits her."

"I wanted to talk to you," Bronwyn began. Her palms began to sweat. How to tell someone their life may be in danger?

"What is it?" Mabel looked at her with narrowed eyes.

"I heard a rumor that the crown was taken."

Mabel laughed. "Is that all? I heard it too. Lady Morwenna told me. But she thinks your mistress had something to do with that." She put a hand on her hip. "Did she? Are you going to turn her in to the empress's guards?"

"No. I'm not," Bronwyn said. At Mabel's raised eyebrows, she added, "I mean, she didn't take it. She didn't do anything."

"Oh. Then why are you here? Your mistress need something?"

"I heard that someone's looking for the crown, and they think you might know where it is."

Mabel's eyes widened. "Me? Why would I know anything about a crown missing?"

Bronwyn shrugged. "I don't know. It's just what I heard."

"From who?"

"I can't remember. One of the maids, I think." She looked away.

"It'll be Joan, I bet. She's always been jealous of me. If she thinks she can steal my position and become the favorite, she's dead wrong." Mabel's teeth clenched.

"It might not have been Joan. I can't remember who said it."

"Well, never mind. If someone's got a bone to pick with me, I'll let 'em have it." Mabel hoisted a pile of dirty laundry in her arms. "Anyway, I'm too busy to steal a crown. Lady Morwenna wants her dresses and bedding washed constantly. Fleas." She shook her head.

"You're not afraid?"

"No. It's probably just the maids trying to stir up trouble. No one would suspect me. What would I do with a crown?" She laughed. "I'm off."

Bronwyn moved aside to let her pass. "You'll be careful, won't you?"

"Sure, sure. But no one in their right mind would suspect me. It's not like I'd go around wearing it." She walked off.

THAT EVENING, AFTER the cooks and servants had had a sparse evening meal and once the knights, ladies, fighters, and prisoners had eaten, Bronwyn was preparing to lie down by the fire when Rupert appeared. Her heart skipped a beat at the sight of his shy yet sunny smile.

"Walk with me a moment?" he asked.

Bronwyn looked longingly at the campfire but said, "All right."

They walked some distance away from other people. The night sky had fallen and the chill wind blew through the camp, but it did not have the bracing cold as before. It was chilly but not freezing, which was a relief. Bronwyn rubbed her hands together. "What did you want to talk about?"

"You know." He paused. "What we were discussing before, before Lady Morwenna interrupted."

The crown.

"Lady Alice was being assaulted over it. Tell me what you know," he said.

Bronwyn relayed quietly what had transpired, from Lady Alice revealing its whereabouts to hiding it herself, when he interrupted.

"Wait a minute. *You* hid the crown?" His eyes were wide. "Yourself?"

"Yes." She put a hand on her hip. "You didn't think I could?"

"No, it's not that. I'm shocked, really. Why on earth would you put yourself in such danger?" He closed the distance between them and stood close enough that she could smell his scent, mingled with the wood smoke from the campfires that hung in the air.

She breathed in ever so slightly. "She asked me to."

"Your loyalty does you credit, but, Bronwyn... You could have let her deal with it on her own. It's dangerous. Where is it now?"

"Somewhere safe." She met his eyes.

He put a hand on her shoulder. "I...... don't want anything to happen to you. That you would be so foolish......" He shook his head.

She moved her shoulder away.

"I understand now why Alice didn't want to be alone in this. She needs someone she can trust, and I can't be there for her all the time. I'm glad she has you as a friend. Especially as whoever is behind all of this trouble has clearly targeted her." His mouth set in a frown.

Bronwyn frowned at him right back. She didn't like being called foolish. She explained about the attack on Lady Alice and her naming Mabel as being involved.

Rupert exhaled. "Why didn't Alice tell me this herself?"

Bronwyn shrugged. "I don't know. Maybe she was afraid of what you might think. Or that you wouldn't be able to help her."

His expression darkened. "Just because we have different loyalties doesn't mean I don't care. Of course I would help her." He ran a hand through his golden curls. "We need to warn Mabel immediately."

"I already tried. She thought it was all a great joke."

"She often likes to flirt with the men. I could have a word with her," he said.

"I suppose. She'll probably take it better from you than me." She pouted. Had he no shame? For all that he declared he cared for Lady Alice and herself, that certainly didn't stop him from flirting with Mabel to gain information.

"She doesn't like you?"

Bronwyn shook her head. "She fancies herself to be of higher rank as she's Lady Morwenna's maid, and in her eyes, I serve Lady Alice."

"But do you? Or are you just being kind? I don't understand," he said.

She scratched her head. "To be honest, I'm not sure. When we were back in Lincoln and at the castle, she hired me for a time as her maid, but it was to help me. It gave me a chance to talk to knights who wouldn't have seen me in the kitchen, and it let me prove my father's innocence when he was accused of murder."

"I remember. You wore a blue dress."

"Oh." She blushed, glad for the darkness. "Yes, I suppose."

"And now?"

"When I joined this camp, I didn't know anyone. I'd only met Lady Alice again a few days ago, and you at the battle when you saved me. I think we just fell into the same pattern without really thinking about it, of her as mistress and me as her maid."

But the lines of their relationship had blurred, like stretches of color across a sky, and she didn't know anymore if they were friends, equals, or employer and maidservant. Lady Alice certainly wasn't paying her, and she did ask for her help but not demand it.

"I see. I shall leave it to you and Lady Alice to figure that out." He paused. "What are we to do about the crown?"

Bronwyn smiled, taking heart from the fact he'd said 'we.' "I have an idea. We put it back."

"What, the crown?"

"Yes."

"How?"

She told him. "When the time is right, we act. I think you and Lady Alice create a diversion, and I'll slip into the back of the empress's tent and put the crown back."

He crossed his arms. "I don't like it. Too much could go wrong."

"Have you got a better idea?"

He scratched his head and thought for a moment. "No. Fine. What about until then?"

"Keep looking after your master as if nothing out of the ordinary is happening."

"None of this is ordinary, Bronwyn."

She snorted. Her entire life for the past few months had been out of the ordinary.

That night, Bronwyn couldn't sleep. She obsessed and envisioned herself, Lady Alice, and Rupert getting caught with the crown and killed. And surprisingly, Theobold filled her dreams as well. She got up, her eyes wide open and alert in the darkness.

The campfire's embers had burned low and smoke hissed and whispered in the air, carrying the delicious smell of wood smoke that often pervaded the camp. She sat up and winced, feeling aches in her neck and back. Sleeping on the bare ground wasn't romantic, and it certainly wasn't comfortable. What she wouldn't give for her own straw pallet back in her family's bakery, the warmth of being indoors, and a blanket of her own. The hard ground made for a sorry bed, and it wasn't the first morning she'd woken up with sore muscles from the outside elements.

She used the privy, snatched her new purple dress from Lady Susanna and walked down to the riverbank, taking some rosemary and lye soap she'd managed to steal. She wanted to bathe, and even just a soak would be welcome after sweating in the cooking tents and shivering at night. But the footing was treacherous, and in the early hours before dawn, it was light enough to see but still a bit dark. She slipped off her dress, socks, and shoes and trundled down the bank, but her right foot slipped on some mud and she slid down, cascading into the water with a great splash.

Rocks and pebbles grazed her skin and soaked her instantly. She cursed and dropped the clothes she held, as well as the rosemary and lye soap, and fumbled, river water filling her nose and mouth. Bronwyn scrambled, her feet kicking at the riverbank floor.

It wasn't too deep where she was, but she didn't know how to swim. She clawed madly at the water for purchase, striking at the surface and grasping at river weeds, but these seemed to tangle around her legs and bar her way. Her plain shift felt heavy on her body and weighed her down, making every step and movement like ploughing through mud. Then her foot slipped and she fell under the water for a brief, terrifying second. River water filled her mouth and nose, and she clawed madly at the surface, her shoes feeling like weights in the river bottom as her head broke the surface.

She gasped for air, coughing and sputtering, reaching for something to grab on to, but her dresses sank and became filmy like silk as she scrambled for anything solid.

A pair of hands hooked under her arms. "Stop struggling," a man's voice said, and with a great tug, he pulled her backward, free of the river and its tangling weeds.

Bronwyn gasped in fresh, clean air, coughing and hacking in

the early dawn. She was dragged onto the bank and released. She rolled over onto her stomach, holding on to the ground, her numb fingers grasping rocks, pebbles, and bare, slick earth on an incline with her left hand, and with her right, the sodden thigh of a man.

She looked up, coughing with bleary eyes. "Theobold?"

He smiled at her. "At your service. Are you all right?" His gaze traveled along the length of her body, taking in the sight of her bare feet and shift. "You're safe now. The river won't eat you."

She nodded, coughing up bits of water, and snatched her hand off his thigh. She coughed again and lay back on the ground, breathing in great lungfuls of air.

When she got her breath back, he asked, "Mind telling me why you were trying to become a fish? Not that I mind the view." His eyes darted to her chest.

She croaked, "I slipped and fell in."

"You should be more careful. It's treacherous footing, especially if you don't know the river. There're places it's safe and places it's not. What were you doing out here, anyway? You're lucky I saw you walk down."

"I wanted to bathe," she said, and sat up. "My dresses are in there."

They floated downriver.

"Hold on, I'll get them." He got a stick and carefully waded in, not too far, and pulled the dresses out. He handed them to her, but they looked like sodden, limp rags. "You sure you want these?"

Bronwyn took the dresses from him with a small sigh. "They're the only ones I have." She took the sodden bundle in her hands and gave a little sigh. "They're dirtier now. And I lost the rosemary and soap I'd taken to make them smell nice."

His eyes were kind. "There are worse things."

"True." The fact that he had probably saved her life made her blush. How to thank a man who did that and then fetched her dirty dresses for her? "Um, thank you."

"Anytime." He rose. "Say, it looks like you missed some. How many dresses were you planning to wash?" He peered out at the river.

"Just two. Why?"

"Look at that." He pointed.

As the dawn's early light brightened, they could see the floating shapes of a dress and more clothing to be laundered, gently wavering back and forth on the river's surface. But not far away, stuck on some weeds, floated something else.

"What is that?" Bronwyn asked.

"I'll see. Stay here." He ventured out again with his stick, and the water quickly swirled around him, enveloping his body almost to his neck, as he pulled and tugged the thing free. It loosened from the weeds and he yelped and slipped back.

"Theobold!" Bronwyn called, hurrying down to the riverbank's shore.

He sprang to the surface, spitting out a mouthful of water. "Stay back," he warned. He tugged at something, towing a handful of wadded up clothes across the river. It was heavy and slow going, but as they grew closer, Bronwyn got a better view.

"Why, that's..."

"Stay back, Bronwyn." He dragged the thing up on the shore. "Do you recognize her?" He pulled back some of the clothes.

Bronwyn gasped.

The lifeless eyes of Mabel stared back at her.

✦

Chapter Nine

BRONWYN FELL BACK against the slippery ground, dropping the dresses. Her hands slid against the mud and pebbly shore, the rough stones digging into her palms. She gasped. "That's Mabel."

"Who?"

Mabel's bloated face gazed up at her. Bronwyn felt like her dark eyes were accusing, looking straight through her.

"It's Mabel. Lady Morwenna's maidservant."

Theobold cursed. "This is bad. What was she doing out here all alone?"

Bronwyn nodded toward the clothes floating in the river. "Likely the same as me, wanted to bathe or do some washing." She paused. "But that's odd. When we last spoke, she was off to do her chores yesterday afternoon. It was still light when we parted ways. Someone would have seen her if she'd fallen in."

"Maybe, maybe not. There're always people in the river, but there's also a lot that can happen that goes unnoticed."

She tilted her head at him.

He wiped his hands on his trousers and looked down at Mabel's body, his wet, curly black hair dripping on her corpse. "I'm surprised Lady Morwenna hasn't noticed her gone. I wonder when this happened."

Bronwyn asked, "What do we do?"

"We'll have to report it. Can you stay with the body? I won't be long. I'm going to fetch some men. The empress needs to hear about this."

"Yes."

He gave her a sharp nod. "I knew I could trust you. I'll be back soon."

Theobold strode up the riverbank, his long legs carrying him up and over the top. His head of black hair disappeared, leaving Bronwyn alone with the body.

She made the sign of the cross, said a quick prayer, and leaned over the body, looking.

Mabel's wispy, blonde hair lay plastered across her cheek and neck. Her face was bloated and her eyes glazed over, but her mouth was open. Water trickled out of it, making Bronwyn tense and shudder.

"Mabel, what happened to you?" she whispered.

She picked up the stick that Theobold had dropped on the bank and used it to gently move Mabel's body. It bore no trace marks or blood, just sodden and tangled from river weeds and the detritus of the water.

Bronwyn peered at the morning light, a quiet, pink glow that began to rise behind the black, scraggly trees. The sky began to lighten gradually, as it did sometimes. The darkness had faded to a deep, dark grey, and now a lighter grey, revealing the shoal of the riverbank, the moving waters, the outline of rocks and the slick tracks in the mud of where she'd slipped.

She looked at the ground. She knew that she had left tracks in the dirt and mud from where she'd fallen in, but had Mabel? Could it have been an accidental fall?

Try as she might to find evidence of an accident, there were too many pairs of footprints that dotted the shore, particularly at the water's edge. Any number of people might have come by. The earth was no help. How could Mabel have died? Had she tripped and fallen, and like Bronwyn, gotten stuck in the river and couldn't swim? Bronwyn's own experience had shown just how easily that could happen, especially if she'd been alone. It could all have been an accident.

But something about the timing of it made her think otherwise. For Mabel to have died so soon after Lady Alice had been attacked and named her as being involved in the crown's theft, it was too timely to be a coincidence. Theobold knew, but who else could she tell?

She heard footsteps approach and realized she was still standing there in her shift. She quickly wrung out the wet dresses and put her old one on over her head, shivering. She held the new purple dress at her side. She'd try washing both again later. She smelled like the river, but it was better than being dead.

The footsteps heralded the arrival of Theobold, followed by a pair of guards, as well as Sir Ranulf and Sir Miles, and the young healer, Edmund. The men surveyed her and then the body.

She bowed her head and stayed quiet as the men discussed the situation.

"What happened?" Sir Ranulf asked. A middle-aged, heavyset, stocky man, he wore light mail over his tunic and fiddled with the sheathed sword at his belt. He looked bleary-eyed and rubbed sleep from his eyes. He peered at Bronwyn. "You're here? I should've known. You're as bad as him." He nodded toward Theobold. "All right, who died?"

"It's Lady Morwenna's maid," Theobold said.

He glanced at Mabel's body. "What is that to me? Find the woman another. Or better yet, let it be a lesson to her to take better care of her maids. The girl shouldn't have worked in the river before light. It's dangerous."

The guards agreed. Bronwyn eyed Sir Miles, who stood quietly. Sir Miles was of an average height for a man, but he was slim and wiry, and he seemed taller. He had a thoughtful expression. Judging by the way his eyes darted around the scene, taking in the sight of the scattered clothes on the river surface, Mabel's body on the shore, and Bronwyn standing by, she knew that he missed nothing.

Bronwyn watched as the young healer, Edmund, stepped

forward and inspected the body. Seemingly having no qualms about death, he touched the woman's head, turning it this way and that. "There're no marks on her neck or face, nothing to suggest anything other than drowning. I think she probably slipped and fell and couldn't swim. An unfortunate accident."

The men nodded. Sir Ranulf farted and belched, scratching at his belly. "I'm headed back to bed. Don't wake me unless it's actually important."

Bronwyn stepped forward, her face scrunched up in a frown. The death of a person, however low in rank, mattered. Mabel had mattered, and this had been more than just an unfortunate accident.

The men looked at her. Sir Ranulf said, "You have something to say?"

Bronwyn swallowed. "I wonder if she was pushed."

The men exchanged glances. Edmund stood as the guard said, "Why are you here? Besides, the healer says she drowned."

"I came here to bathe when I fell in. Theobold pulled me out of the river and found her floating," Bronwyn said.

The men shot Theobold a few looks. Sir Ranulf grinned. "You two were down by the river together alone, eh?"

Theobold rolled his eyes whilst Bronwyn put a hand on her hip. "It's not like that."

"Never mind why you two were here together—no one cares about that. Why would you think the maid's death wasn't an accident?" Sir Miles assessed her.

"No reason. She's making up tales," Theobold said, shooting Bronwyn a hard stare. "Don't worry yourself about this. I'm sorry you had to see this. You can go."

Bronwyn's mouth dropped open. "But…"

"Go on. I'm sure your mistress is waiting for you." His tone was pleasant, but his eyes were hard. There was a clear message there. *Go.*

Bronwyn frowned and her cheeks flaming, she turned to go, conscious of the men's eyes on her.

"Nice bottom, that one," one guard said. The men laughed at this.

Bronwyn grimaced as she trudged back up the riverbank. She washed her hands in the grass that was damp with dew and hadn't been eaten by the horses yet. Sighing, she wrung out the water from her clothes—again. Both dresses were damp and smelled, and those were her only woolen socks. If she ruined them, she'd be running around in her bare shift with hardly a stitch on.

She wrung out her hair and realized she'd lost her kerchief in the river. She normally tied it around her neck, but it had come away. Now she'd need another to tie her hair back in the kitchen tents when she worked. Her shoulders slumped. How had life suddenly become so hard?

She rejoined the camp and sat on a log, thinking. First things first, she had to tell Lady Morwenna that Mabel wasn't coming back. It was barely dawn, and as she looked in on the ladies-in-waiting, they were all sound asleep.

She instead went back down to the river. Mabel's body had disappeared, as had the men. But Theobold's stick was still there on the side. She used it and spotted her kerchief floating downriver. She managed to hook it on the stick and reach it—just. But to get it, she had to get her shoes and socks wet again. Still, she almost retrieved the kerchief. She'd just reached it, when it slipped off the stick and sailed away, downriver. Bronwyn sighed and cursed. That was a bit of bad luck. So much for her kerchief. Now she just needed to figure out what to do next.

She washed both her dresses quickly and sitting in her shift on the bank, wrung out her socks, whipped them around to try to air-dry them, and once she was satisfied they were just a touch damp, joined the makeshift kitchen to help prepare the morning meal. But as she began chopping vegetables and preparing dough for bread, she lost track of time and in an hour or so, she heard the head cook Mary say, "Did you hear? A woman's drowned in the river."

Bronwyn turned. So the consensus was that the maid had drowned. She thought quickly. It must have been at least an hour, maybe two, since dawn. She had to tell Lady Morwenna and the other ladies. Lady Alice needed to know.

"It's true. A servant was found in the river this morning. Must have slipped in and fell. That's what the men say. They're telling all of us not to go swimming or wade out too far, in case we fall in and can't swim. It's a strong current, they say."

"Who was the woman?" a cook asked.

"Some maidservant. Mabel?" Mary shrugged and walked away.

Bronwyn dusted off her hands and quietly said to the nearest cook, "Can you take over? I need to speak with my mistress."

The cook, a middle-aged man with thinning hair and burst blood vessels around his cheeks and bulbous nose, looked at her with watery eyes. "Aye. But I'll not be doing all your work for you. Come back and take care of this. If Mistress Mary sees you slacking off, she'll kick you out."

Bronwyn nodded. "I'll be fast."

She darted away, conscious of the cook rolling his eyes. She darted through the camp, reaching the ladies-in-waiting tent. The ladies were definitely up, for it was noisy, and Lady Morwenna could be heard from outside.

Bronwyn took a breath and went in. Lady Morwenna paced inside her tent. Seeing Bronwyn, she said, "You. You had something to do with this, didn't you?"

Bronwyn took in the scene. Lady Morwenna sat with Lady Susanna, who looked at her with suspicion. Lady Alice sat nearby, twisting a bit of bedding in her hands.

"You've heard."

"Yes, I've bloody well heard. My maid goes and drowns herself in the river rather than serve me. It is a slight and an insult to my good name, and I won't have it. Serves her right for trying to be so stupid as to wade into the river at that hour. Of course she would die." Bronwyn stiffened and shut her mouth like a trap.

The woman didn't spare a thought for her maid dying. How cruel and uncaring. She wondered if that same lack of concern for others hinted at a great guilt. Could she have killed Lady Eleanor? "Lady Morwenna, I do not think—"

"No one is paying you to think, baker. Get out. Unless you wish to be her replacement and serve me? I'm sure Lady Alice wouldn't mind." Lady Morwenna gritted her teeth.

Lady Alice, who had been sitting quietly, stirred. "I... Bronwyn, let us go outside. There are some things I need to discuss with you."

She rose and motioned for Bronwyn to go out. Once they stood outside the tent, they heard Lady Morwenna screech, "And what was she doing in the river so early in the morning? Washing my clothes, I heard. But now they're gone. My dresses are gone! As if it's not bad enough she's dead, now I've hardly got anything left to wear."

Bronwyn breathed in noisily and walked with Lady Alice some distance away.

"You heard about Mabel," Bronwyn said. "Are you all right?"

"No. I'm terrified. What if they come after me next?" Lady Alice bit her nails.

Bronwyn wanted to console her, but she couldn't. Whoever was behind this might well target Lady Alice next. She rubbed at her nose. It was Lady Alice's lie that had led to Mabel being targeted. She could at least spare a thought for the dead maid.

"Be on your guard," Bronwyn said. "Stay with people at all times. Stay by Rupert's side, or the empress. No one will attack you there."

Lady Alice nodded. She still wore Rupert's cloak as if it were a suit of armor, and she wore one of the dresses Bronwyn had cleaned beneath it. "I am lucky, I suppose. You were at least able to wash my dresses and not die." She looked at Bronwyn. "Do you think it was an accident?"

Bronwyn shook her head. "No. I tried to warn Mabel—but she wouldn't listen. Didn't believe me. Rupert was going to talk to her too to try to convince her."

"You and Rupert? Why both of you?" Lady Alice's brow wrinkled.

"I told him about the crown and—"

"You should leave him out of this. I don't want him getting hurt," Lady Alice said.

Bronwyn gave her a sideways glance. "Lady Alice... We need to talk about something."

"What? How you're keen to involve my man in your schemes?"

Bronwyn stared at her.

"Don't think I don't know. Lady Morwenna told me. She thinks you fancy him. I told her it's an utter falsehood because of course, he is allied to me, and you are just my maidservant. She said to watch you, as stranger things have happened." Lady Alice sighed. "I don't know what to think."

Bronwyn said, "Lady Alice."

"And now I hear that you're involving him in this plot. Why? Why do you seek to endanger him?"

"He's a good man and I trust him. And we need help." *Besides*, she thought, *you thought nothing of endangering me.* "We need to talk about our... arrangement."

"What arrangement?" Lady Alice looked at her.

Bronwyn had her full attention now, and yet Lady Alice looked so lost as she pulled Rupert's cloak closer around her, Bronwyn felt pity for her. But she had to tell her. "I'm not your servant."

Lady Alice started as if she'd been struck.

"I'm not here to wash your clothes, or sew your hem, or to clean up after you. I'm here trying to survive, the same as you. I'll work in the cooking tents and help you when you ask, but it's because I... I think we are friends, and that's what friends do for each other. But I'm not your maidservant."

Lady Alice sat very still, as if she were carved from marble. "I see." She rose as Bronwyn opened her mouth to say more. "Very well. I've heard enough. I clearly misunderstood you and our relationship. I thought we were mistress and maidservant."

"We're not. But I—"

"Did I hear right? You two are friends?" Lady Susanna said.

Bronwyn tensed. *To whom was Lady Susanna truly loyal?* she wondered.

Lady Alice said, "Of course not. This doesn't concern you." She waited until Lady Susanna shrugged and walked away, humming off-key.

Bronwyn said, "I only meant to say—"

Lady Alice said, "Don't interrupt. We certainly are not friends, or anything else, as you've made it clear. I could never befriend a servant like you." She swept the cloak around her as if she were a queen in her own right. "As we have no relationship to speak of, I don't see the need to talk with you any longer. Good day, Bronwyn Blakenhale." Her voice carried. She turned and walked straight past her as if they were strangers and back into the tent.

Bronwyn stared after her, feeling her cheek warm despite the chilly morning. She sat the tent flap close behind her, and some wicked laughter rang out across the air shortly afterward. Why did she feel so alone, and as if she'd lost a friend?

Bronwyn returned to the kitchen and took up where she'd left off, rolling out balls of dough to be made into soft rolls. With her absence, they'd started to dry out and get a dry crust on top, so she rolled them out again. They would be a denser bake, as she'd knocked some of the air out of them, but they would do. It was no more than simple bread and would do nicely for serving the people in the camp.

Bronwyn did as she was asked and barely spoke a word to anyone, not joining in the gossip. That day, it swirled around the subject of Mabel's death. Some people believed the servant had killed herself, rather than serve Lady Morwenna any longer. Others who had come across Lady Morwenna's sharp tongue and rude manner thought aloud that maybe Lady Morwenna had killed Mabel herself, while others thought it had likely been just an accident. Bronwyn thought it wasn't an accident. For someone to attack Lady Alice and then have Mabel's name as a suspect, it couldn't have been a coincidence that the young woman now lay dead. It had been murder. And Lady Morwenna was definitely involved, somehow.

Bronwyn was just taking the rolls off the hot stone and set them on a wooden platter when there was a slight cough at her shoulder.

"Bronwyn?"

She turned. It was Theobold. "What do you want?" she asked rudely. She turned back to her rolls. They were dense but would taste well enough.

"I suppose I deserve that," he said. "I've come to talk to you."

"What for? I'm just a silly, empty-headed maidservant. You have no reason to talk to the likes of me." She heard a cheerful titter and glanced over. Some of the servants were eyeing Theobold, the young women especially.

One young woman went up to him and asked, "Are you hungry, sir? We've just got these rolls fresh from the heat." She offered him the platter.

Bronwyn made a noise of astonishment. She'd literally just baked those rolls. If she wanted Theobold to have one, she'd offer them to him herself. She scowled.

"No, I'm fine," he told the young cook. "I would like a word with Bronwyn here."

Bronwyn turned her back on him, feeling his eyes on her between her shoulder blades. "Excuse me."

"Where are you going?" he asked.

"The privy," she said, walking away.

One of the women said to Theobold, "You can talk to me if you like. I'm much nicer than her. And I don't smell like the river."

Bronwyn stiffened and kept walking. She did go to the privy, and when she'd finished, she wiped her hands on the wet grass, drying them with her dress. Her clothes were mostly dry now from her running around.

She began to walk back, when Theobold stepped into her line of sight.

She sidestepped him and kept walking, but he stood in her way again.

"Move," she said.

"Not until you talk to me."

"I *am* talking to you. Move out of the way."

"Not until you listen."

She put her hands on her hips and glared up at him, her eyes raking along his long body. He wore long, brown leggings and a plain, dark tunic over that, with a jerkin and a sheathed sword at his belt. He was handsome—there was no denying it. Especially when a black curl threatened to fall into his eyes, and she wanted to reach up and smooth it away. She expected to find him annoyed, but instead, he smiled at her. A part of her wished to smile back, but she restrained herself.

"What do you want?" she asked.

"To apologize. I'm sorry for what I said earlier."

She cocked her head. "When you acted like I was a nobody, and just a silly, empty-headed servant."

"To those men, it's better if that's exactly what they think you are."

"Why?"

He stepped closer, closing the distance between them. "They're dangerous. All of them."

"Even the healer?" She thought back to how he'd been slightly suspicious of her as he'd treated her cut, and how he'd disliked her asking questions. Was he someone to suspect?

"Yes. No man goes into his line of work without knowing the safe drugs from the poisonous ones. He may care for the sick, but he does not have a kind heart. I wanted you out of there and gone from that situation. Is that so wrong?"

"I can look after myself," she said.

"Except when you decide to turn into a fish, or did you forget what happened this morning? If I hadn't been there to rescue you, you might have died alongside Mabel."

The mention of the other woman's demise made Bronwyn shudder.

"I'm sorry. I shouldn't have said that. But it's true. You could have died. You have to be more careful, Bron."

"'Bron'?" she repeated.

"You don't like it?" He smiled.

"My name already sounds like a boy's name and now you've shortened it. It sounds even worse now," she grumbled.

He laughed. "Is that what you think? Believe me, Bronwyn, no one who looks at you will think that. You're pretty, even if you think you've got a boy's name." His cheeks flushed. "I mean… I, um…"

Bronwyn's eyes widened.

He blushed furiously. "Just ignore me. I say that to all the girls. Women. Um. Anyway. I meant to say, there's to be a bonfire tonight. And I wondered if—"

"A bonfire? Why?" she asked. It might prove the perfect distraction for her to return the crown.

"Her Grace wants us to have a short celebration before we break camp tomorrow. We leave at dawn for Gloucester." He ran a hand through his unruly, black curls. "Bronwyn, I wanted to ask…" He mumbled something unintelligible.

Her mind was going a mile a minute. The bonfire. She had to speak with Rupert and Lady Alice. They had to act tonight, at the bonfire, while everyone was distracted—"Wait, what?"

"Wouldyouliketodancewithmetonight?" His words came out in a rush. "I wondered if you were planning to attend the bonfire tonight. There will be dancing and… I wondered if…"

"I, um, can't. I'll have a lot of cooking to do if we're to cook for a celebration. I may be too busy to go." She began to walk on.

"Surely, the cooks will let you go." He kept pace with her.

"I doubt it. Mistress Mary is quite…… Um. We'll see. But I'm sure I'll be too busy."

"Bronwyn." He stood in her path. His steps were uneven. "Do you… not want to go with me?"

"No, it's not that."

"Is it the dancing you're afraid of? Maybe you need a dancing master to teach you?" He grinned.

Bronwyn shook her head. She needed the time to sneak into the empress's tent and return the crown. Dancing with Theobold by the bonfire was not part of her plan. "I just know I'll be busy cooking, and……"

"I'll come ask for you if they don't. Say I've got special permission to take you to the bonfire," he called after her.

She waved a hand goodbye and kept walking. Why was she smiling? Why was she still thinking about his black hair?

She thought back to Lady Alice's dismissal. It had hurt. But she had more to think on now, like the bonfire. As she began to return to the kitchen, a voice said, "Bronwyn." A hand touched her shoulder.

"What is it?" She whirled around, her blonde braid whipping around her shoulder.

Rupert raised his hands. "It's only me. Why are you so angry?"

She bit the inside of her left cheek.

"Let me guess. You told Lady Alice you no longer wanted to be friends, and she got angry with you."

Bronwyn blinked. "No."

"Then why is she acting like you broke her heart?"

"I didn't. I told her I thought we were friends, and I'd do her favors because she asked, but that I wasn't her maidservant to order around."

"Oh." He stared at his feet. "So you two are having a fight."

"She said we weren't friends. I don't think there's any relationship there to warrant a fight." At those words, she teared up suddenly. "Oh." She turned away, holding her hand to her eyes. She would not cry in front of him. Why had those words suddenly made her tear up? It was unconscionable.

"Bronwyn," he started, "it's okay. You can talk to me."

"We need to return it. The you-know-what."

"I know. So when?"

"Tonight. Find me once the celebrations start, and I'll need you and Lady Alice to create a distraction."

He nodded. "See you then. But, Bronwyn, where is it hidden?"

She shook her head. "Somewhere safe. Better that you don't know."

THAT NIGHT WAS to be a celebration, as the empress had grown tired of Lincoln and planned to move on with the dawn. There was much cooking, and revelry, and by the early evening, there was not a pig, chicken, duck, or hare that hadn't been hunted and cooked for the feast. Great platters went around with food, scenting the air with their rich oils and juices. As a change from their usual potage, Bronwyn joined the others in having bits of hare on crusty bread. It was delicious, if not exactly filling.

The bonfire began, and with it came music played on drums, voices raised in song, and lutes. People danced and as the fading sun sank, and as the sky's hues deepened to the purple of twilight, Bronwyn slipped away from the cooking tents, where the cooks were packing up for the morning ride. They had enough potage and hard biscuits to take for the journey, as well as any leftover meat and food from that evening.

Darkness fell, and the great flames of the bonfire leapt to a great height, crackling and giving warmth to those who danced around it. Bronwyn sought out Lady Alice to speak to her about the plan, but she ignored her, preferring to sashay with ladylike grace before Rupert.

Rupert saw Bronwyn standing off to the side and came up to her. "Hullo. Do you like the bonfire?"

"Yes, it's very nice. We need to… put that item back."

"What are you two talking about? Oh." Lady Alice approached them and stopped. "Rupert, I want to dance. Come dance with me."

"But now is the perfect time. We need to—" Bronwyn started.

Lady Alice huffed and walked away.

Bronwyn watched her go, and Rupert said, "She's not talking to you. I tried talking to her about it, but she won't say anything more, just that you owe her an apology."

Bronwyn rolled her eyes. "We don't have time for this. We need to do this now, before someone sees."

"I agree. Lady Alice?" he called.

Lady Alice came over. "What?" She crossed her arms over her chest, a move not unnoticed by Rupert.

Rupert whispered in her ear, and she frowned. "Fine. We'll distract the guards, somehow. But for what it's worth, I think this is a foolish plan."

"Have you got a better idea?" Bronwyn asked.

"I'm not talking to you," Alice said to no one in particular. To Rupert, she said, "I'm doing this for you. No other reason." She pointedly avoided looking at Bronwyn.

Bronwyn snorted and refrained from rolling her eyes again. Lady Alice had brought her into this mess in the first place, and now she was acting juvenile. Bronwyn was losing her patience. This was to save all of their skins; it wasn't a whim or a walk in the countryside. She leaned forward to Rupert. "You remember the plan?"

"Yes."

"Give me five minutes and then let's go. I'll see you afterward," she said.

"Godspeed, Blakenhale."

She met Rupert's eyes, the bright-orange flames of the bonfire reflecting and playing shadows against his solid features, like he'd been cast from stone. "Good luck."

Bronwyn hurried back to the tree with her purple dress from Susanna and dug into the roots, finding her apron with the crown and bundling it in her arms. It was too conspicuous. What to do?

She looked down and untied her apron. It was dirty and needed washing, but it would do in a pinch. She tied back her hair, saying a quick prayer and thanking the saints she had thick hair, before putting on the crown and tying it up with her hair in the apron around her head, like a makeshift kerchief. The crown was small but heavy, and it settled on her head with a solid weight.

The thought struck her of the audacity of her plan; she was literally wearing the empress's crown. The very thought sent a chill through her. If discovered, she would surely pay with her life. But there was no other way for it. She had to act—and fast. Now was the moment. There was no time to waste.

Securing the apron tightly around her head so it wouldn't fall, she tried walking. It was slightly awkward, as she wasn't used to the crown's weight. Just taking a few steps felt odd, and as soon as she re-entered the mix of people, she was jostled, and her would-be kerchief wobbled. She held a hand to her head then realized how odd she must have looked.

Bronwyn moved around the dancers and people milling about, talking, drinking, laughing, and eating, then hastened away from the bonfire and toward the tents. The empress's tent was clearly in sight, for it was guarded by a pair of guards in front and had torches lit. Small cooking fires dotted the area nearby, but none got too close to Empress Maud, for fear of disturbing her, Bronwyn supposed.

She got closer and saw Rupert and Lady Alice walk by, on their way to the tent. She was about to join them when a thin form stood in her path. "There you are. I've been looking for you."

Bronwyn looked up. In the torchlight stood Mary, the head cook. "Yes?"

"*Yes?*" she mimicked. "Yes, mistress, is what you say to me. We need you back in the cooking tents. Get to work."

"But I already worked today."

Mary snickered. "Doesn't matter. I say you work, you work. Go on now."

"But—"

"No *buts*. Go." She made a shooing motion with her hands.

Bronwyn turned and, locking eyes with Lady Alice, began walking back toward the kitchen, feeling Mary's eyes on her.

She waited until she was hidden by the next few tents, then hid. Mary walked past a few minutes later, humming off-key to herself. Bronwyn darted forward, nodded to Rupert, and walked around to the back.

Her heart began to beat in her throat. Empress Maud's tent was lit well enough, from a single torch inside the tent. Bronwyn snuck close to the back of the tent flaps and slowly lifted one up.

Rupert said, "Here, thought you two might like a drink. It's not fair you can't join in the festivities."

"Cheers, mate," one of the guards said.

Bronwyn heard the light clink of cups and moved closer.

Rupert said loudly, "Anytime. Say, do you want to go enjoy the bonfire? There's some pretty girls dancing over there. I'm a squire. I'm happy to watch the entrance here if you like."

"Clear off," a guard said.

Bronwyn slipped inside the tent, her apron wobbling dangerously on her head.

"All right, all right. It was just a friendly offer."

"I say, you're being very rude," Lady Alice said. "He was just trying to be nice."

"Who are you?" one of the guards asked. "I've seen you around here before."

"I am Lady Alice Duncombe, one of the empress's ladies-in-waiting."

"And who's he?"

"A squire. I work for the empress," Rupert said.

"So do we all," the guard said. "What's your name?"

"Rupert. Everyone knows me. I'm friendly with most of the people here at camp."

"That's fine, but no one comes in here. You heard him. Off with you," the other guard said, tossing his cup to the ground.

"Suit yourself," Rupert said.

Bronwyn lowered the tent flap behind her, quiet as a mouse. She unloosened her apron from her head and lifted off the crown, giving it a quick wipe. It was a relief to have it off, but it was very heavy—and fortunately not damaged from its time beneath the tree.

There before her were big, heavy chests. She quickly darted in front and opened a large one, which opened with a creak.

She froze as Rupert met her gaze. One of the guards started to turn when Lady Alice's eyes flew up in the back of her head and she fell to the ground.

"What's happened to her?" a guard asked.

"She's fainted," Rupert said. "She needs a healer."

"So fetch one."

"She's my lady. I can't leave her. Can one of you go?"

Bronwyn rose to look past the chests at Lady Alice. Was she all right?

Lady Alice briefly opened one eye and winked at Bronwyn.

That was all the incentive Bronwyn needed, and she quickly put the crown in the chest, closing it slowly. Once closed, she tiptoed back around the chest and knelt down as one of the guards left, leaving Rupert and Lady Alice with the remaining guard.

Bronwyn backed away but then froze as she heard footsteps circle around the back of the tent. There was someone there. She stiffened. She couldn't go out the way she'd come in and couldn't leave through the front of the tent without the guard noticing. She stiffened and hunkered down lower on her haunches, feeling very like a deer caught in a trap.

One beat, then two. Lady Alice gave a little cry. "Oh, what happened?"

"You fainted," Rupert said.

"There's no need to speak so loud, we can all hear you," the guard said, "You all right, Lady Alice?"

"I—" She paused. "I am very well, thank you. Rupert, help me up. I must have taken a turn."

Rupert must have complied, for Bronwyn heard some shuffling.

"Thank you. So sorry to have troubled you. Good night." Her voice was sweet.

"It's no trouble, lady," the guard said. "Oh, here's the healer."

The familiar voice of the young healer, Edmund, spoke. "I heard a lady fainted. Is that you?"

"Yes, but I'm better now. Just a turn."

"I see," Edmund said.

The voices chatted and then Rupert said, "All right, Lady Alice, let's go back. I fancy more ale."

"Of course you do. As long as I get my dance," she said.

Bronwyn heaved a sigh of relief as they departed. She was about to move back when a hand clamped itself over her mouth, and a thick arm pulled her close to a muscular male body. "Don't move," a voice whispered in her ear. "Don't make a sound. They'll hear you."

Chapter Ten

BRONWYN TENSED. WHO was this man who'd covered her mouth? Should she bite? Scream? Would he slip a knife into her guts or worse, turn her in to the empress to be tortured? Had it all been for naught?

She struggled and the arm tightened around her waist, pulling her closer. Whoever it was, the man smelled of the river, sweat, ale, and horse. He murmured, "I'm going to move my hand away. Don't bite me, and don't scream." He slowly removed his hand.

Bronwyn turned her head. "Theobold?"

"Sssshhh." He held up a finger for silence.

She clamped her mouth shut and not a moment too soon, for there inside the tent walked a few men. She peered through the gap in the chests and as the light increased—for one of the men carried a torch—she spotted the familiar faces of Sir Ranulf de Gernon, one of the two men who had fooled the chatelaine of Lincoln Castle into letting him and his knights in, leading to the Battle of Lincoln. With him walked Edmund the healer, as well as Sir Miles FitzWalter.

Bronwyn swallowed. These were dangerous men. She barely breathed, barely made a sound.

"What was that trouble just now? Some squire and his lady?"

"Aye," the guard said. "Got ourselves a pair of lovebirds wandering around. Just being friendly."

Sir Ranulf snickered. "Just as well you turned them away."

Sir Miles shot him a dirty look. "Friendly how?"

"The lad offered us drinks."

"You're sure that's all they were after?" Sir Miles asked.

"Yes, sir."

Bronwyn's muscles began to ache. She shifted slightly and her hair brushed against Theobold's face.

He sniffed, too quickly.

She knew that telltale sign. In seconds, he sneezed.

"What was that?" Sir Ranulf asked. "Is there someone else here?"

"Come out now, whoever you are," Sir Miles said calmly.

Theobold leaned back and rubbed his nose. He looked at Bronwyn and motioned for her to get up. When she shook her head, he said loudly, "Come on, love, there's no use hiding." He stood and pulled her up.

"Theobold. What are you doing here?" Sir Miles asked.

"What's it look like?" Theobold gave the men a lazy smile. He wrapped an arm around Bronwyn's waist, and she looked up at him in annoyance. He shot her a wink and a look that said, *play along*.

The men exchanged amused glances. Sir Ranulf laughed. Sir Miles was less amused. "I see. Theobold, you do choose curious places for your dalliances. But then, I don't imagine there's many who would take you willingly, knowing your family. Even with your looks."

Bronwyn sensed Theobold grew angry. His body stilled as if cold, but waiting, as if in the breath before a fight. She touched his arm and said, "I'm sorry. We were looking for somewhere quiet to be alone, and…"

"How did you get in here? There are guards posted outside."

The guards peeked at her and frowned. "Who are you?"

"She's with me," Theobold said, pulling her closer against his side. "I let her in through the back. Just wanted to impress her and find a place we wouldn't be disturbed."

"What a curious choice. You didn't fancy bringing the girl to your own tent?" Sir Miles asked.

Theobold swallowed.

Bronwyn felt Sir Miles's eyes on her, assessing her. "Sorry. It was foolish of me. I'll go."

"*We'll* go. I'm not letting you out of my sight that easily," Theobold told her, his eyes looking into hers as if she were the only one in the room. The only one who mattered. She could imagine falling into those dark eyes of his and never wanting to leave. A black curl fell into his eyes and her fingers itched to smooth it away.

Sir Ranulf coughed. "All right. All right, already. I've seen enough lovers for one night. Clear off, the pair of you. Find somewhere else to fool around. We're here on the empress's business, as you well know, Theobold. Out."

Theobold pinched Bronwyn's rump. She squealed and jumped, smacking him on the arm.

The men laughed, and she glared at Theobold, her cheeks flaming. He grinned and pulled her by the hand, away from the back of the chests and out in front, around the men.

"Gentlemen," Theobold said, not letting Bronwyn's hand go.

A quick flip of the tent flap and they were back in the open night air. The darkness was lit by the bonfire, and dark shapes of men and women dancing and drinking filled her vision. The air was warm from the warm bodies and the ground crunched under the weight of dozens of dancing feet.

She tried tugging her hand free, but he wouldn't let go. "*Theobold.*"

"Wait. We need to talk."

She let him pull her through the crowd of people, past the dancers and couples. He ignored the admiring glances of young women, and some had crestfallen looks as they saw him pulling her by the hand and probably assumed the worst, whereas other people watched and gossiped, talking.

It wasn't until they'd cleared most of the crowd, past the

bonfire, and approached the trees, that he let her go. They were mostly alone as they stood away from all the people. The air was cold here, and at the outskirt of the woods, it was pitch black and her visibility was poor. She shivered yet did not feel afraid of him, only as if she were in trouble.

"Talk," he said, crossing his arms over his chest. "Why on earth were you in the empress's tent hiding? I saw you go in with that apron on your head. If you're in that great a need of a kerchief to tie your hair, I'll get one for you. But imagine my surprise when I go in and you're no longer wearing it. What's the meaning of this, Bronwyn?"

She looked at him. He was tall and looked pale in the slim moonlight. "I, uh…"

"Don't lie. It doesn't suit you. I'd like to know what you were doing there, why you involved Rupert and a lady-in-waiting in your plans, and just what you thought you'd accomplish."

She cocked her head. She realized then that he was quite smart. He'd seen right away that it had all been a ruse to allow her to sneak into the tent.

"For God's sake, Bronwyn, I'm on your side. What do I have to do to make you trust me? I just saved you—again. Possibly from execution."

She glared and walked up to him. "By pretending we were lovers. You made me look a fool."

"No, I made you look innocent. I saved your life. Do you know how serious it could have been if they'd discovered you without me? If they'd found you there alone, they'd have taken you in for questioning, and I can't have that. I won't." His expression was grim.

She lifted her chin, frowning at his dark eyes. "By pinching me and putting your arm around my waist?"

"It was an act, Bronwyn. They know I'm popular with the ladies, so they believed the lie. I saved you." He snorted. "Why are you angry? There're worse things that could happen. And there are a lot of young women who would *love* to be in your position."

She laughed. "Yes, I know it's a lie. I heard you telling Lady Morwenna the other day you'd never be with someone like me. A servant."

He stared. "That's what you're annoyed about?" He laughed.

She turned her back on him.

He said behind her, "Bronwyn. I said that to her because Lady Morwenna has the mouth of a fishwife, and no secrets of her own. She respects no one but perhaps the empress, and if I were to say I fancied you, then she would make life miserable for us both, believe me."

Bronwyn whirled around and put her hands on her hips. "I— oh."

They stood very close.

"That's no reason to make the men think we are lovers," she whispered.

The right side of his mouth curled into a smile. "I can't believe that's what you're worried about. Not the fact that you could have been imprisoned." He shook his head. "I suppose I should be insulted, but I want to know. What were you doing there in the first place? Why did Lady Alice pretend to faint?"

She looked at him. "You won't tell a soul? On your honor?"

He looked back at her. She felt his eyes searching hers, as if for an answer. A beat, then two.

"On my honor, I shall not tell. But I want to know, Bronwyn, what is it I'm keeping a secret."

She told him. Starting with the crown reappearing amongst Lady Alice's bedding and her begging Bronwyn to help hide it, leading up to her plan to return it.

Theobold stared at her, eyes wide. "*That's* what you were doing?"

"She was being framed. I think Lady Morwenna planted it in her bedding and that's why she accused Lady Alice."

"No. Don't start on that line of thinking. You're wrong."

"And why is that?"

"I know her. Lady Morwenna can make mistakes, but she wouldn't be so brazen as to steal a crown and then try to blame it on someone else. Besides, Lady Alice has been suspected for a while now."

"What do you mean?"

He glanced this way and that. "I mean, that what I heard was that she was in Stephen's court for a time. Got pretty comfortable over there with some of the men."

"Only Rupert."

"Aye. And who does he serve? One of Stephen's men. That alone puts her under suspicion."

"But she's innocent. She didn't do anything."

"No, of course not. Except shove the crown at you and leave you to clean up the mess. Never mind it got one maidservant killed and put you in danger." He cursed. "God, Bronwyn. You knew I was tasked with searching for the crown, so why didn't you tell me?"

"I didn't know you that well. I didn't know if I could trust you." Her mouth went dry.

"And now?"

She could feel his eyes seeking hers. When he took her hands in his, she didn't stop him. They were warm, and a part of her felt safe. "I...... I couldn't be certain who to trust."

"So you decided to try and use your friends and handle things yourself." He dropped her hands and ran a hand through his curly, dark hair. "Of all the hare-brained schemes... I can't believe you were so foolish. So you thought you'd simply return the crown, yeah?"

"Yes. It *did* work."

"Only because I helped you. If you had been caught..." He shook his head. "I can't believe you. And Lady Alice. Both of you. But shame on her for getting you into this mess."

"It's not her fault—it's Lady Morwenna's, for stealing it in the first place," Bronwyn said.

He grew quiet. "You can't think *she* is behind this?"

Bronwyn nodded.

"All right. You're wrong, but I'll play along. What makes you say that?"

"She has disliked Lady Alice from the start. Jealous, I think."

"But stealing the crown and planting it in her rival's bedding?" He frowned. "Lady Morwenna often plots and schemes, but I've never known her to be so cruel as to endanger the life of another person. No, you cannot be right. Lady Morwenna is many things, but she's not a killer."

"Why do you defend her?" Her limbs trembled.

"I am not. I'm only speaking the truth, from how I know her. We are… well-acquainted." He looked away.

Bronwyn raised an eyebrow, but as it was dark, she knew he likely wouldn't notice. "I think you're wrong. No one dislikes Lady Alice so much as she does. Morwenna was so certain that Lady Alice had it. Why would she be certain Lady Alice was behind the theft, and why would she think it was hidden in her bedding? Unless she'd put it there herself." Bronwyn paused.

"Also, she didn't care that her own maidservant died. There are rumors that Lady Morwenna killed Mabel herself."

"Why would Lady Morwenna kill her own maid?" he asked. "Just dismiss her and take on a new one."

"Maybe to keep her quiet about what she'd seen?"

"Maybe, but all you have is rumors and guesses. Those do not make Lady Morwenna guilty of attempted murder. Have you looked at the other ladies-in-waiting?" he asked. "Lord, Bronwyn, you're like a dog with a bone. Fine. Hunt this down, and prove me wrong. I might just call you 'Mistress Bloodhound' instead of 'Mistress Baker.'"

She stepped on his foot.

He grinned. "Step on my feet all you want, but the name fits. Besides, you have no proof that Lady Morwenna stole the crown in the first place. All you have is an empty theory you came up with because Lady Alice found the crown and left it with you. Lady Morwenna was possibly acting on rumors. You're so keen that Lady Morwenna is behind this. Did you stop to think that maybe she'd heard a rumor that Lady Alice had stolen it and hidden the crown in her bedding? What if another person had fed Lady Morwenna lies to get them both in trouble?"

Bronwyn gaped at him.

He grunted. "How do I know *you're* not lying?"

"Why else would I be in the empress's tent?"

"Maybe you stole the crown yourself. Maybe Sir Ranulf had the right idea and you were in on the whole thing. Maybe Lady Eleanor was a thief, got cut down, and you saw an opportunity and helped yourself."

"And where would I have hidden it? I'd only been there a moment before you all came in." Her knees felt weak.

"Your apron, maybe? I don't know."

"That's a lot of maybes and no proof. You're guessing. Besides, you would have noticed the crown-shaped bulge in my apron." She put a hand on her hip.

"See? Now you know what it feels like, to be acting on guesses and little evidence. You need more than that before you go around pointing fingers at people, Bronwyn."

His eyes darted to her lips.

She swallowed and looked up at him. She shivered. "I know one thing to be true. We are not lovers."

A slow smile spread across his face. "There is only so much I can say about that rumor. Sir Ranulf loves a bit of gossip, and he's worse than the court ladies. He's likely spreading the tale far and wide to anyone who will listen."

Bronwyn clapped her hands to her mouth. "Oh, no."

His smile fell. His voice grew quiet. "Is that so disagreeable, the idea of being with me? Am I so hideous?"

"Theobold..." She started.

"Save it. Save your pretty words for someone else. Your lady, perhaps."

"Lady Alice is no longer talking to me," Bronwyn admitted.

"Now, why am I not surprised?" he said with disgust before

walking off into the night.

THAT NIGHT, BRONWYN slept in a circle with other women curled up on her side. They were huddled around a campfire, one of scores of fires that lit up the night like miniature orange beacons, crackling in the darkness.

When she woke, she was warm and had a long man's cloak curled around her. She opened her eyes and saw a woman shivering near her, eyeing the cloak with envy.

"Morning. Uh… How did I get this?" Bronwyn asked.

The woman curled up next to her said, "Some man came and put that on you while you were asleep. Said you'd know who it was from." She raised an eyebrow at her.

"Did he have black hair?"

"Mm-hmm. So you do know him."

"Yes." Bronwyn blushed and handed the cloak to the woman, who was shivering. "Take it. I'm fine."

That morning, she rose and helped cook, doling out spoonfuls of potage into bowls as people queued for food. Their bellies full of the steaming-hot mixture, horses were fed and watered, and wagons were loaded as the group broke camp and set out for Gloucester.

Having concluded her business in Lincoln, Empress Maud now would take her followers with her, to where Stephen would be properly received at her court, as befitting a royal prisoner. It was said the empress was positively gleeful at the idea of how it would look and wondered whether to receive him in chains, or just at spearpoint in her court.

"Ever one for appearances, our Maud," a knight was heard saying.

But Bronwyn wasn't so sure. She cast one look behind as they left the grounds of Lincoln, trying to memorize its walls and gates. She stared hard, shielding her eyes from the morning sun that rose, as she tried to memorize in her mind the streets and alleyways she'd take to reach her family's bakery, or the market, where they would sell bread on market days.

She felt a pang of regret that she was leaving, and now, she was losing any chance she might have of finding her parents and Wyot. She felt cowardly, but she wouldn't have wanted to search for them alone. Not after what she'd seen at the old bakery. It was no longer a home, but a shell of a home, and she wouldn't have known where else to go. She had no one, and nowhere, to call home.

They were on the move. Rupert stayed close by the prisoners, to ensure his master was as comfortable as could be expected and was being well-treated, whilst Lady Alice rode in a wagon with the other ladies-in-waiting and the empress.

Bronwyn walked behind the wagons of food with other servants and refugees who had joined the camp. She felt there was a certain safety in numbers, should any bandits wish to attack, but she had been in two battles now and did not hold out a strong hope of her chances of survival should another battle or skirmish occur.

The casualties and fatalities she had seen were too often older men, women and children who were unarmed and defenseless, unable to protect themselves. She may just have been a humble baker, but she wanted to survive. She wanted to learn to protect herself, but how?

But there was safety in numbers, and here, every spare hand and helping body was needed. There was something always that needed doing in the camp, be it stirring sauces or cleaning pots in the cooking tents, mending linen, or caring for the sick and injured.

She marched, in a slow and orderly group with the other cooks. The older people and children rode in the wagons, whilst the fighters rode ahead and a handful behind to bring up the rear. By midday, Bronwyn's feet were sore and ached from hours of walking. But she didn't complain.

Still, at the first sign of stopping, she sat where they stopped, sitting on the ground. The grass was damp, but she folded her apron into a small bundle and sat on that to protect her bottom from getting wet.

She chatted briefly with the other cooks and they unloaded baskets of premade meals for luncheon. Mostly the fighters, women, elderly, and children, along with the sick, ate. Food was not readily had, so many of the servants went without. Bronwyn was one of those. She could afford to skip a meal here and there. Some of the children looked so hungry, she felt almost ill at the thought of taking a bit of bread for herself.

They were just packing up and preparing to start the trek again, when Theobold trotted up on his horse. "What are you doing here?" he asked. "And where's your cloak? Don't tell me you lost it already."

She squinted up at him, shielding her eyes from the midday sun. "So it *was* from you. No. But there was a woman who needed it more than I did. Thank you, though. It kept me warm at night." She paused. "I didn't expect such kindness."

He rolled his eyes, then let out a noise of exasperation. "Just because we had a disagreement doesn't mean I'm uncaring. I walked by the camp in the night and saw you were cold, that's all. Besides, that's the second time I've tried to give you a cloak. Are you just averse to accepting gifts, or is it me?"

"What does 'averse' mean?" she asked.

"It means you dislike something."

"I thought we already agreed I didn't like you."

He flashed her a winning smile. "So we did. I'll just have to try harder to convince you of my charms."

She snorted. "Good luck with that."

He grinned. "Do you want to ride with me for a bit? You look tired."

She shook her head. "I'm fine."

"Maybe next time you won't refuse my gifts."

"Maybe."

He leaned forward and whispered, "Did you hear the news? The empress has found her crown."

Bronwyn tensed.

"It's almost as if it never went missing. She thinks she must have misplaced it, or it had gotten lost. Quite miraculous, you might say." He gave her an even look and rode on.

"He's got his eye on you, that lad," one older cook said.

Bronwyn shrugged. "Doesn't matter. We're from different worlds."

"Not so different, I think. Doesn't the empress have you deliver her rolls by hand?"

"Yes. So?"

"She doesn't have anyone else do that. Only you. Gives you special treatment, eh?" The cook nudged her with his elbow.

Bronwyn laughed. "Oh, yes, I love being called on to deliver things myself, to a room full of noblewomen who stare at me, make little snide remarks, and dismiss my clothes." She snorted, then realized the cook was right. She was privileged.

There were many who would love to be in that position. Perhaps not to have their looks dissected by some discerning ladies-in-waiting, but to be asked personally by the empress to come and to wait on her. That alone was a privilege, bestowed on very few. She was lucky, indeed. She just needed to see that.

WITHIN THREE DAYS, they had crossed from Lincoln and down the countryside, away from London, down to where the land was no longer so hilly but the landscape changed. It was marshy and often rainy and wet. More often than not, they got rained on as they walked, and Bronwyn shivered in the misting rain that drummed against the hard ground and pattered against the covered wagons and carts. She dearly wished for Theobald's cloak or her old coat and jerkin to wrap around herself, but she had naught but the old purple dress from Lady Susanna, her apron, her socks, and her shoes.

It was quite a change from the life she'd known before, she reflected. It made the miles pass easier, thinking about other things, and at times dwelling on the life she'd led before the Battle of Lincoln. She had liked to experiment with pastry and create small designs, often leaves and flowers out of pastry, to make them pretty pieces of delicious art atop pies and tarts. The customers never really noticed, but she thought they were charming, even if her stepmother had declared them at times to be fanciful and a waste of good pastry.

That was the good thing about working in her family's bakery, she decided. There was no waste. Every spare bit of beer, milk, eggs, and pastry were used, down to the last yolk and egg white. At least they had never gone hungry, which was more than she could say now as she walked in a group with the other cooks and servants.

By midday on the fourth day, they reached Gloucestershire, and with it came a sense of excitement and relaxation amongst the servants, knights, and people in the train. The sun broke through the grey clouds that hung overhead.

They entered the city of Gloucester, where the roads were wide and the buildings tall. It was a fair place, Bronwyn surmised, as she craned her neck and looked all around.

The farms outside the city were well tended, but there was a crowd of people at the gate leading into the city, and a wall of noise that struck Bronwyn's ears when they passed through the high gates and within the stone walls.

As they were in the empress's city, people crowded around as if for a parade at the empress's entrance, waving and cheering. It gave them something to do, to celebrate the arrival of their empress.

More and more crowd-goers appeared, craning their necks to see the empress and her knights and cast an eye at the fair ladies-in-waiting who traveled together in the covered carriages.

Bronwyn couldn't help it—she grinned. The city held a festive air and the sun shone. The place was full of good cheer and she waved along with the servants. She held her head just a little bit higher and smiled brighter as people noticed them and waved.

As they brought up the rear of the train of the empress's

entourage, there was less excitement to see the servants, but people were still jolly. Bronwyn laughed at the small children running along behind the parade of people, and dogs trotting around the groups of crowds, nosing for food.

But then came a quiet, along with whispering, boos, and hisses. People seemed to realize that one of the wagons held King Stephen prisoner and began to boo and talk loudly, making their displeasure known. Whether it was anger at his fighting the empress for the crown, or anger at his being imprisoned when he was a king, Bronwyn didn't know.

But she was aware that the parade of people picked up the pace, and that the wagon surrounding the imprisoned king and his loyal men was heavily guarded by knights and armed footmen. In a riot, he would be torn to pieces—or rescued—but the guards carried halberds and dangerous-looking spears, and so people were wise enough to mutter angrily and whisper, but not to try their luck.

She and the other servants waved and followed the train through the streets and to the palace across the city, through another set of gates and into a courtyard, where the festive air disappeared and all was back to business. Her feet were sore and her body felt bone-tired, but she was curious and wide-eyed at her new surroundings. So this was Gloucester, and the palace.

It was very grand. Solid, stone walls. A large, noisy, bustling courtyard. The air was filled with the sounds of men calling out orders to grooms and more servants, whilst knights disembarked from their horses and pack animals were led away from the group to be watered and fed, their burdens relieved by busy servants. Men and women called out, and Bronwyn stood by, waiting for someone to notice her.

One of the cooks was approached by another woman, a large woman with wide arms that reminded Bronwyn of hams; a large, round bosom; and a plump face with a double chin. She wore her hair tied back in a kerchief and had on a crisp, clean, white apron, her hands on her hips. She eyed the servants who stood with

Bronwyn and gave orders for them to unpack the wagons of food and supplies and follow her.

Having traveled all that way, Bronwyn and a few others were given the chance to sit and work, whilst space was made for them to have a place to sleep. There were sauces to be stirred; chickens, game hens, pheasants and quail to be plucked; wild hares to be skinned; boars to be butchered and smoked; hams to be steamed; and great haunches of meat to be turned on large spits that required two boys to handle—carefully.

Down in the castle kitchens, Bronwyn was quickly put to work. She didn't mind at all, especially when she was given a chance to sit and rest her feet. A small cup of ale was put into her hand and a small, wooden bowl of potage with a piece of crusty hard bread passed to her, as the large woman, the second head cook, known as Mistress Agnes Dunbar, gave orders for all the new incomers to be fed.

Mary, who had held court with such a dominant manner in the camps, was quickly overruled at the castle, and she went to work with much muttering under her breath and dark looks. But her comments were largely overlooked by the others in charge, and she soon faded from Bronwyn's notice.

But before she and the other new cooks and servants could get situated, an order came through that was extraordinary: they were being called to the throne room.

Bronwyn stared. She looked at the page, who announced it to the kitchen. The boy repeated the order, louder this time, and said, "The empress bids you all to come to the throne room. Right now."

Bronwyn set down her cup of ale and empty bowl of potage and followed the stream of servants out of the kitchens and up the steps, leading the way through the corridors and up and out, to the castle proper, where there were many dozens upon dozens of people filing into a grand room. Guards were posted outside the walls and as Bronwyn entered, it briefly took her breath away.

It was a large room, larger than the throne room at Lincoln

Castle. But what struck her was the richness and opulence of the furnishings. Large, colorful tapestries, depicting scenes of battle, adorned the walls of the room. Beneath the tapestries was solid-wood paneling, and guards were posted around the room. They also lined a sort of walkway to the dais of the throne. People milled and walked about, murmuring and talking.

Crowds of people were already present, being directed to one side or another of the room and told to stand in place. There was nowhere easily to go, or to leave, for that matter, if she wanted to quit the room. That thought struck her and a slight shiver went down her spine as she looked around the room. Was the crowd making her nervous? A little.

This was a new feeling, however. She had never minded crowds before. But with the bodies pressed in tightly around her, the air soon grew warm and stifled, and more people were entering the room. It was a decent-sized room. Smaller than a great hall, but bigger than other rooms she had seen. At the far end of the room stood a great throne, on a raised dais. It was a great, wooden chair with armrests that commanded the space.

But then tall people stood in front of her, and she couldn't see well. Being an inch or two shorter than average height for a woman, she looked here and there and resigned herself. Whatever was to take place in this great room, she would see little of it but the person's shoulder who stood in front of her.

The chatter and noise grew as people wondered loudly what this was all about. Bronwyn turned to the cook next to her. "Do you know what this is about?"

The cook shook his head. He was a short, plump man with thinning blond hair in his mid-twenties, she guessed. He rubbed his eyes.

"Does the empress do this often? Make announcements like this?"

"No. I've never even been in this room before, and I've lived at her court for three years," he said. His accent was different to hers, which surprised her a little. But then, of course, she was from the north, and they were now in a more western part of the country, not far from Wales, she'd heard. His accent was rounded and almost musical.

Then the doors to the hall closed, and the guards nearest the doors stamped their spears. "Silence." Their voices boomed. "Silence for the empress."

The people quieted. Bronwyn and the cook exchanged a look but said not a word.

Then, toward the side of the room, a part of the wall opened up, and Bronwyn stood on her tiptoes to see. A stream of knights entered, about ten, wearing not armor but mail over their tunics. They walked almost in formation, each taking a stance as a barrier in front of the throne. Almost like an extra human layer of defense, the sight of them was impressive indeed, as each man stood armed and at the ready. As if to add a bit of theater, each man unsheathed his sword to the sound of a great hush from the crowd and planted the point of his sword into the floor. Not hard, but it was an impressive sight. Adding to the intensity of the moment, the men did not speak, but only stared straight ahead.

The ladies-in-waiting were next and filed into the room one by one, hardly speaking. There were all three of them: Lady Morwenna, Lady Alice, and Lady Susanna. They stood on either side of the throne and looked around at the crowds. If they were nervous to be the center of attention, they did not show it.

The young cook beside Bronwyn unconsciously patted his hair and pulled up his sagging trousers at the sight of the ladies-in-waiting.

Bronwyn smiled at the sight. But then she watched as the people shuffled and suddenly, she was able to see. No longer standing on her tiptoes, she looked and saw as two pairs of trumpeters and drummers entered, taking places before the knights. This was to be a treat, Bronwyn realized. Music. Perhaps there was to be a feast, or a dance?

It didn't have that same celebratory feel, however, as none of the people there were speaking. The drummers started drumming, a steady beat, and this built to a crescendo rather quickly, when the trumpeters raised their horns and blasted loud notes into the air. They were not in tune with each other and one played faster than his fellows, but the effect was stirring. The men lowered their horns and stood off to the side, as there was a small gasp.

The empress entered the room, wearing a dark-burgundy dress that looked rich and thick. This was no woolen gown, and it was cut well to suit her figure. She wore a gold belt that hung at her waist, and a headdress that covered her head, with her golden-brown hair pinned back and plaited. She did not wear a crown, but there was no mistaking that this was Empress Maud.

Flanking her was Sir Robert of Gloucester, Sir Ranulf de Gernon, Sir Miles FitzWalter, and Theobold, who all took places on the dais, at either side of the throne. In a short amount of time, there were a lot of people, and Sir Robert escorted the empress by the hand and led her to the great, wooden throne. She stood before it, looking around at everyone, her eyes surveying the crowd. Once satisfied she had everyone's full attention, she sat, and it was as if a collective breath was let out.

It struck Bronwyn at that moment that she was at court, but something serious, possibly momentous, was to happen. But what?

She did not have to wait long, for the empress's husky, alto voice called out, "Bring in the prisoner."

It echoed in the hall, which was warm, and heads turned, as the pair of guards at the main entrance stamped their spears against the floor again and this time opened the doors with a great and mighty creak.

Heads craned to see, as did Bronwyn. And then she saw it.

King Stephen, standing at the entrance, in chains.

Chapter Eleven

THEOBOLD'S HEART BEAT in his throat as clear down the length of the room, the foul traitor who called himself a king, Stephen, stood quietly yet commanded the attention of the entre assembly. He was heavily guarded, with six guards surrounding him. It was a bit much, but Theobold knew the empress loved her bit of pomp and ceremony, and so it came as no surprise to him that she'd decided to treat the man as if he were a wild beast.

This was not his first time seeing Stephen, but Theobold thought the man did bear himself well. He watched from his viewpoint on the dais, watching the crowd. He didn't see Bronwyn, but he hoped she was there.

He smiled to himself. Mistress Bloodhound, more like. He enjoyed teasing her and liked seeing her annoyed expression. She liked him—he could tell. But he thought she hadn't realized it yet. And it wasn't easy when she was friends with that sorry excuse for a squire, Rupert Bothwell.

He hadn't liked the young man as soon as he'd seen him. It was more than the fact that they were on opposite sides of the war, and both knew it. They'd had a mutual dislike, almost upon first meeting. Rupert with his easy smile for everyone, he worked hard at charming the men and women alike. Honest and friendly, he'd be every man's good friend and flirt with and wink at the women. Theobold disliked him, and the more Rupert spent time with Bronwyn, the greater his dislike grew.

Rupert seemed to have a good word to say for everyone, and that couldn't have been true. He was false, and Theobold wanted to wipe the smile off his face at the first opportunity. It was just as well they often faced each other in the practice ring. He'd look forward to the next practice fight, just to see Rupert's face in the dust when he bested him.

But never mind that now. The empress was holding her fanfare, and he had to pay attention or suffer her ire later.

"Approach," Empress Maud said, with a slight beckoning of her hand.

Stephen walked down the length of the room, his chains jingling. Theobold looked closer. The empress had been busy since they'd arrived. It wasn't just that she'd bathed and changed her dress from her travels—she had her cousin chained at the wrists and ankles, so that like a court jester with a bell, or minstrel, all might know when he came near. It was an insult, and Theobold didn't like it.

But she did like her theater, and this was a prime opportunity to show her dominance and prove that once again, she deserved to rule.

Stephen approached the dais and was stopped by the guards coming short. Two of the guards before him moved apart so that he might face the empress better.

"Well, well, Cousin," Empress Maud said. "I somehow knew that the next time I saw you, it would be with you in chains. What a shame I was right."

Stephen looked tired, old, and dirty. He smelled of unwashed body and worse, and his light locks, which Theobold had once heard described as "comely," now hung greasy and to his shoulders. His beard had grown long, unkempt, and uneven, and it needed a trim. He looked slovenly, but then Theobold supposed that was the point. How could anyone follow this man into battle and believe he was the true King of England?

Then Stephen raised his head, and it was like a hawk had entered the room. His eyes were sharp, his shoulders squared as if facing an enemy head-on, and he straightened, as if wearing a cloak that none but he could see. In that moment, the crowd held its breath, and Theobold could see that this was indeed a ruler.

"Well met, Cousin. The dress you wear suits you." Stephen's voice was dry and raspy, as if he needed a good drink.

Empress Maud leaned forward in her chair. "I would say that the throne suits me."

Stephen bowed his head. "On that, I must disagree."

"You'd like that, wouldn't you? To see me be the one in chains begging at *your* feet like a dog. Well, I—" She lapsed into French.

Theobold's French wasn't strong, but he caught the gist of her words. They were argumentative—and angry. He frowned. This was not how this exchange should have been happening. He glanced at Sir Ranulf, who scratched his beard idly. Beside him, Sir Robert cleared his throat.

It was a simple noise, but it had the desired effect. The empress stopped talking and leaned back, as if realizing she was not just in a heated argument with her cousin, but a star player in a very public performance that was not going her way. She sat up straight, settled herself in the creaking wooden throne, and said loudly, "I call you all here to witness the sight of my cousin, Stephen, who seeks to usurp my throne."

All eyes fixed upon Stephen, who stood quietly, staring straight ahead.

"I must say, I am surprised at you. I hear your own men betrayed you at the Battle of Lincoln and ran away like sheep at the sight of my warriors. Is that the kind of leadership you expected to bring to this country?"

Theobold grinned. She was baiting him. He'd been at that battle and she was right, at the sight of her men—knights and hired mercenaries from Wales—a good number of Stephen's men had fled. It was a sorry sight, and the battle had soon ended after that. Stephen was a good fighter, however. He'd fought until the very end, cleaving at the air and slicing into enemies with that old

Northman's axe of his, until he'd been caught.

"I am one who commands the hearts of true warriors, and I do not have to hire them from other nations to fight my cause." Stephen's words were chilly. "But I bow to your greater knowledge of how to tempt men to your side, Cousin. Pray tell, now that you sit upon the throne, where is your crown? I thought to see it on your pretty head."

The empress was incensed, Theobold knew. This would not end well.

He wasn't the only one who sensed it. A few of the knights stiffened. From his viewpoint at the side of the throne, Theobold could see the empress's mouth wither, then curve into a smile. "You may insult me, Cousin, but my men will not stand for it. And neither should the people of England. I will wear the crown when the time is right."

Stephen snorted.

"I call upon you all to witness Stephen, a false pretender to the English throne, bequeathed to me by my father, King Henry. It is Stephen's fault we are at war because he would not listen and obey the laws set forth by our previous king."

"I do obey the law. But your claim is not without fault, and I have a legitimate claim. A woman cannot rule. It is not right, or legal." He set his jaw.

"Not right? Legal? My father the king, declared it to be so. *You* are the one who went against divine rule." She raised her voice.

Stephen bowed his head. "For that, I am sorry, but your father was wrong. I would not want good Englishmen to pay the price for his folly, but neither would I see the crown placed upon the head of a woman unfit to rule." His words were cutting, and they lanced through the quiet hush of the room like a surgeon's knife through a boil.

Theobold might have been made of stone, but the empress was like a lion. Her petite nostrils flared and she looked ready to rip off her headdress and stalk toward her cousin, regardless of his chained state. She gritted her teeth and her eyes narrowed.

"Get out. Let us see if a ransom on your head will pay back toward some of the men's lives you stole in fighting this senseless war. Guards." She motioned, and the guards resumed their places around him, aiming their spears at him from six different directions.

A lesser man would have quailed or shown some kind of nervous reaction, but not Stephen. He was like ice, and stood quietly, calmly. When he spoke, he sounded tired. "My quarrel is with you and you alone, Maud."

"I am an empress. You will address me as such."

"I will not."

"Guards. Take him away. Let us see how you like your new chambers in our jail. Perhaps they will offer you a new look on life."

"You will not get away with this, Maud," he said tiredly.

She mimicked his words in a nasty tone. Theobold felt it was beneath her. She was taunting him like a childhood bully.

"Guards." She waved a hand, and all watched as the guards removed him from sight, leading him at spearpoint down the length of the room, past all the dozens, maybe even hundreds, of faces that watched him leave in disgrace, the former man who would be king.

Theobold stood, watching him go. In that brief exchange, he had seen a bit of Stephen's mettle. He was middle-aged and tired from his days of captivity, but that was to be expected of any prisoner. But he had not expected for Stephen to show such calm, or steadfastness, even when at the height of what had been intended to be public humiliation. He hadn't seemed like a cruel or power-hungry man. He'd almost seemed good-natured.

The empress rose. "He speaks with honeyed words, but he would have you all believe he has a heart of gold, whereas I do not. But do not forget, it is he who has destroyed your homes and killed your husbands, your sons, your children. He does not believe a woman can rule, but we will prove him wrong. He has no real claim to the throne and by my divine right, I will claim what is rightfully mine." Her voice rang out, echoing in the hall.

It took no time at all for the knights at the front to start the chant. "Empress! Empress! Empress!"

This built into a few loud chants and then grew into a solid roar, with people clapping, shouting, and stamping their feet.

Empress Maud watched them all, cheering. She smiled at the crowd and stuck her chin out in defiance at the shadow of Stephen's departure, as if his shade still lingered, and turned and left, leaving through the side wall, as quickly as she had entered.

Theobald followed her, falling in line behind Sir Robert of Gloucester, Sir Ranulf, and Sir Miles, her cousin. As he passed through the wooden door and into the shadows, he could tell his mistress's mood from the sharp, staccato sound of her shoes against the floor. Her skirts subtly swished as she moved almost as if stalking, or like an angry cat. All that was missing was the warning swish of the tail and he'd be sure to watch out.

He and the other men followed her into a private room, where she bid them close the door. In the room stood himself, his lord, Sir Robert of Gloucester; Sir Ranulf; and Sir Miles, as well as a handful of her ladies-in-waiting.

The door had barely closed behind them before the empress began spouting profanities in French. Theobald knew a few, but not all. He shuffled his feet and glanced at the other men, who looked uncomfortable. Their faces were telling. Sir Robert stood as if carved from stone, but Sir Ranulf openly grinned. The other knights present exchanged disapproving looks before quickly hiding their reactions behind polite expressions. Theobold recognized them, unfortunately; they were disapproving of the empress and her unladylike ways.

It was unseemly for a woman of her status and regal bearing to be swearing like a sailor. She paced up and down the wooden floor, her small feet creaking against the floorboards, as she gesticulated with her hands and glared at them all, cursing in her native language.

The ladies-in-waiting all looked at each other and away,

probably unsure of where it was safe to look. They reminded Theobold of a flock of geese.

Finally, the empress wore herself out and sat in a chair, not bothering to sit up straight. She slouched and rested her hands languidly on the armrests.

"Well, that could have gone better," Sir Ranulf said.

The empress glared. "Do tell."

"The way I see it, you shouldn't have let King Stephen annoy you like that." He picked at a bit of lint on his shirt.

"Shut your mouth, Sir Ranulf," Sir Robert said.

Sir Ranulf looked up and saw Sir Robert's look of warning. He seemed to stop himself when the empress held up her hand.

"No, I want to hear. Do tell, de Gernon. How could that assembly have gone better?" Her voice was soft and quiet, almost sweet. Theobold knew that if Sir Ranulf were a smart man, he would take his father-in-law's advice and shut his mouth.

Sir Ranulf said, "It's like any shouting match, Your Grace. A man like King Stephen always knows what to say."

"Oh? *King* Stephen does, does he?" She seethed.

"Yes. He's had practice. He's had to speak to crowds before. It's harder for a woman—"

"Get out." Her voice was cutting.

"But, Your Grace..." Sir Ranulf started.

"I said, *get out*. Leave, all of you." Her voice rose.

Theobold nodded to his lord, and they began to leave. As the ladies followed, Empress Maud said, "Bring me some of those white rolls that Stephen's wife is so fond of. I will have something of hers tonight."

"Yes, Empress." Theobold nodded and followed the men out. He belayed the order to a servant and entered a side corridor, where Sir Robert of Gloucester cuffed Sir Ranulf on the shoulder.

"Ow, what was that for?"

"Your stupid tongue, you fool. Do you have any idea how foolish that was, telling the empress that due to her sex she lost that exchange with Stephen? And for God's sake, stop calling him 'the king,' unless you want to lose your head."

"Well, she asked, and I was just saying—" He stopped mid-stride.

"She didn't ask your opinion, idiot. You gave it and she was toying with you. God. What my daughter saw in you, I don't know."

Sir Ranulf gave him a dazed look.

"Go. I would talk with my squire alone. There are some matters we need to discuss."

Sir Ranulf smirked. "Oh, yes. No doubt there is some horse dung that needs shoveling. Glad I'm not a squire anymore." He left, whistling.

Once he had left and Theobold and his master stood alone in the corridor, Sir Robert said of his retreating form, "That man is a fool. He's going to lose his head someday, thanks to that big mouth of his."

Theobold wisely kept his mouth shut.

"Tell me what you've found out about the crown. Why was it ever missing?"

"I can't tell you much more than I already have. Once it had gone missing, one of the ladies accused another of stealing it. But the guards and I both found nothing to suggest it was anything other than idle gossip."

Sir Robert snorted. "Those ladies-in-waiting are like a vipers' pit. They play games with each other's lives."

Theobold nodded grimly. "But as I told you, the crown reappeared in the empress's personal effects. I saw it myself on the morning we left for here."

"Then either some good Samaritan returned it, which seems unlikely, some poor fool found it and got too scared to demand a reward for its return, or... I don't know. We can guess why it was taken in the first place. Stephen has his supporters wherever we go. But... why do you think it was returned?"

"I couldn't say. But now that it's back, the empress can continue to London to be crowned."

"Yes. And yet… I do not trust this order of events. Why was it stolen at camp, and a ransom demanded, only for it to reappear the day we travel? It does not make sense."

"I wonder if the guard talked, or if someone else found it and decided to return it, in support of the empress," Theobold said.

"And not ask for a reward? I doubt that. The world is full of good Samaritans, as long as there is a quick payment in return." Sir Robert smiled. "Well. Let us hope there are no more surprises in store for us. Tonight's feast should be a good event to gather the people together."

Theobold agreed and turned to go.

"Oh, and Theo…" Sir Robert started.

"Yes?"

"Look after my horse. Tell the grooms he needs grain, a farrier to look at his hooves and…" He gave Theobold a knowing look.

"And shovel the horse dung." Theobold nodded, bowed, and left, giving a slight sigh.

THAT EVENING THE castle held a festive air. As the outside was chilly, people gathered inside the castle, aristocrats and their families alike. Servants went to and fro, pages darted around, and squires stood by, looking after their masters.

After looking after Sir Robert's horse as he'd asked, Theobold had indeed relayed orders for the horses to be fed and watered and then shoveled the dung himself, ensuring their stalls were clean. There were groomsmen enough for the chores, but his master didn't always trust the grooms and preferred Theobold to do the work himself. *It builds character,* he'd said. Now Theobold just went and did it, rather than raise a fuss.

It was hot and sweaty work, so he washed and cleaned his clothes before shaking the water off them and wringing them out. He didn't have many clean shirts with him, but he had one that would suit for the feast tonight. It was dark blue and woolen, with a bit of embroidery at the cuffs and neck, courtesy of his sister, Winifred. He paused, thinking of her as he rubbed his thumb against the delicate but not exactly matching embroidery.

How was she doing at home? Was she all right? She was only sixteen. No doubt their mother and father would be planning her marriage to someone, but in his mind, she was just a girl with plaits, running after him as he said goodbye before joining Sir Robert of Gloucester as his squire. She would be a young woman now. But he hadn't seen her in three years, and he missed her. He missed his parents too. But a life squiring and seeing the world was better than the family trade, and his father knew it. His father talked about being an executioner as a calling almost, but one that Theobold thankfully didn't listen to. His brother had been the same way, with that adventurous look in his eye. So when Theobold had been old enough, his family made an agreement with Lady Morwenna's to put up him as a squire and pay his way.

So much he had seen, and so many stories he had to tell. But not tonight. He saved this shirt for special occasions, and as he pulled the woolen cloth over his bare skin, he was conscious of how the sleeves were tighter across the arms and his shoulders.

He didn't have a looking glass in the spare room he shared as sleeping quarters with the other squires and instead raked his fingers through his black curls and thought of Bronwyn. Perhaps he'd ask her to dance tonight, if she was willing.

She was a funny creature, that woman. He liked her well enough, but she puzzled him. She wasn't like the other young women he'd met. For one, she didn't seem the least bit interested in him. That was odd. But she wasn't immune to his charms, he could tell. And she had eyes, for she'd stared at his muscular arms and chest after he'd practiced wooden swords with Rupert that one time. She found him attractive, he was sure of it. He grinned at the thought. She might deny it, but her eyes told a different story.

And God help him, all his thoughts and plans and promises to the empress fled from his mind when he looked at her. Whenever he took in the sight of her fair skin, blessed by the sun, with a freckle or two, her blue eyes and rosy lips, she almost took his breath away.

He blinked away the thought. She was pretty, yes. But so were many young women, and the empress's camp had plenty. The castle at Gloucester had more, as men and women flocked to the empress's flag. So what made her different from any other? Why did she reappear in his thoughts time and time again? He'd dreamt of her at night and woken up thinking of her face.

He thought on this as he walked down the corridor and down a set of circular stone steps, picking up speed as he made his way to the ground-floor level, where the large banquet hall was set. Servants milled about, the air smelled of rich food and wine, and he almost stepped on a page or two. Women wore their best, the men strutted around chatting and looking important, and minstrels played quietly nearby.

The banquet hall was well-decorated, or as much as could be done in late February. The fine walls hung with large tapestries, depicting battle scenes that must have taken skilled ladies months to make. Great tables sat in the center of the room, with benches that stretched long. Small torches dotted around the room, adding golden gusts of light that flickered with warm glows, and candles sat interspersed on the table. There was a large grand fireplace that was so big, people could easily walk inside it. Great logs cut down from some poor tree now added fuel to the healthy blaze there, and it made a room already warm from so many bodies even warmer.

Men and women chatted and laughed with good cheer, and Theobold found himself idly chatting with the other squires whilst keeping an eye on his master. Sir Robert was present and had bathed after his travels as well, for Theobold had been the one to organize the wooden bathing tub and hot water for him.

That was one lesson he'd passed on during their time together. Bathe at every opportunity. It bred good health and made any foul airs or miasmas they might have picked up on their travels depart. Plus, the ladies didn't seem to mind. Not all knights felt this way, and some, like Sir Bors, prided themselves on their manly odor, as a sign of their strength or virility, perhaps.

In any case, Theobold found himself smiling at one or two young women in the room, then blinked and made himself stop. By all reasoning, he should inform the empress immediately that the crown had been found, and of Bronwyn's involvement. The fact that she'd put it back was a mark in her favor, a sure sign of her loyalty, and yet something made him pause. A voice in his mind told him that the empress would not see it that way, and to speak of Bronwyn getting in the way at all would put her in danger. His loyalty first was to God, then the empress, then his master, and to his family. So why was he pausing? Why did his feet stop short, when his head demanded he report to the empress about the crown? He knew what he should do. His loyalties required his action. And yet he couldn't.

He was on a mission for Her Grace to find out what he could from Bronwyn, and he needed to get close to her, not flirt with the other young women. What would Bronwyn think if she knew?

Instead of going to report, Theobold helped himself to a cup of wine and winced at the taste. It was a mix of sour and sweet, and it held sediment that filled his mouth. If this was the work of the local brewer in the castle, he might go without. He spat the sediment back into his cup and reached for pale ale instead.

Then the empress entered the room. A hush fell. The empress smiled, for she enjoyed being the center of attention and liked it when those present stopped what they were doing. She stood quietly, waiting for all to take notice. With her hands clasped, Empress Maud almost looked demure.

Once satisfied, she took her place at the head of the table, flanked by Sir Miles, Sir Robert, and Sir Ranulf, as well as the turncoat Sir Bors. Theobold didn't like the man, for he along with Sir Gilbert, Sir Baldwin of Clare, and Sir Grossetete had sided with Stephen's court. The three knights now sat imprisoned along with the rest of Stephen's men, but Sir Bors was an opportunist and had been quick to switch sides back again.

Theobold didn't trust him, especially since Sir Bors had been attacked in the tent where the crown had been stolen. His recent return to the empress's court, combined with him being in the tent at that time, seemed too much of a coincidence. But the empress had welcomed Sir Bors back, and so the man strode into the room, boldly as ever, no doubt stinking of horse, sweat, and gritty wine.

Sir Bors wore a clean shirt and tunic, belted with his sword at his waist. He'd combed his hair, but his beard looked as scraggily as ever. He was tall and barrel-chested, and he liked to challenge men to wrestling bouts to show off his skill. Theobold had fought him once, and the man fought dirty. He didn't wish to face him again.

Sir Bors took a place on the benches amongst the knights, many of whom ignored him. Theobold stood back behind his master and brought him a cup of wine. He disliked the stuff, but his master enjoyed a good vintage. As Sir Robert turned and motioned to Theobold to bring him another, Sir Ranulf de Gernon, sat across from him and next to Sir Bors, eyed the cup of wine and said, "Here, boy, bring me one too."

Theobold gave de Gernon a level look. "I'm not your boy." He motioned to the nearest page to pour him a cup of wine. He noticed Rupert standing there, quiet. *No doubt awaiting his moment to prove himself, the swine,* Theobold thought. He ignored him.

Sir Ranulf's timing was excellent. He glanced back ever so slightly, just in time to raise his hand and knock the cup from the page's hands, sending it and the wine falling to the floor. Amongst the noise from the people present, it was not so noticeable—spills and accidents happened all the time—but Sir Ranulf fixed a smile at Theobold. "Clumsy. Fetch me another."

A page stepped in to help and Sir Ranulf said, "No. I want him to do it." He motioned to Theobold.

Theobold held his gaze. People were starting to stare, and he knew it.

"Why are you ordering around my squire?" Sir Robert asked, his voice even.

Sir Ranulf glanced at his father-in-law. "Well, we're family, so I don't see why not. What's the problem? I'm thirsty."

"You're clumsy and ordering around my squire. He serves me." Sir Robert's voice was calm, but authoritative.

Theobold stood at his master's shoulder. Sir Robert was even-keeled, especially in the quiet before a fight.

"So what? He can serve me too. We are related, after all."

"You know the rules. Squires serve their masters. He may help others if *I* say so."

Theobold blinked. His master had never put his foot down like that before. He'd never needed to. Theobold had simply helped out where he pleased and he had trust from Sir Robert that it was a job well done. Any complaints or reprimands were done in private.

"Oh, for goodness's sake, why are you two arguing over a mere squire?" the empress said. "Such rules and rigidness. I do not care who serves whom, as long as the job is done and my men's bellies are full. You there, step in for these clumsy pages and assist de Gernon."

A page stepped forward when Rupert moved in front of him. "Allow me, Your Grace."

Empress Maud simpered. She watched as Rupert deftly took a pottery jug and poured a cup of wine, setting it by Sir Ranulf's thick hands.

Sir Ranulf snatched up the cup and drank the wine, sediment and all, whilst gazing at Theobold. His eyes narrowed, and Theobold knew this wasn't over.

Lady Alice glanced at Morwenna, who was taking her seat. "Why, Lady Morwenna, your hands. Were you sampling the honey? They look sticky."

Lady Morwenna's cheeks flushed as she reached for the table-cloth to wipe her hands clean. "Yes. You caught me. That's what I was doing. How good of you, Lady Alice, to closely keep an eye on what all of us do in our off moments. I wonder, do you plan to watch me use the privy, too?"

Lady Alice looked away, and Lady Morwenna laughed. She wasn't the only one. Lady Susanna tittered as well, her gaze darting between the two of them.

Empress Maud clapped her hands and stood. "Welcome, everyone. I'm so glad to see so many of you here tonight. We have had a long journey in coming here, and it has not been without its share of trials. But now is a time to celebrate. So I ask you to eat, drink, and be merry. Enjoy the meal and the wine— and laugh. Let this be a happy time. We have returned."

The knights all clapped and thundered their feet beneath the table, some banging the table and bumping into platters, trenchers, and cups with the noise. It was like a drumming that grew into a frenzied roar, and the empress laughed and sat down.

A servant set a cup brimming with wine down before her, and she raised it to her lips. "To our return to Gloucester, and soon to Westminster. We will travel to London for our coronation and show the people of London what it means to have a real ruler to rally behind."

At that moment, Sir Bors and Sir Edward came into the room. Sir Bors carried something on a pillow, covered with a silken cloth, judging from the folds and the way it caught the light.

"Ah, there you are. What kept you?" Empress Maud asked.

"This, Your Grace," Sir Bors said. He whisked the cloth off the item with a flourish.

The crowd instantly *ooh*ed. It was the crown. Gleaming, polished, shining with great stones in the light. Instant applause and cheers filled the room.

Empress Maud's face lit up with a broad smile. She clapped her hands and motioned them forward. Smiling benevolently, the empress inclined her head, waiting for the moment when the crown would rest on her scalp.

"Why don't you do the honors, Sir Edward?" Sir Bors asked.

Sir Edward nodded and picked up the crown. "Ow." He snatched his hand away. "That's odd. It tingles." He looked at his fingers. "Something scratched me. Like a needle."

Blood dripped from his fingers. He sucked one, then he crashed to the floor.

Empress Maud shot up from her chair. "Sir Edward!"

Theobold dashed around to see. Sir Edward thrashed on the floor, choking and clawing at his throat. "The crown…" His eyes were wide and he gasped for air.

"Fetch the surgeon—now." Sir Robert said to the nearest page.

"Somebody help him!" Empress Maud said. "Sir Edward, stay calm." She knelt by his side.

Sir Bors stood stock still, clearly horrified.

The crown lay on the floor, discarded.

Sir Edward gasped and choked and coughed, and then all was still.

Theobold went over to him and bent down to assess him. His eyes were wide and bloodshot, his chest had stopped rising and falling, and his mouth hung open, slack in mortification. Theobold took hold of his wrist and then pressed two fingers to the man's throat.

"Is he….?" Empress Maud asked.

"He's dead."

Someone gasped. Guards pulled the empress away. She batted their hands off and cried, "Stop this. Unhand me!"

The men stopped. She stood stiffly, quietly. "Someone, pick up my crown."

People hesitated. No one wanted to touch the crown, especially as a man had just died holding it. Theobold could easily predict their thoughts. What if by touching it, they died too?

The knights looked askance at each other, until Theobold snatched the silken cloth from Sir Bors and carefully wrapped it around the crown. There came a hush and then whispers as he picked it up. Theobold ignored the murmurs and holding it carefully, turned the crown this way and that.

"What are you doing?" the empress asked.

"I want to check something. Sir Edward said something scratched him, like a needle." Theobold carefully turned the crown over. There, affixed to the inside of the crown was a needle. Not so big, but its point was bloody and stained. He stopped. Could Bronwyn...... He didn't want to think it, but his thoughts ran like mad, refusing to let him ignore the possibility. He'd been with Bronwyn as she'd put the crown back in the empress's tent. Could she be behind this? Had he misjudged her? He knew she liked Rupert. Had he put her up to this? Or had she been acting alone? What if she was innocent, and someone else was behind the tampering of the crown? If so, who?

He approached the empress and said quietly, "Your Grace, this crown has been poisoned."

"What?" She shied away as if she'd been slapped. "Are you certain?"

"Yes. Look here." He pointed to the tiny needle affixed to the inside rim of the crown. "This is what scratched Sir Edward. I have no doubt it was meant for you. When you would have worn it, the needle would have scratched your head—"

"Killing me instantly." Her face turned pale. "Right." Loudly, she called, "We shall hold a mass for our lost knight. Sir Edward was a good man."

Theobold stood by as she said quietly, "Remove him. Lay him out in the church. We will bury him once the ground softens."

As if awoken from a dream, her knights snapped into action. Some of the knights calmed the others around them, urging the pages to refill cups of wine, the minstrels to play on their lutes, while Sir Ranulf organized for Sir Edward's body to be removed.

As the body was taken away, Sir Bors bowed. "I am sorry, Your Grace. I had no idea what Sir Edward planned."

"What? What do you mean?" Empress Maud asked.

"Well, it's just, he came to me and said it would be a treat to bring you the crown, now that it's been cleaned and all. It was his idea to crown you before everyone at the meal. Put it in their minds."

"Put what?" she asked.

"That you're the rightful ruler. I had no idea what he was planning, honest."

Theobold surveyed him thoughtfully, and his mouth went dry. He felt relief that people had handled the crown after Bronwyn had returned it. And of course they had, for someone would have packed it for traveling to Gloucester. His shoulders relaxed. If she had poisoned the crown, most likely the servant packing the empress's things would have been killed right away, unless they'd been in on the plot. That seemed highly unlikely, which meant that whoever had poisoned the crown had done so after they'd arrived at Gloucester Castle. Bronwyn was innocent. He felt a wave of relief come over him that he'd not told anyone about her involvement with the crown.

"Very well. But this displeases me greatly. I am most unhappy." She clapped her hands and motioned him away.

Sir Bors gingerly held out the pillow. He avoided Theobold's eyes.

Theobold gave a slight snort and replaced the crown on the pillow, carefully. Sir Bors bowed again and followed the men out.

Empress Maud let out a sigh, retook her seat, and picked up the cup from the table. "We are most saddened by this loss. Let us hope that we face no more tragedy in this war, as my cousin seeks to strike us down."

An unsatisfied grumble emerged from the men present as she took a ladylike sip of her wine and then grabbed a dainty piece of meat and a great big mouthful of bread, popping it all into her mouth. She chewed and then she coughed. Once, twice, thrice—and she began to have a coughing fit.

The men shot to their feet. "Where is that blasted surgeon? Fetch him," Sir Robert said to Theobold. He put his hand on Maud's back and thumped her hard.

She kept coughing, as the men cried, "Help!"

"Where's the healer?" came another cry.

"Fetch help, quickly."

Theobold hurriedly looked around for a healer. The place was filled with cries for help as the empress kept coughing and pointed at her throat. She gasped.

Rupert ran forward and shouldered Sir Robert out of the way.

"What are you doing?" Sir Robert asked.

"Let me."

The empress gasped and coughed, her face turning pale. Rupert put his arms around her.

"What in God's name are you doing?" Sir Robert demanded, his mouth falling open.

Rupert put his arms around the empress's middle and tugged hard, inward, toward her stomach, his hands clasped together in a fist.

She gasped and expelled a breath.

He pushed hard, inward and upward again.

"Let her go. Guards!" Sir Ranulf shouted.

"Get your hands off her." Sir Robert had his hand on his sword.

The knights were like children, none knowing what to do.

Theobold stared, transfixed, as Rupert gave it one more mighty push, and the offending piece of bread shot out of Empress Maud's mouth, flying across the table. It landed in a cup of wine with a great splash, sending the wine cascading over the rim of the cup.

The empress gasped and slumped forward, putting her hands on the table as she coughed, her body wracked with hacking sounds as she breathed in fresh air.

Rupert stood back and let the guards grab hold of his arms, restraining him at spearpoint. Sir Ranulf had his blade at Rupert's throat. "If you killed her, boy…"

"I didn't," Rupert said. "Look."

He was right. The empress coughed, took a fresh sip of wine, and swallowed, emitting a loud breath. She stood, leaning a hand on Sir Robert's arm. He gripped her arm in return and asked, "Are you all right?"

She nodded weakly and coughed again. The empress released his arm and sipped the wine, beckoning a servant for more. When she had drunk her fill, she said, "I am now."

She turned toward Rupert, who was still being held by the guards. "You. Who are you?"

He met her gaze head on. "Rupert Bothwell. I serve Sir Baldwin of Clare."

"Baldwin? I know him. He was one of my knights," she croaked, her expression falling into a frown. "You are his squire?"

Rupert nodded.

"How did you… know what to do?"

"You were choking, Your Grace. I've seen it before. A man was choking in the market one day and another man came up behind him and did the same movement. Saved his life. He could have died but for that bit of fish."

"So you saw me choking and leapt into action. What quick thinking on your part."

Theobold crossed his arms. Of course, Rupert would act the hero. But why would he save the empress, the leader of the opposition, when he served Sir Baldwin of Clare, one of Stephen's close knights?

Sir Ranulf turned to the servants. "Get the head cook in here. I demand to know why they sliced the bread so thick. We'll have his head. He almost killed the empress."

Empress Maud waved her hand, negating his order. "No. I was the one who tore off a bite too big to eat. It is no one's fault but my own."

Sir Ranulf turned red, but Maud didn't care. Her attention was fixed on Rupert, much like a snake on an unsuspecting mouse.

"You may have saved my life."

"I only did as any man would, Your Grace. If my master were

not sitting in prison right now, I know he would have done the same for you."

She snorted. "Ha. Sir Baldwin made his choice. He is with his master now. Why are you here?"

"I wanted to make myself useful."

"And so you will." She surveyed him thoughtfully. "You are a squire. You will serve my man, Sir Ranulf de Gernon, and still look after your Sir Baldwin. You may go."

She waved her right hand, and the guards released him. Sir Ranulf brightened and opened his mouth, but the empress spoke first.

"Tell the cooks to prepare a handsome meal for Sir Baldwin, and bring it to him in the prison. As a thank you for the actions of his quick-thinking squire. Perhaps a decent meal might make him reflect on his life choices, and think about just whose prison he rots in." She clapped her hands. "Now, I will have music. Play us a tune."

Theobold clenched his teeth and retook his stance behind his master, Sir Robert. He tried to keep his face calm and composed, but all he wanted to do was punch Rupert in the face. He wasn't just a flirtatious chap who liked Bronwyn, now he was a rival at court. *I'll need to keep a close eye on him,* he thought darkly.

$$\begin{array}{c} \text{Chapter Twelve} \end{array}$$

Chapter Twelve

T HE WORD OF Sir Edward's death and the failed attempt on Empress Maud, followed by her almost choking to death, spread like wildfire. Servants were questioned about the crown, particularly those who served within her immediate household, led by Sir Miles. Sir Bors led the investigation into the attempted poisoning on her life, and for the next few hours, cooks were questioned, guards demanded answers, and the castle was in an uproar. All over a crown and a piece of bread.

Bronwyn worked in the kitchen, her eyes and ears open to all the court gossip. But each time a servant was questioned under armed guard, she tensed and couldn't concentrate. What would she say when they asked her? That the crown had been poisoned was news. How could someone poison a crown? She froze amidst wiping. Had the crown been poisoned when she'd had it at the camp? She'd touched it so many times. Admittedly, it had been mostly wrapped in her apron or the dresses at the time, but she had worn it once. Had she unknowingly risked her own life in handling it? She needed to learn more.

She wiped down the worktables with trembling hands and helped clean up after the evening meal. But soon her turn came.

A guard approached and said, "You. Come with me. You're wanted for questioning."

A lump rose in her throat. She followed the servant into the adjoining cooking space and saw that they'd meant to question her in the kitchen, at the table where the cooks and servants ate. She blinked. They couldn't be able to get much information out of people when they practically had an audience. Anyone could listen.

She sat at the long, empty, wooden table, where Sir Bors had made himself comfortable with a cup of ale. "You. You're always at the center of trouble, aren't you?"

Bronwyn shook her head. She opened her mouth, then shut it. She had a feeling that anything she said would only be used against her, depending on Sir Bors's mood.

He noticed her shut mouth and grinned. "Smart. Now. What do you know about this business with the crown?"

She froze. "I don't know anything."

"And I don't believe you. Tell me what you know. Now." He leaned back on the bench.

She shrugged.

"Did you know the crown was poisoned?"

"No."

"Did you happen to touch it?"

She cocked her head at him. "When would I have done that?"

"I know the empress wanted you to find it. Failed at your mission, didn't you? Maybe you got jealous and wanted to hurt her after somebody else found the crown and you didn't. It had a needle stuck to it. You know something about that? You missing a needle?"

"No. I don't have any." She didn't want to suggest he speak to any maids, either. She didn't want to implicate anyone innocent. Unlike Lady Alice and poor Mabel.

"Fine. And this bread that the empress ate. You bake that?"

"Probably. We all have a hand in the cooking, usually."

He crossed his arms over his chest. "Maybe you wanted her to choke. Maybe you purposely made the bread so hard, you hoped she wouldn't be able to swallow it."

"I didn't do any of those things. We always make the bread the same way." She was thinking very rude thoughts now but didn't speak them. It wasn't her fault the empress had taken too large a bite and almost choked to death.

"A likely story. It'd have been easy for you to get some poison, I bet."

"How was it poisoned? I heard a knight died."

"Sir Edward."

Her hand darted to her mouth. "The man who was in love with Lady Eleanor."

"The very same."

"How did he die?"

"He touched the crown and it pricked him. Now listen here, I'm asking the questions." He glared at her. "You're trying to distract me, aren't you? Who's to say you and Theobold didn't get together and—"

"We're not together," she said.

Sir Bors laughed, a loud, ringing sound. He waggled his eyebrows at the guard by his shoulder. "'Course you're not. You two just happened to be having it off right there in the empress's tent the night of the bonfire. You lovers, I swear." He chuckled.

"We are not lovers," she said hotly.

"Sure, you're not," Sir Bors said, "and I'm made of cheese. All right, I'm wasting my time here. But you hear anything, you tell me. Yeah?"

She nodded.

"Let's go. These servants don't know anything," he told the guards. He rose, stretched and finished his ale, then belched loudly.

Bronwyn went back to the worktable, which was clean already, and picked up the damp rag she'd been holding.

If that was how Sir Bors went about investigating, it was no wonder he hadn't found anything. He was hopeless. But she had learned a few things. First, poor Sir Edward had died, pricked by poison. But how? She had touched the crown so often, she likely would have poisoned herself rather quickly at the camp if it had been poisoned then.

She tried to focus on her work while thinking. Rumors spread that it had clearly been an attempt on the empress's life. Others said King Stephen had broken free of prison and forced her at spearpoint to eat it or give up her throne, whilst others said it had been mere clumsiness on her part. She'd simply eaten a piece of bread that had been too big to swallow, and being hard, it had stuck in her throat. It was not the first time a person had died from choking, nor would it be the last.

A lesser woman might have feared for her life, or having had two near-death experiences, be a bit rattled. Not Empress Maud. If anything, she was more focused, more driven, more demanding that actions fall into place to secure her rule.

THE NEXT DAY, a page tapped on Bronwyn's shoulder in the kitchen. "Yes?"

"A squire wants to talk to you," the page said.

"Oh." Her spirits lifted. Was it Rupert? She wiped her hands on her apron.

The head cook waved her out. "Don't take too long. We've got luncheon to prepare."

Bronwyn nodded and followed the page out of the kitchen.

Seeing Theobold standing in the corridor, she said, "Oh. Hullo."

He nodded at the page, who left. Once he was sure they were alone, he said, "Don't look so disappointed. We need to talk. Walk with me outside?"

"All right."

They exited the castle, their shoes crunching on the stiff ground. Theobold said, "You'll no doubt have heard about the death of Sir Edward and the empress almost choking."

"Yes, everyone knows. Someone tried to kill the empress."

"I was there. Sir Edward's death was an accident. When he brought the crown to her at dinner, someone had affixed a poisoned needle to the inside of it. The crown was stained with Sir Edward's blood when I looked at it, but it also bore a different kind of stain. I thought we might speak with the healer about it together."

She let out a small sigh of relief.

"What?" he asked.

"So it was poisoned after we arrived in Gloucester."

"It looks that way. Oh. Oh." He cursed and ran a hand through his dark curls. He gripped her shoulder. "Good God, Bronwyn. If it had been poisoned before…"

"I'd be dead already." She turned a shade paler. "At least you know it wasn't me."

"No. It was likely poisoned after you returned it. But I can't say I didn't suspect you."

She glared at him. He removed his hand.

"Only for a minute. I realized it couldn't have been you. And…… I didn't think it was." He faced her. "You may not like me, or like the idea of being with me, but we are mixed up together in this mess. I think we know each other well enough to know that neither of us would willingly commit murder."

She met his eyes. But both of them had killed before. She had in defending herself and the empress, and he in rescuing her during the battle outside Lincoln. "Neither of us is a poisoner, I believe that."

"Good enough. I…… didn't tell anyone you had the crown."

"Thank you. But why?" Her fingers touched her parted lips.

"I don't think you meant the empress any harm. Besides, you had the crown for days. During that time, you could have sold it, ransomed it, collected enough money to start your life over. But you didn't."

She paused. She'd never even thought of doing any of those things. But they were wrong. To knowingly sell a crown that wasn't hers to begin with, it amounted to stealing, to selling stolen goods. That was not her way.

Bronwyn met his eyes. There was warmth, and kindness there. "Thank you."

He smiled faintly and a slight blush colored his cheeks. "Anyway. Thought you'd want to come along. It's not my usual choice of how I'd spend time with a pretty woman, but it'll do."

She rolled her eyes at that and tried not to smile. "Lead the way."

He took her to another part of the castle, where the surgeon had a sort of hut, filled with low-hanging bushes and vines of herbs. It was a proper workroom, with many shelves laden with jars and pots. The surgeon and his assistant from the camp were there, along with Sir Robert of Gloucester, a hooded figure, and stretched out on a worktable, a body.

Bronwyn tensed. It was Sir Edward. Gazing upon his corpse was chilling. She recognized his thinning, blond hair turning to silvery grey, and the cut of his clothes. A pang of sadness filled her for the loss of him. First Lady Eleanor and now him. Two good people dead. It didn't make sense.

The surgeon stood by with his assistant and beckoned them to come close. "Close the door," he said.

Sir Robert asked Theobold, his eyes darting to Bronwyn, "Why is she here?"

The hooded figure waved at Sir Robert and hissed. "We do not have time for this. Continue, Master Surgeon."

Theobold extended his arm to Bronwyn, as if they were at a dance. "You can hold on to me if you wish. If you feel over-come."

A part of her wanted to laugh at him, then she realized he was being serious. "No, I'll be fine."

Once they were gathered around the body, the surgeon said, "I do not like this."

"Tell us what you have found," the hooded figure said.

"Look here." The surgeon beckoned them forward and pointed at Sir Edward's right hand. He lifted it up and said, "If you look closely, it looks to me like a bite, or a pinprick. You'd never have guessed it was the work of a sewing needle."

The hand was discolored and the area around the index finger was black and purple. It smelled, but that could also have been the body decomposing.

The hooded figure held up a spray of flowers before their face. "So, it was in fact a sewing needle that did this. Not a knife or a blade."

"No. When I looked at the crown, it was an ordinary needle. It's of a type you could find anywhere. Most servants would have one. I think Sir Edward must have pricked his finger on it."

"Sir Bors said it was Sir Edward's idea to bring the crown to the dining hall in the first place, to show them all I was the rightful ruler. But Sir Edward has never been one given to flights of fancy," the hooded figure said, now revealing a husky, womanly tone, tinged with regret.

"Your Grace?" the surgeon enquired.

The empress lowered her hood, revealing her light-brown hair in long braids and covered by a thin veil and different golden circlet. "He was not the most original of men, let us say. A good fighter, and an honest and loyal soldier. But for this to be his idea surprises me. I would not credit him with it."

"You think Sir Bors was lying?" Sir Robert asked.

"I do not know. I do not wish to consider the idea that any of my men would lie to me. It is unheard of."

And yet, Bronwyn thought, *someone took the crown and fixed a needle inside. So small as to not be noticed right away, until it was too late.*

"This was clearly meant as an attack on Your Grace," Bronwyn said.

The empress met her eyes with a stiff nod. She turned to Theobold. "But you weren't harmed when you picked up the crown."

"No. I had a cloth."

The empress crossed her arms beneath her chest. "We need to find out who did this. Now two of my loyal subjects have been killed. I think it's obvious what is happening here."

The others looked at her.

She snorted softly. "Someone from within my court is trying

to kill me. They want to disturb my faith in my fellow subjects, especially those close to me, so they are killing off those loyal to me, one by one. It is a dastardly practice, and when I find out who is behind this plot, I shall have them drawn and quartered."

Bronwyn breathed in. A gruesome punishment. She'd never seen it before, but she'd heard of it happening, in dire circumstances. She glanced at Theobold, who paled. He looked as if he liked the sound of that torture less than her, and the very mention of it filled her with distaste.

"What was the poison used?" Bronwyn asked.

"Who are you again?" asked the surgeon.

"She's nothing but a servant," Sir Robert of Gloucester said, avoiding eye contact with Bronwyn.

"She is helping me," Theobold said.

The empress raised an eyebrow.

"Bronwyn Blakenhale," said Bronwyn. "I work in the kitchen."

"Yes, very well. Hullo, Mistress Blakenhale," said the surgeon, who still seemed confused about the kitchen servant's presence. "The poison used came from our own stores, I'm afraid. When we were traveling with the camp from Lincoln to here, our traveling stores were broken into and some things were stolen. Among them was our supply of monkshood."

"What is that?" Bronwyn asked.

"A poison, if fallen into the wrong hands. I make an ointment, made from the wolfsbane plant—you might have seen it with blue or purple flowers. It is good for soothing aching joints, but if eaten or taken in the blood, it is highly poisonous."

"Would it kill this quickly?" Theobold asked.

"Yes. The roots and leaves are toxic as well, so it must be handled carefully. Whoever stole this knew what they were doing. Or they knew enough to put it on the needle and not get pricked themselves," the surgeon's assistant said.

"So we are looking for someone with a knowledge of monkshood," Theobold said. "Come, Mistress Blakenhale. I'll walk you back to the kitchens."

Bronwyn nodded and curtsied to the group, following Theobold out.

Once they stood outside the surgeon's workshop, he said, "This plot keeps getting more complex."

"Do you think the empress is right, and that someone is trying to remove those people close to her?"

"It's possible. Sir Edward and Lady Eleanor were known to be steadfastly loyal to her. Lady Eleanor was often her confidante amongst her ladies and helped keep them in check. Without her, the empress will be without a friend."

"Does an empress need friends?"

"No. But she does need loyal subjects, and people she can count on. You helping me in this will help prove to her that you are smart, and useful."

"I work in the kitchens. I'm already useful."

He faced her. "Not to mention beautiful."

She rolled her eyes. "Stop that."

"What?"

"Saying pretty things like that. Your face and your voice take on a certain look when you do it, and I know you're just saying it, when it's not true. Or it's not how you really feel."

He started, "Bronwyn…"

She held up a hand. "Save it for the next pretty woman. You say these pretty words and act like I'm lovely, and then behind my back you talk with Lady Morwenna and act like I'm nothing, like I'm nobody." She let out a shuddering breath. "I always thought I was nobody, even after I saved the empress's life. No one acted like I'd done anything special, and my life didn't change. But once Lady Eleanor died and the crown went missing, then you started acting like maybe I was somebody worth knowing. More than just a woman. But now, I just don't know anymore. And I don't know if I believe anything you say."

"Bronwyn, I need your help in this," he said. "I never would have thought to ask the question about the poison."

She shook her head sharply, her thick, blonde braid thumping hard against her shoulder. "I'll help you because I want to know who is doing this. But not because I like spending time with you, or because I want to hear more of your flirting. You're wasting your breath with me." She walked away, sniffing. She idly wondered if he might come after her, but he didn't.

THE NEXT FEW days passed quickly. No matter how many meals she prepared, breads baked, or worktables cleaned, she could not clear her mind of Theobold, Rupert, the attempts on Empress Maud's life, and the crown. That golden circlet was at the center of it all. And she needed to find out who was behind this, for whoever it was, they had traveled with the party at camp back in Lincoln and now were here. She might very well have served them dinner. And with a stolen poison on the loose, who knew who might end up poisoned next? And she wished, right down to her bones, that she would be taken seriously on her own merit, without needing a man to speak for her. And that those who did like her liked her for herself, and not any other. But perhaps she was asking for too much. Maybe most men did have wandering eyes, or maybe she'd just been unlucky and fallen for two men who were equally flirtatious.

It was early March, and to her surprise, she'd been paid a wage.

The empress had minted coins, with her own image on the face, and each servant, knight and man at arms, had been paid. There was some discussion as to whether the coins would be worth much, but in Gloucester, the coins could be used in the local market. In her off hours, which really meant before bed, Bronwyn had taken to mending the old, purple dress that Lady Susanna had given her. She wasn't very deft with a needle, but she'd managed to mend it enough that it was serviceable. She spent a happy hour down at the farmer's market after mass on Sunday, looking at the wares and finery for sale.

Food hawkers called out for people to come and see the

fruits, and even spices, whilst there was no mistaking the smell of blood and meat that came from the butcher's stall, where great carcasses hung and fresh lamb legs, beef shoulders, steaks, and bacon were sold. Bronwyn's mouth watered, but then she walked past some of the bakers' stalls and had to take a look. Some of the rolls looked small, others had a sandy look about them, as if the bakers had weighted them with sand, rather than using the full amount of flour that should have been used. To cheat customers like that was wrong, but she decided she wouldn't get involved. She had enough to worry about.

She looked longingly at the gloves, the bolts of cloth, the shoes and even the pretty ornamental knives. Not that she could afford to buy such finery. In the end, she bought some thread to hem the purple dress and had just purchased a plain kerchief, when she saw Rupert walking with Lady Alice. They looked like proper lovebirds, and she turned away and hurried back to the castle, not wanting to see more.

A DAY LATER, a page came up to her and cleared his throat. His voice squeaked. "Mistress Bronwyn?"

She looked at him, her hands full of dough. "Yes?"

The boy was about age ten and wore a page's livery. "Lady Alice Duncombe wants you to meet her in her quarters, now."

Bronwyn looked toward Agnes, one of the head cooks, who raised her eyebrows at the request. "She's a bit high and mighty, ordering around one of my bakers. Bronwyn?"

"I've served her before."

"All right. Go and see what she wants. But if she wants more than a plate of rolls, you send her to me. I'm the one who gives orders in the kitchen, not a lady. I don't care how many acres of land she owns. The kitchen is my province." Agnes crossed her arms beneath her chest.

Some ten feet behind her, Mary, the former head cook at the camp in Lincoln, glowered at Bronwyn.

Since they'd come to Gloucester, Mary's cruel teasing and

snide remarks toward the others had subsided, due to them all being so busy, as well as Mistress Agnes's seniority. She brooked no unkindness or unfairness amongst the staff, and when a servant did well, she praised them publicly. It was a pleasure to see, and it fostered goodwill amongst those working in the kitchen.

Bronwyn wiped her hands clean and followed the page up two floors to where the ladies-in-waiting stayed. He led her down a corridor and to a room.

Bronwyn breathed in through her nose. They hadn't spoken since their heated discussion back at camp, before arriving at Gloucester. Perhaps they would be friends again. Maybe Lady Alice missed her. Maybe…

She knocked on the door and walked in. "Lady Alice?"

"Shut the door, Bronwyn."

Bronwyn's hopes at a reconciliation of their friendship sank. Her shoulders slumped, she let out a tiny sigh and closed the door. "Yes?"

She looked around the room. It was a decent-sized living space, with a grand four-poster bed and traveling trunks set before it. A small table for writing or cosmetics stood against the left wall with a looking glass, and a squat, wooden stool.

Lady Alice sat at the edge of the bed and rested her hand on one of the wooden posters of her bed. "I wanted to talk to you."

"I thought you didn't want to see me again."

Two spots of color blossomed on Lady Alice's cheeks. She waved a hand airily and said loudly, "That was then. This is now." She motioned for Bronwyn to come closer.

As Bronwyn approached, Lady Alice motioned for her to come closer and closer, until they stood just a foot apart. "Lady Alice?"

"I've come into some information, and I could use your help."

Bronwyn crossed her arms. "It's not something else that's gone missing, is it?"

"No. It's…" Lady Alice looked around the room, as if the very walls watched them. "Stephen is trying to escape."

"What? Now?" Bronwyn stepped back.

"No. He's testing the guards, to see who will help him. He's offering gold, and lands, and position, to any man who will help free him and secure him safe passage from Gloucester."

"How much is he offering?"

"Enough that a man who is either greedy or foolish will take him up on it. Fortunately, all the men Empress Maud posted to his cells are loyal, but… I think every person has their price. It would not surprise me if some dream of more and agree to help him."

"How'd you hear about this?" Bronwyn asked.

"I heard the men talking. I didn't recognize who they were. All I know is they're planning to break him out soon."

"Why come to me with this? Have you told the empress, or Rupert?"

"No. I know he now serves two masters, but…… This information is important. I can't risk it falling into the wrong hands. There are very few people I can trust here at court. Consider yourself lucky that you are one. Rupert is another. Even if he does now serve Sir Ranulf." Lady Alice's upper lip curled in distaste. "There are better men he could serve, but never mind."

"You know the crown was poisoned."

Lady Alice started, a dainty hand flying to her mouth. "So it was? I heard a rumor but didn't think it was true. Who would poison the crown, and how?"

Bronwyn put her hands on her hips. "From what I understand, you were there. You saw Sir Edward fall."

"Yes, but I didn't hear much. There was a lot of commotion and noise." Lady Alice froze. "You don't think it was poisoned when we were at that dreary camp outside Lincoln, do you? I… touched the crown when I found it in my bedding. Could I be poisoned?" She swallowed.

"No. Otherwise, we'd both be dead," Bronwyn said flatly "It

was poisoned here."

Lady Alice stared at her. "I don't like your tone." When Bronwyn didn't reply, Lady Alice said, "You don't think I had anything to do with that, do you?"

"Did you?"

"No." Lady Alice's voice was firm. "And I'm surprised you even had the gall to ask. I certainly didn't. I love the empress, like any loyal subject should. I would never." She cocked her head. "Did you?"

"No."

"So if we didn't, and now Sir Edward is dead, then who would have wanted to kill the empress? You don't think he would want to have done her harm, in revenge for Lady Eleanor dying?"

Bronwyn shook her head. "I don't think he blamed the empress for her death. And it defeats the purpose, since he poisoned himself. He didn't know the crown was poisoned. Otherwise, he'd have worn gloves or not handled it at all."

"So who was wearing gloves that night?"

"I don't know. We could ask Rupert and Theobold. They were there."

Lady Alice smiled. "I don't see why we have to do anything at all. The empress is fine, Rupert has a place in the empress's court, and Stephen is behind bars. All is well. Sort of."

"And yet you called me here to tell me about the plot you heard of to free Stephen."

Lady Alice looked away.

Bronwyn stepped closer. "Why bring me here to discuss it if you don't want to act? And why do you care so much for the empress?"

Lady Alice met her with a solid stare. A moment passed, then two. She raised her chin and said, "The empress...... gives me an opportunity to better myself. To raise myself and do more than sit and make civil conversation, or spend my hours doing embroidery. She gives me a chance to help my family, and raise us up in the world. To have the empress's good faith is everything. And... I believe in her. The crown belongs to her. These men fight amongst themselves and raise armies against her because she is a woman. If she were a man, Stephen would not have raised such a fuss or been so quick to try and claim her birthright for himself."

She spoke with such strength, such fierceness, Bronwyn thought. She rather admired Lady Alice at that moment.

"Fine. So what to do about this rumor you heard?"

"I cannot bother the empress with just a rumor. She'll laugh me out of her chamber. I need proof if I am to get credit for saving Stephen's life," Lady Alice said. "What about this poisoner at court? What do we do? They could kill us in our beds."

Bronwyn scratched her head. "I don't think we are their target, unless we get in the way. I wonder if Lady Eleanor, Mabel, and Sir Edward were accidents."

"They killed three people by accident?"

"No, but they weren't the intended targets. Each time something happens, there's usually an event to tie it to. Like whoever is behind this plans their actions around an event, in the hope that people are so distracted, no one notices."

"What makes you think that?"

"The first attack at camp came with the theft of the crown. We returned it. The attack on Lincoln Castle came during the feast day of the Purification of St. Mary. Why does nothing happen on an ordinary day, like Tuesday?"

Lady Alice smirked. "Perhaps traitors have favorite days of the week like we do."

"In any case, I bet if he does convince someone to break him out, it will come during a feast day or event. When is the next feast day?"

"You would know better than me. I like a good feast, but I never remember the church holidays. You tell me."

Bronwyn thought quickly. "Lent is coming. There is Shrove Tuesday, and then Ash Wednesday."

"That's in two days," Lady Alice said.

"Then we have to be ready. We have to tell someone."

"Who? Lady Susanna is sweet but cannot keep a secret, and Lady Morwenna has a foul temper. And the men...... Sir Miles and Sir Robert would want proof, Sir Bors is a bore, and Sir Ranulf makes my skin crawl. I cannot trust anyone here, except for Rupert and yourself." Judging by Lady Alice's wary glance, even that level of trust was only just there.

"There are good people here."

"Just like there are fools stupid enough to decide to take Stephen's word and help him. He'd have convinced the guards watching his jail cell." Lady Alice brightened. "All right, we'll talk to Rupert. We can have him speak to Sir Baldwin in the cells. Rupert would have a reason to go down there, anyway, to check on his master. He can find out who the traitors are."

"But Sir Baldwin made his choice. He's cast his lot with Stephen. Why would he tell Rupert just to get in trouble and betray his king?" Bronwyn asked.

Lady Alice pouted.

"Exactly. He wouldn't. Not unless he had something to gain, or lose, by Stephen getting free. Otherwise, there's no reason for him to betray Stephen."

"Unless he thought it was part of a greater conspiracy to kill him," Lady Alice said brightly. "If we have Rupert tell Sir Baldwin that there is a plot to kill Stephen on the road, so he's better off staying in prison, then he could relay who Stephen's been bribing and we could report them. Then I get the credit for saving Stephen's life and the empress has me to thank. He's too valuable a prisoner."

"I don't like the idea of asking Rupert to lie. I don't think he would do it. And not to his master."

"Then you don't know him very well at all. Rupert would do it for me," Lady Alice said confidently.

"No. Let's find some other way. It's not right, asking him to lie."

Lady Alice frowned. "You act like it's some great crime I'd be asking him to commit. All it would be is a little, white lie."

"There's no way we can prove he's trying to escape, anyway," Bronwyn pointed out.

"That doesn't matter. Of course he's trying to escape. It's a king. They'd be surprised if he wasn't trying something."

Bronwyn had to agree with that. It'd be an odd king who was content to sit in prison. "We need to find out who Stephen is bribing and if they will really help him or not."

"And when they're planning to release him."

"We know it must either be tomorrow night for Shrove Tuesday or Ash Wednesday. We need to learn more. Who is planning to help him. We'll need names."

"I'll ask Rupert," Lady Alice said brightly.

"Fine, but don't have him lie. Do you think he'll tell the empress once he learns who is involved?"

Lady Alice put her hands on her hips. "I'm not sure. He'll have to decide which of his new masters is more important. Just as long as he credits me with handling this delicate information. You'll have to speak with her too, just in case. And be sure to let the empress know I should get the credit for finding out this plot. But I'm sure Rupert will do as I ask. I think I know how best to handle him. Don't you?"

Bronwyn wisely held her tongue. She felt rebellious—and slightly pained at the mention of Lady Alice knowing Rupert so well—but strangely enough, her thoughts drifted toward…

"I bet I know who's got you staring dreamily like that. It's that squire, Theobold. Sir Robert of Gloucester's man." Lady Alice smiled. "You have good taste, I grant you. He is handsome."

Bronwyn looked away. "I don't know what you mean. That's not what I was thinking."

"Sure, it wasn't. Your cheeks just *happened* to turn pink at the mention of his name." Lady Alice patted a spot on the bed beside her. "I know you too well, Bronwyn Blakenhale, and I can recognize when a man has caught a young woman's eye. Tell me, I want to know all. What has he said to you? Has he paid court to you? Does he know you like him?"

"I hardly know what that means," Bronwyn said, sitting next to her.

"Ugh." Lady Alice rolled her eyes and looked up at the four-poster bed canopy. "There is so much you need to learn about men."

THE NEXT DAY was Shrove Tuesday, and that meant, for everyone, attending church. It also meant removing all edible delights and temptations, particularly of the food variety. No more sweet pies, meat haunch, or sweetened rolls. It was a time of contemplation and confessing one's sins before Lent.

Empress Maud was especially religious, having a reputation of being a particularly devout Christian, and it became known to all that she was attending Mass that morning. Bronwyn laid down her paring knife from the apples she was carving and followed the other servants to Mass.

Together, they went to Gloucester Cathedral, which was an exceptionally grand building. With soaring spires and great, glass windows that the morning light shone through, Bronwyn felt especially inspired. Whilst not everyone had to confess their sins, it was encouraged, so Bronwyn stayed back to wait. But the queue for confession was quite long, and after waiting for almost an hour, Bronwyn stretched and thought something very un-Christian before turning to leave. She decided to return later. God would understand, she hoped.

As she passed by the nobles who waited their turn, Lady Alice coughed and dropped a handkerchief.

Bronwyn stooped to pick it up and hand it to her, when Lady Alice coughed again and murmured, "The guards Christopher Stockly and Adam Granger have agreed to free the prisoner tonight. At the feast. You might tell the empress if you get a chance. Traitors' names have more weight than a rumor, and I don't think our friend with two masters has done anything." She took the handkerchief and said, "Thank you, girl."

Bronwyn's heart sank. So now she knew which guards would help release Stephen. This was going to happen. She wanted to speak with the empress somehow. But then, to whom was she loyal, Stephen or Maud? She wasn't sure. A part of her wanted to walk away and never turn back, but the cathedral offered such peace, it would be nice to talk to someone about her inner dilemma. Perhaps confession might work. As she hurried out of the cathedral, the queue of people from the castle and the city of Gloucester stretched out the door. It was enormous. There was no way she'd be able to confess her sins today. She'd come back tonight, perhaps, she decided.

The day was spent in using up the remaining eggs, cheese, butter, and dairy that was left. Normal dairy foodstuffs were expressly forbidden once Lent began, and so it was a day of cooking and creating lots of dishes. Pies were stuffed with capons; chickens were baked with golden-crusted pastry; meat pies and small rolls were cooked; great haunches of pig, beef and mutton were roasted and turned on the spit; and great jugs of ale were passed around.

Bronwyn liked her ale as much as the next person, but she knew the dangers of drinking too much. Drinking water was unsafe, so she either drank milk or ale, usually. Wine was reserved for finer folk, but the servants had nicked some of it before. When she'd tasted the liquid, it had been unexpectedly sour and bitter and had left her with a mouthful of sediment. She was not keen to try wine again and so watched herself as she took orders and baked dozens upon dozens of bread rolls.

The haunches of the roasting meats produced great vats of drippings for sauces and gravy, and this was collected beneath the spits with great trays. This was one of those days where the castle kitchens smelled so wonderful, the air itself was perfumed with the interweaving scents of roasting meat, slowly roasting enough to make a person's mouth water.

That early evening, she nipped outside to use the privy and thought it would be a good time to visit the cathedral again. She hurried outside and found the cathedral largely empty, but for a guard or two snoring against some of the pillars.

She nipped inside the confessional and sat down on the small, sturdy bench.

"Father?" the husky, feminine voice spoke.

Bronwyn knew that voice. "Empress?"

"Who are you?" the empress demanded. "How dare you interrupt my solitude? I'll have your head for this."

"Please, I meant no harm," Bronwyn said. "I didn't know you were here. I thought the priest was."

"A likely story. Get out." She uttered a noise of disgust. "Stupid guards. I bet they're either gambling or asleep."

Bronwyn rose, the seat creaking beneath her, then paused. This was the moment to speak, if ever there was one. "Your Grace, there is something you should know." She told her of the plan to spring Stephen from prison.

The empress hissed. "You are the second person to tell me this. Your information is old, little baker. Sir Ranulf has already informed me of Stephen's plan, and the plot to kill him on the main road. I know all about it."

Bronwyn tensed. So she did know. And learned about it from Sir Ranulf, Rupert's new master in the empress's court. Most likely Lady Alice had told Rupert of the plot, and he'd told Sir Baldwin, who had revealed the guards who had been bribed, in order to save Stephen's life. Lady Alice hadn't listened to her, after all, and she'd made Rupert complicit in the lie. Her shoulders slumped. And there had been no mention of Lady Alice. Perhaps Rupert had done it to protect her, in case the plans went sour?

The empress said archly, "But how very good of you to tell me so yourself. Now I wonder if it is such common knowledge that even the cooks know of his plan."

Bronwyn winced. "I'm sorry, I... No. I am sorry to have disturbed you, but I'm not sorry at all to tell you, even if you already knew. They plan to release him tonight." She gave the traitorous guard's name.

The empress laughed. "Let them try. They will see what happens when they try a plot under my nose." The empress sniffed. "Now, for God's sake, get out. Or I will see to it that you are scrubbing chamber pots for the rest of the year."

Bronwyn left. When she quit the confessional, the two guards were awake and stood talking with a priest. They quickly cornered her.

"What were you doing there?" one asked.

"I…… got lost. I was looking for a priest when……"

"Off with you," the other said.

Bronwyn fled.

The feast that evening was a grand affair. There was chaos, from what Bronwyn could see from sneaking away to peer into the main hall, but it was somehow organized chaos, like the flight and flurry of bees.

Pages scurried to and fro, bringing in jugs of ale, wine, and beer. The long tables groaned under the weight of many serving platters of different types of roast meat, with dozens of Bronwyn's rolls to dunk and mop up the drippings, sauce, and gravy from the wooden and stale bread trenchers. The steam of the hot food mingled deliciously with the smokiness of the fire burning in the grand fireplace, and minstrels played and walked around the room, strumming guitars, playing lutes, and tossing balls. First the meal, then dancing. It would be a great evening.

Bronwyn watched from the shadows and gave a quick sigh. Just once, she wouldn't mind dressing up as a maidservant again and mingling with the finely dressed people. She might dance, laugh, and be jolly. But there was a lot of clean-up to do back in the kitchen, and she had hours left to go before she might return to the room where she slept with the other women servants.

But the music lightened her soul, and she crept away, humming offkey. It wasn't until she was sent to bring some food down to the prisoners that she wondered what had become of the plot to release the king. She took platters of leftover meat and potage and with another pair of servants brought them all along with jugs of stale beer down circular, stone steps to the jail.

The air changed; it was cold and chilly. The walls had lost their warmth and bore traces of dankness, a wet, moldy chill that threatened to sink into one's bones if left too long. Bronwyn followed the other servants down carefully, but they were stopped.

"What's going on?" Bronwyn asked.

The guards were busy, walking up and down the corridor with the cells, barking orders and demands.

One of the cooks ahead of her said, "Oi, we've got food for the prisoners. What's the problem?"

The guards faced them. "Get back to the kitchens," said one, a tall, middle-aged man with an impressive mustache and bushy eyebrows. "Stephen has escaped."

Chapter Thirteen

Bronwyn stared and almost dropped the trencher of food she held, so she gripped the sides hard, feeling the stale bread trencher almost crack beneath the pressure of her fingers. She lessened her grip. "'Escaped'?"

"Aye. Go away if you know what's good for you."

Bronwyn and the other servants turned to go. They began to make their way up the stairs and back into the corridors when there came an order to deliver the food to the rest of the prisoners. Bronwyn and a handful of servants went to the kitchen and returned with trenchers of food and cups of stale beer. She faced a cell full of knights, who ate hurriedly, the smell of the smoky, roasted meat and potage a brief respite from the smell of unwashed male body, urine, and feces that hung in the air. The straw on the floor did nothing and was damp and wet beneath her shoes, and more than one mouse and rat scurried by, darting and squeaking around her ankles.

Bronwyn had never been scared of rodents, but this many around made her feel nervous. She waited for the men to finish eating and drinking, took the empty bread trenchers and stood back as the guards marched a man in chains through the corridor, the chains clinking and ringing, echoing through the space.

Bronwyn and the other servants kept quiet as the men marched King Stephen into the walkway, and one held an open door.

Stephen walked through, his locks hanging limply by his face. His beard was long and scraggly, the smell of him made Bronwyn wrinkle her nose, and he walked as if with a great weight upon his shoulders. He looked up briefly, seeing the servants there, eyeing hungrily the sight of the empty trenchers and jugs, and walked into the cell.

The guard slammed the iron door shut and locked it tightly. "Serves you right for trying to escape. No one escapes."

"I did. For a time," Stephen said.

The guard spat on the straw that rustled and squeaked beneath his feet. "No one escapes for long. We could smell you a mile away."

"That is not my fault. It seems my cousin's hospitality does not extend to allowing her prisoners to bathe."

The guard smirked. "Least now you stink like the ruffian you are. Never seen a king smell like horse dung before."

Stephen was silent.

The guard grinned and left. Bronwyn waited for him to pass, then took one of the remaining trenchers that still had food on it and told one of the servants, "Go. I'll catch up."

"Suit yourself," he said, leaving with the rest of the servants.

Bronwyn went to the king's cell and tapped lightly on the iron bars. She held out the trencher and waited. Peering into the darkness, she knew there were men on the other side of the bars and yet no one came near.

Finally, a few footfalls approached. A man stood before her. Tall, stocky. He smelled.

"You witnessed my humiliation just now. Yet you would feed me?"

She looked up into where she thought his eyes must be. What to say to a king? Especially this one, who a month ago had imprisoned her father for a crime he had not committed and would have hanged him? She owed him no loyalty, that was sure. So why was she standing there, holding out the trencher so he might eat?

"You have to eat, Your Grace," a male voice said from within the cell.

"I was not addressing you, Baldwin. I have not forgotten your treachery," King Stephen said.

Bronwyn wondered at this. How had Stephen found out about the plot?

A heavy sigh. "Your Grace, it was the only thing I could do, to save your life. I would sooner serve a live king than a dead one." Sir Baldwin of Clare, Rupert's master, said.

Bronwyn said, "It's Shrove Tuesday. We're getting rid of all the meat, anyway. It's not poisoned, I promise." She froze. Would he even remember that she was the baker involved in a plot to poison some bread rolls from months ago? Would he accuse her of being behind it all?

There was a pause, then a thin hand reached out and took some of the bread and meat. He chewed and swallowed, as if trying to savor the bites, but was so hungry, he could not help himself, and he ate quickly. He groaned, rubbing his stomach. "Thank you."

Bronwyn nodded. "I am sorry." He did not seem to remember her, after all.

He looked at her, and she left, trying to ignore the moving rushes beneath her feet, and the squeaks and flurry of tiny mice and rats that scurried around.

THE NEXT DAY, Bronwyn awoke to screams. She shot up, conscious of the still-sleeping forms of the women servants near her. They slept on straw pallets on the floor and blankets. It wasn't quite a bed like Lady Alice's, but it was a thousand times better than sleeping outdoors with only a fire, a thin dress, and the bodies of those around her to keep warm.

There came another cry. Bronwyn threw off her thin blanket. "Did you hear that?"

Most of the servants were now awake, aside from those who could sleep like the dead.

"Eh, it's probably a lord getting his leg over," one man said. "Get on with your chores. We've got enough work to do without disturbing a lord and his lady."

Bronwyn shot him a dark look and ran out of the room.

She spared a thought for the fact that the strings of her woolen, brown dress around her bodice hung loose, as was her blonde hair, and that in her hurry, she hadn't put on shoes. But those things didn't matter now. She ran toward the sound of the screams.

The sound came again, closer this time.

She ran in the direction and hurried up the stairs. The cries took her to the ramparts of the castle, where the air was decidedly cold, windy, and chilly. She shielded her eyes against the rising sun and was surprised at the loud cawing of crows, birds, and flies that buzzed near the edge of the walls.

She saw nothing. No one was there. Was it all a trick? A spirit?

"Help! Somebody help me!" a woman cried.

Bronwyn dashed to the edge of the ramparts, where two thick ropes were tied around narrow pillars. Hanging on to one of them for dear life clung a familiar face.

"Lady Morwenna?" Bronwyn said.

"Oh, thank God. Help me, please." She turned a tearstained face upward. The fear in her eyes was real. "Please, help me. I don't want to die."

"Oh, my Lord." Bronwyn bent down and, leaning awkwardly between the parapet pillar stones, she reached for her.

Lady Morwenna gritted her teeth and grasped her hand. The woman's hands were soft, smooth, and sweaty.

The women worked together, with her tugging and Lady Morwenna climbing until she got a handhold on the stone, her cheeks pink with exertion, her eyes wild.

Bronwyn helped pull her over. Together, they collapsed on the stones, breathing hard.

"What happened?" Bronwyn asked, once she'd caught her

breath.

"I… came out for a breath of fresh air. I like to take the air here sometimes. It's refreshing." Lady Morwenna's voice was tight.

Bronwyn looked at her. "And you just happened to trip over the side?"

"No, I…"

"Are you all right?"

The woman turned around. Lady Morwenna's face was tear-stricken.

"What really happened?" Bronwyn asked.

"I… L-Look." Lady Morwenna pointed.

Curious, Bronwyn gripped the stone and planted her feet solidly so she wouldn't slip. She leaned over just enough to see.

There around two of the stones hung ropes. At the end of the ropes hung the lifeless bodies of two guards.

Her right hand darted to her mouth. These were likely the guards from the previous night who had helped Stephen escape. Christopher Stockly and Adam Granger, she supposed.

Bronwyn leaned away, took two deep breaths, feeling light-headed, and was sick. As she heaved her guts out onto the stones and breathed in gasps of fresh morning air, she noticed something.

The scent of roses hung in the air.

Bronwyn sank to the stone floor of the ramparts, breathing hard. She could still taste the vestiges of bile on her tongue, and spat, wiping her mouth clean. She felt the solid, cold weight of the stone against her back and was glad of it. That and the blustery wind plastering her hair around her face made her feel awake, even if her legs felt wobbly. She closed her eyes and took deep breaths.

"Do you wear a rosewater perfume, Lady Morwenna?" she asked.

"Uh, no. No, I don't," Lady Morwenna said, sounding farther away.

"Bronwyn. Are you all right?" a familiar voice asked, and a shadow fell over her face.

Bronwyn opened her eyes. "Rupert. What are you doing here?"

"I heard the screams. What happened? You're pale."

She motioned with a shaking hand. "The ropes… Don't look. There are bodies."

Rupert ignored her and leaned over the parapet. He cursed. "Good God. Who did this?"

"I don't know."

"Wait a minute," he said. "Those are guards. They…"

Bronwyn pulled him away, a safe distance from Lady Morwenna, whose eyes widened while a slow smile grew on her face as she watched them.

"I think it's the men Stephen bribed to let him out," Bronwyn said.

"How do you know about that?" he asked.

"Lady Alice told me."

"Me too. I told Sir Baldwin about the conspiracy to kill the king once he was free. He told me who the bribed guards were and I relayed it to de Gernon and—"

"Sir Ranulf de Gernon? Why him?"

"I'm serving him now, as well as Sir Baldwin," Rupert said.

"I heard that from Lady Alice. Why?" She frowned.

"I have my reasons. Anyway, he told the empress of the plot."

Bronwyn's shoulders slumped. "I told her too. She said she already knew."

"Via Sir Ranulf, yes. Thank goodness Sir Baldwin told me which guards were at fault. Now the king is safe."

She looked at him. "But he wasn't in danger."

His eyes squeezed shut. "What do you mean?"

"There was no plot to kill him on the road. That was fabricated by Lady Alice. She—"

"Bronwyn, you're not making sense. Of course there was a plot. Lady Alice said—"

"She lied to you, Rupert."

"She wouldn't do that." He shuffled backward.

"She did. We argued about it before. I… told her not to. That we'd find another way." But Lady Alice hadn't waited for her, or thought of any other way herself. Then she realized, Lady Alice had simply assumed Rupert would give her credit for handling the intrigue when he reported it. But he hadn't.

"Lady Alice used me in her scheme? But why?" Rupert's voice was tight.

She didn't want to reveal the truth, that Lady Alice wanted credit for the intrigue, and they were both just pawns to her. "I couldn't say."

"Try. One of you is lying. Which is it, you or her?" He looked at her, his eyes hard. "Bronwyn, I—"

"You there. What's all the noise?" Theobold's voice called out.

Bronwyn looked past Rupert.

Theobold's mouth withered when he saw them together. "Bronwyn? The screaming was you? What happened?" He crossed the walkway when Lady Morwenna cried out and threw herself into his arms.

Theobold's eyes widened as he held her. "Lady Morwenna, what are you doing here?"

Lady Morwenna trembled and wept in his arms. He gave her a comforting pat on the back whilst looking daggers at Rupert and Bronwyn. "Will somebody tell me what's going on?"

"There're bodies," Lady Morwenna said tearfully. Her thick, brown hair tickled Theobold's nose and he sneezed.

More figures appeared at the entrance to the parapet. "What's going on here?" Sir Ranulf asked.

"Oh, my lord Sir Ranulf." Lady Morwenna ignored Theobold and hurried to his side. "It's the most terrible sight. Two men are dead."

"I know. Empress's order. Now they've learned the cost of betraying Empress Maud," he said. "Come away, girl. This is no sight for a lady." To Rupert and Theobold, he added, "Theobold, see to your master. Rupert, pack my saddlebags. Tomorrow we're off to escort the prisoners to Bristol Castle."

"Bristol?" Theobold said.

"Aye. We leave at dawn. The empress wants the false king to have a special meal first." He departed, escorting Lady Morwenna down the steps.

Theobold came over. "Bronwyn, are you well?"

She nodded and wiped her mouth on her sleeve. She noticed his eyes dart to her chest and realized the strings of her dress were undone. In her haste to find the source of the screaming, she hadn't attired herself properly. She quickly turned and did up the laces and stood, conscious of her stocking feet cold on the stone. She brushed down her skirts.

"I came when I heard the screams. I found Lady Morwenna hanging off of the stone."

"What?" Theobold's mouth dropped open.

"I helped her up. Then we saw the bodies. I was sick," she said.

"Yes, I can see that." His voice was chilly. "What was she doing up here, alone with two corpses?"

"I don't know. She didn't say." And she wondered how Lady Morwenna had fallen in the first place. The stone parapets were high enough that a person would have to be very unlucky to trip over the side, unless they'd been pushed.

"I don't like this. You're at the heart of this mess, for sure. Trouble just follows you around." Rupert shook his head at her.

Theobold gave him a hard stare. "Right. Bronwyn, you'd best be going. No doubt they'll need you in the kitchens."

She ducked her head and walked away. Instead of leaving, though, she entered the exit and paused just inside the entrance, hidden in the shadows.

"What say you and I have a little talk, Bothwell," said Theobold.

"As it please you," Rupert said.

"What is your interest toward the kitchen maid?" Theobold asked.

"You mean Bronwyn? We are good friends." His voice rose.

"Is that why you comfort her and instead treat your Lady Alice with coldness? I saw you at the dancing. You stood by and ignored her wishes to dance."

"My master would have minded."

"Your new master wouldn't. And why is it that you inserted yourself into the empress's affairs? Saving her life like that was a bold move."

"I only saw her in distress."

"She is the leader of the opposition to your side. You could have let her choke to death."

"No, I couldn't. She is also a woman, and a person. Even if I disagree with her policies." But his voice sounded unsure, and Bronwyn was not the only one to notice.

"You want to gain the empress's favor. I should have known. A word to the wise, she doesn't care for turncoats. You'll have to do more than save her from choking to gain her full trust. She'll have forgotten about that incident within a day. Good luck with that."

Rupert retorted, "Why are you questioning me about whom I curry favor with? And you have no business questioning my relationship with Lady Alice. Besides, I thought you fancied Bronwyn."

"Me, fancy a kitchen maid? Don't be ridiculous. I don't like a man with stratagems, especially when it involves the empress. Just keep out of my way."

Bronwyn hugged the shadows and crept into a small archway not far from the entrance. She did not wish to hear more. So neither Rupert nor Theobold liked her as more than a friend, and even that was questionable. Oh, to be beautiful, when she was anything but. She blinked hard and wiped away a tear. Never mind love, or desire. She would have none of it. Bronwyn thought to herself, *I am a baker, and I've got a mystery to solve. I have more important things to do than fancy two men at once.*

She learned from the guards that the bodies had been hanged there the previous night, as punishment for helping Stephen escape, and as a warning to all who dared help him. They might have been hanging over the side of the castle, but the news spread and everyone, lord and lady and servant alike, knew of the guards' fate within hours. Apparently, the empress wanted the bodies to stay up longer, but the message was loud and clear, and it had spread without needing fresh corpses to look at over breakfast every morning. They were to be removed in a day or two, Bronwyn heard. She hoped rather than trusted that this would be the case. Something about this move didn't sit right with her. It was ugly, grisly.

Once Bronwyn had returned to her room and properly attired herself for the day, she went to the kitchens to begin work. But her energy was dull, and she felt slow, her mind dwelling on the sight she'd seen early that morning. No man deserved to be strung up like that, like a sad puppet. It was beyond humiliating, for it was public humiliation after death. There was something unconscionable, even un-Christian, about that, it seemed.

A page walked into the kitchen with a funny look on his face. He whispered something to one of the cooks, who stared, asked him to repeat it, and then cursed. He frowned.

"What is it?" Bronwyn asked. It wasn't like the day could get any worse.

The cook said, "We'll not do that. We'll send him a plate, same as anyone else."

She approached. She did not know the cook's name, for there were many dozens of staff in the kitchen alone, not to mention the rest of the castle household. "What's wrong?"

He ran a floury hand on his apron. "Direct order from the empress." He paused, looked at the floor, then back up at her. "She wants... In return for his attempted escape last night..." He let out a noisy breath. "It's Ash Wednesday. The start of Lent."

"Yes. Did she want a meal sent up?"

"Aye, but not for her. For Stephen in the cells."

"That's nice. So what's wrong?"

He looked pale. Sweat dotted his forehead. "She wants a platter of rotten fish guts and bones to be sent to him. As a farewell gift. Fish gut soup."

Bronwyn felt ill. "But that's… wrong. That can't be right."

"That's what I said. But the boy said it came from her own mouth. Do we dare disobey her order? She is the empress."

She frowned. "No. We do what she asked."

His eyes widened. "But to do that… No, I couldn't. And those fish guts…" He glanced at the pile of them on a platter nearby, where flies buzzed.

"I know. We use the bones to make a stock broth and pass the liquid through a sieve to clear it away from any remaining bones. Serve it with a bit of old bread and it'll be a strong fish broth."

The cook nodded. "Smart. I'll do it now. Then we can say we did it, and no one's the wiser."

She agreed. "I'll help if you like."

"No, I'll do it. I took the message."

Within a few hours, Stephen was delivered a bowl of hearty fish stock, complete with fish heads floating on top for effect. Aside from the grisly topping of fish heads, the soup smelled delicious. *With a bit of crusty old bread, it won't be so bad,* Bronwyn thought.

THE NEXT DAY at dawn, she rose early and crept into an empty room. Bronwyn stood by the windows on the first floor and watched as a small group of knights escorted a covered wagon away from the castle. From any ordinary viewpoint, it would appear as though it were a simple cart, perhaps containing food or market wares. No one would know it would bear a rebel king and his loyal knights inside.

She spotted Sir Ranulf and Rupert, along with a handful of other armed men, riding out. She turned to leave when a sharp voice said, "There you are. Just the maid I've been looking for."

Bronwyn turned around. "Lady Alice?"

"I suppose it is too much to ask you to speak to me with a civil tongue, since you obviously bear no respect for me at all," Lady Alice declared, entering the empty room.

"What are you talking about?"

"You and your stupid, insipid, busybody ways. I know you told Rupert about the lie about the plot on the road. That was none of your business." Her upper lip curled.

"You shouldn't have lied to him," Bronwyn said.

"That's not your concern. I'll speak to him however I want."

Bronwyn glared at her. Lady Alice glared right back.

"As your friend, I'm telling you—"

"We are not friends. When are you going to get it through your thick skull? We were never friends. I once thought different, but your actions have made it clear you were never a friend to me. Only to him. I should have seen it for what it was. Did you think that Rupert would like you if you told him the truth? Trust me, Bronwyn, no one likes bad news, and especially not the messenger."

"Lady Alice. I didn't mean…" Bronwyn started.

"Save it. He's broken it off with me. Says we need some time apart, if you can believe it. All thanks to you."

"I didn't know you were courting." She felt a tightness in her throat.

"Well, we are. We were. It was never said but implied in his every word, and… Never mind. It's over now." Lady Alice's dainty fists clenched.

"I'm sorry." Bronwyn felt a pang of regret for her, in spite of herself. "But you shouldn't have lied to him."

"That's all you have to say? He blames me, when all I did was help him save his blasted king's life. He should be thanking me. Instead, I don't even get credit for the blooming scheme. Sir Ranulf does. And now Rupert's… Never mind. I only wanted to tell you to leave me be, Bronwyn, and I'll not speak to you again.

Let us part. It was wrong of us to let our worlds intersect." Lady Alice shot her a glance, her dark eyes flashing to match her shining, black hair, and left.

Bronwyn sighed. And now what did it matter? Stephen was alive and relatively safe, but she'd lost a friend. And broken up a happy couple. She walked back down to the kitchens and threw herself into her work. And based on Stephen's treatment of her father previously, where he'd been preparing to hang him for a crime he hadn't committed just a few months ago, she was surprised she cared at all. *Maybe the man would be better off dead,* she thought darkly. But she couldn't shake the feeling that this was not up to her, and even if he wasn't quite a king, Stephen deserved better treatment than what he was getting here.

This was the second day of feasting, but the foods were quite different. Being Ash Wednesday, there was no more meat from four-legged creatures, and the emphasis was on fish. The day was spent either gutting fish, deboning fish, making fish sauces, boiling fish in milk, and frying fish over hot pans. Along with fresh bread, it was to be the first Lenten meal of the season.

For Bronwyn, it was quite a learning experience. She'd only ever worked as a baker before this year and had only limited experience working with fish in the kitchen. It was exciting and she'd never learned so much about cooking in such a little time. She'd come to understand that in the city where she'd grown up, being a baker meant learning a trade in a certain set of skills, but working in the castle kitchens was like an entirely different world.

Here she did a bit of everything, and it was invigorating. There was just one problem: her mind kept getting diverted by what she'd witnessed and heard on the roof that morning—and all of the strange things that had happened since she'd joined Empress Maud's camp.

Why had Lady Morwenna been holding on for dear life to the ropes above hanged traitors in the first place? Had she tripped? Could it have been an accident? What had she been doing on the parapets at such an early hour?

Bronwyn thought to herself as she slowly stirred a broth. She mentally stepped back to the start of the events that had taken place and pondered the order of what had happened.

Lady Eleanor, loyal to the empress by all accounts, had most likely interrupted men stealing the crown, and in her fighting with the guards, she'd been killed for her trouble. Or, if Sir Bors was to be believed, she had been attempting to steal it herself, and he'd stopped her, but he'd been struck from behind. His account was odd, though, considering how big and strong he was, and everyone's description of the lady as the empress's most trusted friend. There was also the scent of roses she'd smelled at the time, a scent that Lady Eleanor did not wear.

Bronwyn excused herself, went to Lady Alice's room and knocked on the door. She rapped and rapped until a sleepy Lady Alice said, "What? What do you want?"

"Does Lady Morwenna wear a scent? Like a floral scent?" She walked into the room.

"You bothered me to talk about perfume? Lord, you're unbelievable. And if you haven't forgotten, I'm not currently speaking to you. We are no longer friends, Bronwyn. We are nothing."

"Yes, yes, I know. But answer me this. Lady Eleanor wore lavender scent, but do any of the other ladies?"

"Well, Lady Susanna likes the smell of apples."

"That's not what I mean."

"I know. But you seem to know enough already. Yes, Lady Morwenna likes to smell like roses. She had a rosewater she would often wear at camp, more so as she said the place smelled terrible, but she ran out of it and wishes to buy herself some or make some more. Why do you care, and why did you wake me up at the crack of dawn to ask about her toilette?"

"Because. When I first came across the scene of Lady Eleanor's death, I smelled roses in the air." Bronwyn realized Lady Morwenna had lied to her when she'd denied wearing the scent.

"So? There might have been flowers present." Lady Alice yawned.

"Lady Eleanor was the only woman there and there were no flowers. It was February."

"Oh. Well…" Lady Alice sat on her bed, thinking.

"And just this morning. I found Lady Morwenna at the top of the castle on the parapet, screaming. She was holding on to a rope that…" Bronwyn felt sick.

"Are you all right? You look pale."

"Yes, I'm fine. I found Lady Morwenna, but she smelled like roses. I'm sure of it. But when I asked her, she denied it."

"Hmm. You think she had something to do with Lady Eleanor's death?" Lady Alice asked and tapped her chin.

"I think she might have been there, right before I found Lady Eleanor."

"Then why didn't she say anything?" Lady Alice asked.

"That, I do not know. Maybe she was afraid she'd be suspected of the crime. Maybe she saw Lady Eleanor die and it was too late to save her, and whoever had done it threatened her," Bronwyn said.

Lady Alice said, "She was clearly trying to frame me for the theft of the empress's crown. She's up to no good at the best of times, I think. Perhaps she took the crown the night Lady Eleanor died. Or there's the more obvious solution."

Bronwyn raised an eyebrow. "Go on."

"Maybe Lady Morwenna killed Lady Eleanor."

Chapter Fourteen

THEOBOLD STRAINED AND blocked as his opponent's wooden sword sliced at him in an impressive arc. The sharp clap of the other squire's sword against his sent a small shock up his right arm. He used his small, wooden shield to block and slice at his opponent, when the youth stepped away. The squire stopped, looking past Theobold at something.

"What are you doing? Why aren't you fighting back?" Theobold asked.

"There's a woman here. I think she's waiting for you." The other squire motioned with his sword.

Theobold turned and ran a hand through his dark hair. "Bronwyn? Oh. Never mind." He spotted Lady Morwenna watching and ignored her. "We can still practice."

"I'm tired, anyway," the squire said.

They bowed to one another and the squire left him as the small crowd of knights, squires, pages, and other servants dissipated. Two other squires took up their discarded wooden swords and shields and took their places on the grass.

For a wet day in March, it wasn't the warmest, but practicing short swords outside did give Theobold the chance to burn off some energy. Theobold stood back and to the side as the other squires began to fight.

Lady Morwenna came to him. "Hullo."

He grunted.

"I wanted to talk to you. Can we talk?"

"You already are."

"You're being beastly," she said with a frown.

He shrugged. He didn't care what Lady Morwenna thought. He'd hoped it would be Bronwyn. Instead, he was faced with her, with whom he had history, and whom he didn't particularly care for. "What do you want?"

"I don't want to talk here. Can we go somewhere?" she asked.

"Fine. I need to check on the horses, anyway." He walked away from the group, leaving her to walk after him. His long legs easily ate up the ground at a fast pace, and she had to hurry to keep up.

"Slow down," she said.

He slowed.

"I think the castle isn't safe anymore. Could you... help me travel home?" she asked.

He glanced at her. Gone was her overabundance of self-confidence, her coy and flirtatious smiles. Her round, doughy face was thinner, and her dark eyes looked haunted. Shadows hung beneath her eyes, as if she'd hadn't had a restful night's sleep.

"Why do you want to go home?" he asked. "The castle is plenty safe. Safer than that camp we traveled from, anyway. And there are plenty of knights here to protect you. Besides, Stephen and his men are on their way to Bristol. No harm will come to you here."

"I just want to go home. Will you take me? I can't make the journey alone."

He cocked his head. "Give me a good reason why. I'm not saying *no*, but I'll have to ask permission from my master and he'll want to know."

"I just..." She looked around as they approached the stables and tossed her head. "Fine. If it's too much trouble, never mind. I clearly asked too much of you."

"Lady Morwenna, what is it? Why are you... Are you scared of something?" He crossed his arms over his chest.

She paused. "No, of course not."

He faced her. "What's wrong?"

"Nothing's wrong. I just want to visit my family."

"So early in the year, when the empress needs you?"

"She doesn't. She has ladies enough."

"She lost Lady Eleanor and her own life was threatened just the other day. She would want to know why you would abandon her like this."

"I'm not abandoning anyone," she declared. "I'm just looking out for myself."

"Tell me why," he pressed. "Cousin, what's frightened you?"

"Nothing."

"I don't believe you." He waited, then when she remained silent, he asked, "What were you doing inside the tent the night Lady Eleanor died?"

"What? Nothing. I wasn't there. I didn't do anything."

"Then why did Bronwyn smell your rosewater perfume?"

"I don't know. Her nose must be mistaken. I wasn't there," Lady Morwenna said, her head held high.

"Lady Morwenna, we have known each other too long. I know when you're lying."

"I'm not." She turned her head.

"I think you are." He entered the stables and approached the stall with his master's horse. "Once upon a time, we didn't keep secrets from each other."

"That time ended long ago," she said bitterly. "You made it clear you weren't interested in me. Has that changed?"

Her question hung in the air. He breathed in and glanced at her. He gave a stiff shake of his head.

The rejection seemed to sting her like the prick of a bee. "I see. Well, then, I see no need to tell you anything."

"Tell me what is bothering you and I can try to help."

"You can't do anything. You and that kitchen maid of yours can't do anything. You're always skulking around corners together. Doesn't she know you're only getting close to her in order to watch her, in case she does something suspicious?"

There was a soft gasp.

Lady Morwenna's head turned. "Did you hear that?"

"No." He had, but he decided to pretend he hadn't. It was Bronwyn, he was sure of it. Who else would be lurking in the shadows, spying? He entered the horse stall, closed the door behind him, and began brushing down the horse. His chin dipped low to his chest. Bronwyn now knew of the empress's order. Would she still speak to him?

Lady Morwenna wrinkled her nose. "You don't really like her, do you?"

"You've already declared it to be a farce," he said.

She smirked. "As I thought. You always were such a flirt, Theobold. I... Have you ever fallen for the wrong person?"

He looked at her. "What do you mean?"

A door creaked, and a horse nickered softly. Someone else was in the stables. It had to have been Bronwyn. He'd speak to her shortly and explain. Maybe with a kiss.

"What was that?" she asked.

"A groom or stablehand, probably. It doesn't matter."

Her expression clouded. "I should go."

He put a hand out, barring her escape. "Lady Morwenna. Tell me what is wrong. I can tell something troubles you. What is it?"

"Nothing." She shivered and stood closer to him. Her eyes were questioning, assessing him. "I can't tell you. I thought it was nothing, but I didn't realize until I was too mixed up in things. And now it's too late. I can't get out."

"What are you talking about?"

"Don't you understand? If I breathe a word of this they'll kill me, Theobold. Me. The little push over the parapet this morning was a warning. Thank God that maid Bronwyn found me or I might have died. But then they don't care about who gets hurt. I used to think I was important, but now... I'm afraid."

"Of whom?" he asked.

She continued as if he hadn't spoken. "I'm terrified I'll end up dead, just like my maidservant. They were behind her death, I'm sure of it. I was training her, you know. Now I have to find someone else."

He cocked his head. Her passive and emotionless way of speaking about her dead maid disturbed him. Had she so little care for her previous maid?

"What are you mixed up in, Lady Morwenna?" he asked.

"Nothing, I—" She stopped and hissed, "If you won't help me, then be smart and ignore what's happening right under your nose, like you always do."

"Lady Morwenna..." he started. "Tell me what this is all about. I can help you."

"Oh, Theobold, you can't even help yourself." She gave a little laugh, ducked beneath his arm, and quit the stables.

Theobold didn't go after her. He waited a moment, then turned toward the direction of the sounds he'd heard. He stepped quietly, his boots barely making a sound on hardpacked earth, until he found the other person in the stables, calmly stroking a horse. He tensed. It wasn't Bronwyn at all. His shoulders scrunched up by his neck. It wasn't her, but someone certainly close to her, who could reveal everything. "What are you doing here?"

"I like to go to the stables. Brushing down horses helps me think. They're better than people sometimes, even if they smell worse." She sniffed.

"And how much did you hear?" he asked.

Lady Alice's eyes were dark and accusing as she tossed her glossy, black hair. "Enough."

"Are you going to tell Bronwyn?"

"I should. But then from what I heard, you don't care for her, so perhaps she won't think anything of it."

He gazed down at his boots.

"Why do you profess to not care for her at all, when it's so obvious you do?" she asked.

"I could ask you the same thing. Why do you pretend you

aren't friends, when you so clearly care for one another?"

They stared at each other, neither wishing to look away first.

"I heard you were attacked, back at the camp. Bronwyn told me. And about hiding the crown."

"Of course she did. Ever the opportunist."

He raised an eyebrow. "What did they want?" he asked.

"Some man came after me and demanded to know where the crown was. I didn't know. Bronwyn had hidden it at that point, and I was scared, so I gave him the name of Lady Morwenna's maid." She shuddered. "I didn't know they'd kill her. I just didn't want Bronwyn to get caught."

"You wanted to save your own skin, you mean."

She glared at him.

"And hers, I see," he added. "You were protecting your friend."

"We are not friends. Friends do not betray each other."

"What did she do?"

"She and I knew of the plot to help Stephen escape, but not which guards were helping him. I told Rupert a little, teeny, tiny white lie about a plot to kill Stephen on the road after his escape, which led to Stephen's own man ratting him out and the guards being discovered."

"They were gutted and hung out on the parapets. We found them this morning."

Lady Alice stared. "I know. I figured they would be punished. I didn't know they'd be fodder for the crows."

"Let me guess. Bronwyn didn't want you to lie to Rupert?"

"No. She thought it was a bad idea. But she told Rupert about it, and he and I had a falling out. So I told Bronwyn we were done. Our acquaintance is at an end."

"That is a shame. From where I'm standing, you could use a friend right now," he said, crossing his arms over his chest.

Lady Alice snapped, "What do you know about it? You belittle your relationship with her every chance you get. At least I am honest with her and don't toy with her emotions. It is not right, you know, what you are doing. You take her on horse rides and even act like you are courting, then pretend she is nothing to you in public. It is hurtful. It is deceitful, and..." She looked away. Two spots of color rose on her cheeks. "It is not right."

"You disapprove of me. Of our relationship. Because I am a squire and she is a maid."

"I disapprove of your treatment of her. She is more than just a kitchen maid—you know that. So much more. And even if we are not friends now, she... Look. If you are going to do nothing other than be warm and caring toward her one day and cold and rude the next, I'd rather you stay away from her completely, thank you. She's a strong young woman. She'll get over it."

"Quite a defense for someone who isn't your friend."

"Just heed my words, squire." She huffed.

He couldn't think of what to say, so he left.

That evening, he learned from the men that the empress had received word from Henry of Blois, King Stephen's younger brother and the bishop of Winchester, that he had accepted the empress's plans and would call a council at Winchester shortly to discuss her coronation as queen.

The empress's reminder to Theobold stuck in his mind. The empress was in a good mood that evening, which was good for him, as he'd learned nothing more about the culprits behind all of the suspicious activity as of late. But that didn't stop her from asking.

She motioned to him at the evening meal and when he came to her, she asked quietly, "Have you found who killed Sir Edward and Lady Eleanor yet?"

"No, Your Grace. But Mistress Bronwyn and I are working on it."

"Good. And has she done anything suspicious we should be aware of?"

"No, Empress. I believe she is innocent," he told her.

"Very good. I think it was wrong of me to tell you to get close to her. Before he left, de Gernon was full of gossip, saying you two were a romantic pair and that they'd caught you both together in one of my tents at camp. Is that true?"

"Yes, but I was only watching her. She thought she might catch whoever killed Lady Eleanor."

Her fair expression clouded for a moment, the slight pang of pain passing over her noble, feminine features like a raincloud. "I see. Well, there is no need for you to continue your attentions to her, I'd say. When we return from Winchester I had better know more, Theobold."

"Winchester, Your Grace?"

"Yes. You and Sir Robert will accompany me, along with a handful of my men. We go to Winchester to meet with Henry of Blois, the Bishop of Winchester. He has the pope's ear and is pleading my case to have the church formally recognize me as the rightful ruler. There will be a sort of coronation pre-ceremony, ahead of my official coronation in London."

"Yes, Your Grace."

"Do not look so downtrodden, Theobold. I am sure there are as many young ladies to charm in Winchester as there are here. Pack a bag. We leave tomorrow." She motioned for him to leave her.

His heart beat in his throat. He needed to talk to Bronwyn. But how, and what did he say? He thought on this as he looked after his master at dinner and afterward, making sure his master's bags were packed and ready.

Inside his master's room, his thoughts ran wild. He wasn't sure how best to speak to her, which was odd, as she was just a young woman. He'd spoken and charmed young women since he'd turned fourteen. But Bronwyn was different.

It wasn't until he approached his master's bags that he noticed that they were already packed, but badly so. The clothes were so badly stuffed in the bags and hung out, it was a poor servant who'd tried to assist, clearly. They didn't know Sir Robert's preference for tidiness.

Theobold took up the first bag and pulled the jumble of

clothes out, then began folding a spare shirt and jerkin into a bag. His hand brushed against something and he paused. He felt in the folds of the jerkin, brushing against not one, but two wooden handles. Strange. These were like wooden toggles, connected by a strong thread, like wire. He tensed and swallowed. He gingerly picked them up and held them in the light, a lump rising in his throat.

The door to Sir Robert of Gloucester's room opened and in stepped his master. "Oi, Theobold. I meant to say—what is that?" He stared.

There in Theobold's hands, dangled a garrote.

⚜

Chapter Fifteen

THEOBOLD DROPPED THE garrote like it was a snake. "Is this what I think it is?"

"If you mean an implement to kill someone, yes. Why do you have it, boy?" Sir Robert asked.

"I don't. I mean, I found it in your jerkin when I was packing your shirts."

"What?" Sir Robert's eyes widened. "Why? Did you put it there?"

"No. I didn't know what it was until I picked it up."

"What was it doing in my shirt?" Sir Robert asked.

"I don't know. I came in and saw that someone had packed your bags already."

"Who did this?" Sir Robert asked.

Theobold shrugged. "A servant, perhaps? I couldn't say. I pulled the first bag I saw and began redoing it but then felt the handle and took it out to see as you came in. Honest, sir. I wouldn't."

"Where did it come from?"

"Search me."

Sir Robert's face clouded. "Remind me, how did Lady Eleanor die?"

Theobold swallowed. "Bronwyn said she died by a garrote, judging from the hard, red lines on her neck."

"And now we find one amongst my things." He breathed in

noisily. "Someone is playing a dangerous game. They have put this in here, hoping to cast suspicion on me." He shook his head.

"What do we do with it?"

"The garrote? Hide it. Get rid of it. No doubt whoever hid it is hoping it will be found and I'll be labeled as a culprit and blamed for Lady Eleanor's death. Whoever they are. Give it here."

Theobold handed the garrote to him and Sir Robert quickly approached the small stone hearth in his room, then thought better of it. "Come to think of it, let's keep it."

"Why?"

"To use as proof," Sir Robert said. "Someone came in here and planted this. They want me to look the fool and likely thought that like so many other servants, you would be lazy and not notice that someone had packed my bags already. I want to be ready when I am accused of murder."

"Who would want to frame you?" Theobold asked.

"Isn't that what the empress wants you to figure out? You and that maidservant, or kitchen maid, whatever she is. Find out who planted this and you'll have your murderer." Sir Robert's face was grim, and he stroked his short beard. It was brown fading to grey, and bristly.

Theobold took back the garrote and felt revolted at its touch. He didn't want to touch the thing, especially as its thin thread was stained red. He stuffed it in a spare cloth and put that in his shirt.

Sir Robert saw his discomfort. "Remember you are not your family, boy. Their trade is not yours, and it doesn't have to be. You don't need to have any part in it. The empress values you for your sword and your mind, as I do."

Theobold nodded. It still bothered him, to know that a murder weapon was now on his person. He hated it. The garrote was a tool to kill, to murder. A sword and shield were used for defense and had saved his life before. He felt dirty just having touched the garrote.

"As for who might want to ruin my good name, I should

think any of the empress's knights, or Stephen's. But for this, I would say it's only a handful of men. Think of this: Stephen's men are in jail or on their way to Bristol. Sir Ranulf and that new squire of his among them. But even fewer men knew that Lady Eleanor died of a garrote."

"So that means…" Theobold started. "Only those in the tent after her murder could have known."

"Unless Sir Bors was telling the truth, and if there was a second guard there, then he killed the good lady with the garrote and fled, then put it here to frame me. But he'd have needed to know for certain that the empress knew how Lady Eleanor died. So…"

"That means one of the people in the tent with us did it."

"Now you're using your head. Find them, and you'll have your killer."

Theobold packed the rest of Sir Robert's bags and then hurried to the kitchens. Arriving almost breathless, he ran into a cook, who stopped him with a hand. "Oi, what are you doing?"

"I need to speak with Bronwyn. Please, it's important."

The cook grumbled. "All right. But only for a moment. The woman's worn out from cooking for the feast, like the rest of us. She'll be asleep on her feet soon."

"I won't be long." He moved past the cook and approached the familiar feminine shape of Bronwyn, who was wiping down a worktable. "Mistress Baker," he started.

Bronwyn stiffened and turned around. Her expression was frosty. "If you're hungry, there's some leftover bread and a bit of drippings over there."

"That's not why I'm here." He came toward her.

She swallowed and looked up, her rag in her hands.

"I need to talk to you," he said, stopping a few feet away.

"I think you've said enough, don't you?" Her eyes narrowed.

"What do you mean?"

"Lady Alice told me. Apparently, you two are very close, and when she asked if you…" She looked away. "She overheard you saying I was just a servant. A nobody. Just someone the empress told you to get close to because she suspected I knew too much about Lady Eleanor's murder. A silly kitchen maid you were supposed to charm, like any other woman. Is it true?"

His cheeks burned. He noticed her eyes were red. "Have you been crying?"

"Tell me the truth. Is what Lady Alice said true?"

He met her gaze then could bear it no longer and looked away.

Bronwyn stared at him. Her eyes had been so full of hope, but now they filled with unshed tears. Her voice was dull. "So it is. I should have known. Lady Alice wouldn't lie. Not about this." She turned away when Theobold caught her wrist.

"Let go of me," she said.

"Listen to me." He dropped her wrist. "I found the weapon used to kill Lady Eleanor."

"What? Where?" Her eyes darted around, looking to see who had heard.

"I was packing up my master's bags for tomorrow—"

"What's tomorrow?" she asked.

"We go to Winchester, for Empress Maud's pre-coronation ceremony. The men of the church are to recognize her and the nobility are to come. But that's not important. What *is* important is that I found the garrote used to kill Lady Eleanor in my master's things."

"Sir Robert? He did it?" She gave him an incredulous stare.

"No. He found me and was as surprised as I was. I was surprised because his bags were already packed after he asked me at dinner to pack them, and when I went in they were done, but messily. Like someone had just thrown the clothes in. He's always been of a steadfast nature and likes things done a certain way, down to how his bags are packed. Neither he nor I did such a poor job, so when I went to unpack and pack them again properly, I found it."

He felt it, sitting there in the bolt of linen cloth against his skin. His skin started to crawl at the thought of it. An implement of torture, of death. He hated it.

"What does this mean?" she asked.

"Someone wanted it to be found in his things. Perhaps to accuse him later, or if his bags were searched, for it to be found."

"Like Lady Morwenna when she accused Lady Alice of stealing the empress's crown. She was so sure, and she was furious when there was no sign of it."

"Yes, exactly," he said, taking heart at the excited gleam in her eyes. Then he grimaced. He should have known Lady Morwenna was up to more than just foul tricks. "Whoever did it meant to get my master in trouble, but also, they would have had to have known that Lady Eleanor had died by the garrote, and that we knew how she'd died. Otherwise, they'd have planted the weapon for no reason. That means only a small number of people would know—those in the tent when she was found."

"That's a small number of people," Bronwyn said.

"Yes. We're close to figuring it out. But I have to go. We're leaving in the morning."

"You still are set on that? But you can't leave. Not when we're so close to figuring out who did this." She pressed her lips together.

"It's why I wanted to tell you first. So you would know and be on your guard."

"How much time do we have?"

"Not long. The empress already asked me about our progress in finding the culprit. She's given us till her coronation in London," he said. "Bronwyn, I..."

She looked at him, her expression pained. He wanted to do more, to tell her how he felt. How he'd been an idiot, a fool, unquestioningly following his empress's orders to get close to her, and how was in serious danger of losing his heart in the process. He wanted to...

The moment was gone. She huffed, "Well, then, that's your problem to solve. I'm just a simple servant, after all. Safe travels."

She left him.

His shoulders slumped. He wanted to take her hands in his, flour and all. But he didn't dare. Not when she'd been hurt so utterly, again and again. He mentally cursed Lady Morwenna's gossiping tongue, and himself for falling into her traps. By wanting to protect Bronwyn from Lady Morwenna's tormenting, he should have known someone else had been listening. He'd lost her now, possibly forever. "Farewell, Mistress Baker."

He quit the kitchen then, furious with himself with every step. He was a fool, and what was worse, he knew it.

Theobold traveled to Winchester with the empress the next day but learned nothing, and frustration ate away at him. He hardly noticed much, aside from the grey and rainy days that bled from one to another, as March blurred into April. Many times he'd taken a pen to parchment, wanting to write Bronwyn a note, but when he had a quill and parchment before him, ready to take down a word, his powers of persuasion failed him.

He felt like a coward. He, Theobold Durville, tongue-tied at what to write to a young woman. When he could smile and charm any woman between the ages of fifteen and thirty. He didn't understand it. What was this hold the kitchen maid had over him? When he rested his head on his saddlebag at night, her face greeted him, and it was the last lingering thought that dwelled in his dreams when the morning broke.

Winchester was… disappointing. Part of it was the rain that drummed against the oilskin saddlebags and his hooded jerkin, running in rivulets down his back and his horse's legs as they made a slow and steady march through roads that turned to mud.

He had formed part of the empress's entourage as she'd visited with Henry of Blois and paid her respects to the church, but to her surprise, not all the nobility had been there to recognize her in her pre-coronation ceremony.

Theobold had watched quietly as the empress, whilst putting on a polite and serene face in public, took issue with this before the men. She raged and threw objects in private. More than once, he'd had to duck and dodge as crockery dishes, plates, and vases were launched at the walls, shattering against the stone and jangling his nerves. This wasn't a queen, this was an empress, and she was volatile.

Even worse, the treasury she was to inherit was empty. At the time when Henry of Blois had told her, she had laughed and said, *"Is this a joke?"*

The bishop's silence had answered her, and her smile had fallen. As had her goodwill. Theobold had exchanged a knowing look with the other squires as they'd stood by silently, conscious that another rage was coming.

Her courtiers, for there were always some, had been quick to try to placate her. The rain and foul weather had delayed many traveling, especially on the roads from London. But she'd eventually gotten her approval from the church, on the proviso of some deal she'd struck with Henry, and earned her ceremony in Winchester, before dozens of nobility. The London delegation still had not arrived.

On a fine day in April, she wore a fine dress and Theobold wondered what Bronwyn would think of it all, the pomp and ceremony, as she was announced empress and future Queen of England.

The hall filled with the applause and cheers of her knights and noble families. But as Theobold looked around the great hall, he wondered how many of them would actually stand by her. The noble families wore plastered smiles and toasted the empress, but would they still if they knew the treasury was empty, and she'd sent the bishop's own brother to prison?

That night after the ceremony, a feast was held in her honor. Theobold served at table, monitoring his master for anything he might need, and remained quiet as he ignored the admiring looks of the ladies present and the maidservants. He had no interest in their smiles, and it surprised him. After the meal, he took his time to chat with a few and recognized a few not-so-subtle invitations to sneak into some dark corners to steal kisses, but when faced with the possibility, something in him turned cold.

He no longer wished to plant his lips on just any young woman's willing face. He had no interest in their hair, lips, or bodies. He wanted only one: the bright-eyed, frowning face of Bronwyn Blakenhale, whose blonde braid swung like an angry cat's tail when she was angry, and whose eyes flashed when she was annoyed, a thing that happened often. He missed her, he realized. Why had his cousin, Lady Morwenna, had to go and ruin things?

But then, he'd played a part in that and had only himself to blame. Why had he told Lady Morwenna such lies? But he knew why. He just didn't want to admit it out loud.

He was beholden to Lady Morwenna's family, the Banburys, and had been since he'd been a small child. His own family was poor, and what money they did have went to their survival. But his uncle, Lady Morwenna's father, didn't have a son, only daughters, and wanted to do right by him. Their family had connections and sometimes sponsored young men who showed promise, like Theobold, when he'd shown an interest in stepping outside his own family's traditional profession. His uncle had taught him how to serve as a page and when he'd turned nine, introduced him as a potential page to Sir Robert of Gloucester, who had been visiting and as luck would have it, whose page had recently died of illness.

Theobold remembered that night, serving at the table in clothes too big for him, his shoes shuffling, almost slipping as he'd carried wooden trenchers heavily laden with steaming meat, straight from the kitchen. His uncle had arranged the introduction and after serving for the evening, the young knight had turned on the bench and surveyed Theobold.

"How old are you, boy?" the man had asked. He'd had a full, thick beard and had been broad-shouldered.

"Nine."

"Can you fight? Are you strong?"

"Yes." Theobold had curled up an arm to show off his mus-

cles.

The man had grinned. *"Can you ride a horse?"*

Theobold had nodded.

"You'll do." The man had waved him over to fill up his cup of wine and said no more.

The next day, Theobold had been visited by the man on a great horse, who'd told him to bid his family goodbye. His mother had clasped him close to her breast, tearing up, whilst his father had clapped a hand on his shoulder and squeezed. "Be strong, and of good faith, lad. Do what your master says, and you'll see the world."

His sister, Winifred, had shyly watched from the doorway and given him a flower goodbye. He'd lost it in the first week, but whenever he saw the purple tops of thistles, he thought of her.

That had been years ago. He'd aged since then and had visited but rarely. Attracted by the idea of adventure and serving a knight, he'd grown up in the employ of Sir Robert. Once Lady Morwenna had become one of the empress's ladies-in-waiting, and she'd come bearing a missive from her father, his patron, Theobold realized they'd hardly needed to ask. Of course, he would look after her and make sure she settled well into the court. It would do them good to know a family member was nearby if she needed help, and it reminded him of his obligation and debt to his patron.

But the Lady Morwenna at age nineteen was not the same woman as the wide-eyed, black-haired girl he'd known as a child. She was simpering, she was mocking, and even mean. She ordered other people around like servants, when there was no need to, even the fellow ladies-in-waiting at times, and hardly a 'please' or 'thank you' ever passed her lips. And worse, if he showed too much romantic interest toward any one woman, she made their lives miserable. He didn't dare reveal how he cared for Bronwyn. Theobold didn't want to give Lady Morwenna the satisfaction, or see what horrid plans she would plot for her. He liked Bronwyn too much for that. But how to tell Bronwyn? Her hurt expression made no bones about it: she was offended and no doubt angry at him for keeping the empress's orders a secret from her. He wasn't likely to tell her that he'd been instructed to flirt with her and get into her good graces, but he could see why she felt betrayed.

The sharp step and foul cursing of the empress drew his attention away. She cursed a blue streak in French, her native language, and said words he did not know, but he was rather glad he didn't.

She was followed into the private room by Sir Robert, Sir Miles, and a handful of other knights. Theobold stood at attention as she raged and paced the room, her hands clenching and unclenching. She approached Theobold. "Give me your sword."

He unsheathed the blade and handed it over without question.

She took it from his hands and wove it in a large arc, attacking the nearby table. The heavy blade struck the wood with a loud *thunk*, chipping small pieces of wood into the air.

Theobold stiffened and looked at his master, stunned. He rubbed his forehead. The empress might have a right to anything she wanted, but she was damaging his sword and he began to fret. Swords were expensive.

Everyone in the room stared in amazement as the empress hacked and swore, slicing and chopping at the wooden table in her anger. She railed and stabbed at the long table with the sword, which was heavy for her to bear. In moments, she became tired and tossed the sword away, panting. She shouted a swear word and leaned over the table.

Theobold quietly picked up his fallen sword. It wasn't meant to be used as an axe. It hadn't taken any major damage, but he'd need to hone the blade and clean it again for sure.

"Empress?" Sir Robert started.

She looked up.

"If the table offends you, I'm happy to find you a proper axe."

She glared at him, meeting his eyes for a solid minute, then let out a throaty laugh. "No, the table does not offend me. The London nobility does. They have not come to hear me announced as the queen, and it is a grave insult. I am insulted, as should all of you be. Who do they think they are?"

Sir Robert walked toward the pitcher of wine on the table, filling a cup and handing it to her.

She drank thirstily, then set it down. "They also insult me by taking their time. The roads are clear, the rain has all but stopped. Why have they not come? They have missed the ceremony entirely. Did they even mean to show their faces?"

The men were silent. Sir Robert bowed his head, as did Theobold. Silence reigned in the room, when a voice said, "They do not respect you, Empress."

Empress Maud's head snapped toward the sound. "Who said that?"

Sir Miles spoke up. "I did. The fact is they do not believe you are worthy of their respect, so they dally and delay. You need to make them sit up and take notice that you are their rightful queen."

"Yes. But how? I already had my ceremony here."

"Be crowned in London. Make them pay," Sir Miles advised. "Charge them for their loyalty, demand their fealty with a cost to their purses, and they will take you seriously."

Theobold's mouth set in a firm line. That strategy sounded like a good way to make the people of London dislike her.

"Empress, I must disagree. The London nobles are late, but that's no reason to punish them. They will not take kindly to this." Sir Robert said.

"I do not care. They should have treated me with respect if they wanted respect in return. No, Sir Miles is right. They need to be taught a lesson. I will make them pay for their rudeness with every coin they have. I am Queen of the English, and they will recognize my legitimacy." She looked at Sir Robert. "We will be crowned in London. First, let us return to Gloucester and get more men. Then we go to London."

DAYS LATER, IN early May, the empress summoned him. "Theobold. Are you still close with that kitchen maid?"

Bronwyn was never far from his thoughts. "Yes, Empress."

"Good." She rubbed her hands together. The empress's smile was warm, but her eyes were calculating. She gripped a small note in her gloved hand. "I have here a letter from Matilda, Stephen's wife. She writes to beg for her husband's release from prison."

Theobold glanced at his master, Sir Robert, who gave a slight shake of his head. His frown was apparent.

"I will do no such thing," said the empress. "He is a danger and is better off where he is."

Sir Miles stood by, his hands resting behind his back. "A wise decision, Empress. While he lives, he poses a threat to you and all you stand for. The nobles will not respect you unless you show strength. Come down on them hard, demand their respect and their coin, and they will give you their loyalty."

Empress Maud nodded. "I want to give Matilda a little surprise. I will write back and invite her to London, to witness my coronation as rightful ruler. She will not call herself 'queen' for much longer. And having her favorite, little kitchen maid there, seeing her amongst my people, my followers, will be all the better for it. We will travel there for June." She turned to Sir Robert and Sir Miles. "Call the men back from Bristol. Let us make the arrangements for my coronation."

Theobold schooled his face to display no change of emotion. But this did not bode well. For the first time in a long time, fear bloomed in his heart.

Chapter Sixteen

B RONWYN HURRIED TO the castle courtyard to see. The men were returning from Bristol, and she would see Rupert again.

She moved as fast as her feet would take her. But then she stopped. It felt wrong, somehow. For many nights, since he had left for Winchester with the empress, she had thought not of Rupert, but of Theobold. But her lips pursed in a frown. The very thought of him annoyed her.

He had hurt her so, more than once. Theobold was hard to follow. Warm and caring one moment, and cruel and harsh the next. He seemed to value her opinion, and had even asked for her help in finding out who killed Lady Eleanor and Sir Edward. So why would he go to such trouble to seek her out and spend time with her, only to declare she meant nothing to him? It pained her worse than eating bad fish. But then of course, he'd only taken an interest in her because the empress had ordered it. That hurt more than anything, to know that he had been fake all along.

She stood in the shadows as the column of men entered the courtyard. The air filled with sound as grooms, stableboys, pages, and porters came out to meet them. She was glad she stayed back, for Lady Morwenna walked out, followed by her fellow ladies-in-waiting, Lady Alice among them.

The ladies stood not ten feet from where Bronwyn watched, talking amongst themselves. Lady Morwenna said, "Well you must be excited, Lady Alice. You'll see your squire again. Although why you lower yourself to dally with a mere squire, I'll never understand."

One of the ladies tittered at this. Lady Alice's cheeks turned pink.

Bronwyn noticed Lady Alice held her tongue. Why was that? She was normally quick to respond, especially to perceived slights and insults.

"But then perhaps he has forsaken you. I did see him talking with that kitchen maid Bronwyn before he left," Lady Morwenna said. "And I saw them walking together more than once before we came to Gloucester. Perhaps he has thought of *her* on those chilly nights instead of you."

Lady Alice said nothing and stared straight ahead.

"In my family's household, no servant in her right mind would dare show her interest in a man I fancied. But then, he will be a knight someday, and soon. There's no clear sign that will ever happen for your dear Rupert. And I heard that now he serves his old master in Stephen's court *and* Sir Ranulf. Is he hoping that one will raise him to be a knight if the other doesn't?" She laughed. "But I suppose we shouldn't begrudge you an idle fancy. Theobold is handsome, at least. Do you know, I once told a servant that if she kept talking to Theobold, she would catch the pox? She ran away that day and it took five servants to convince her to return. She wouldn't even go near him if he was nearby." Lady Morwenna giggled. "Stupid girl. At least she knew better than to try her luck with him again."

Bronwyn's eyes widened. Maybe it was a good thing that Theobold didn't fancy her. If he had, she'd have to put up with Lady Morwenna's jibes and intrigues, and they could be deadly.

"You fancied Theobold the squire?" Lady Susanna asked.

"No, of course not." Lady Morwenna avoided Lady Susanna's gaze. "He is simply a pretty face, and we grew up together as cousins. He is indebted to my family for arranging his position with Sir Robert of Gloucester. He has long admired me, but he is only a squire, so he is not worth my time. Once he becomes a knight, however, then I will consider his suit."

"Has he made you an offer of marriage?" Lady Alice asked.

For a second, Lady Morwenna's look was like daggers before she was smiling thinly. "No, not yet. But he will, once I give him a sign that I will accept him. He's only waiting for the right time."

Bronwyn's shoulders slumped. No. If what Lady Morwenna said was true, he was *her* champion and always had been. Bronwyn had no business thinking of him in that way. And for a second time, a man she'd had hopes for in fact fancied another woman. Maybe she should swear off love entirely and become a nun.

She stood by and watched as the knights, men at arms, and squires returned with the empress's carriage in the company. Men stood at attention, weapons ready, as Sir Miles escorted the empress from her carriage. Sir Robert stood by with their squires.

"Oh, there he is," Lady Morwenna said excitedly.

Sure enough, Theobold, moving slowly with fatigue, his black curls disheveled and clothes wrinkled, took up a place not far from his master and stood at the ready.

"And look, there're the men from Bristol. They must have followed the empress from the main road. Lady Alice, where's that squire of yours?" Lady Morwenna asked.

Bronwyn watched Lady Alice closely. Something was wrong with her, but she couldn't tell what.

"He's not my squire," Lady Alice said flatly.

"Oh, right, of course. You two had a falling out, I heard. What a shame, considering how close he is with that kitchen maid. But then I always say, like attracts like. If he's choosing to spend his time walking with her rather than with you, you shouldn't waste your time."

Lady Alice turned and saw Bronwyn watching, and her eyes widened. She whirled back around, raising her chin. Her shoulders were stiff, as if expecting an attack, and Bronwyn knew better than to try to say anything.

Bronwyn wanted to go to her, reassure her, but a part of her also felt pleasure at Lady Morwenna's words. So Lady Morwenna had learned that Lady Alice and Rupert had parted ways. Did that mean it was okay for Bronwyn to tell Rupert how she felt about him? Her mind raced, searching for an answer. How *did* she feel about him? She touched the wooden frame of the doorway she hid by, watching. She wanted to feel something solid, as her feet felt unsteady beneath her, mirroring her thoughts.

Did she still care for Rupert? She felt like to express her fondness for him would betray Lady Alice, even though they had most recently fought. Were they even still friends? Had they ever been? Lady Alice seemed to think not. So were they acquaintances? She didn't know.

As the men followed the empress through the courtyard and into the castle, Theobold was looking around for someone, as was Rupert.

Lady Morwenna embraced Theobold, whilst Lady Alice went to greet Rupert, a big smile on her face. Both young men reacted warmly, which sent a dagger through Bronwyn's heart.

She kept to the shadows and slunk away to the kitchen. She'd talk to the young men later. She didn't want to see their romantic embraces with other women.

The next day, Bronwyn spotted Rupert and Lady Alice walking together, their heads close together. Lady Alice seemed animated; Rupert did not. Lady Alice caught Bronwyn's eye and touched Rupert's arm, her eyes never leaving Bronwyn's.

THE FOLLOWING AFTERNOON, Bronwyn spotted Lady Alice and Rupert together again, and the day after that. She grew sick of seeing them together. If it wasn't seeing them looking happy and in love, it was seeing Theobold and Lady Morwenna walking together, arm in arm.

She tapped a foot angrily. She'd seen Theobold around and yet he had made no move to speak with her. Not a single word as to whether he'd learned anything about the murders since they'd last spoken. It riled her, but not as much as seeing Lady Morwenna laughing and wrapping her hands around his arm.

Bronwyn stayed in the castle kitchens and rose only to do her work. She wanted to figure out who had been in the empress's tent during the night of Lady Eleanor's murder and thought on it whilst making rolls, skinning animals, and stirring soups. Anything to take her mind off of the loving couples who strolled the castle grounds, laughing and talking together.

She felt so alone. She had no friends. Her family, if they still lived, was likely hundreds of miles away in Lincoln, and she had no one whom she could trust. She longed to have someone to whom she could speak honestly, and bare her soul. But she didn't. All she had was herself to rely on, her mind, her wit, and the baking skills her family had instilled in her. She would solve Lady Eleanor's and Sir Edward's murders—and Mabel's, too, since it probably had not been an accident. Lady Eleanor had been so kind to her when they'd met; she couldn't bear to see their murderer go unpunished.

She thought. That night, there had been herself, Theobold, Sir Bors, Lady Eleanor, Sir Robert, Sir Ranulf, and Sir Miles in that tent. Sir Bors had said that he'd found Lady Eleanor attempting to steal the crown for herself and tried to stop her, when he'd been hit over the head by a guard.

But if what the empress had said was to be believed, and there was no reason Bronwyn should not believe her in this, then Lady Eleanor had been innocent, and she would have no reason to steal. Had she simply been in the wrong place at the wrong time? Why would she have gone to the tent?

Something must have caught her attention. She might have gone in there to hide during the battle, or to look for the empress. For whatever reason, she had been there. So why had Sir Bors been there? Had he been telling the truth, and he'd caught Lady Eleanor trying to steal? But the empress seemed to mistrust his account, and with one guard dead and another gone, there was no way to tell what had really happened.

Then the person had killed Lady Eleanor with a garrote and stowed it away in Sir Robert of Gloucester's saddlebags, to possibly be found later. That seemed like a calculated move, for if the person had wanted to dispose of the garrote, they could have easily dropped it in a ditch somewhere long before that day. They must have had reason to want to discredit Sir Robert, but what? The only reason she could think of was that he had the empress's ear, and by discrediting him in her eyes, that would leave the avenue open for another person to gain prominence in her circle of advisors.

She was returning from the privy, her eyes on the stone walls, when a familiar set of ladylike slippered feet matched her pace. Bronwyn looked up.

Lady Alice said, "Come with me." She took Bronwyn's hand and led her into a small alcove. It was only a small area, cut away into the stone, that offered a place to stand by a slim window, but it offered a scant bit of privacy. The view of Gloucester an impressive sight, even from the narrow window. But Lady Alice wasn't minding the view.

Lady Alice said, "Lady Morwenna has been telling tales. At first I didn't believe it, but…… she seeks to make me believe that Rupert likes you, and you like him. This is nothing more than childish japes, of course. I told her it's a load of nonsense, but she laughs and is like a viper. Tell me, is there any truth to her words?"

Bronwyn met her gaze. Lady Alice bit her nails, then caught herself doing it and brushed down her skirts, plucking at stray lint that wasn't there. Her jet-black hair hung loose and lovely around her shoulders, and her expression was alert and wary.

"I care for him," Bronwyn finally said.

"I know. You are good friends. He told me so himself."

Bronwyn swallowed. "And you two are…"

"We made up over our little squabble." She stepped closer. "Bronwyn. I know he and I are of different worlds apart, but I… like him. I care for him too, but not just as a friend, like you do.

And I don't want him getting the wrong idea. The very thought of you two together is laughable. A squire, well on his way to becoming a knight, and a kitchen maid? The idea is ridiculous."

Bronwyn's mouth opened, but the words she wanted to say died on her tongue. She closed her mouth again. She felt cowed, and hurt, and even more alone. "I thought you wanted to talk to me in private so we could be friends again."

"I couldn't be friends with someone whom I can't trust. No, I'm simply letting you know that we are together again, and I don't want you getting the wrong idea about him. Rupert and I are together, and that's that."

Bronwyn walked away.

"Don't walk away from me. Come back," Lady Alice called, but Bronwyn had had enough. She'd stepped into the alcove, wanting to find her friend again. Instead, she'd been met with distrust and insults. She'd figure this mystery out on her own. Maybe she didn't need friends, after all.

That didn't stop Lady Alice, however. The next day, Lady Alice sent for her specifically, to deliver a set of pastries to her in the castle courtyard. Bronwyn went, plate in hand, to find Rupert and Lady Alice kissing on a bench, Lady Alice's hands in his reddish-golden hair.

The roll Bronwyn had munched on her way there felt like ash on her tongue. She stood by, feeling useless, then set the plate down on the ground beside the bench. They could help themselves. She wasn't going to stand there watching. Just being there pained her.

"Oh. Sorry, I didn't see you there," Lady Alice said, smiling. Her cheeks were rosy and her skirts were in slight disarray as she entwined her hand with Rupert's.

He grinned at her, his hair mussed, then blinked at Bronwyn. "You brought rolls?"

"Lady Alice ordered them."

"Why bring them yourself? Surely, a page could've done it."

Bronwyn raised an eyebrow at Lady Alice, who giggled.

"Thank you, Bronwyn. That will be all." Her aristocratic tone was so clipped and overly formal, Bronwyn couldn't stand it. She walked away, fuming the entire time back to the kitchen.

As she passed by, Bronwyn spotted some of the other ladies giggling at the scene. Her cheeks turned pink. She'd not only had to witness Rupert and Lady Alice kissing in a public space, but her humiliation at being ordered around had been seen by others. For once, she wished for a bit of privacy, or that the earth might swallow her up, just for a few moments.

But soon it was nearing the end of May, and she was no closer to figuring out who was behind the deaths. She felt stumped. She wanted to talk to Rupert, Theobold, or even Lady Alice, but felt they were all too involved with their romances to spare time to see her.

Theobold had avoided her since he'd returned, and when she did see him, Lady Morwenna was not far away. Soon, Bronwyn took to avoiding him and instead welcomed her time in the kitchens. It was different each day. She learned new things about cooking, cleaning, and food preparation, and it kept her busy for hours at a time. Part of her mind gave her a treacherous thought. She could just forget about it all. The mystery of Lady Eleanor's, Sir Edward's, and Mabel's deaths could just fade away like a bad dream. There was enough to be getting on with, after all, what with the empress's plan to go to London.

But the plot to poison Empress Maud's crown bothered her and kept her up at night. She wanted to know who would have taken it upon themselves to kill a kind woman, and then steal and later poison a crown. It wasn't right.

She was stripping a chicken's carcass of feathers, when a familiar voice cut into her thoughts.

"Mistress Baker, I've been thinking…" Theobold's low gravelly voice said.

She looked up. "Oh. Hullo."

He blinked, as if surprised she hadn't noticed him. "You are preoccupied, I see. I won't trouble you."

"No, stay," she said. She knew she should be mad at him, but she couldn't help it. She still liked him and wanted him there, even if they just talked about murder. "I'm thinking. What were you going to say?"

"Only about this business with the crown. We'll need to figure it out in time for her coronation in a few days if Empress Maud is to safely have her coronation in London."

"You will, you mean." Her posture was stiff, her tone sharp. He hadn't come to her before and now he wanted her help. She let out a small sigh.

"Uh, no. You will too. You don't—" He glanced at her, eyes widening. "No one told you. The empress is taking a retinue to London, and you're to be part of the company. She specifically wants you amongst them. I forgot to say." His arms hung at his sides.

"Me? Go to London?" She paused, the chicken in her hands.

"Yes."

"But why? I'm nobody."

"I..." He gave a little sigh. "The empress knows that Stephen's wife will be present. She wants to flaunt you and others in front of her, to show her supporters."

Her brow wrinkled. Would she always be a pawn to be used by others? "That seems unkind."

"This is war, Bronwyn. War isn't kind, or caring, or compassionate. The sooner you come to understand that, the sooner you'll comprehend your place in it all." His voice was curt.

She leaned away from him slightly. "Did I offend you somehow?"

He ran a calloused hand through his dark curls. "No. Can we talk about this whilst you're not holding a chicken?"

She set it down.

"There's something I need to tell you," he said, leaning closer. His voice had grown quiet, his eyes warm.

"About what?" Her breath hitched.

His eyes darted to her lips, her throat.

"Theobold, there you are. I need you. Right now." Lady Morwenna's voice carried across the kitchen.

Bronwyn looked across to see Lady Morwenna sniffing and holding her nose in the air, staring and turning her nose up at the servants as they worked. She wore a pretty, green dress and approached them. "Oh, Bronwyn, how good of you to be already preparing for our dinner. Mind you roast it good and tender—I do love chicken. But none of your spices in it; I hate seasoning." She touched Theobold's arm. "Theobold, come. There is a private matter we need to discuss."

"What is that?" he asked.

"It's private, and I would not have the kitchen maids listening to our affairs. Now, will you come or not?"

Theobold let out a small sigh and followed her out. He glanced back once at Bronwyn, catching her eye, then left.

Bronwyn picked up the chicken and resumed her plucking. London. Another great city in England. Another adventure and yet...... She didn't want to go. She felt comfortable here, and she didn't want to go be a part of the empress's scheme. But she was getting sick of seeing all the happy couples around her. Maybe a change of scenery would do her good.

An older cook came over, an average-sized woman with grey hair cut short and a heavily lined face. "Those friends of yours always treat this kitchen like it's their own dining hall. Tell them to keep out, especially Lady Morwenna. She's a nasty one."

"They're not my friends."

"Pft. That squire Theobold comes in here most days, looking for you, even if he don't say so. And I even seen that squire who's romancing Lady Alice; he's come around here too looking around."

"When was this?" She froze, feathers falling from her fingers. Rupert and Theobold had both come looking for her and she hadn't been here? A part of her cringed.

"When you were out tending the castle gardens and gathering herbs. I heard what that Theobold said. So you'll be joining the servants going to London. That's a treat. You'll enjoy that."

"What's it like?"

"London? Unlike anything you've ever seen. People every-where. Animals, churches, streets that wind around alleys and walkways and the food…" The cook smiled. "You'll enjoy it. Just remember to come back and tell me all about it."

They chatted a bit more about London. Bronwyn kept an eye out for Theobold, but he never returned, much to her regret.

In a few days' time, Bronwyn rose at dawn and joined the retinue of knights, men-at-arms and fighters, along with ladies-in-waiting and other chosen servants, to begin the trek from Gloucester to London.

She yawned, squinting in the early morning light. The season had changed and now it was June. They walked, and it was a long train of people, making periodic stops along the way. But then the ground changed. Gone were the wonderful shaded woodlands of Lincoln and winding roads and hills she'd come to know so well. These were replaced with wet, damp marshland and rivers, and firm, hard-packed roads that were dry on some days and thick with mud the next.

She saw a great many people, travelers, who stood off to the side as the roads cleared of people to watch the party's arrival. Her feet were tired and sore from days of walking with little rest, but they entered through a large, stone gate and passed through the great walls of the city.

It was so loud, and full of people, much more so than Lincoln, where she'd grown up. The buildings were so numerous, they were practically stacked on top of each other, and the streets were filled with people, animals, refuse, and the smell.

Bronwyn wrinkled her nose at the smells, which once had been as familiar to her as breathing, and the sounds of city living, but this was like two-fold what she'd known and had expected.

Some people cheered; others were quiet. It was not every day an empress rode in the streets of London and yet from the people's glowering faces, Bronwyn wasn't sure how welcome they were.

They walked through the city, stopping eventually in a place called Westminster, to take residence in the palace. Apparently, it had been constructed less than one hundred years earlier by Edward the Confessor, along with a grand abbey, called Westminster Abbey.

Bronwyn looked up at the fine stone walls and impressive glass windows. She had been in awe since they'd arrived, but to be here, in London, it was like out of her wildest dreams. She had never left Lincoln before this year and now in just a few months, she had seen Gloucester and now London. What a feat.

But that evening, as she and the other servants worked with the castle staff to prepare for a feast, Bronwyn was called over by one of the cooks. "You're Bronwyn?" The cook, a beefy man with thick, brawny arms, looked her over.

"Yes."

"The empress wants you to serve at table tonight. You're to serve her ladies-in-waiting."

"Me? Why?" she squeaked. The idea of serving in front of so many people made her nervous, and yet she remembered Theobald's words of warning. This was all part of the empress's game to put her on display before Queen Matilda.

She didn't like the idea of being used but didn't have a reason to refuse, nor did she feel she could do so. "All right."

In a few hours when the food was ready, Bronwyn removed her apron and unbound her hair, brushed herself down and helped carry in a platter of meat and bread, freshly baked.

As soon as she'd entered the grand dining hall of the palace, she felt eyes on her. She carried the platter with both hands, conscious of the strands of damp, blond hair that stuck against her cheeks.

She followed the pages and servants to the tables and set the platter down on a table. The tables were arranged in the shape of a horseshoe, with the empress and her men at the center. On either side sat ladies-in-waiting, knights, and some faces she did not recognize, likely members of the nobility.

Jugglers walked around the room juggling, musicians played lutes and pipes in light, playful music nearby, whilst people talked and laughed. There was a light atmosphere in the room, but this was no ordinary party, for armed guards stood posted at the entrance and at the exits, with spears at the ready.

"Well, well. If it isn't Bronwyn Blakenhale, here to grace us with her presence, straight from the kitchens." Lady Morwenna smirked.

Bronwyn looked up.

Lady Morwenna sat beside Lady Alice and Lady Susanna, with others looking on. Bronwyn felt their eyes rake up and down her dress, her hair, and finding her wanting. But a fire kindled her in belly, and her spirit rose. She cocked her head and stared at Lady Morwenna's mouth.

"What are you looking at?" Lady Morwenna asked loudly.

"You have food stuck in your teeth."

The ladies giggled and tittered behind their hands, and Lady Morwenna's face turned red. Her eyes narrowed, her mouth pursed, and she quickly took a large swallow of her wine. She pushed the empty cup at Bronwyn. "Get me a drink."

Bronwyn fetched a pitcher from a passing servant who carried two and poured a fresh cup for Lady Morwenna. She felt their eyes on her and didn't dare react, but when her gaze lifted to see Lady Alice, she was pleased to see her former friend smile.

She took a place behind the ladies as the knights began to slowly pound their fists on the table—first just a simple thud, a pound, and then it increased. With the thudding and the thumping, the tables jostled and bounced beneath the force of the knights' fists, drinks jumped and spilled, and platters shook. The men didn't care. The sound increased in speed and volume, until it was a loud thumping, thunderous, a cacophony of noise as the men cried out Empress Maud's name.

Empress Maud grinned and slowly rose to her feet, taking a moment to enjoy the attention. As the pounding stopped, she raised a hand and began a speech about why they were here.

Bronwyn looked about the room. Beside the empress sat Sir Robert of Gloucester, Sir Ranulf de Gernon, as well as Sir Bors and Sir Miles. Behind them stood Rupert and Theobold, ready to serve.

She reflected on this. The same people who had been present when Lady Eleanor had been found dead, and when Sir Edward had presented the poisoned crown which had killed him. She felt more than ever that the secret lay behind one of them. But who would want to steal a crown and then poison it?

Lady Morwenna motioned for her to bring more wine, and Bronwyn poured her a fresh cup. Lady Susanna said, "Lady Morwenna, you should slow down. You'll get drunk if you're not careful."

"What do I care about that? You should have a care more for yourself and stop sticking your nose in other people's business. Don't think I haven't noticed where you've been going off to. You should be glad I don't tell the empress about your little dalliances."

Lady Susanna's face clouded. "You said you wouldn't—"

"And I won't, provided you stop fretting about everyone around you. Stop worrying. Everything will be fine." Lady Morwenna drank her wine.

Bronwyn felt her eyebrows rise. So Lady Susanna was seeing someone as well. Was everyone finding true love but her? She gave her head a tiny shake and got back to work, serving as often as the ladies wanted.

At one point, Lady Alice dropped a knife on the floor. "Bronwyn, pick that up for me."

Lady Morwenna grinned.

Bronwyn went to her side, when Lady Alice turned her head and murmured, "You should speak to Lady Susanna alone. She often stays late at church after Mass."

Bronwyn picked up the knife. Why would Lady Alice tell her this, unless she thought it useful? What did Lady Susanna know, and could it be related to the murders? And why was Lady Alice involving her again in court politics?

"Wipe it clean and give it here. I've no time for you to fetch another," Lady Alice said.

Bronwyn did as she asked and stood back. The evening passed quickly. She purposefully did not look over at Rupert or Theobold, who both served the knights, just a few feet away. If they wished to speak to her, then they would have to make the first move. She would not be going to them.

After the meal had ended, she'd helped clear away empty platters, and returned with more wine from the cellar, Bronwyn passed by Theobold in the corridor. They did not speak, but he eyed her and opened his mouth, as if he wished to say something.

Well, she thought, *if he has nothing to say, then neither do I.* She kept walking and continued to supply the guests, particularly Lady Morwenna, with wine. Lady Morwenna burped and belched loudly, wavering in her seat. She lurched at Theobold as he passed by and crashed to the floor.

Lady Alice looked on in dismay, as did Lady Susanna. Theobold rushed to help her up, and Lady Morwenna babbled in his face, making him frown. He looked at the ladies. "I need to help her to her bed. Where is it?"

"I'll help her." Lady Alice rose.

"Uh, I need the privy. A chamber pot. Anything." Lady Morwenna grabbed the empty wine jug Bronwyn was holding and vomited into it, loudly.

Bronwyn stepped back and let her retch. Theobold helped her stand, and with Lady Alice, they took Lady Morwenna's arms and led her from the room.

The funny thing was, this caused little upset from the others. The empress chatted with her knights gaily and the men and women began to rise, to dance. The music grew louder, and Bronwyn turned to leave, gingerly picking up the now-used wine jug from the floor, holding it at arm's length.

"Bronwyn," Rupert said behind her. "Dance with me."

She looked at him. "Rupert? I'm a little busy…"

"Yes, picking up a wine jug filled with bile. It will wait. Come dance with me."

"I don't know the dances." Her heart beat in her throat.

"Yes, you do. They're the same ones you'll have grown up with."

"I never really danced as a child."

"Don't be silly. Every child dances, at some point."

Bronwyn faced him.

He touched his hair and met her eyes with a smile. "You are out of excuses."

She swallowed and looked up at him.

His eyes twinkled and he held out a hand. She took it, and they moved around the tables to join a set of other dancers.

He was right. They were group dances that she knew from a younger age. The music was better and the men and women were dressed finer than her stepmother and father had been in the bakery when they'd taught her how to dance, but they hadn't neglected her schooling very much. Her stepmother had been sure that the key to a man's heart was through his stomach and had been keen to teach Bronwyn to become a very good baker. But failing that, she'd needed to learn to dance, and move, and with a pretty step and a sense for timing, she might also attract a man.

Such had been her stepmother's hope, long ago. But that had been before Lincoln had fallen to Empress Maud's men.

Rupert led her in the dance, and she soon lost herself in the row of dancers, moving to and fro. As they clasped hands, her heart raced. His fingers, so warm and gentle, almost seemed to caress hers. She blushed and worried he might see. If he noticed, she'd say it was the wine, or the heat from the fire.

He turned her in a circle and said, "I think you've been avoiding me."

"I haven't." Her voice rose.

"You have."

"You've been busy. Everywhere I go, I see you and Lady Alice together. I don't want to disturb you."

He smiled. "She is very beautiful. I can't believe how lucky I am, that a woman of her rank… fancies me. I'd never have expected it. Not in my wildest dreams."

He was a man in love, Bronwyn realized, and a part of her heart seemed to crumble in regret. She'd been falling for and admiring a young man who was in love with someone else. It pained her, and she felt as if clouds had cast a shadow over her heart, when just being with Rupert had felt like dancing with the sun.

She smiled faintly. "I'm glad you are happy."

"I am. But that's not why I asked you to dance. I mean, I've wanted to dance with you, but… I wanted to tell you something that occurred on the road."

"What's that?"

"I was traveling to Bristol Castle with King Stephen—" He looked around and lowered his voice in case he was overheard. "With Stephen and his men, including my master, as well as the knight I now serve."

"Sir Ranulf?"

"Yes. On the way, Sir Ranulf seemed pleased with himself, and once we got back and were all in the empress's private chamber, he asked Theobold if he had gotten any further with the investigation about the empress's crown. Especially whether he knew about the garrote used to kill Lady Eleanor."

She breathed in through her nose. Her chest felt tight. "Oh? What did he say?"

"Theobold put him off. Sir Ranulf seemed amused at this but wouldn't say why. Time grows short, Bronwyn. I do not think Theobold had an answer to give, so I wanted to ask you. Who do you think did it?"

Conscious that they were surrounded by others, she gave a slight shake of her head. "I do not know."

"Well, I know something that might help."

"What's that?"

"When I was traveling, I rode with the healer's assistant. We came to know one another during the journey and he told me about when their stores had been broken into, back in Gloucester. He told me about how the monkshood had been stolen. What he said was so strange was the scent of the scene."

"What scent?"

"He said that even though some jars and pots had been disturbed and broken, the tent had smelled like roses. But they don't often use roses in their medicines, as that's more for cosmetics and dyes. And roses are out of season. So…"

"So we find out who wears a rose scent, and we'll have our thief." Bronwyn smiled for the first time that day. "Rupert, I could kiss you."

He started. His gaze dropped to her lips.

Bronwyn blushed. "Sorry, I meant—"

Lady Alice's voice cut through their exchange. "I think you can leave that to me, thank you."

⚜

Chapter Seventeen

Bronwyn cringed and shuffled her feet. "Sorry. I was just excited."

Lady Alice sniffed, her dark eyes wary. "Go back to the kitchens, Bronwyn. They need you. You shouldn't be dancing here, anyway. Not when there's work to be done." She smiled sweetly, but her eyes were like daggers.

Bronwyn nodded and backed away, happy to let Lady Alice take her place. She was too excited to care. She needed to act, but then she bumped into a wall of hard muscle. "Oh." She whirled around.

Theobold's expression was suspicious. "Dancing, Mistress Baker? And here I thought you didn't dance. Or maybe you just choose not to dance with me."

"What?"

"You don't remember? I asked you to dance the night of the bonfire, and instead, I found you... elsewhere." His eyes narrowed.

"I'm sorry."

"Don't be. I'm just glad I know the truth now. It's not that you dislike dancing—you just had a different dance partner in mind. Far be it from me to get in the way of your happiness." He voice was gravelly, his expression stone. His dark eyes were filled with hurt, when Lady Susanna touched his arm.

"Theobold, I should love to dance. Will you dance with me?"

she asked.

"Gladly." He turned his back on Bronwyn.

Bronwyn heard Lady Alice laugh, and walked away, darting around whirling couples and back out around the tables again.

"Oh, Bronwyn, don't forget to take the jug Lady Morwenna was sick in," Lady Alice called.

Bronwyn's cheeks heated and she ignored Lady Alice, keeping her back straight and her head held high. Laughter followed her, but she didn't care. She felt embarrassed enough, anyway, although not by Lady Alice's dismissal.

Rupert had looked shocked when she'd made that slip of the tongue and said she could kiss him. Physically shocked, as if the very idea was unheard of. Was she so repulsive? Was the very thought of kissing her so horrible? And yet it had been an innocent slip of the tongue, for her mind did not dwell on him, but on the murder, rose scent, and Theobold.

She'd hurt his feelings, but knowing him, he would soon have another admirer on his arm already, if Lady Susanna's attentions toward him were any indication.

That evening, there was no more investigating to be done, as she had no desire to spy on the lovers. She waited until the dancing ended and people dispersed, then helped clean up, happy to have something to do. She would have wanted to tell Theobold what she'd learned from Rupert but was too mad at him, and she wanted to be sure. Lady Morwenna had stolen the poison, she was sure of it. But then why had Lady Alice suggested she spy on Lady Susanna?

The next day, she slipped out of the kitchens and went to Mass. Bronwyn wasn't the most religious or devout woman, but she did believe in God, and since the fall of Lincoln, had prayed most nights that she might see her family again.

She hung back and waited for people to leave, having spotted and watched Lady Susanna through most of the service. As Lady Susanna stayed longer than most of the parishioners, her head bowed in prayer, Bronwyn came to stand behind her.

"Lady Susanna," she whispered.

Lady Susanna's head shot up. She turned. "What do you want?"

"To speak with you. Lady Alice said—"

"Oh, not you too. You've come to tease me as well, eh? Laugh at me for my choice of lover? Well, don't bother. I get enough torment from facing Lady Morwenna each day."

Bronwyn cleared her throat. "No, I don't know anything about that. "I thought you might be able to help me."

"With what?"

"Find out who might have killed Lady Eleanor."

Lady Susanna's face grew long in regret. "I did like her. She was so kind. Do you know, when I first arrived, I could barely string two sentences together in French, and she spent time teaching me so I wouldn't make a fool out of myself? I'll never forget it. Especially when she might have preferred to go walking with her man."

"Sir Edward."

"Yes. It's a horrible shame what happened to him."

"Were you there?"

"Yes. I saw the whole thing." She repressed a shudder. "I don't want to think about that."

Then why had Lady Alice said to talk to her, Bronwyn wondered. She pressed on. "Lady Susanna, do you know something about what happened that night, to Lady Eleanor?"

The other young woman paused.

Bronwyn was about to speak, when Lady Susanna said, "I don't see why I should tell you. You go around asking a lot of questions. Why is that?"

"Because I want to find out who did it."

"To what end?"

"So that Lady Eleanor didn't die in vain. Is that not enough?"

"Is that all? It's not to attract Theobold?"

Bronwyn shook her head. "He doesn't care for me. He's Lady Morwenna's man."

Lady Susanna snickered. "No, he's not."

"What do you mean?"

Lady Susanna was about to turn and face her, a wide-eyed grin on her face, when a monk walked past, watching her. She turned back to face front and said quietly, "Lady Morwenna likes Theobold. She always has. And she makes it as though she has a claim on him, but she's playing him false."

"How?"

"She's not interested in him at all. Or if she is, she's hardly showing it. She's bragged about seeing another man. An older one." Lady Susanna covered her mouth, as if it were a great secret.

Bronwyn wondered, what about Lady Morwenna's teasing about Lady Susanna's lover? Could this be her taking a bit of revenge? "What do you know about him? Was he involved in Lady Eleanor's death?"

"All I know is that when the battle broke out that night in the camp, Lady Morwenna knew it was happening. The rest of us huddled together for protection and shelter, but she ran out. I went after her and saw she'd gone to the empress's tent."

So Lady Morwenna *had* been there.

"And Lady Eleanor?"

"She wasn't there. Lady Morwenna went in, and then Lady Eleanor came to check on us, and went to see after Lady Morwenna. That was the last I saw of her." Lady Susanna sniffed. "She was so kind to us all. Life at court isn't easy, you know."

"So Lady Eleanor and Lady Morwenna were in the tent."

"I suppose so."

"Did you see the guards who were there?"

"There was only one guard."

"How do you know that?"

"It was something I overheard in passing; some of the men were discussing the guards needed to be put to better use. One man said, 'There's naught but her clothing and bedding in that tent; she doesn't need a retinue of guards for that. One will do.'

And the other man agreed and said he'd make the arrangements."

"Who was it you heard?"

"I couldn't say. They sounded familiar, but I didn't know who, sorry."

Bronwyn asked, "And Lady Morwenna wears a rose perfume, does she not?"

"Yes. How did you know?" Lady Susanna cocked her head.

Whilst this wasn't new information, hearing it from another source was interesting. Lady Morwenna had been in the tent when Lady Eleanor had died, and she most likely had broken into the stores of the healer. But why?

For love, Bronwyn realized. "Who was Lady Morwenna's lover?"

Lady Susanna simpered. "That's the odd thing, I don't know. She would talk about him but was secretive; she wouldn't say his name. Only that he was very high up in the empress's camp among the trusted men. I thought she meant Theobold, but she denied it was him."

So Bronwyn needed to figure out who Lady Morwenna was seeing. She had taken serious risks, and all for what? To please her lover, but why would he have her do such things? Was she acting alone or was she playing a part in a greater scheme? And why had she been dangling from the stone that morning back in Gloucester? Had she tripped, or had her lover pushed her?

"Thank you, Lady Susanna."

"Don't thank me. I hope you find out whoever did this. And Bronwyn?"

Bronwyn paused, halfway up out of her seat.

"Lady Morwenna isn't all bad. She just has a certain way of doing things and her own particular view of the world. She doesn't mean to be unkind."

Except when she's stealing, accusing Lady Alice of theft of the crown she may have planted herself, or teasing others for their romantic affairs, Bronwyn thought. She thanked Lady Susanna and left.

⸙

Chapter Eighteen

THE NEXT DAY, Bronwyn woke up. Her pallet of straw was different somehow, even though she lay on the floor and shared a room with other women servants. She rubbed dried sleep from her eyes and yawned, staring up at the ceiling, comprised of heavy, wooden rafters.

The sounds of the other maidservants sleeping, their slight snores and heavy breathing, deep in slumber, made her stay quiet. Then she realized, they were in London, at Westminster Palace, where the night before, the empress had been enjoying a great feast. She wanted to tell Theobold everything that she'd learned and had confirmed, but she was still mad at him. And…… considering their history, she wasn't sure he would believe her when she revealed Lady Morwenna's guilt. What if he turned on her? He could. That more than anything kept Bronwyn from going to tell him immediately.

Bronwyn quietly rose, fixed her braid, pulled on her shoes, shed her thin blanket, and crept around the sleeping bodies of the maids and cooks, tiptoeing until she slipped out the door of their room.

She joined the cooks and staff who were up in the early hours for a quick bite to eat, then set about the day's baking. Word came down from the empress that she wanted sweet white rolls made with honey, which Bronwyn immediately remembered as Queen Matilda's favorite. The games were already starting, she realized.

She baked the sweet rolls as asked and put them on a plate, with word to a page to deliver them directly. He returned ten minutes later, saying the empress wanted her to make more for midday, and to bring them herself to Empress Maud at the palace, in the great hall.

Bronwyn's eyebrows knit. She had an idea of what this was about but did as was asked.

By the time midday had come around, she had a plate of rolls ready. Two armed guards and pages escorted her, along with a cook who bore a pitcher of wine, and together, they marched to the great hall, with its immense stone pillars; smooth, worn, polished floor; and stained-glass windows that let in the light.

The rows of the hall were filled with nobles, as Bronwyn saw a sea of faces, watching her every move. She noticed Rupert, Lady Alice, and the Ladies Morwenna and Susanna there, as well as Theobold, who briefly met her eyes. They might not know if she was a servant or a prisoner, but this was like theater; all were watching, and every move was like that of a puppet on a stage.

Empress Maud sat on a great chair at the far end of the room, presiding over it all. She was sitting quietly, amused, as a lady was talking.

As she and the other servants drew closer, Bronwyn recognized the voice, for she had heard it numerous times just a few months ago. It was Queen Matilda, the wife of Stephen, and she was giving an impassioned plea.

The queen was short, but her stature was great. She had presence and moved with a feminine grace, from the slow movements that were almost like a dancer, to the demure bowing of her head. That day, she wore a rich, blue dress of a deep color, like the darkest ocean, accessorized with long sleeves and a gold belt at her waist. She had her dark hair pinned back in waves beneath a thin, golden circlet.

"I beg you all, we must come together in unity and rid England's fields of bloodshed. Let us return to the way things were, when there was hope, and peace among us. But that starts with having the rightful ruler in place, and my husband is just that man."

The empress laughed and bit into an apple, chewing loudly.

Matilda continued. "He is one of you, but raised by God, with a divine right to rule. He must not be allowed to languish in prison. That is why I beg you, all of you, to convince this woman to free him. It is not right," Queen Matilda said. "I ask that each of you think of this injustice, weigh it in your hearts. Stephen is the true ruler."

Bronwyn listened and heard with only half an ear, for she watched Empress Maud's face during this, and she was in part amused, and partly livid. She wore a pretty smile, but her eyes were flinty, her mouth fixed, almost a rictus grin. Bronwyn could tell by the stiffening of her back, sitting rigid and straight, the hard set of her jaw, and the way her nails dug into the wooden armrests of her chair, a great, hulking wooden beast far too big for her petite form, meant for a man.

The view of the would-be throne, and how it was meant for someone so much bigger, made Bronwyn think on this. But then Empress Maud began to clap, haltingly, almost sarcastically, sharp barks of a clap that rang out and echoed in the great hall, as if it were empty, rather than full of hundreds of men and women.

The air was warm, but Bronwyn stood stock-still as if frozen in time, as Empress Maud rose from her wooden seat and addressed the gathering. "My dear cousin's wife makes a pretty speech, but these are nothing but fine words, meant to distract you from the truth. You know in your minds how best to separate falsehoods and design from what is real, and the truth of the matter is that I *shouldn't* be queen."

Gasps sounded. Bronwyn blinked, stunned. What was she saying?

Empress Maud waited. The air hung still, as the nobles strained to listen. She clasped her hands together, almost as in prayer, and said, "By right, it belongs to my brother, William

Adelin. But fate took him from us, him and so many others that day on the White Ship."

She said, "They will never be forgotten, but the consequences of that voyage mean that my father, your former king, Henry, decreed that I am his heir, and your rightful ruler upon his death. The right to the Crown is mine, and I will claim by right what belongs to me." Her voice was cutting.

"So many of my dear cousin's men flock to my camp and proclaim their support. Why, even when his deadly forces took over the humble city of Lincoln, the very cooks and people living there fled to me and my encampment for help." She motioned for Bronwyn and the page to come forward.

Bronwyn swallowed and walked ahead, together at pace with the page, who held the wine pitcher and cup. Bronwyn held out the plate of rolls, and the empress smiled and, taking her by the shoulders, turned her around to face the gathering.

There was a quiet gasp of recognition.

Bronwyn's eyes darted to Queen Matilda. Their eyes met. Bronwyn's were full of apology, but Matilda's only held pity.

Bronwyn kept her eyes on the ground and Empress Maud said, "You remember this humble maidservant, a cook in the royal household, and a very good one." Her voice grew louder. "But when this innocent, young woman's father was accused of a murder he did not commit, Stephen threw him in prison and forced his daughter to work in the kitchens to work off his debt. Is that how we repay innocent Englishmen?"

The crowd murmured at this. Empress Maud continued. "You may recognize this young woman, Matilda, or not. I would not begrudge it if you had no memory for servants' faces, as you clearly do not care for them. Please, do try one of her sweet rolls. They are delicious." She nudged Bronwyn forward with a little push.

Bronwyn stepped forward uncertainly and walked a little distance over to the queen. She held out the platter nervously, her hands trembling.

Queen Matilda looked at the plate of rolls as if they were snakes. She whispered, "It's all right, Bronwyn. I forgive you your part in this farce."

Bowing her head, Bronwyn returned to the empress's side. She wasn't sure to whom she felt loyal at that moment. Matilda was the woman who had willingly imprisoned her father for lack of another culprit, but she also felt anger at being used by the empress.

Empress Maud grinned. "What is the matter, Matilda? Are you too high and mighty to eat good, honest bread?"

"Alas, I have no appetite."

"What a shame." She hastened Bronwyn to come closer. "Give the rolls to the men and women in the front row."

Bronwyn did, offering the plate out as if serving at a feast.

The nobles took and bit into them. "Delicious," said one man, wolfing one down.

The rolls quickly disappeared.

"You see what comes of a little faith? And good hard work and honesty? This young woman made these rolls specially for today, but Matilda is too good to eat them. She raises her nose up at the very idea of it."

"That is not true," Matilda said, eyeing the now-empty plate.

"You had your chance. Now it is too late," Empress Maud taunted. "I ask you, all of you, to help me put an end to this fighting and help me rebuild England for you all. We need peace, but that requires funds. We need money if this campaign is to succeed, and if you are to have a nation at peace again. Stephen's forces have trampled the fields, bled the towns and villages dry. What is to prevent him from coming after your castles next?"

"My husband does not—" Matilda started.

"Your husband is in prison, where he'll rot," Empress Maud snapped. "He is a traitor. A traitor to the Crown, to my father, and to England. He tries to steal something that is not his and worse, he lays claim to the very crown, which my father bequeathed to me. I am a good and honest woman, and I obey where my father leads. Can you say the same?"

"I…" Matilda faltered.

"Speak up, Matilda. We cannot hear you. If you are a queen, as you say, then let us hear you," Empress Maud bellowed. She earned some laughs from the crowd and grinned.

Queen Matilda's cheeks turned pink. To the nobles, she said, "Please, I beg you. Please help me rescue my husband. He is the true and rightful leader. He—"

"He is a prisoner of war and deserves only your censure for a poorly run campaign. He does not deserve your respect, or your support. He cares little for loyalty, and his men know it. That is why so many of them come to me." Maud turned. "You are the noble families of England. Know that this decision belongs to you. You will decide who is right. A man who attempts to steal his way to the English throne, or the rightful ruler, with a legal and divine right. My right." Her voice rang out.

The nobles murmured and talked amongst themselves.

Empress Maud said, "I trust you will make the right decision. That is why I invite you all to my coronation tomorrow, where you may witness firsthand the makings of history."

Queen Matilda opened her mouth to speak.

Maud added, "And I will be hosting a feast tonight, the likes of which you'll never have seen. It will be one to defy all who say we are not a great nation." She smirked at Queen Matilda. "I would invite you, dear Matilda, but I fear you will have no appetite."

Queen Matilda bowed her head. "I have said what I needed to say." Her eyes flicked to Bronwyn for a second, then she lifted her head and with her shoulders straight, she walked down the long open walkway through the crowds, past the hundreds of people there, and out of the great hall.

The empress rubbed her hands together and said quietly, "Excellent."

HOURS AFTER THE empress's declaration, Theobold shifted in

place. It was like a chill had crept down his spine, and he wanted to hunch his shoulders together and lower his head like a snapping turtle. He almost wished he wore armor, but that was silly. Especially as it was June—and hot. But inside the palace walls and the room that Empress Maud had commandeered as her throne room, it was hotter.

She sat on the makeshift throne, resting her hands on the wide, wooden armrests. Her hair was long and braided, and her veil and gold circlet on her head looked pretty, but her expression was anything but. Her smile did not meet her eyes, and her gaze was dangerous. It sent a chill through him, more so than the coldest wind.

This would not end well, he just knew it. He felt for Bronwyn. It wasn't her fault she'd fallen into the empress's court, and she did not deserve to be paraded about and used in such a way. From Matilda's reaction to seeing Bronwyn and her rolls, it was clear they knew each other. He wondered what Stephen's wife had said to her. Whatever it was, she'd handled herself well and walked with poise. She was a promising young woman, if a bit headstrong at times.

At that moment, a small delegation of noblemen, representing the noble families, had come to beg an audience with her in private, away from the prying eyes of the hundreds gathered at the assembly earlier.

He stood along the other knights and guards, ready to defend her if necessary. But these well-dressed noblemen were fat and like sheep, down to their sleepy eyes and self-assured grins. They did not realize they were in the presence of a she-wolf, and she was hungry.

The head of their delegation, Lord Wains, was a middle-aged man in his early forties. He was heavy-set and round about the middle, and he wore clothes of rich material that strained against his bulk. There was a simple coin purse at his waist but no blade, such was his trust in the men around him. His round face bore a smile, and he addressed the empress.

"You see, dear lady, that simply cannot happen. Taxing England's noblest families to feed your army would not merely rob us out of our house and homes, it would make us poor. We would no longer be able to look after our own families, or the serfs who serve us. Would you have us starve to pay for your war?"

The empress leaned forward in her seat, but before she could speak, he *tsked* and shook his head.

"Of course not. You wouldn't be so unkind or heartless toward the good men of this country. Perhaps it is different in France, but here in England, we do not rob the rich to pay for foreign wars."

"This war is on English soil," Sir Robert pointed out.

That earned him a hard look. "Yes, I am well aware. But the fact of the matter is, Sir Robert, your great lady asks too much. We can and will pay some, of course. But we cannot risk starving ourselves and have nothing left for winter. We cannot give what we don't have. You understand."

Theobold became keenly aware that the empress was trembling. Her fingers gripped the wide, wooden armrests like claws, digging into ornate, carved designs. The way her fingers curled and she leaned forward ever so slightly, her chin jutting out, he recognized the signs. She wasn't just angry. She was furious.

The nobleman, blissfully unaware of this, was saying, "You simply cannot act so… unwomanly. It does no credit to you, your husband the duke, or his cause, to see you demanding things. You cannot just demand people pay for you to go to war. It is not done. There are proper ways to go about these things. But I wouldn't expect a woman to understand."

Theobold exchanged an anxious glance with his master, who said, "Thank you, Lord Wains. You may tell the delegation that the empress will consider your words most carefully."

The empress rose from her seat and hissed, "You, Sir Robert, do not speak for me."

"Begging your pardon, Empress, I—" he started, but he fell silent at her murderous expression.

"You, Lord Wains, listen here. I am your empress, and tomorrow, I shall be crowned queen. I fight this war, not because I want to, but because it is my divine right, as bestowed upon me by God, and rightfully due to me from my late father, your king. My cousin is no more than an interloper and his scheming wife seeks to pull the wool over your eyes, but, my good man, we are at war, make no mistake about that."

The nobleman stared as if struck. He took a step back at her ferocity, blushed at his action, and stepped forward again, reddening more.

"Dislike me or not," she said, "hate me or not, but our army must survive if we are to free England from the clutches of my cousin, and by God's good grace, you will pay."

"My good lady, you don't—" he started, but she got in his face.

"You seem to be mistaken about your role in this matter. I am not *asking*. This is not something you can *deliberate over*. I am *telling* you, you noble families will pay whatever amount I ask. I do not ask. I demand it."

The man's mouth dropped open.

Her eyes blazed, and she was never more furious, or glorious, in that moment, Theobold thought.

"You will pay. That is all. I shall see you tomorrow at my coronation. Good day." She turned her back on him, returned up to the dais to retake her seat on the throne, and waved her hand imperiously.

"Well..." The man grunted and cleared his throat. "I... um."

The guards led him away.

Once they were alone in the room, without noblemen present, Sir Robert asked, "Was that wise, Empress?"

She snapped at him. "Do not question me. You would not question my husband, so why are you questioning my commands?"

"You are mistaken, Empress. If a leader of mine was in danger of making an ill judgment, I would question him too."

"I am not one of your fighters, Sir Robert. I am your empress. And tomorrow, I will be queen. Do not plague me with your questions. You're worse than Elea—" She stopped.

Her face clouded at the mention of her dead friend, and her eyes snapped to Theobold. "You."

He stiffened. She knew his name. But not acknowledging him signaled something far worse. She did not seem to bother with names at times like this. It was like she stopped caring about honorifics during times of stress. But honorifics were different from names. He wondered if he mattered to her, would she use his name?

"Yes, Empress." He stepped forward.

"I don't need to tell you how important tomorrow is. It is *my* coronation. I want no trouble, no mistakes. Make sure my crown is safe and not tampered with. If anything goes awry, I am blaming you." Empress Maud's voice was hard; her eyes were crystal clear. Her stare was for him alone.

A lesser man might have been distracted by her cold beauty and dismiss her concerns, like Lord Wains had. They would be fools to do so.

Theobold nodded. "Yes, Empress."

"Do not fail me, Theobold."

He swallowed and stepped back into place, in line with the other guards. He noticed Sir Ranulf grin but made no mention of it. The man was ignorant, rude, and self-serving.

Theobold waited for the empress's audience to conclude, then he exchanged a look with his master, who motioned for him to approach. Sir Robert said quietly, "Go check on the crown. Don't let it out of your sight. Even if you have to sleep with the bloody thing, nothing can disturb the coronation. Too much is riding on this."

Theobold nodded, accepted a set of iron keys from Sir Miles, and quit the room. He heard footfalls behind him and turned. "What are you doing?"

Rupert said, "I'm coming with you."

"Why?"

"You know as well as I do, the empress's success hinges on tomorrow's coronation going well. Like she said, no mistakes. I don't know about you, but I don't trust that something won't go wrong."

"What do you think *you* can do?" Theobold appraised him.

"I can help. Two heads are better than one. Besides, I don't trust everyone in that room. Aren't the men there also those who were present when the empress's friend died?"

"Yes."

"Then they all know what she wants, and what she's charged you to do. I wouldn't put it past any of them to try to sabotage you, then sit back and let you take the blame."

Theobold rested his hand on his sword pommel at his hip. "You have a calculating mind."

Rupert shrugged. "Now, are you going to get Bronwyn, or am I?"

Theobold raised an eyebrow. He clenched his teeth.

"She's at the heart of this and she can think these things through better than I can. How do you know you won't be attacked tonight and the crown stolen?"

"I'm one of the empress's trusted men. No one would dare."

"You've got a high opinion of yourself." Rupert snorted.

"It's not an opinion when it's the truth," Theobold said.

Rupert rolled his eyes and cuffed Theobold on the shoulder. Theobold swatted his hand away and gave him a punch back, and they laughed, teasing one another as they walked to the room where the empress had her crowns and circlets locked away. Most of her crowns and circlets were back at the castle in Gloucester, but for the circlet she wore currently, and the crown with which she was to be made queen.

But as they entered the room, they stopped. "What is it?" Rupert asked.

"This door should have been locked."

They entered cautiously, looking around.

"Where are the guards?" Rupert asked.

"We don't post any guards for a locked room."

"Who has the keys?"

"Sir Miles. But he gave them to me once she ordered me to look after it." He fumbled the keys in his hands, unlocked the door and tripped, dropping the keys on the floor.

"Look at that," Rupert said.

As the two entered the room, the large box that held the crown was empty.

"It's gone. Again," Theobold said dismally.

A noise, a footstep. A rustle of cloth. Almost like the whisper of skirts against the floor.

"Who's there?" Rupert asked, looking.

"Huh?" Theobold turned and heard a feminine titter. A hint of skirts swished past the opening. "Wait." He rushed forward as the door slammed shut. Keys turned in the lock.

Rupert ran at the door, banging on it. He called for help.

Theobold ran a hand through his hair and cursed. "No one's coming. We're locked in."

Chapter Nineteen

A HAND TOUCHED Bronwyn's arm. She startled, jumping in her sleep, when a hand covered her mouth. Her eyes flew open.

Lady Morwenna held a finger to her lips and whispered, "Come with me."

Bronwyn swallowed. Lady Morwenna had found her whilst she'd been sleeping. Was she wise in going with her, away from other people? She hesitated, then thought to herself, *I want to learn more.* What if like Lady Susanna, Lady Morwenna had more information to share about the night Lady Eleanor was killed? She could not picture the woman being so brazen as to attack her, even if she'd been up to no good.

Bronwyn rose silently, pulling on her dress over her head and slipping on her shoes. She tiptoed out of the room, past the sleeping forms of the other maids and kitchen girls.

Once outside the chamber, she shut the door and whispered, "What is it? Why did you wake me?"

"Time is growing short, and I need someone I trust won't throw me to the wolves. Can I trust you?"

Bronwyn blinked. "Lady Morwenna, what are you talking about?"

Lady Morwenna pushed back a strand of dark hair from her face. "You don't understand. Today is the coronation."

"I know. We've been cooking till late last night to prepare for the feast afterward."

"There won't be a feast, unless it's for a funeral. They're going to kill the empress. Today."

"What? Who? How?"

"The crown, you silly. They've poisoned it again. Don't you know anything? I thought you were smart. Isn't that why the empress and Lady Alice like you?" Lady Morwenna rolled her eyes.

Bronwyn was too tired and curious to be annoyed at the slight. She also noticed that Lady Morwenna didn't say who was involved in this supposed new poisoning. "Tell me what's going on."

Lady Morwenna put her hands on her hips and sighed, then motioned for her to follow.

"Where are we going?"

"Somewhere quieter. I don't want anyone to hear what I have to say."

Curiosity ate at her. Bronwyn nodded slowly and followed her down the corridor and down the main staircases, to the very depths of the castle, where the air was cold and damp and a dank smell chilled her.

"This way. I need to talk with you in private," Lady Morwenna said.

"What is this place?"

"The jail. I thought we would be safe here." Lady Morwenna led her into one of the cells.

Unease crept at the base of her spine. "Lady Morwenna, I don't think—"

"The crown is missing."

Bronwyn's mouth dropped open.

"I wanted to tell you, but I never got the chance. You ruined their plan earlier, back at the camp outside of Lincoln. The night of the battle, they plotted to hide the crown, but then when it wasn't found amidst Lady Alice's things, that messed up all their plans to discredit the empress."

"You took it that night, didn't you? I could smell your rose perfume in the tent when I found Lady Eleanor. You were there."

Lady Morwenna gave a stiff nod.

"What were you doing there?"

"What do you think?"

"I think you were part of a plot to steal it. You weren't working alone. Your partner had already killed the one guard there. Lady Eleanor caught you taking the crown and demanded to know what you were doing, and when you tussled, your partner strangled her with a garrote."

Lady Morwenna looked sick. "I... I did, for a time, regret it went that far. I went to Theobold, you know. He told me he was only romancing you to get close to you, upon order of the empress. She doesn't trust you." She laughed bitterly. "She doesn't trust anyone. Even me, when I've obeyed her every want and need. And what do I get? Nothing. To sit in her presence and play music and read French. I don't even like French." She gritted her teeth.

"When I found you dangling from the castle parapet, that was a warning, wasn't it? You'd gone to Theobold for help, to escape, and he'd turned you down. The man you were working with found out about it and gave you a warning."

Lady Morwenna paled. "You think you're so smart. You don't know anything. If you're so smart, who do you think did it? Who killed Lady Eleanor?"

"I think your partner was Sir Bors. That night in the tent, after he killed Lady Eleanor—with your help—he heard people coming and had you hit him so he looked injured, then told you to flee. But your perfume stayed."

Lady Morwenna smoothed down her dress once, twice. She kept at the motion so it was almost frantic.

Bronwyn continued. "Sir Bors had been a turncoat before, and with Stephen on the losing side, he'd be open to promises of riches and wealth. I think he hired some mercenaries to stage an attack on the camp and create chaos, as a distraction for your true purpose, to steal the crown. Like you wanted to discredit Lady Alice by hiding the crown in her things, he thought to do the same by hiding the garrote in Sir Robert's clothing for the journey to Bristol. No doubt he accused the man of having it, but like your own search back at camp, this would have turned up nothing. What I wonder about is Sir Edward's death, and that of your servant, Mabel. Lady Eleanor had been in the wrong place at the wrong time, but why kill them?"

"Mabel was unfortunate. Lady Alice told Sir Bors my maid had taken it, and then when he cornered her down by the river, she fell in. Mabel practically drowned herself, from the way he tells it. But then, she had seen him and knew who he was, so she could've reported us both. He had to get rid of her. It was easy." Her voice was flat.

"And Sir Edward?"

"An accident. I took a spare sewing needle, coated it in the monkshood, and affixed it to the inside of the crown with tree sap. Couldn't wear gloves, as it was so delicate. And it was supposed to kill the empress, not Sir Edward. Today will be different."

"Why? You're one of her ladies-in-waiting." Bronwyn's hands shook. She'd worried she'd been taking a risk, going off with Lady Morwenna. She began to feel nauseous.

"I have my reasons." Lady Morwenna looked behind Bronwyn. "Heard enough?"

A grunt was her only warning. Bronwyn whirled around and a fist punched her in the head. She fell to the ground and felt the loop of a hard, waxed line come around her neck. She stuck her right hand against her neck as the loop pulled, choking her instantly.

"Think you're smart, eh, girl? Not too smart to see me coming." Sir Bors's breath, stinking of cheap beer and onions, was in her nostrils as he pulled the garrote tight.

She coughed, gasped, and bucked, her legs thumping against the floor as she tried to fight back, but all she saw was Lady

Morwenna's piteous expression as she said, "I'm sorry. You're too smart for your own good. It had to be done."

Then everything went black.

SOMEONE WAS SLAPPING Bronwyn's cheeks. A weight pressed against her chest, and lips blew air into her mouth. Sensation fluttered in her brain, skittering like mad fireflies in a summer night. Her head and neck hurt, and her mind was dark. Her eyes fluttered and when the weight pressed against her chest again, she moved a hand.

"Oh, thank God."

Her eyes opened and she gasped and coughed, flailing at her neck. She grabbed at the looped coil, but it was gone.

"It's gone, it's gone, Bronwyn. Breathe." Lady Alice knelt in front of her.

Bronwyn coughed, gasping, and felt at her neck. Her throat felt raw. She swallowed painfully and croaked, "What happened?"

"I'll tell you on the way. We've got to go, before he wakes up." Lady Alice looked to her side.

Bronwyn saw Sir Bors lying beside her, a tiny bit of blood darkening his blond hair as it dripped on the floor.

"Come on."

Bronwyn took Lady Alice's proffered hand and got up.

Bronwyn glared at the man and coughed. Her throat hurt. She swallowed and after a few tries, croaked, "He tried to kill me."

"He would have too, if I hadn't hit him with this." Lady Alice picked up a chair leg. "Let's go."

Bronwyn followed Lady Alice from the cell. "Thank you."

"Don't mention it. There're a lot of nobles here, so we ladies-in-waiting have had to share a room. Lady Morwenna got up early and was acting strange, so I waited and then followed her. When I spotted her leading you here, I knew something was wrong, but I stayed back to see what she had planned. I knew you'd draw the truth out of her."

They looked down at the unconscious form of Sir Bors.

"What do we do with him?" Lady Alice wondered.

"Lock him in. We'll tell the guards and the empress and they can try him later for his crimes."

"Good idea. Once a turncoat, always a turncoat."

They closed the cell door behind them, making sure it was closed.

"Lady Morwenna fled, if you're wondering," Lady Alice said. "I don't know where she's gone."

"Never mind her," Bronwyn croaked. "We need to stop the coronation. She said they would try again to use the crown to poison the empress."

"So, you're on our side, now? Loyal to the empress?" Lady Alice asked.

Bronwyn shrugged. "Let's stop the coronation first."

The young women ran up the steps. It was past dawn, and the servants were already up and the kitchen was busy.

Servants, pages, and maids went past, all with orders, as noblemen, guards, and knights walked by with purpose. Bronwyn tried to get one's attention but was ignored.

"What can we do?" Lady Alice wondered. "Everyone's so busy, they'll just ignore us. Should we find Rupert or Theobold?"

"There's no time," Bronwyn said. "Lady Morwenna stole monkhood from the healer's workshop. They plan to use it to poison the crown again. They might've already done it. We have to go to the coronation and stop it there. See if we can spot the crown before it's used, before it's too late."

Together, they went to the great hall, which was packed with families and nobility trying to edge their way to the front. However much they might disagree with the empress, being present at a coronation was not an event to miss, and many were dressed in their finery.

Bronwyn spotted jewels and necklaces on women to dazzle the eye, soft silks and satin that clung to bodices and shapely calves, whilst the men looked on and laughed, conversations going on all around them as the noise in the abbey rose to a clamor and people angled to get the best seats.

Then there were trumpets, drums, and great fanfare as everyone rose to see. Bronwyn and Lady Alice were shoved out of the way, moving to the side as people shuffled back to let the procession pass.

"Come, we'll join it," Lady Alice said. "Look, there's Lady Susanna. We'll join her at the front."

"What?"

"Bow your head and at the end, fall in line behind them. We'll have a better view from the front if we're part of the parade."

"All right, but you're out of your mind."

"No more than you, going along with Lady Morwenna to a jail cell. What were you thinking?"

Bronwyn reddened. "I wasn't." She paused. "I wanted to know the truth. I knew it was risky, but I didn't think until it was too late that I might be in any real danger. I never thought she could hurt me. I was—"

"Too full of yourself, clearly," Lady Alice snapped. "Sorry. I would've gone after her too. I'm just glad I was there to rescue you."

"Thank you," Bronwyn rasped.

The procession filed past. The empress wore a white, satiny gown that shimmered in the light. The effect made her look angelic and almost holy, and her long hair had been combed out to cascade down her back in silken waves. She wore a deep-red cloak trimmed with ermine and shot Lady Alice and Bronwyn a questioning look as she walked by, but then paid little notice.

The trumpets and horns blared the signal for people to watch, and Bronwyn could hear the roar of people outside cheering. To say it was loud was an understatement; the horses and people outside sounded like a swell of noise, a cacophony of sound.

Then Lady Alice grabbed her hand and whispered, "Keep your head bowed and keep pace with me. It's strange—I don't see

Rupert or Theobold anywhere."

They joined the end of the procession, their heads bowed as if in prayer. Bronwyn and Lady Alice followed a small procession of servants and pages dressed in bright livery who held banners and flags. Soon they were led up to the front and stood off to the sides of the group surrounding the throne, just thirty feet away from the empress.

The horns and drums rose to a crescendo and then stopped as Henry of Blois and members of the clergy began the ceremony.

Bronwyn stood, looking around the crowd. She couldn't see the crown anywhere, and the room was very warm. The abbey was stuffed full of people and quiet, despite the noise from outside. The abbey doors soon shut, sealing the group in.

The bishop intoned from a great book, and sometime later, the empress was handed a rod and scepter, and gave many oaths to look after the people and counties of England. Bronwyn felt her eyes getting drowsy and had begun wavering on her feet when Lady Alice elbowed her in the gut, jolting her awake.

"Look," Lady Alice whispered.

Sir Ranulf approached, holding the crown on a pillow, a smile on his face as he walked toward the empress.

Time slowed, and to Bronwyn, it felt as if she were trying to run through mud. She saw him get ever closer and she shoved and pushed her way past people, calling, "Stop! Stop the crown! It's poison!"

People stopped and stared at her. Sir Ranulf froze and, flashing a look of annoyance, continued to approach.

Bronwyn's arms were gripped by two men, but she kicked one and head-butted the other, slipping from their grasp. She got away and, stumbling on her hands and knees, flew toward the raised dais, where the empress was on her knees before the bishop, who stared at her in dismay.

Bronwyn and Lady Alice together charged at Sir Ranulf. Bronwyn shoved a guard away and was tripped by another, when Sir Robert stepped in and shoved one aside, letting her pass.

Bronwyn dodged, finally knocking into Sir Ranulf with her shoulder.

It wasn't much force, but it was enough, and he stumbled, the crown flying from the pillow. The crowd of nobility gasped and shouted, people called out for her head, but all Bronwyn could see was the golden crown, lying on the floor. A servant went to pick it up.

"Don't touch it! It's been poisoned."

The servant paused.

"You stupid girl," Sir Ranulf backhanded her across the face, making her ears ring with the force of his gloved hand across her cheeks.

Gasps rang out at the sight of him striking her. She fell back, staggering, and Sir Robert caught her. "I've got you," he said, holding her up. His tone was calm, but his hand gripped her arm. She wasn't going anywhere, she realized.

"Stop him. The crown," Bronwyn rasped.

"What is going on? What is that girl talking about?" the bishop asked.

Lady Alice said, "The crown has been tampered with. It's a plot by Sir Bors to kill the empress."

People looked over.

Sir Ranulf snorted. "The girl is telling tales, Empress. And just where is Bors now?"

"We've locked him in a cell in the castle. He tried to kill Bronwyn. She figured it out," Lady Alice said.

"Figured out what? We are in a ceremony, young woman," the bishop said angrily.

Empress Maud held up a hand. "I would hear what they have to say. Ladies, come here."

Sir Robert released Bronwyn's arm, and she and Lady Alice approached the empress.

"Tell me what you have found," Empress Maud said.

Bronwyn croaked, "Sir Bors was part of a plot from the start, to use the battle at the beginning to steal the crown. If you had no crown to be crowned with, there couldn't be a coronation. He used the opportunity to steal it, but he and Lady Morwenna were interrupted." "What happened to your voice? And Lady Morwenna? What has she to do with this? Lady Susanna, where is Lady Morwenna?" Empress Maud gazed around the room. "I don't see her. Funny, I don't see those squires, either." She glared at Sir Robert and Sir Ranulf.

There was a scuffle, and a lot of shouting as Theobold shouted, "Let us through. I am squire to Sir Robert of Gloucester!"

"And I am squire to Sir Ranulf de Gernon."

Lady Alice looked at Bronwyn and practically cheered. "Rupert."

Bronwyn grinned.

The voices carried, and grew nearer. "I don't care who you are. Both of you are ruining the empress's coronation," a clergyman said.

The squires, followed by a few angry nobles and clergymen, interrupted the procession and made their way to the front. The clergyman bowed and said, "I'm terribly sorry, Your Grace, but these two men—"

"Enough." Empress Maud held up a hand. "Let them approach. I know them." She glared at the squires. "Why did you decide to come late and interrupt my coronation?"

Theobold bowed. "Apologies, Your Grace. We were locked in where you keep the crown. It's gone missing."

"You were careless with the keys?" Sir Ranulf grinned and a few men laughed.

"No, Your Grace," Rupert said. "We found the crown gone when someone locked us in. We had to force our way out."

"I see. Theobold, why on earth didn't you tell me what you'd discovered about the crown? I tasked you with finding the blasted thing and you didn't. Then it was poisoned and I almost died. I've lost too many good people now, thanks to your incompetence. And now you've let yourself get locked in a room? What is wrong with you?" The empress seethed.

Theobold swallowed and inclined his head. "Your Grace, I...... We knew it had been stolen and then returned but didn't know who was behind it. We had suspects, of course, but no real proof. Not until now. I have been working with Mistress Bronwyn to find out."

"And yet I told you to keep an eye on her in the first place." She rolled her eyes and let out a noise. "You're as bad as my guards. Well, while you two squires were breaking down doors, I was hearing how Lady Morwenna was supposedly involved in all of this." To Bronwyn, she said, "Pray, continue."

Bronwyn spared a glance at Theobold, who looked at her stonily. She said, "The night of the battle outside Lincoln, Lady Morwenna was stealing the crown whilst Sir Bors killed the guard. But Lady Eleanor caught them, so he killed her."

"What proof have you of this?" the empress asked.

"None. The girl lies, Empress," Sir Ranulf said.

Bronwyn glanced at him. Why was he so keen to defend Sir Bors and Lady Morwenna and put the crown on the empress's head? She noted he was wearing gloves. Perhaps he was in on the plot too.

"He killed her with a garrote and hid it in Sir Robert's things to try to accuse him later on the road to Winchester. But it was disposed of, and he used another to try to kill me, earlier today," Bronwyn croaked, coughing.

"It's true," said Lady Alice. "This morning, Lady Morwenna led her to a cell and confirmed it when Bronwyn revealed what she knew. Sir Bors tried to kill Bronwyn, and Lady Morwenna would have just let it happen, if I hadn't saved her."

"How did you do that?" Empress Maud asked.

"Hit him with a chair leg. He's in the cell now. Lady Morwenna fled."

"Guards, go investigate the cells and bring him to me." Empress Maud turned to the young women. "So it was the two of them behind this?"

Bronwyn coughed and rasped, "Not entirely. I think she was

working with someone, not just Sir Bors. He's not smart enough to do this on his own. But Lady Morwenna's perfume could be smelled in the tent where I found Lady Eleanor, and again in the healer's stores when it was broken into and the monkshood taken. It was easy for her to steal a needle, and she affixed the poisoned needle to the crown with tree sap."

"It's true, Empress," Lady Alice said. "You recall how she complained of her hands being so sticky, and she said it was from eating too much honey—yet she refused to lick her fingers. She reached for the tablecloth instead."

"I do recall. It was a strange moment. Her table manners are normally impeccable."

Bronwyn added, "Lady Morwenna told me herself: the target was always you. Lady Eleanor simply got in the way, and Sir Edward's death was an accident. They even killed Lady Morwenna's maidservant when she—"

Lady Alice stepped on her foot.

"—when she found out too much," Bronwyn finished.

Lady Susanna gasped.

"And now?" Empress Maud asked.

Sir Ranulf talked over her. "Now I've heard enough of these tall tales. We are here. Are we going to have a coronation or not?" He stood at the empress's right shoulder and said, "Your Grace, there've been enough interruptions already. The crowd will not stand for this forever. They want to see a queen today. You."

"Yes. But first, Sir Ranulf, mind you pick up the crown and show it to me," Empress Maud said.

"Fine. But this is all a load of nonsense," Sir Ranulf said. "I've never heard such fantastical stories in all my life. Mark my words, Empress, we'll be laughing about this later."

"I doubt that. Show me the crown."

"But remove your gloves first," Bronwyn said.

Sir Ranulf glared daggers at Bronwyn and slowly removed his gloves, tossing them to the floor. He gently picked up the crown and put it back on the pillow that was on the ground. He held out the pillow. "Empress."

"Turn the crown over," she said.

He gingerly picked it up and turned it over.

But as she leaned in, there was a sound of breaking glass. Heads turned. Rocks, bricks, and sticks flew through the stained-glass windows of the abbey, along with shouts and cries.

"*Mon dieu*. What is happening?" Empress Maud asked.

A crossbow bolt sailed through the air, slamming into the wooden chair, where the empress's head had been just seconds before. It pinned her ermine robe to the chair and she slipped it off, revealing a slice on the shoulder of her white dress, staining it with blood.

"The empress! Help her." Sir Robert's voice cried.

In seconds, chaos reigned. The doors to the abbey flew open, and crowds of angry Londoners, noble and peasant alike, entered the building, armed with pitchforks, cudgels, sticks, pikes, maces and stones.

Women cried and men charged, shoving and pushing. The crowd surged and soon they were surrounded on all sides.

Shouts and yells filled the air, and the crowd was like a moving, living being, coming at them almost like a wave. The air they breathed grew hot and stifling, and Bronwyn trembled, for she did not see a way out. There was no escape, and every real chance they might die. Would she die from a spear point, a rock, or trampling from hundreds of feet? Or worse, lack of air?

A tear rolled down Bronwyn's cheek as the people drew closer, and Lady Alice took her hand and squeezed it tightly. "Do not worry, Bronwyn. We are not going to die today."

"How do you know?"

"I just do." Lady Alice gripped Bronwyn's hand. "Don't let go."

The knights and guards formed a circle around the empress and them by extension. Bronwyn's pulse was in her throat, as the guards aimed their spears and brandished swords at any rebels who came too close.

The men hustled them all in a tight circle, and Bronwyn and Lady Alice held each other tightly as the poisoned crown lay forgotten. They were moved along as Empress Maud, the bishop, the knights, and the squires moved through the back of the abbey, farther and farther away from the crowds and out a side entrance, a small door. Sir Robert tore off the fine, red ermine cloak from the empress's back. At her yell, he threw his cloak over the empress to hide her face and gown and hustled her out.

Outside, the noise was worse as hundreds of people clamored about, throwing knives, stones, bricks, dirt—anything they could—at the abbey, and flooded the entrance, trying to get in. Bronwyn staggered and was helped up by Lady Alice. The small group of defenders loyal to the empress leaned on one another and huddled close as the men got the empress on a horse, holding on to Sir Robert. They formed a small, makeshift band of warriors and led the empress away as fast as they could.

Bronwyn saw her look back once, before Sir Robert kicked the animal's sides. Empress Maud's face was terrified, angry, and a little bit heartbroken and forlorn. Her chin quivered, and she let out a strangled cry. In that moment, Bronwyn could see that the woman who called herself "empress" had desperately wanted this all to go well, to claim her birthright and rule England. Instead, she was fleeing, the wind whipping her hair against her face as she rode bareback on a horse, being jostled down the muddy roads. On what should have been a day of celebration, Empress Maud hid under a cloak as the people of London revolted. She heard later that Queen Matilda rejoiced.

Epilogue

THE AIR WAS hot, and sweat trickled down Bronwyn's back. She rode on horseback in front of Theobold, with his arms around her, holding her close. A part of her relished the intimacy. Another part of her was just happy to be alive.

They'd managed to find some horses from nearby stables and the men had paid handsomely, far too much for ordinary horses, but the grooms hadn't asked questions or looked too closely.

Empress Maud and Sir Robert had taken the first horse and fled into the morning sunlight, leaving the rest to follow. They had flown like the wind, and it was all the others could do to catch up.

So now she rode, gripping the mare's mane, which felt like strands of silk in her fingers. The mare took a ground-eating pace and the wind rifled through her hair, pulling baby-fine hairs free from her thick, blonde braid. The wind from the horses galloping whipped her face as Theobold expertly urged the mare on, the hooves striking the dirt road as they tried to catch up with the empress and her men.

The horses slowed as they passed through roads filled with people.

They were on the road again, this time back to Gloucester. London had been a disaster. No one spoke of the calamity that had been the coronation. Empress Maud began calling herself the Lady of the English, and no one dared oppose her. She was in too foul a temper to be reasoned with. And woe be it to any crockery or weapon that came too close. Any plate, piece of armor or utensil was quickly thrown or smashed to pieces—such was Empress Maud's fury.

They followed at a slower pace, now that they had gotten some distance away from London. With each step, Bronwyn relaxed slightly. She had felt a very real danger inside the abbey that she might die, and it had shaken her.

Theobold broke the silence. "Are you all right?"

"I think so. What will happen now?"

"She won't be crowned queen, if that's what you're wondering," he muttered in her ear.

Sir Robert called a halt, and they gathered together and dismounted, keeping close by.

"Bronwyn, you should know. I never… That is, I… never meant to hurt you," Theobold said, helping her down from the mare, his hands on her hips.

She slid from the horse's back and faced him. She tried not to think about how warm and strong his hands were. He had lifted her down as if she weighed nothing at all. "Why did you get so close to me, then? It was the empress's orders to get close to me, I understand that. But I thought we were… friends at least. Did you really suspect I had something to do with all this?"

"Not since the second or third day. As soon as you began asking questions about Lady Eleanor's death and wouldn't let it go, I knew you were innocent. A guilty person wouldn't work so hard to find out the truth."

She faced him, very conscious that his hands were still on her hips.

His hands dropped to his sides, but they stayed facing each other, barely a foot apart. His brown eyes sought hers.

She caught him gazing at her mouth, her lips, and swallowed. "If you thought I was innocent, then why did you stay? Didn't you think I would find out I had been a suspect?"

"Maybe. I didn't think that far ahead. I only did what my

empress had asked me to do, but…" He ran a hand through his thick, black curls.

"And do you only do as your empress, or your master, asks, or do you ever think for yourself?" she asked, fire in her belly. She'd gotten sick of him taking orders and wished to see the man stand for himself, not because another had told him to.

His head shot up. He met her glare for glare. "Of course I have a mind of my own. I stayed close to you because I fancy you. Is that what you want to hear?"

Bronwyn snorted and walked past him. "So you felt a passing fancy. Lady Morwenna, should I ever speak to her again— unlikely, since she aided in my attempted murder—would tell me otherwise."

"If I hadn't been locked in a room, I never would have allowed that to happen."

"Lady Morwenna stole the crown, was an accomplice in Lady Eleanor's death, and stood by as Sir Bors tried to kill me. If Lady Alice hadn't rescued me, I'd be dead."

He swallowed. "I'm sorry I wasn't there. Rupert and I were locked away all night. I…… think it was Lady Susanna."

She stared. "What?"

"It was a woman who locked us in. And I know Lady Morwenna's build. Her movements. This was different."

"But why? Why would Lady Susanna lock you both in a room overnight?"

"To prevent us from interfering with the crown and the coronation," he said.

Bronwyn's mouth opened a little. "My God. I never suspected her."

"None of us did."

Bronwyn let out a breath. Lady Susanna. Perhaps her secrecy in the plot was tied in with her secret lover, whoever that was. Someone higher up, and close to the empress. *Who could it be?* she wondered. If only she had looked closer at the young woman.

"Why do you refuse to think poorly of Lady Morwenna? I

know she is your cousin, but I could have died," Bronwyn said. "Do you love her?"

"No."

"Are you two…?"

"No. But that's not stopped her from trying."

"Then why are you so loyal to a woman who doesn't care who lives or dies? She liked Sir Bors, anyway."

Theobold pressed his palm to his eyes. Was he relieved? "We are connected. Her family and mine. They arranged my living, brought me into a life and learning that I love, away from my family's legacy."

"Of death, you mean."

"Yes. I don't want to become a hangman like my father. Lady Morwenna's family gave me a way out. But in return, I look after her when we are together. I owe her family everything. My life."

"But what about what *you* want?"

He chuckled, and it was bitter. "We both serve the Crown, Bronwyn. You know as well as I do that we aren't allowed to have our own wants or desires."

"That sounds like a poor life, Theobold." She reached out to him.

"It's not all bad. I get to flirt with all the pretty kitchen maids I like." He took her hand and raised it to his lips.

She started, eyes wide, as a warmth filled her from head to toe. He held her hand as he lowered his lips to hers. His touch was featherlight as her eyes closed. It was a fleeting kiss, but when she opened her eyes, she felt a blush coming over her, and saw that she wasn't alone. His cheeks were rosy, his eyes dark. Then he stepped back.

"I have to go after her. Find her."

"Who?" she asked, dazed. It had been a good kiss.

He grinned. "Lady Morwenna. Thief or would-be killer or not, she disappeared, and her family will be worried. I have to find her and make sure she's all right."

"What about the empress?" Bronwyn asked.

"She'll be all right. She will understand."

"What about... me?" she whispered. Her heart thumped loudly in her chest.

He squeezed her hand. "I don't know how long I will be gone. May I have your favor?"

"My favor? What do you mean?" She bit her lip.

His gaze darted to her mouth. "A token of yours so I might think on it during the night and take comfort. Favors help keep men alive, you know. During jousting and battle."

A gentle blush warmed her cheeks. "I have nothing. I am poor."

"You are not. What about that kerchief you use to tie up your hair?"

She felt at her neck for the scarf. It smelled of rosemary. "This cheap thing?"

He laughed. "Yes."

She unbound the scarf and gave it to him, feeling shy and awkward. It was sure to be sweaty, especially in the damp heat. Her blonde hair hung low on her back.

He tucked the kerchief away in his left sleeve. "See? Now I am protected."

The words came to her tongue without her thinking. "Now you will come back."

His eyes widened. "I will."

"Good."

He flashed her a smile and climbed atop the mare. "Mistress Baker." He nudged the horse and took off at a gallop, the mare's hooves a steady beat down the dirt road.

Lady Alice quickly came up to her. "Did I just see what I think I did? He kissed you. And you gave him your favor?"

"Um... yes?"

Lady Alice let out a noise. "Oh, how romantic. You're not all cooking and breads, after all. Rupert, did you see that?"

Rupert joined them. "I saw Theobold leave. Sir Ranulf says he's gone after Lady Morwenna."

"Not that, silly. He kissed her. In front of everyone. And he has her favor." Lady Alice gave a small, wistful sigh. Bronwyn grinned.

"Yes, well." Rupert coughed and cleared his throat. "I still don't trust him." He had a stiff posture.

Bronwyn met Rupert's eyes. She didn't know what to think. She still liked Rupert plenty, but at the same time, Theobold had tugged at her heartstrings a moment ago, and she didn't know what to think anymore.

"The empress will be so pleased. She loves a bit of court gossip. Just wait till I tell her this." Lady Alice went in search of the empress, leaving them alone.

Bronwyn turned and watched Theobold disappear into the distance and did not see Rupert frown.

"Do you care for him?" Rupert asked.

"I'm not sure."

"You don't need to throw your lot in with his," he said. "There are good men here. Men who would look after you."

She snorted. "I have nothing, Rupert. No dowry. My family is gone. I have no friends, no money, barely a roof over my head, and I've just ridden out of London, where the people were throwing stones and I thought I might die. You think I'm really weighing my chances at romance right now?"

He grunted and scratched at the slight scraggly hairs on his chin. "I'm just saying, you're not alone."

"Oh, really? Because it sure feels that way."

"You're not." He took her hand. It was warm. "You have me."

A flash of cognition hit her, strong as lightning. He liked her. But as a friend, a sister, or something more? Her pulse quickened at the thought.

They stared at one another as Theobold's mare's hoofbeats faded into the distance.

Historical Note

In the historical accounts I read, there is little information on Empress Maud as a woman, quite possibly because these accounts were all written by men.

It's our task as amateur historians to piece together what she might have been like as a person, but the historical records vary in their criticism of her, from ignoring her accomplishments to outright dismissing her attitude, calling her aggressive, demanding, and arrogant, and suggesting she acted in a manner that was "unwomanly." These accusations of her overbearing behavior toward the men around her sound not so dissimilar from the double standard that many women can encounter in the workplace today. When I started writing this series, I didn't know what contemporary historians thought of Empress Maud, and so to learn she was remembered so harshly made me want to learn more.

This story sparked an idea—she is due to have a coronation in London as queen, but what if there was no crown to crown her with? The coronation couldn't take place. That idea is what began this story. In this tale, I tried to breathe life into some of the experiences that Empress Maud might have encountered as she pushed forward, just to have a coronation.

I purposely paint her behavior in contrast to her opponent, Queen Matilda, not just to highlight some of the sexism of the day, but to also point out that these were two women in powerful roles who accomplished great things in their own right and who deserve to be written about, warts and all.

If I have made any errors in my interpretation, those are mine and mine alone. I have looked at twelfth-century contemporary accounts of battles and descriptions of these women and the men who surrounded them, but in the end, artistic license must be taken. I hope you enjoy reading this series as we see more of the struggles these women face in a push for the Crown.

Acknowledgments

Big thank you to the lovely team at Dragonblade, my fearless and hardworking editor, Amy, and my wonderful fellow writers, Aviva, Theresa, Lois, and S.E, as well as my husband and family for their constant support.

About the Author

E. L. Johnson writes historical mysteries. A Boston native, she gave up clam chowder and lobster rolls for tea and scones when she moved across the pond to London, where she studied medieval magic at UCL and medieval remedies at Birkbeck College. Now based in Hertfordshire, she is a member of the Hertford Writers' Circle and the founder of the London Seasonal Book Club.

When not writing, Erin spends her days working as a press officer for a royal charity and her evenings as the lead singer of the gothic progressive metal band, Orpheum. She is also an avid Jane Austen fan and has a growing collection of period drama films.

Connect with her on Twitter at twitter.com/ELJohnson888 or on Instagram at instagram.com/ejgoth.

www.ingramcontent.com/pod-product-compliance
Lightning Source LLC
Chambersburg PA
CBHW070525310726

48976CB00002BA/542